ONE MAN GAVE HER EVERYTHING— ANOTHER DEMANDED ALL

Lenard pulled Megeen up against him. "Let us lie down together on the bed. It's such a waste if my father does not use it. Someone should."

Megeen moaned softly, "Lenard, no! Please let me go!"

"You need more coaxing? Come, I'll make you want it as you never have before." Lenard's mouth found her lips, then her tongue. Megeen made no effort to pull away now. She was imprisoned not only by his arms but by her own urgent need. All the lonely nights were erupting now. Now she was the one who inched backward toward the bed, drawing him with her. . . .

And as the sudden ache of desperate hunger took hold of her, Megeen knew in her heart that it was too late to free herself from this wave of passion that was enslaving her, from this fever of love that would surely bring her to ruin. . . .

Big Bestsellers from SIGNET

NIGHTINGALE PARK

By

Moira Lord

A SIGNET BOOK

NEW AMERICAN LIBRARY

TIMES MIRROR

*NAL books are also available at discounts in bulk quantity
for industrial or sales-promotional use. For details, write to
Premium Marketing Division, New American Library, Inc.,
1301 Avenue of the Americas, New York, New York 10019.*

First Signet Printing, August, 1977

1 2 3 4 5 6 7 8 9

 SIGNET TRADEMARK REG. U.S. PAT. OFF. AND FOREIGN COUNTRIES
REGISTERED TRADEMARK — MARCA REGISTRADA
HECHO EN WINNIPEG, CANADA

SIGNET, SIGNET CLASSICS, MENTOR, PLUME AND
MERIDIAN BOOKS are published in Canada by The New
American Library of Canada Limited, Scarborough, Ontario

PRINTED IN CANADA
COVER PRINTED IN U.S.A.

NIGHTINGALE PARK

Chapter One

The light in the small kitchen, dull and dusty gold a short time ago, was blurring into dingy darkness. The outlines of the people around the table, with its hand-embroidered cloth, lost their sharpness. To Megeen, now more than ever, the other three seemed to be strangers: the two men she had met only a short time ago and her sister, the handsome girl with her glittering eyes and quivering mouth.

Conversation languished, revived, became strained and awkward. When Annie rose to take a kerosene lamp from an open shelf, it caused a welcome diversion.

"Can I help you, ma'am?"

"Come, love, let me do that."

Both men rose, but Martin Mulcahy sank back quickly into his chair. Tom O'Flynn put himself in his wife's path. Then he slid behind her and fastened his big hands around her waist, almost circling it. Then he pulled her against him and rubbed himself against her buttocks.

Annie's face flamed into a bright flush and her indrawn breath sounded harsh.

The villain! The words were in Megeen's mind but as clear as though she said them aloud. Married three months and he's still like a rutting animal. And tormenting the poor girl so!

Annie's need and impatience must be like a fever inside her. Her dark-red hair was tumbled and strips of it fell across her forehead. She had lovely eyes, wide and the color of the sky on a bonny morning. Now they looked dazed, like those of a sleepwalker. Her creamlike skin was hidden by the ugly, mottled blush, and as she lighted the lamp, her hands were unsteady.

Tom O'Flynn made a chuckling sound deep in his throat. "Those that've never had it before like it the best."

He seemed unable to keep his hands off his wife. He began

, to caress her shoulder, her long and graceful throat, then slid down to squeeze her breast.

The playfulness would go on until he took Annie to bed, of that Megeen was sure. And although Megeen had slept in the same room with her parents, as Annie and the younger children had done from time to time, she had never seen such a lack of decent manners before.

He was a rare one, indeed—this Tom O'Flynn. Megeen had never seen a finer-looking man.

Tall and with broad shoulders and a great mass of black hair that seemed to burst from his head. His untidy eyebrows looked as though they had been left there by an explosion. and the eyes of the man were wicked, with their bright glinting. The women would be after this one, to be sure. Poor Annie would have her hands full; Megeen envied her not at all.

Martin Mulcahy, who must be sharing Megeen's embarrassment, shifted in his chair and turned his eyes away from the two. He spoke directly to Megeen.

"Did you mind the long journey then, Miss Ahearn?"

"I managed to endure it, sir."

She spoke shortly, wondering why he was there on this, her first night in the new country. He was a quiet man, neat and clean-shaven and with his sand-colored hair parted precisely down the center of his head. He had the short upper lip and the turned-up nose that was the mark of many Irishmen. All in all, he was not too unfavorable to look upon.

But Megeen refused to meet his eyes. The goings-on of her sister and brother-in-law shamed her into shrinking farther into her chair.

"Ye've all come the same way," she mumbled. "It was no tea party, as well ye know. I'd as soon forget it, if ye don't mind." Rising, she said, "And ye'll excuse me, for I'd as soon have a bit of a wash and climb into bed."

Too late she realized that mentioning such intimate things as washing and going to bed was sinfully immodest with two strange men to hear, and she stood up so hastily that she was suddenly whirled about in a spell of dizziness.

She had spoken the truth. She wanted to forget that long ocean voyage. She had been both seasick and homesick. Into every inch of that plunging ship had been squeezed vile-smelling, travel-sick men and women with their fretful babies and children.

The journey had ended in the numbing disappointment of not finding Annie waiting for her. All those long weeks she had yearned for the sight of her sister, whom she had always loved above the others. Worse still, there had been no joy at her coming, no glad welcome.

All Annie O'Flynn's feelings, it seemed, had been burned away in the heat of her passion for this man who was thinking only of the pleasure her body could give him.

Megeen grasped the back of a chair. The others were standing now, too, and she looked very small beside them. She had not been favored with her sister's spectacular coloring. Her hair was a rusty shade of red, her eyes were lighter blue. Whereas Annie's skin was as soft and pretty as a flower, Megeen's was sprinkled with freckles, and her chin was too sharp and her jaw too stubborn for anything resembling beauty.

"It is time for me to take my leave, too, and I thank ye for your hospitality."

Martin Mulcahy's voice had in it the lilt that was familiar to Megeen, and she turned to smile at him briefly. For the brogue had brought into the small, dreary kitchen a touch of home. The voices of the other two, thickened by their driving desire, were not at all familiar as they bade the man goodbye.

His footsteps faded as he went down the two flights of stairs. Annie, nodding in that direction, said, "You could do a lot worse than Marty Mulcahy, Meggie. His father owns the saloon on the corner. Mulcahy's Irish Bar, it's known as. When the old man dies, it'll all be Marty's. His wife will never want for anything. Seems you could have been a little bit more friendly."

Megeen's stubborn, prideful chin rose an inch or so. "I've no wish for you to be matchmaking for me, Annie, if you do not mind. It was not to find a husband that I came all this way, especially one who's a saloon keeper. Makin' a livin' on the destroyer. Often Marm told me—and you, too—that it's the whiskey that rots a man's soul. Now if ye can bear to lose my company"—a note of irony crept into her voice—"I'll take my rest. For come mornin' I must see about the job Mr. Gilligan promised I would have."

"'Twas a fine thing he did, meeting you at the boat." Annie was already unfastening the buttons of her bodice. "I'd have gone down—honest, I would have—but Tommy comes home for lunch every day and. . . ." The flush was rising from her throat again. "Well, it seemed best to have Packy Gilligan there, for such is the way it's done, Meggie. He meets each greenhorn. That gives him a chance to look them over so's he can see where they would best go for a job. He's a fine man, is Patrick Gilligan."

Megeen kept her own opinion of the man to herself. She wanted to go on talking to her sister, but Annie would care for nothing she might say. Had she listened, she would have heard of the lost, frightened feeling that had grown to panic when Megeen had found herself alone in the swirling crowds on the wharf. And how startled she had been when a man she had never seen before spoke her name.

Dazed and bewildered, she had been led by his hand on her arm through the pack of people, some laughing, some crying, all seeming to be chattering at the same time, to where his wagon was waiting.

"I know who ye are, lass." His voice rose over the noise. "From what your sister told me. I'm Patrick Gilligan, at yer service. I'm to take ye to the home of Mrs. O'Flynn. It will take no time at all, at all."

Everything about the man was exaggerated. To Megeen's ears his brogue sounded false, as though he were making fun of all the Irishmen in the world. But maybe it was kindly meant, something to make the newcomers feel more at home.

But she sensed that Mr. Gilligan had motives that were of benefit only to himself. And what a dandy dude he looks, indeed, Megeen thought. He wore a square, pearl-gray derby and a fine coat buttoned high about his chest. His cravat was a dazzling shade of green.

By the time they reached his wagon, it was already crowded. Two long seats facing each other held more than a dozen greenhorns like herself. Most of them she had seen aboard ship, but there was no friendliness now between them. It was as though, having arrived at where they were going, they wished to repudiate one another.

The ride was a short one, as Mr. Gilligan had promised, but it was long enough for Megeen to see the narrow, dirty streets, the fish markets along the wharves, the dismal tenement houses.

The jolting of the wagon brought a sour taste to her throat. She gritted her teeth, and when the horse was pulled to a stop, she drew a long, shuddering breath and said a silent prayer to the Blessed Virgin for having delivered her safely to her sister's house, disappointing and unprepossessing as it was.

Mr. Gilligan had climbed down from his seat beside the driver and had come around to the back of the cart to help her from it. He steered her with his hand at her elbow across the dirt sidewalk. Then he groped in his pocket and drew out a few scraps of paper. Squinting, he held one of them at arm's length and then handed it to Megeen.

"There's where ye're to go in the mornin', lass. Easy enough to find, it is. Nightingale Park, number seventeen. Real high-class neighborhood, that is."

His voice took on the cadence of genuflection, but he was quickly businesslike again. "Agnes Callahan, the cook there, is in need of a kitchen maid, the last one havin' been bounced out for havin' sticky fingers, so they say. Let it be a lesson to you, me girl." His jowls quivered piously. "Honesty is the best policy, a little sayin' I made up not long ago. Now you're to tell Aggie it was me sent you. Ye'll have no trouble landin' the job at all."

His left eyelid fell in a wink so brief that Megeen wasn't sure she had seen it. "To be sure I get a small token of gratitude from them what I put in positions. I'm a generous man, ye'll find, and all I'd expect from a green girl like yourself ... well, let us say half of yer first month's wages. But most important is the votes. To me and me friends, that is. We'll have the town run by the Irish afore long."

There was no mistake about the wink this time. Megeen, edging impatiently toward the recessed doorway, said, "But I know naught about votes, sir. Am I not still a subject of Her Majesty's?"

"Queen of the lobsterbacks!" Mr. Gilligan spat into the gutter. "Ye'll get nothin' from that quarter. While with us— But ye're wantin' to see them what is waitin' impatiently for a glimpse of your face. So I'll be biddin' you farewell."

He removed his hat and flourished it with a wave of his hand. The wagon clattered off a moment later, and Megeen was left feeling desolate and just a little frightened at the bottom of a dark staircase. She could scarcely believe that she would find her sister there at the top of the two flights of steps. She had waited so long, dreamed so constantly of this moment. Now that it was here small, nagging doubts began to nibble at her mind. Annie's last letter, written after her marriage to Tom O'Flynn, had contained no phrases urging her sister to join them in their new life.

After Martin Mulcahy's departure, Megeen's feeling of being unwelcome became even stronger. She wished that Annie would listen, understand, and reassure her. Drumming in her mind were the worries. What if she did not get the job in Nightingale Park? She had in her purse only a few coins. If Mr. Gilligan were to be given half her first month's wages, how was she to send Marm the money she had promised?

"This Nightingale Park then? How will I find it, since I know not a single place in this city?"

"Morning will be time enough to tell you."

Annie's eyes shone brilliantly in the gentle light of the kerosene lamp. Her tongue licked relentlessly across her lips. Sprawled in a kitchen chair, Tom O'Flynn growled, "The pair of ye gonna blabber all night?"

As Megeen went down the hall and groped past the bigger bedroom, she was careful not to look into it. She'd had a glimpse of it earlier in the day, and the brass bed seemed to dominate it. On the wall behind the bed were a framed marriage certificate and a picture of a cherubic baby.

At the back of the flat was a smaller room that contained only a pallet—borrowed from a neighbor, Annie had told her—a commode, and a straight-backed chair.

On the chair was a bundle, a knitted shawl bulging with the things she had brought with her and everything she owned in the world. Her First Communion prayer book. Two changes of underwear. Three pairs of woolen stockings. Two nightdresses. A small framed picture of the Sacred Heart. Three strips of flannel held together with safety pins, to be used when she had her monthly period. And the brown homespun dress that she had worn almost continuously throughout the long, dismal sea voyage.

These were the only things that held her to her home, and she wished that she and Annie might have a long, comforting talk about Kerry, that lovely spot God must have favored above all other places on earth, about their mother and the younger children whom she missed with a dull, bruising pain. To speak of them would, in a sense, have brought back the lost ones for a little while. Memories shared with her sister would be balm to an aching heart.

Annie, who had made the journey not two years ago, must know how Megeen was feeling on this woeful night. But she seemed to have put that other life well out of her mind. She wanted nothing else, Megeen thought desolately, except her lust-maddened husband riding on her naked body.

Annie appeared only briefly at the door of the small bedroom. She held a candle that she placed on the top of the commode. She did not meet Megeen's eyes.

"In the morning, when you go to that place you're to work in ..." She hesitated, as though trying to remember something she had been instructed to say. "In a job like that, you'll live in the house. So you might as well take all your things with you and not have to come back for them. To be sure, you'll be making visits here now and then."

Still without meeting her sister's eyes, she turned and slipped quietly out of the room. The noise began an instant later, Annie's teasing laugh, her pretended cries of "No! No!" and sounds of a scuffle.

A warm, tickling sensation between her legs reminded Megeen that she needed to go to the outhouse in the backyard, but she was afraid to go down into the strange, unfriendly darkness. She looked for and found a chamber pot in the bottom of the commode, and she used that. Then she washed in the water in the basin, the same water that she had washed in earlier that day; her petticoat had to serve as a towel.

Nothing was as she had expected it to be. She had not come all these thousands of miles to live no better than one of Marm's pigs, she told herself. Through the magic of money she would learn how to be a lady.

She would bathe all over every single day and have hot water every time she fancied it; and she would eat good, tasty food, for she'd had enough of withered potatoes and dry oat cakes.

She did not know how all this was to come about, but she would find a way. The saints, if she prayed hard enough, would help her and watch over her. She would not ask from Annie or her husband a single small coin. She had no wish to become a beggar, either.

Her besetting sin was pride—the awful, stubborn pride of the Irish. So Marm had told her. But she had no other protection in this bewildering, unfriendly place.

While on board ship she had found the means to wash her clothes each day, and the rough cotton nightgown she put on was clean at least. She knelt beside the pallet but she could not keep her mind on her prayers, for the noise in the next room had risen in volume and now there were no restraints in the young couple's lovemaking.

First there came Annie's delighted laughter; then that died away in a gasp so loud that it might have come from the throat of someone in physical pain.

Then there was Tom's muffled growl. "You want it, luv. Tell me you want it. Say you gotta have it!"

Annie was groaning. "Give it to me, sweetheart! I'm beggin'. Oh, there! I can't stand it. Please, please!"

But he went on tormenting her, laughing when she cried out. The bed creaked with their thrashing about, and finally both their voices rose at the same time, his grunting in steady rhythm and hers in frenzied screams.

Even if she had not known that there was no place for her in the O'Flynns' tenement already, Megeen would have realized now that this could never be her home. She could not imagine what her new one would be like, and she dropped into troubled sleep whispering the address on the scrap of paper that Patrick Gilligan had given her.

Chapter Two

Annie was listless and short-tempered in the morning, like someone who had been drunk the night before and was suffering aftereffects. Long after Tom had left for work, Megeen came through the kitchen on her way to the outhouse and Annie had for her sister only the curtest of greetings.

It was not until Megeen had come back upstairs, pumped water at the sink, and put the kettle on the coal range that there was any conversation between the two.

"Oversleepin' the way I did!" Megeen wailed. "It could be that I've missed gettin' the job in Nightingale Park. I'm sorry indeed that I could not get to sleep for a long time."

She had not meant to sound accusing, but bright color swept into Annie's face. "You see how it is then," she said waspishly. "I can't deny my husband his pleasure, even if there's someone close by. It's a tiresome job driving the horsecars and a man's got to have something to look forward to when his day's work is done."

As you do yourself, Megeen thought. She had not needed Annie to tell her that her absence was more to be desired than her presence.

When she had washed and combed her hair and put on the brown homespun dress, she made of her other things as neat a bundle as possible. She would look a greenhorn indeed with the bulky, shawl-wrapped burden. Already she knew that much, and that having to find a strange street in a strange city would slow her down so that she would arrive even later at the house in which she hoped to work.

"Now if you'll tell me how to get there, Annie."

Her sister gave her sketchy directions. "All I know is that it's somewhere in the South End and real high-toned. You go right straight ahead toward the center of the city. Ye'll be walkin' down Dorchester Street to where other streets meet, and then over the bridge. Beyond is the cathedral and ye'll see that well enough."

"This is where you go to Mass on Sundays?"

The flames were in Annie's cheeks again. "No, to St. Augustine's. When Tom is not too tired to get up, that is. Or has other ideas."

Megeen felt the jolt of shocked dismay. Could this be true? Annie, the most pious one in the family? The pet of the nuns who had taught her exquisite needlework and gently hinted that she might be one of them? Who had prayed for hours to be shown her true vocation? Surely she would not be lolling abed on a Sunday morning, not too tired, Megeen was sure, to sweat and squirm under her husband's body.

"You're to write nothing of what goes on here to Marm." Annie's eyes seemed to be shooting little sparks. "Not about . . . me and Tom. Nor anything else. I did stretch the truth a bit about the furniture. Some of it we got at the junk man's place. I said nothin' about that in my letters. I most likely gave you all the wrong idea, making it sound like we were comfortable and well-off."

She tossed her head and her hair broke free of its pins and swirled untidily around her shoulders. "Tom will soon have a rise in pay, for it's a good job he has on the horsecars. Packy Gilligan says it'll be for a lifetime, so we have no fear, for he's one of the smartest men in the city, that Packy. To be sure he is."

Her face softened as Megeen started toward the door. "You might better take the cars, Meggie. Do you have the fare then?"

Megeen did not know what the fare might be, and even if she had, she was determined not to spend the last few coins in her purse.

"I am well able to walk, thank you. And it looks to be a pretty day outside."

The heaviness of sorrow still pressed upon her heart when she reached the street. Then fear took its place, fear that she kept hidden behind a stiff, proud face.

It was as though she were two Megeen Ahearns, the one who walked along with her head held high and the other the quaking girl whose insides seemed to be filled with ice.

There was much to be afraid of; she could feel and see the dangers around her. A team of monstrous brewery horses with tassels of hair on their forelegs seemed to loom up out of nowhere as she started to cross a street. She drew back quickly, her heart drumming. Their driver, seated high upon a beer keg, waved his whip at her and grinned impudently. A man in dirty clothing came lurching out of a saloon, muttering something she did not understand.

As she tried to follow the directions Annie had given her, she saw that there was a saloon on every corner; and from the noise inside them, muffled only slightly by their swinging doors, she guessed that they were crowded with drinkers even at this hour of a Saturday morning.

What Marm would have said to that! She hated, with a deep and terrible hatred, the drink that had killed Clement Ahearn, their beloved Da who died penniless so that two of his daughters must travel across the sea to find a kinder and more prosperous life.

The day was too warm for the woolen cloak Megeen was wearing; she pushed back its hood. The sun was hot on her head and it polished her hair a brighter color. It was her hair that brought a little knot of half-grown boys trailing after her, young lads who might be free from school and were undoubtedly bent on mischief.

Their piping voices cried out, "Red, Red, stayed too long in bed!"

She tried to walk faster, but her bundle struck against her

legs and she could put no distance between her and her tormentors. They began to dance around her, singing their loathsome song until she was forced to stop and try to squeeze past them.

They did not listen to her when she begged, "Let me by, if you please. I have a job to go to and should I be late, I may lose my chance."

Her words were lost in the rising volume of the chanting. She had hoped that one of them at least would hear her appeal and be moved by it, understand the importance of her errand, for they were all poorly dressed. Their long black stockings had holes at their knees, and when one of the boys pirouetted in front of her, she could see the half-moons of flesh at both his heels.

Appealing to them was merely furnishing them with heartier amusement. The whirling figure made one last turn in front of her and then, with dirty hands clasped at his chest, piped in falsetto, "Oh, dear little boys, have mercy upon me, I pray!"

His companions doubled up with laughter. One of them collapsed at Megeen's feet holding his sides in spasms of glee. She reached down with her free hand, hauled him to his feet, and glared down into his face.

"Do you not know, foolish boy, what I am? I'm a witch and that's the truth. A witch as were my mother and her mother before her. How do you dare to mock my red hair when all witches have upon their heads hair the color of mine? Ignorant boy, don't you know that I can put upon you a curse—still your tongue or blind your eyes forever? And so cursed, ye'll be that way to the day of your death. Begone now, all of you, for I have the power to put the spell on more than one."

The chanting had petered out while she was speaking. The boys exchanged uneasy glances. They were all marked by the features of their ancestry: turned-up noses, fair skin with the color close below it, the green-blue of their eyes, and the thickness of their black lashes.

Megeen guessed that they'd heard the stories of the little people and evil spirits and curses. She put as much fierceness into her expression and voice as she possibly could. "Run away now, little imps, or ye'll never again see your homes or your marms."

They backed away and fled, and now it was her conscience

that bothered her. "Dear Lord, forgive me, but there are times when naught but a lie will serve the purpose."

As she came closer to the center of the city, the stench of fish and mud flats filled her nostrils. She tried to hurry, but the bundle seemed to have grown heavier and her boots felt as though they were made of lead. She was still nervous. What, she worried, if she was not going in the right direction and had to go back and start all over again?

She could be lost all day in this big city, with its warehouses and smoke-belching factories. When she saw a man with a pushcart on the road in front of her, she ran to overtake him and asked where she was and if by following this road she would come to Nightingale Park.

He directed her with gestures. Then, reaching over to pinch her bottom, he showed her his yellow, broken teeth. "Sure that's all you want from me, lass? I got something else you might like."

Anger, quick and burning hot, made her want to strike at that grinning face. There was no room for fear in the boiling of rage, in spite of the fact that there seemed to be no one else close by at that moment. This she had never been afraid of—that a man would try to force her to let him have his way with her.

When she had been fourteen, her mother had given her a wicked-looking hatpin and told her, "Use it if you have to." At St. Monica's school, the gentle, angel-faced Sister Melitas had lifted the skirt of her habit and demonstrated to her senior class of girls the way to knee a man's groin.

Megeen cried in savage tones, "It would be hard up indeed I'd be to want anything from a disgusting wretch like you!"

She walked on stiff-backed and came to a more crowded area where wagons and carts passed her, and there were a few carriages, hacks carrying people whose faces were blurred behind the windows, rigs with trap doors, and some with drivers perched high in the air. Never had she seen so many vehicles.

Finally, she reached the cathedral. She slowed her steps as she walked past it, awed by the size of its great doors and the height of the spire, its golden cross gleaming in the sunlight.

She longed to enter it and kneel before its altar, needing now, as she had never before, the comfort of prayer, but she could not delay any longer and so she made a promise to herself; no matter how far this imposing edifice was from the house where she would be living, she would come here every Sunday to Mass.

And no matter how rich she became (for she was still clinging stubbornly to her dream), she would make this her spiritual home.

The distance would not be too great. She learned that a few minutes later, when she came upon Nightingale Park. She had been thinking of it in terms of the great, wide-flung parks with the castles of Kerry standing upon them. And so her first glimpse of the two rows of houses around a strip of grass filled her with disappointment.

The grassy area was surrounded by an iron fence, its pickets resembling spears thrust into the ground. A few trees inside the enclosed space were coming into bloom and were decorated with the green ruffles and frills of their new leaves.

As she walked along beside the fence, Megeen saw that there was a gate halfway down its expanse. It was securely locked and an impressively lettered sign warned against trespassers.

PRIVATE PROPERTY. THIS PARK IS TO BE USED ONLY BY RESIDENTS AND OWNERS OF BORDERING HOUSES. OTHER TRESPASSING UPON THESE GROUNDS WILL BE PROSECUTED BY DUE PROCESSES OF THE LAW.

Megeen tossed her head. Who would want to sit in their park? There were only three benches along the border of the path that cut through the new grass. Indeed, it was nothing to make a person long to break the law.

Still, the stern wording of the sign had a chilling effect. She hoped that she would find more warmth and friendliness in the house on the other side of the oval. For she had found it easily, No. 17 Nightingale Park, the place that was to be her new home.

Chapter Three

The house was almost in the center of the block, well-marked with brass numerals marring the beauty of its fanlit door. It was tall and narrow, as all the houses around the park were, four-storied and with balconies jutting from the downstairs windows, their grillwork as delicate as black lace.

It was attached to the other houses on each side of it so there were no alleys that would have led to a back door; this puzzled her, for she was sure that those seeking a servant's job were not to walk up those fine marble steps and hope to enter the house through the elegant front door.

Then she saw the areaway. Steps led downward, and at their bottom was a door almost hidden by the shadows. The stairs needed sweeping. She saw that with a critical eye. Scraps of paper, broken twigs, and dried leaves littered the corners. The knocker, which she lifted and then let fall, was tarnished. A pity indeed, Megeen thought indignantly, that even this part of such a lovely house should not be taken care of properly.

Inside it was worse. The middle-aged woman who opened the door was slatternly. Her apron was soiled and limp. Wisps of gray hair escaped from her cap, which looked as though it had been accidentally dropped down upon her head from some place far above her.

"Agnes Callahan?"

"None but the same. And what would you be wantin'?"

The woman had a lean face with a long nose and a sharp, pointed chin. Her eyes, too close together, gave her a sly and disagreeable expression.

"Mr. Gilligan sent me."

"Another of them! Well, I only hope ye'll turn out better than the last one he sent me. And that ye'll keep your hands off of what don't belong to you. Ever done housework before, have ye?"

Megeen's direct gaze did not falter. "At home I ran things almost alone, for Marm was often bedded with the backache. I can cook well and scrub and do the washing. And I learned from a magazine a lady loaned me on shipboard how to set a table."

"Did ye now!" Mrs. Callahan cackled. "Well, there'll be few fancy chores for you here, my girl. If ye're hired, ye'll be workin' in the scullery, for Tessie, she who calls herself a parlor maid, is findin' the scullery chores beneath her."

The small, bright eyes traveled over Megeen's body, but if she saw what she was looking for, she gave no sign. During the short silence, Megeen let linger in her mind the things Agnes Callahan had been saying, not concerned so much with their meaning but the way she had spoken, the coarseness of her voice, the pronunciation of words that revealed ignorance and lack of education.

There had been educated people aboard ship. Simply because a person was born in another part of the world, it was not necessary to cling to the worst features of the native language. It was at that moment that Megeen became determined to lose her brogue and to enunciate more carefully as the nuns had taught her to.

"Tessie's run down to the market," Mrs. Callahan said on a whining note. "Me health is poor and will not allow me to go that distance. And she's always eager to go. Deny it though she may, I think she's got a suitor down there. The good Lord alone knows when she'll be back. Well, come along in then."

Absorbed in her grumbling, she did not notice Megeen's shocked expression at her first glimpse of the kitchen. She tried to keep her dismay from showing, but what she saw when she darted quick glances around the basement kitchen amazed her.

Cooking pots and pans hanging on the walls were filmed with grease. Coffee grounds had been dumped into a sandstone sink and left to discolor it. Dish towels were dingy and the oilcloth on the long table needed a proper scrubbing.

Such a big room with so many fine things in it: a butter churn and a monstrous stove with nickel-plated trimmings that could not have been polished for a long time; a dish cabinet with a glass door so dingy that the articles on the shelves behind it were almost hidden.

Megeen's glance returned to the woman who stood with her hands on her hips.

"Then what will my duties be, ma'am?"

"Ye've not been hired yet, so 'tis early to be talkin' of duties. There's a small matter we must be settlin' first of all. Did Packy Gilligan make it clear to you that girls I put to work here show their gratitude with a little present? Half a month's wages is what goes into me pocket. Does that fail to suit you, we'll forget the whole matter. You can look elsewhere, for there's greenhorns aplenty comin' over all the time who'd be glad to pay that triflin' sum for a good job in a fine house like this one."

"But Mr. Gilligan . . ."

She did not get a chance to say that Mr. Gilligan had already spoken for his "little present." One half of her month's wages to him and one half to Mrs. Callahan, greedy-eyed as she waited for Megeen's answer—then how was she to live all that time with scarcely a cent in her purse?

And how was she to take orders from this woman, whose nose twitched like that of an animal smelling game and whose coarse voice rasped in the ears?

"Anyway, it'll be himself who'll decide in the end. Ye'll say little to him, nothin' at all about me and my kitchen. He leaves me alone, I'll give him that. I could count the times in the past year that he's set foot down here."

She straightened her cap and smoothed down her apron. " 'Tis only a courtesy more or less, to be goin' up there at all. He'll say it's up to me, as he always does. But he must pay yer wages, to be sure, and were he to meet ye in the hall, 'twould be well if he knew who ye were!"

She crackled a laugh, seeming pleased with her own weak humor. Then she motioned Megeen to drop her bundle. "No sense in yer seeing yer room until the matter's settled. Come along with me then, Maggie. No better time to see himself than now, for the two of them are at their lunch, only workin' half a day on Saturdays as they do."

She began to make shooing motions toward a back stair-case, but Megeen remained standing where she was.

"You are miscalling my name, Mrs. Callahan. Perhaps Mr. Gilligan gave it to you wrong. Megeen it is. I care not for Maggie at all, and you will favor me by not using it when you speak to me."

Mrs. Callahan cast her eyes ceilingward. "Oh, hoity toity, indeed! There's much ye don't know, Maggie, my girl! Ye'll learn that the nose-in-the-air people of Boston favor certain names for their servants. In every one of their kitchens, there's a Maggie or a Lizzie or a Kate or a Bridie or a Delia. Used to those names, they are, and it keeps us in our places. Me, I'm Cook, and they must call me with a 'Mrs.' for that's me station in life."

Megeen felt a touch of pity for this woman, whose only claim to dignity and distinction was the usage of such a title before her surname. She wore no wedding ring, so perhaps the title did not actually belong to her. . . .

"Ye'll get nowhere daydreaming. So leave the bundle there, Maggie, and leave off yer cloak. We've not all day if we're to find the master at lunch."

As she led the way up the back staircase, Mrs. Callahan talked in a low voice as though to a fellow conspirator.

"The missus died a year ago and there's only the two men now. Sad it was, her only forty. Mr. Vickery's been mourning her ever since. Tonight'll be the first time he's even had people in to dinner."

This, then, was the reason the Vickery kitchen was in such a deplorable condition. There was more here than the carelessness of servants, Megeen thought. There was the lack of a firm hand of a mistress.

It could have been a beautiful house if anyone had cared to make it so. As they crossed the first-floor hall, Megeen looked from side to side, catching glimpses of deep, velvet chairs and a marble fireplace in the drawing room, a doubly curving staircase covered with a rose-patterned carpet.

The door leading to the dining room was open and Mrs. Callahan went through it, motioning Megeen to follow her. It was a long, narrow room, seeming to have been built to accommodate the long, narrow table at which two men sat facing each other and very far apart.

They both looked up, and it was then that Megeen felt panic grasp at her insides and squeeze painfully. So much depended on what would be said during the next few minutes. If Mr. Vickery took an instant dislike to her! If he had intended to cut the expenses of the household and decided that a kitchen maid was not absolutely necessary for his comfort!

What, then, would she do? She felt the tightness and coldness that settled in her face. She was unable to stretch her mouth into a smile, although the elder of the two men, seated at the head of the table, smiled gently at her.

He was a man favored with good looks. Forty or more, he was thus on the edge of old age in Megeen's opinion. His hair, which had undoubtedly been pale gold in his younger years, was dulled with streaks of gray. His face was bony, the sweep from the point of his jaw to his chin a little too sharp, the eyes gray and deep-set were lively, the long mouth soft for a man's, yet not feminine.

She had only to glance at the other end of the table to see how Alexander Vickery had looked twenty years ago. On this young man's head there was no hint of tarnishing. His curly hair was true golden under the light of the chandelier. He was a finer-looking man than any Megeen had ever seen. His skin was flawless, his nose high-bridged, and his eyes

were framed with good, strong lashes. She found it difficult to
take her eyes from that handsome young face and suddenly
felt Mrs. Callahan's elbow in her ribs.

"Mr. Vickery, sir, I've brought ye a new kitchen maid to
look upon and decide whether or no she'll be employed by
you."

As though I were a piece of horseflesh! The indignant
thought spun into Megeen's mind, but she knew that she must
watch her tongue and control her face so that none of the
other three in this room would guess that she resented bitterly
being put on display this way.

The man at the head of the table seemed to have a gift for
knowing what she was thinking. His eyes were keen and wise
as he studied her. There was something else in them, too,
which was not exactly pity but which made her aware that he
was not seeing her as merely some soulless thing he was contemplating buying.

"You know, Mrs. Callahan, that I never question your
choice or interfere in matters of this kind. If you like the girl,
well and good. Hire her by all means."

His voice fascinated Megeen. It was, she supposed, a com-
pound of the elegant tones of the native Bostonian and the
leftover cadence of the British. In spite of her perturbation,
she made a note of it in her mind and was determined that
from now on she would make it her own. It was not as lilting
as the Irish voice; the vowels were flat and somewhat nasal
and there was no music in it, but if she were to one day be
one of them . . .

Mr. Vickery was saying, "You might tell us her name." He
was smiling again, this time with a faint lifting of the corners
of his mouth. "Surely she has one."

"Yes, sir. 'Tis Maggie. Maggie Ahearn."

Megeen's body stiffened. Never had she been able to keep
her temper in control completely when she was angered. Nor
could she, in times of stress, keep her true feelings hidden.
This was her worst sin, Marm had told her, along with the
stony pride. And now she could not help blurting out, "If you
please, my name is not Maggie but Megeen, and I should like
very much to be called that if you have no objection."

The young man at the other end of the table stirred and
leaned forward in his chair, showing some interest for the
first time in what was being said.

"Well spoken!" There was a note of mockery in his voice.

"What do we have here? A champion of the working classes? Soon they'll be giving the orders and we'll be obeying them."

Megeen turned to stare at him. There was something there under the surface of the look of boredom and the slightly jeering words. She did not try to decide what it was or what was meant by the statement, for she was too appalled by the fact that she had put her job in jeopardy, perhaps even thrown away her chance to work here.

Mrs. Callahan, after an outraged gasp, moved away as though in repudiation of the girl whose brazen outburst might be construed as her own fault.

"Indeed, sir, I beg yer pardon on her behalf. For ignorant as she is—and ye'll excuse it if I say that some of the Irish are thickheaded as mules—she'll not work for me. She can look elsewhere for another job and I'll not bring you another one unless I'm sure."

Alexander Vickery interrupted her with a lift of a white, long-fingered hand. "It does not seem to me that it was an unreasonable request. Our names are our precious belongings. I should very much dislike to be miscalled. Besides, Mrs. Callahan, are you not known also as Aggie? So would there not be a bit of confusion if she were called Maggie? Megeen—that is her name, is it not? Megeen, I am sure, will be an addition to our household. By all means, hire her if she desires the job."

Usually so quick with words, Megeen could not find the right ones now. The first bit of true kindness she had received since landing on the soil of this new country had come from this man, whose eyes were twinkling at her. She did not know how to express her gratitude. But he seemed to expect none, for he rose to his feet and bowed in a gesture of dismissal, exactly as though she and Mrs. Callahan were guests in his house.

As she turned, she found the eyes of the young man at the other table intently upon her, bold and bright.

Embarrassment for having spoken out as she had slid away and a more pleasant kind of confusion took its place. How handsome he was! And undoubtedly as kind and well-mannered as the elder man, who, it was plain, was his father. Megeen could scarcely drag her glance away.

As they reached the threshold, they were stopped while Mr. Vickery addressed the cook with questions and orders.

"Everything, I assume, is in readiness for the party tonight?

As I've already told you, we will be eleven at dinner. You can handle everything, can't you? The best china, of course, and you'll make sure the silverware is polished to its highest shine."

Megeen's spirits went soaring upward. How kind were the saints who were watching over her! They had kept her from being turned out onto the streets to beg for any wretched job she could find. They had guided her to this lovely house, where on her first night there was to be a party.

Even though she would not be attending it, of course, she would be part of the gaiety and excitement and, as a servant, catch glimpses of the fine people enjoying themselves.

Chapter Four

"It will be the first time he's had anybody at all in the house since the missus. A full year of mourning he's had. I'll give him that."

Mrs. Callahan put the heavy tray crowded with silverware in front of Megeen. The girl had never seen such beautiful articles, let alone known how to polish it. But once she was shown, she learned quickly.

The cook sat hemming the skirt of a dark-gray uniform. It was to be Megeen's, once it was shortened and taken in at the seams. Tessie, back from her trip to the market, was rolling knives and forks and spoons of various sizes out of their chamois wrappings.

Except for a sentence slipped in now and then by Mrs. Callahan, Tessie kept up a monologue, repeating gossip she had heard, setting forth her views on various subjects.

She was like someone drunk on the sound of her own voice. She seemed not even to hear the woman's scolding.

"Enough now, ye lazy girl! Ye've a tongue that wags at both ends. Eight months in this household and ye know it all, some of it guesswork and some of it gossip and none of it any of yer business."

Tessie paid no attention. Having found a new listener in-

spired her. She was not an attractive girl. Her big head and
round, lively face did not match her flat bosom and scrawny
legs. There was a slight cast in one of her eyes and her fine-
textured hair flew in all directions.

Although she had never seen Flora Lenard Vickery, having
come to work in the house four months after the woman's
death, she could describe her in great detail.

"The missus was frail, poor soul. You can see her portrait
over the fireplace mantel in the drawing room. Pale and only
a little bit pretty. But highborn. The Lenards was what is
called the cream of the cream. They do say that a man looks
for his mother when he shops around for a wife. True
enough where Lenard is concerned. I heard from the Loverings' upstairs maid—they live right across the park—that he's
sparking Dorothea Lovering. The young master, that is. All
believe that the two of them will be betrothed soon."

Megeen felt something tightening inside her. It caused her
breathing to grow uneven and a sudden, strong lump to form
in her throat. She did not understand it. How could it matter
to her if that handsome young man was planning to marry
someone named Dorothea Lovering, whom he had probably
known since they were children? Megeen knew that she
should have more on her mind than that and she had no wish
to turn as silly as Tessie McNamara, with her sighs and wist-
ful pouting when she mentioned Lenard Vickery's name.

Her sewing finished, Mrs. Callahan handed the garment to
Megeen. "Not that ye'll be needin' it tonight, for ye'll not be
in the dining room once the guests arrive. Tessie'll do the
servin' and she better remember all I told her or God help her!
Where ye'll be is down here, to send food up on the dumbwaiter. Then, when the evening's over, we'll all wash up the
dishes."

The two girls exchanged nervous glances. Megeen had no
idea what a dumbwaiter might be and was amazed when
Tessie showed it to her. Who would believe there was a con-
traption like that, a movable shelf that could be hauled up to
the next floor to save carrying heavy trays of food and table-
ware up the stairs!

So this was to be all of the fine dinner she would share.
She would not even lay eyes on the people who were causing
all the hard work and commotion. She had hoped to write a
letter to Marm on the morrow and describe this beautiful
house she was in and the people who were Mr. Vickery's

guests. No matter. There would be other nights, other parties. Perhaps then Mrs. Callahan would allow her to do the serving.

But Mrs. Callahan was one to keep a grudge. She would receive no favors from the cook, Megeen sensed. Tessie having run out of breath, Agnes Callahan was having her say.

". . . doubt if it'll fit ye right, bein' as how ye're a mite of a thing indeed. Scarcely a pick on them bones and how ye'll be able to do the heavy work I've no idea. Me, I like a good husky helper and one not so impudent as you. Megeen, indeed!"

Her nose was raised as though in a permanent sniff. "Why himself was that easy on you I'll never know. Knocked me off the feet when he said ye'd do."

It was not necessary for her to put it in plainer terms. She would be looking for something to criticize, a reason to discharge Megeen and replace her with someone more easily browbeaten. Her authority had been weakened by the master's coming to the girl's defense. Megeen knew that she had made an enemy, and a powerful one.

Apologies would do no good; she could not force herself to make one at any rate, for she knew that she was in the right.

She said, "Thank you for fixing the garment. If I may take the washtub into my room and fill it with hot water, I could be taking a bath before I change clothing."

"A clean one, are you then? Once a week, my girl, is all the bathin' that goes on around here. For no one wants to leave themselves exposed to germs by scrubbin' their bodies too often. Ye're not to use the water closet on the second floor for washin'. It's all right to use it, should ye feel like climbin' the stairs. Ye'll empty it when you use the slop jar and keep the room in order."

It was a small room, almost as small as the one in which she had spent the previous night. It opened from the kitchen and was full of the smells of fried food, urine, and sweat. There was a bed a little larger than the one in the O'Flynns' spare room. Over the bare mattress was folded a thin quilt; a holy picture hung on one wall.

The picture brought no comfort to Megeen, who was wondering how she was ever to breathe in this airless place. Then she discovered the wooden shutters high on the wall. They opened onto the street beyond, and because the room was below the level of the street, all she would be able to see of passersby was their feet and a small portion of their legs.

A chair beside the bed and the commode across the room puzzled her. Both were delicately carved and stood on bowed legs. She knew somehow, even though she had never seen the likes of these pieces, that they were valuable and did not belong in a dingy place like this.

When she opened the shutters, the late-afternoon sun poured in with a flood of dancing dust motes, and all the dirt and grimy surfaces were exposed without pity. As soon as she had a little time to herself, Megeen vowed, she would give the room a good scrubbing, beg for sheets and a pillowcase, and wash out the stinking slop jar under the bed.

Always offer up for the souls in Purgatory the hard and disagreeable tasks, Marm had told her. But there in that small room it was not of her soul that she thought. Her mind went soaring to the rooms above her that she had seen that day. And to Lenard Vickery, with his golden hair shining under the light of the chandelier that brightened the dining room with its dark woodwork and blood-red wallpaper. She was so lost in daydreams that Mrs. Callahan, her arms full of bedclothes, had to speak sharply to her.

Chapter Five

The guests began to arrive at seven o'clock.

"And such nonsense," Mrs. Callahan grumbled. "Can't eat at a respectable hour, it seems. Them as believes themselves better than any others must sit down at the table at an hour when people should be in bed."

Megeen, who had been polishing glass after glass before she put them on the dumbwaiter, could hear the clatter of horses' hooves on the cobblestones, the high-pitched voices of the women, the heartier, rumbling ones of the men. The front door opened and closed, and opened and closed several more times.

Footsteps sounded over the kitchen ceiling, muffled by the

carpets on the rooms above it. Mrs. Callahan's complaints grew louder. Sweat poured from under her cap and the ragged dish towel she used for mopping her face could not keep pace with its dampness.

Mr. Vickery came downstairs to fetch the bottles of wine he had brought up from the cellar that afternoon and left in a washtub of ice outside the back door. He spoke only to Mrs. Callahan and then only briefly.

"Everything going all right?"

She opened her mouth to begin her litany of grievances, but he was moving quickly and did not stop to listen. There came, a moment later, the faint tinkle of glassware and the sweet, high laughter of a woman from the drawing room above.

It was aggravating, Megeen thought, not to be able to see the owners of the voices and the feet that pattered above her head. Just a peek would have satisfied her.

The chance came later that night.

Tessie, who had been groaning and moaning all night, said finally that she could not stand upon her feet for one moment longer.

"I did my duty as best I could," she whined virtuously. "They've all been fed and no one can expect me to do more. For my insides are torn apart by the curse. Three days late, it was this time, which probably made the cramps worse."

Megeen suspected that the girl was exaggerating her pain. No one could have remained on her feet while suffering the agony Tessie was describing. Mrs. Callahan sighed deeply and said, "Well, go on to bed then. For ye'll be no good to me in that state."

Tessie had no sooner left the kitchen when the woman declared that she, too, was feeling poorly and felt that she had done enough hard work for that day.

"And two flights of stairs to climb and me with me bad legs. It's lucky you are, girl, to have a room and a nice one, too, right here off the kitchen."

"Well then," Megeen asked, genuinely puzzled, "why don't you sleep down here and let me have your room upstairs?"

"What!" Mrs. Callahan's eyes shot barbs of outrage. "Me in that pokey little corner? No, thank ye very much!" She stomped across the kitchen and then turned. "The men'll be havin' their port in the dining room and cannot be disturbed yet. And when they've all left, the glasses and teacups and such will have to be cleared from the drawing room and wherever else. All must be in order before ye can quit for the night."

Megeen's weariness made her bones ache. But at least she was to see something of the party. She waited until she heard the masculine voices coming from the hall as the men went to join the ladies, and then she crept upstairs, slid quietly into the dining room, and moved around the table to a spot where she could glance into the drawing room.

There were five women gathered in a corner of that big room, their heads bent toward one another, their voices rising and falling.

She noticed, first of all, their gowns. Never had she seen such beautiful articles of apparel. Fashions were not becoming to the feminine form that year. Waists must be tortured by tight corsets that pushed women's breasts almost out of their bodices. Huge gatherings of material at the back of the gowns seemed to make postures awkward. But the lamplight streaked with brightness the rich, pearl-gray satin, the delicate old-rose silk, the emerald-green velvet, and the brocade of yellow-gold design.

Trimmings were of narrow, foamy lace, tiny rosebuds, and clusters of imitation jewels.

Thick frizzes of hair hid the ladies' foreheads, and ropes of braids towered on the crest of their skulls or were looped in figure eights at the napes of their necks.

Megeen could see those things but not, with any clarity, the faces of the women. She was curious about which of them was betrothed to Lenard Vickery—Dorothea Lovering. The name had remained in her mind since Tessie had spoken it. But there was no way of Megeen's picking that lucky young woman from among the other feminine guests.

Megeen had almost finished clearing off the table when she heard the rustling of skirts and the light footsteps of the women on their way to the music room.

Someone said brightly, "But, of course, you'll sing for us, Dorothea. I'm sure Lenard would like that, too."

Dorothea demurred prettily, and then she and her companion moved out of earshot. The voices of two other women had in them more serious notes.

". . . never hire another of the Irish, not for house servants; nor will Josiah at his mill. My dear, we pay them good salaries and what do they do? Hand it over to their priests, of course, to be used against us. It is said that they are buying guns and other ammunition and storing them in the basement of the cathedral. When they feel themselves strong enough, they will take over the city and give it to the Pope."

Megeen remained where she was, her skin seeming to shrivel and grow icy. But inside her was a hot rushing of anger and outrage. How dared they! By what right did they speak of God's representatives on earth in such a manner? She stalked to the door so that she might hear better the rest of the conversation, the final words of the calumny.

She heard a fluting laugh. "Adeline, really! Do you actually believe that? They are harmless, the Irish, for they are too stupid to be otherwise. What I have against them is that they are always running to church, no matter if they are upsetting the household. They get drunk and fornicate, and then they go to what they call confession. They tell their sins to a priest and then go back and do the same things all over again. And everyone knows that the priests and the nuns . . ."

Megeen was standing at the door of the dining room, and there was no turning of their heads in Megeen's direction. It would not have mattered to them if they had, she thought with bitterness. All they would have seen was a servant's uniform, a faceless servant.

After she had made the last trip to the dumbwaiter, picked up the last of the party disarray, she sat alone at the kitchen table and tried to pray.

". . . forgive us our trespasses as we forgive those who trespass against us . . ."

But she found it hard to forgive. Again, it was the pride and the stubbornness. Even her favorite saints, those who were to greet her at the gates of Heaven when the time came, seemed to be far away.

She was being drawn down into sleep when Alexander Vickery came down to the kitchen, muttering something about wanting to thank someone for the success of the dinner and the added work that had made it so. She tried to spring to her feet, but her chair toppled backward and fell with a clatter. She could barely see the man's face through the watery swim of her tears.

She blinked rapidly, lest he think she was weeping and did not recognize the outpouring from her eyes for what it was—the result of bone-aching fatigue.

As her eyes cleared, she could see that he was not quite

steady on his feet. And when he said, "Go to bed, girl, you're
up much too late," his voice was as thick as though his throat
were stuffed with flannel.

"But Mrs. Callahan—"

"To hell with Mrs. Callahan! I give the orders around here
and what I shay . . ." He grinned ruefully. "Having a little
trouble shaying shay. But you know what I mean."

She waited until he had weaved his way out the door and
then went gratefully to her bedroom, walking not much
more steadily than he had walked, almost overcome by exhaustion. It was almost completely dark in the small room,
but she was too tired to lift her arms to open the shutters.
She had barely enough energy to undress and put on her
nightgown. She thought about locking the door but did nothing about it, for the few feet from the bed to the door
seemed to stretch like endless miles.

Then, instantly, she was asleep, deeply, dreamlessly asleep.
She did not know if it was a single minute or an hour or
longer when she was wrenched awake by the sound of someone outside her door.

Her body became numb with fear, and she pressed it hard
against the mattress as though she could make herself invisi-
ble. She tried to cry out, "Who's there?" but her throat was
agonizingly constricted, and no sound came from it.

The door opened a few inches and a dim bar of light
stretched its length. A shadow slipped through the opening
and then the door was shut quietly again.

The room was filled with darkness now, and the stillness
was broken by a man's heavy breathing and his unsteady
footfalls. She knew it was a man there in the darkness with
her even though she could not see him as he groped his way
to the bed.

And she knew, her heart banging roughly against her ribs,
why he was there.

She put out a hand in an effort to ward him off and she
felt the smoothness of the silken garment he wore. He opened
it quickly and she could hear its rustling as he shrugged it off
his body. And, naked and sweating, he fell upon her and
clutched at her nightgown.

His hand slid under it. She could feel his fingers seeking,
smoothing, thrusting. There was one paralyzing moment
when Megeen felt as though she had turned to stone. Then,
with a gasp of outrage, she began to thrash from side to side

in an effort to free her body, which he had pinned beneath him.

Her face was under his shoulder, for he was taller than she and so she could not cry out. The reek of liquor about him sickened her, and she was afraid that she would faint, for she could not breathe with her mouth against his bare flesh.

He held her down with one hand while the other went on squeezing and poking and rubbing and exploring, arousing himself more and more until he was like a crazed animal. His groans and grunting, too, sounded bestial.

He forced his knees between hers, and when he had them open, he came up into her with a cry of triumph. A dozen times he thrust into her, going farther and farther into her, until his hardness tore everything that lay in its path.

She was half fainting from the pain and the indignity when, with one last roar, he fell upon her, gasping and sweating. Then he withdrew himself and rolled off her. At last she was free. Shivering in spite of the fact that his hot, damp flesh had warmed her not a minute ago, she pulled the bedclothes up around her. She lay there, hoping that this was a nightmare, that she would awaken at any moment in the kindly darkness.

There was no awakening and no kindness anywhere. She discovered that the man who had violated her had not left the room. He was squatting in the corner and there was something loathsome about that crouched figure, which seemed not to be breathing now but merely waiting to spring at her again.

Not again! Oh, God help me now!

She made a stealthy attempt to slide from the bed, her anguish buried under her terror. There was but one little movement and only the slightest sound as her feet touched the floor.

He sprang out of his corner. He grasped her around the waist and threw her back on the bed. And there he pinioned her shoulders, his knees separated her thighs once more, and he entered her without hesitation, as though he was compelled to force the shame upon her as quickly as possible for fear of being interrupted.

But he was not ready and he was forced to thrust himself into her over and over again until she cried out for mercy.

When he was finished with her, when he had finally poured his semen into her, he rolled off her, snatched up his dressing gown from the floor, and slipped from the room as quietly as he had come.

All she saw of him was that stealthy figure and a face that was only a pale blur in the darkness. It did not matter to her now who he was. She lay huddled and weeping on the blood-stained sheet, feeling its sticky wetness under her.

Finally she got up and made a bundle of the sheet and pushed it under the bed. That small movement drained her energy and she fell onto the bare mattress, panting. Slowly her mind released itself from the horror. She knew that she must cling to her sanity. She was lucky to be alive, for if she had fought too vigorously during those terrible moments, the man might have choked the life from her body; in his frenzy he would not have been denied.

She groped her way across the room and locked the door, too late. It was a flimsy latch at any rate and would not have kept out anyone who was driven by drunken lust.

She lay there for a long time. Some of her thoughts were clear enough and they trailed desolation and fear in their wake. Others were bitter and uncomprehending.

So this was the reason her sister was a bitch in heat in the presence of her husband. And why Tessie McNamara yearned for a suitor. Megeen had felt the want herself; remembering the tremulous heat between her legs, which was like a persistent itching, she quickly stopped her thoughts.

This was how it ended up then? You lay sick and shamed and with your insides as sore as though a stick had been shoved into you.

She had been fooled. Her sister had scoffed at the idea of carrying around a hatpin and told her that no man wants an unwilling piece. Sister Melitas had told her senior girls that they could defend themselves by kneeing a man's groin, but she had never explained that there was no defense against the pinning body of a lust-crazed man.

Megeen fell asleep at last, and when she awoke, the tears had dried on her cheeks.

Chapter Six

Megeen's half numbed mind went groping through the unfamiliar noises: the steady music of a church bell somewhere a long way off, the insistent cheeping of birds outside her window, footsteps on the street above her.

She felt stupid and thickheaded until she remembered where she was and what had happened. Then the bruising pain struck at her again. She pulled herself out of bed, went to the window, and opened the shutters. Sunlight came pouring in, and she stood in its brightness as though it could wash away her anger and shame.

From where she stood she could see the feet that passed the window. There were the buttoned shoes of thin calfskin worn by women, the sturdier boots of children, and the men's boots, which had inserts of elastic at the ankles.

All, she thought bleakly, on their way to some church or other.

It was Sunday and she, too, must go to church, for to miss Mass would put the stain of mortal sin on her soul. No matter what had happened in this vile little room last night, she had a duty to fulfill.

She examined her conscience carefully. Had she, by word or glance, signified that she would welcome the attentions of the man who had violated her? He had been, of course, one of the two men in the house, for who else would be going about naked except for his dressing gown?

If she had done so, then the fault was hers, too. Men had overwhelming needs, especially when they had the drink in them. The young Mr. Vickery—had her eyes betrayed the fact that she found him attractive to look upon?

But she could find no blame to place upon herself. And rising inside her was a flood of anger and bitterness.

She did not put on the uniform that hung on a nail by the door. It seemed to her now that it was a badge of shame, the outward sign of her servitude, which made her vulnerable to the animal needs of a man of a higher class.

The brown dress, much as she despised it, covered her body decently. Her hair combed and her face scrubbed as clean as could be managed in the stagnant water in the basin, she opened the door and walked firmly out into the kitchen.

Tessie and Mrs. Callahan were there in hats and gloves and carrying prayer books in attitudes of piety.

"So ye decided to arise at last! I was about to rouse ye from bed, lazy girl! What do ye think this is, a place to be waited upon when ye've slept half the day away?"

The words made little impression on Megeen. Because they were quickly followed by others that caused her skin to tighten and her breath to hang suspended.

"Himself will be havin' his coffee right away, girl. No breakfast this mornin', he says. Natural enough, that is, for he must be fairly uncomfortable with all the whiskey and wine last night. He's to be served in the gentlemen's room—or the study, as he calls it. Ye're to carry up a full pot there, for no doubt he'll be joined by the young master."

When she and Tessie reached the door, she turned and said, "Me and Tessie is goin' to the Mass that'll start in ten minutes. There's a later one you can attend, if, that is, it suits yer fancy to go at all." She hesitated and then, unable to hold back her resentment any longer, spat out, "Ye did not finish picking up last night for this day I found glasses in the study, dirty ones they were. And the drawin' room was not aired out."

"But Mr. Vickery told me to go to bed."

"To be sure! Ye've found a way to get around him and ye used it again!"

Then, flouncing so that her hat wobbled atop her head, she stamped through the door and up the areaway steps.

Tessie made a little face before she followed in Mrs. Callahan's wake. Tessie would never be pretty or even attractive, but in her blue serge suit and the hat with the wings of a bird spread out over its brim, she looked quite stylish.

Megeen was beginning to realize how sharply her own clothes marked her for a newcomer. When she received her wages at last, Tessie would teach her how to dress.

But that thought died almost before it was formed in Megeen's mind. Such things were unimportant now. And what she must do stretched her nerves so tightly that she felt physically sick.

Alexander Vickery, clad in a dark-blue silk dressing gown, sat with the untidy pages of *The Boston Globe* spread on his knees. He sprang to his feet when Megeen pushed open the door of the study and the sheets of newspaper slid to the floor.

He shoved them aside with his foot and crossed the room and took the tray from her hands. As he placed it on a low table, she glanced around, postponing the moment when she would say what she had to say to him.

In spite of her nervousness, she was able to note that the room was furnished for a man's comfort: well-worn leather chairs, a beautiful desk that she guessed was very old, shelves of books reaching to the ceiling on one wall.

She could postpone the moment no longer. And when she lifted her eyes to Alexander Vickery, all she could see was his dressing gown.

It was of such dark material that it could easily have blended into the darkness of the small room. When he returned her direct look with one of his own, she saw the redness that rimmed his eyes.

Megeen did not know how she was to begin, and although she had turned words and phrases over in her mind in preparation for this instant, they failed to come to her tongue.

The sound of footsteps in the hall diverted her, and she had turned toward the door when Lenard Vickery came through it. Her heart struck hard against her ribs, but she held her ground. What she must accuse one or the other of was to be heard by both.

"I have something to say, and if you'll but listen for no more than a few minutes . . ."

Their eyes were upon her, Mr. Vickery's looking a little surprised, his son's with an expression that told her nothing, blank as it was.

Anger rose like a burning fever from deep inside her, not at either of these two men now but at herself when she heard the servile note in her voice.

"What happened last night . . ."

But she could not go on. She saw that the younger man was smiling now, an amused smile as though he were enjoying her discomfort.

His father said quietly, "Well, what is it? Of course we'll listen if you have something important to say, as it seems you do."

She gave him a grateful glance and then, in a quick spate of words, told them she had been molested twice in her small room off the kitchen, told them how sensitive parts had been violated and her body used as a vessel for a man's outpouring.

She did not even find it embarrassing to tell these two men, virtual strangers. She was too carried away by the awful memories to stem the outburst or pick more polite phrases.

The outburst halted as abruptly as it had begun. For Lenard Vickery, moving about restlessly, came into her line of vision. He, too, was wearing a dressing gown. It was of dark-red satin with lapels of a lighter shade, and there were silken frogs down the front of it.

Was this the smooth material she had felt during that moment before he had discarded it to leave his body naked?

Alexander Vickery drew a long breath and said softly, "My God! What a thing to have happen on her first night in this house!"

"If it's true."

The two men locked glances. "Of course it's true!" Mr. Vickery's voice had become stern. His jaw had tightened and his face grown grim. "Why would she concoct a story like that?"

Now they were talking about her as though she were out of earshot.

"Then, if you believe she's telling the truth, we must find out who the man is. One of our guests, do you think, Father? Did anyone stay after the others had left? I don't remember much of anything after Dorothea and her parents went home."

"There was no one left. Nor could anyone have broken in, for I saw to the doors and windows on the first floor." He spoke curtly and he seemed genuinely troubled. "And I have trouble, too, remembering anything after that."

"Father, are you meaning to imply . . . ?"

Lenard lifted his long hands, palms out, in a gesture of denial. "If you're thinking of me in that regard, Father, you're all wrong. Not that she's not a tempting bit."

He finally looked directly at Megeen, who stood with her hands locked together at her waist. "A mite small and thin for my taste, but the red hair is attractive, I'll own, and there's a wicked sparkle in her eyes."

The sparkle was a furious glare as she cried out. "I'll thank you not to speak of me as I did not exist! And this talk of outsiders is ridiculous. For there was nothing under the only garment he wore."

Her voice petered off and the shame rose again to scald her skin. How could she argue with these two men, who had money and social position and who knew ways to defeat her in a battle of wits?

Lenard said, "We've forgotten about Hanley."

The name was unfamiliar to Megeen and she turned a questioning face to Mr. Vickery.

"Hanley is our coachman. My stable is set up over on Washington Street. The horses and carriages are there and Tim Hanley takes care of them. Yes, he could have come back into the house, but he's a grumpy, taciturn one. Fifty or so."

"It could not have been him, for if he works in a stable there would have been about him the smell of the horses and there could have been no mistaking about that. It was naught but whiskey that I smelled."

Lenard threw back his head and roared out a laugh. "The wit of the Irish! All of them seem to have it."

She said coldly, "I can see nothing funny about it. The worst thing that could happen to a girl happened to me last night in this house. It cannot be undone by a joke. Nor by the attempts of either of you to prove that it was someone from the outside who forced himself upon me."

"What do you want then?" Lenard asked bluntly. "Money?"

Speechless with fury, she glared at him with eyes so hot that they felt as though fire burned behind them. Her voice was broken when finally she was able to say, "I am not to be paid for like a slut upon the streets. You cannot understand what I feel, either of you!"

Mr. Vickery's gentle glance calmed her.

She turned to look at him and saw only kindness in his eyes. But it did not stop her from saying, "This I will tell you now as the truth. Happen it did, then, but never will it so do again. For I saw yesterday in one of the cabinets in the kitchen a collection of wicked-looking knives. And if I am to stay here in this job, every night there will be the longest, sharpest one of the lot under my pillow."

She drew an uneven breath. "Never," she vowed, "will I be at the mercy of a man, be he drunk or sober, who believes that a woman is fair game because she does menial work."

Lenard, grown sober, looked at his father with eyes troubled by uncertainty. "Why don't you fire her on the spot, Father? You can be sure of one thing—she'll be running to church to tattle to the priests about what she says went on last night. And it could cause a scandal. Dorothea and her parents will hear about it and then I'll be in the soup for fair."

"I cannot allow you to speak that way!" Megeen clenched her fists and pressed them together. "The smallest child knows that not a single word passes the lips of those holy men who take the place of God here on earth. The seal of the confessional is sacred and what is heard in it can go no farther."

Lenard honked a brief laugh. "Oh, come now! Holy men indeed! I'll tell you something everyone does know. Your priests and nuns have themselves a high old time together. And the results of that—the bastard babies—are killed at birth and buried behind every convent in the country."

Her anger was misting her eyes, and she could barely see his face. She took a step toward him, but Alexander Vickery put himself between her and the young man.

"Gossip," he said, "does not become a man of your age and station in life, Lenard. I think you had best leave us now, for I can handle the situation better if I could talk to Megeen alone."

She edged toward the door. "I beg pardon, sir, but I had best be going, too. Else I shall be late for Mass."

He said in the same calm, determined voice, "Sit down, Megeen, other things can wait. I know it is foolish of me to tell you that it would be best to forget this . . . unpleasantness. But surely there is something we can do to right the wrong."

She was beginning to learn a certain thing about people like Alexander Vickery. They could show a haughty face to the world and no one could guess what thoughts and feelings were hidden behind those cool, proud exteriors.

"Tell me, Megeen, why did you wish to speak to me today? To give notice? Are you intending to leave my employ?"

"Oh, no, sir! Only to try to make sure that no such thing happens to me again, and to tell you—as I did—how I am to protect myself."

"It won't happen; I promise you that. But I would think that you could not get away from this house quickly enough. Isn't that what we might expect a young, respectable girl to do under the circumstances?"

"Not if her only choice was starving to death."

A faint smile twitched at the corners of his mouth. "Come now, isn't that a rather melodramatic statement? I refuse to believe that such a drastic fate would await you. You're well-spoken, more so than any servant I have ever encountered. You sound like a fairly well-educated person."

"As I am, indeed," she said proudly. "I graduated from St. Monica's Academy, which is a few miles from my home in Kerry. The nuns allowed me to work for my board and a few pence a week. Had I stayed, I might have become a lay teacher, but the pay was poor and much money is needed at home now that my father is in his last resting place."

"And you came to America hoping to find the streets paved with gold?"

"I am not that ignorant," she said icily. "I knew that I could not find a job easily not having worked anywhere before. I thought that my sister, who came here two years ago . . ."

She stopped herself just in time. His quiet attention was making her say things that were better left unsaid. "It makes the difference," she told him, "when you are without two coins to rub together."

He asked her how much money she was earning as his kitchen maid and she confessed that she did not know. "It will be many long weeks before there is anything in my pocket at any rate. For my first month's wages are to be divided between Mrs. Callahan and Mr. Gilligan."

What she was saying seemed to puzzle him. Wrinkles spread across his forehead. So she explained the form of bribery necessary if a greenhorn was to obtain a job. She had had no intention of speaking of that, either, but worry that was almost like despair brought the words from her mouth.

"So that is the way it is done," Mr. Vickery said softly. "Traffic in human beings, almost as bad as the slavery we got rid of not so many years ago. And at what a cost!"

He went to the graceful little desk and lifted from one of

its drawers a gray ledger book. Then he riffled through its pages, and when he found what he was looking for, he kept his gaze fastened upon it for a long time.

Finally he turned back to speak to Megeen and his face was grave.

"Six dollars a month is what we will be paying you. And that will be free and clear; you are to make no payments to anyone, not now or at any other time. If you have any trouble with the cook or the blackguard who lives on the wages of poor young people he seeks out for the purpose of making himself richer, you will let me handle the matter."

Her eyes had widened when he mentioned the sum of her wages. She had not expected to earn such a princely salary, and immediately her thoughts raced to Marm and to plans for sending across the sea at least half of that amount.

Gratitude brought a trembling smile to Megeen's lips. She knew that she would not be able to speak without bursting into tears. The raw feeling in her throat grew more painful when Mr. Vickery unlocked another drawer of the desk and took from it three one-dollar bills.

As he handed the money to her, he said, "This is an advance on your wages, Megeen. If you are needing more, please come to me. I will not permit you to be browbeaten by anyone in this household."

Clutching the money, she moved toward the door. "When the others come back, I will be going to church. I will offer prayers for you, sir, and, yes, the one who treated me so brutally. We must forgive, so it says in the Scriptures, and I shall try to do so, although I fear I'll have little luck that way."

He walked with her to the hall. "Do you actually believe in such things? Prayers, I mean? Do you expect God to answer them?"

His tone was merely curious and she took no offense at the question. Poor man! she thought. With all his riches, he had little enough if he did not know the way to heaven.

"I do indeed, sir. But I do not bother the Creator with my small petitions too much. I ask the saints to intercede for me. I choose the ones who are not so well known. The others ... well, poor St. Patrick must be swamped with prayers, for he is the favorite of all the Irish. And St. Joseph, too, for he is the patron saint of the nuns. Who but me, I wonder, thinks to pray to St. Camillus, who wears the red cross of mercy on his cassock; that he did when he gave his life to the sick and the dying. And St. Dymphna, a young girl not as old as I who was beheaded because she refused the advances of her own father."

Then Megeen turned and met Mr. Vickery's eyes. "Kindness is one of the major virtues, as perhaps you know. So you will have your reward sometime, regardless of—of anything else."

It was not until later, when she put her hand into the pocket of her dress and the greenbacks crackled in her fingers, that the troubling thoughts came back. Six dollars a month—she was sure that scullery maids did not ordinarily receive such high wages.

So, in spite of her brave words to Lenard Vickery when she had claimed that money chould not heal the wounds of her spirit, she knew that she had, in a fashion, sold something in the marketplace of this strange, new world.

Chapter Seven

"... for I have sinned. It is two months since my last confession, Father, but it was not my fault entirely, for I was aboard ship on the long journey and there was no priest even to say Mass. I made my last penance and since then I am guilty of the following sins ﹒﹒."

The list was not a long one and none were other than venial. Neglect of prayers at bedtime. Uncharitable thoughts. The flaring of temper and the stubbornness of pride.

Outside the airless confessional, with its smell of the dusty velvet curtain and the wet clothing of those who had been there before her, were three benches full of supplicants. Afraid of being overheard, Megeen dropped her low murmur to thin whisper.

"Speak up."

The disembodied voice on the other side of the screen was gruff. "I must hear what you're saying, you know."

"Yes, Father. It is just that—that it upsets me to talk about this. Sometimes I think I must have sinned grievously against God, that I have been punished this way. . . ."

When she finished the ugly story of what had happened on that night exactly a week ago, he was silent for a long time. She began to be uneasy, worrying that the people waiting in the pews outside would suspect her of some heinous crime that was taking her so long to confess.

The priest spoke at last. On a gusty sigh, he said, "So they are still treating our girls thus! I had hoped that with the war at an end, feelings about us would change. My child, you must pray not only for your own soul but for those of all in this growing, Godless city. Well, go on, young lady. Was there at any time during the assault upon you that you enjoyed the act?"

"No, Father, truly there was not."

"Then there was no sin on your part. But you must give up your position in that household. Otherwise, you are condoning what was done to you. And you must avoid the occasion of sin."

He did not demand, as she thought he would, that she obey the order or withhold absolution on that condition. Nor did he give her time to explain her method of protecting herself: the knife under her pillow, the chair placed against the door, the latch that she had repaired herself with a screwdriver.

Her penance was not only the twenty Hail Marys he imposed upon her; it was also the daily humiliation of working in a place where the servant in charge never gave her a kindly word or smile. That Mrs. Callahan despised her she was well aware. The meanest, hardest chores were heaped upon her. She was seldom allowed upstairs.

But on a day when Tessie was confined to her room with a toothache, Mrs. Callahan ordered Megeen to clean the drawing room.

"Since ye seem to have such a love for workin'," she said spitefully, "a little more extra should bother ye none."

She was referring to the fact that Megeen, unlike the other two servants, was conscientious about her tasks. She spent hour after hour with scrubbing brush, steaming water, and strong yellow soap, stopping only briefly for meals. Megeen knew that the two resented her more for that than they would have if she had idled the time away and tried to shunt her chores upon them.

The kitchen had become an attractive place because of her labors. The copper pots and kettles shone like objects of precious metal. Behind the glistening glass of the cabinet doors, the chinaware was spotless. She had polished the stove until its surface was like onyx. Its metal trimmings gleamed and the mica patch on its door was the color of a ruby.

"So it's upstairs with ye now and no lingerin', mind. I know how long it takes Tessie to put the place to rights. And be careful what ye touch, for there's things supposed to be worth a lot of money, though, if they belonged to me, I'd not give them houseroom."

Megeen felt a little twisting of pity for Mrs. Callahan, who was blind to the beauty around her, was locked into a narrow world of discontent and absorption with her poor health, real or fancied. Her arms burdened with broom, pail, and dustrag, she turned to look at the woman and saw in the close-set eyes something that surprised her.

It was uneasiness, almost fear. And Megeen realized then what it was that made the woman unable to speak a civil word to her. Mrs. Callahan feared for her job. Alone and growing older and with her energy and vigor seeping away, she must be terrified of losing her job.

Megeen said gently, "I'll hurry. And if you'll leave the laundry, I'll put it on to boil as soon as I come back."

It had been the wrong thing to say. She realized that the moment the words were said. Without intending to, she had diminished Mrs. Callahan's importance in the household. But the laundry had been Tessie's chore and it was a heavy one.

Sheets and pillowcases, table linen and towels, were dumped into great copper tubs filled with scalding water and set upon the stove. A thick, sturdy stick was used for stirring them. The articles, when they were rinsed, were wrung out and hung on lines in the backyard. Then the tub was carried to the sink and the water emptied from it.

It was not an easy task for a woman whose complaints of backaches, swollen feet, the discomforts of the menopause, and pains and aches in various parts of her body, were a never-ending litany.

Megeen knew that they would never be friends, she and Mrs. Callahan, but she was grateful that God had given her the wisdom to see the misery of a soul behind the denfensive bad temper. Having seen it, she would never feel the same about Agnes Callahan again.

The drawing room was beautiful indeed. The marble fireplace had carved into each side of it the figures of angels with lifelike, lovely faces. The hearth was of pale-pink brick and on the mantelpiece were figurines of ivory and what Megeen guessed were jade.

But it was the portrait over the fireplace that caught Megeen's attention and kept her staring upward.

This was the portrait Tessie had spoken of, and it seemed to dominate the room. It was as though Flora Vickery, dead now for more than a year, still was a part of this room, where she had once entertained her guests, chatted and laughed and moved about.

She might have been surveying sadly the neglect of the furnishings. The mouth wore a faint droop. The shawl that lay across her shoulders seemed not to be worn for the sake of fashion but to protect her slender body from a chill.

Flora Vickery: a frail flower whom death had blighted before she reached the age of forty.

Megeen heard the sound of movement behind her and turned quickly. Alexander Vickery was smiling down at her, but there was no warmth in the smile.

"Admiring or just curious?"

A burning flush colored her cheeks. "Both, I'm afraid, sir. I was thinking how sad it is—her such a young-looking, bonny woman. I'm sorry. I know I should not be saying so much. . . ."

His eyes, lifting from Megeen's face to the portrait, became tender. "No reason for you not to speak out. That was the hardest part, you see. My friends, my son—none of them would talk about her to me. No doubt they thought the mention of her name would bring me pain. They didn't realize that it would have helped if we could have talked of the happy times we shared with her. That would have kept her alive for me for a time."

It was a strange conversation for the master of the house and his scullery maid. But she felt nothing of embarrassment or awkwardness, only a deep, aching pity for a husband mourning his lost wife.

"Lenard refused to speak of her at all. The blow was a bitter one for him, for he and his mother were very close. Until the night of the dinner party he would not step foot into this room. It was peculiarly hers, and I am glad it's to be taken care of properly."

She took that for a hint and started her work by sweeping the hearth. But he did not leave. He stayed there, talking of the lady in the portrait; then he began to identify the pieces of furniture by the names of the artisans who had fashioned them. Certain delicate chairs were Hepplewhites. A lovely desk had been the work of Thomas Sheraton. An armchair with curved legs he called a Chippendale.

She listened to it all carefully, filing it in her mind, for she had a fondness for learning new things, bits of knowledge that she had not found in her schoolbooks.

The lesson ended when Mr. Vickery said, "Easter is a week away. Each year at this time Mrs. Vickery sent the servants down to the dry-goods store to pick out yard goods for new dresses. Last year, of course, we were in mourning. But now we shall resume the custom. Mrs. Callahan will tell you where to find the store. It has the Vickery name over the door—one of my business interests. Not a profitable one, but it remains a sentimental weakness of mine. My great-grandfather started in shortly after the Revolutionary War."

He glanced at her briefly and impersonally. She was conscious of the ill-fitting uniform that Mrs. Callahan, an indifferent seamstress, had altered.

"And perhaps new bonnets," he added. "You may tell the others to put everything on my account."

It was an order that Megeen carried out with high spirits. Even Tessie's toothache was cured miraculously by the promise of new clothing.

Megeen was the one who measured and cut and sewed far into the night until her eyes felt like burning coals. Tessie, with the help of a dog-eared fashion magazine, had chosen maroon silk and white rickrack braid and a jabot of filmy lace. She argued for even more trimming, but Megeen convinced her that the gown would look richer by far without it.

Mrs. Callahan could not be persuaded to relinquish her insistence on respectable black, but Megeen added a velvet bow here and there, and in her new brimless hat of shiny black straw decorated by a single rose, the cook made an imposing figure.

Megeen had been tempted by nothing except a soft green merino, and she fashioned it with a slight gathering at the back. It was a subdued sort of style in contrast to the monstrous bustles ladies were wearing that season.

She saw them when she went through the streets of Boston

on her weekly afternoon off. There was a great deal to see and often she returned home speechless with awe.

Life had become pleasant for her. No matter the sarcastic remarks of the other two servants. Never mind her disappointment over her sister and the little spells of homesickness now and then. The saints were watching over her, seeing to it that she was safe and even enjoying her work and the being part of this growing, bustling city.

Easter came and went. The weather was made for the day—bright with sunshine and with the gentlest of breezes—so that the women could fare forth in all their finery. Church bells rang from many church steeples in great harmony, a lovely sound in the morning air.

It was a day when, without knowing why, Megeen felt a change stealing into her life. It was not merely the new clothing but something different, something to do with the feeling that she was becoming an American woman and no longer was a green girl from across the sea.

Her first payment of wages came from the hand of Mr. Vickery himself. The envelope that contained it was sealed, and neither Mrs. Callahan nor Patrick Gilligan made any claims for their share of the money. Megeen guessed that Mr. Vickery was responsible for that, but when she tried to speak to him about it, he seemed not to want to talk about it. Nor would he allow her to repay the advance he had made on her salary. He waved away her offer to do so and said carelessly, "Some other time."

Megeen had become acquainted with the one other member of the household. Tim Hanley, who was in charge of the Vickery stable, sometimes took his meals with the other servants. At first he repulsed all her overtures at friendliness. But gradually the barrier of silence and curtness crumbled; when he talked, he did so rapidly, as though making up for lost time.

He had served in the Union army during the Civil War, had been wounded at Antietam, had seen President Lincoln at close range. He described the draft riots and the country's great sorrow over the assassination of Mr. Lincoln in 1865.

To Megeen the stories were like those read in a book. But she believed them all because she could walk no more than a mile to see that this was a wild, astonishing country; street fights were not unusual, there was always a runaway horse, a fire, or a collision of some sort.

She enjoyed the city and its fast pace, and she was sending bank checks regularly to her mother.

There was only one small cloud of worry in her mind. She had missed one menstruation period and there were signs that she would miss a second.

Chapter Eight

One morning, when she felt a familiar cramping of her stomach she thought for sure she was not pregnant. But her hopes were soon gone when, shortly after, the nausea began and there were spells of vomiting that kept her shuddering over the slop jar in futile efforts to keep the women in the kitchen from hearing the sounds of her shame.

Her pallor and the uncertainty of her steps told Mrs. Callahan enough. But she expressed no horror, no grim satisfaction or even surprise. It was not the first time she had found herself with a pregnant kitchen maid. Women, she would have said had she been able to articulate her thoughts, were at the mercy of men. Loyalty to her own sex kept her silent and even a little indignant.

Megeen refused to accept the truth of her condition for as long as possible. She worked to the point of exhaustion, believing that if she offered up enough mean, disagreeable tasks, she would be rewarded with freedom from what she knew, deep in her heart, was growing there.

She discovered a sad little garden behind the house. One half of the small patch of land was strung with clotheslines. A low fence separated it from the rest of the yard, and there were high fences marking off the Vickery property on either side and at the rear.

The garden was a miniature jungle. Thorny bushes and unrestrained strips of ivy strangulated whatever flowers might have bloomed there. But there were a few hardy plants. A few purple and white irises were showing buds. Morning glories had found a bush tall enough to provide a branch to twine about; violets were almost buried in a patch of moss.

From the first Megeen thought of this as Flora Vickery's garden. She could imagine the woman of the fragile features and sorrowful eyes sitting on the bench against one of the high fences. The bench, fashioned of delicate grillwork, was rusted now and some of its paint was peeling, but at one time this must have been a pleasant place to sit on a warm afternoon.

Whenever Megeen had a little time, she worked in the garden, clearing away the overgrown shrubbery, replanting, digging, training the morning glories and ivy on lengths of twine that she nailed to the wooden fences. She coaxed Tim Hanley into painting the bench and repairing the broken pieces of flagstone that formed a short path through the center of the garden. She never noticed Alexander Vickery watching her from the windows.

One day she found, under the rubble of uprooted weeds and bushes, a small statue. The figure was that of a male child. He held upon his shoulder a water jug, and Megeen guessed that the statue had once been part of a fountain.

She found, too, a small pedestal hidden among the shrubbery, and when she placed the figure upon it, she could force it to stand upright.

With the sun shining upon it, the carved boy looked almost lifelike. But Megeen was embarrassed by his nakedness. She dug a deeper hole and pushed the statue farther into the ground. But still she could not hide more than the feet of the little boy.

She spent almost the entire afternoon there in the garden, transplanting the larger growing flowers—irises, rose bushes, forsythia, syringas—and arranging them at the base of the statue so that they decently covered the private parts of the carved figure.

Alexander Vickery found her there almost at the moment she had completed her exhausting chore. He had, he said, a letter for her, and aware that it had been sent by her mother, he had wanted to deliver it into her hands.

"For I know how welcome it must be. And that you would want to see it at the first possible moment."

Then he took a step closer and his eyes fell on the statue of the little water boy. For a few seconds he looked puzzled, as though he were not quite sure what it was he was seeing. He walked closer and gently pushed aside one of the tall plants.

He threw back his head and a great explosion of laughter burst from his throat. Megeen had not heard him laugh in this manner before. She stood ill-at-ease, making tucks in her apron but not resentful that he found her modesty a source of mirth. Poor man, he had little enough to amuse him! Since the dinner party, which had ended so disastrously for her, no company had come to the house and there seemed to be little companionship between him and his son.

Lenard was absent from the house a great deal of the time, not only during the daytime hours when he and Mr. Vickery were at their law offices on State Street, but in the evenings as well. The romance between him and Dorothea Lovering was flourishing, according to Tessie.

There was little that Tessie did not know—or guess at—about the Vickerys and their neighbors. Megeen learned that you simply could not accept everything the other girl said as the truth. You sifted through the gossip, conjectures, and bits of authentic facts, and selected what was genuine.

What was true was that Mr. Vickery was an attorney-at-law and his son was reading as a clerk. Lenard had been dropped from Harvard University across the river for failing in his scholastic work.

What could only be imagination was Tessie's story of a dramatic deathbed farewell by Flora Vickery, when she pleaded with her husband to take care of their "little boy." Lenard would have been nineteen when his mother passed away. And, at any rate, Tessie had not come to the house until a few months later.

Throughout all those spring and early-summer days, there crouched at the back of Megeen's mind, waiting to overwhelm her, the secret that she knew could not remain a secret much longer. No matter what she was doing—taking long walks on her afternoons off; visiting the new Museum of Fine Arts, where she stood and absorbed the beauty around her; the shopping for inexpensive clothing to replenish her wardrobe—she never felt alone.

Sometimes she daydreamed about the baby. In her mind there was always Lenard Vickery. He came down into the kitchen to claim his one true love, who was bearing his child. The birth was easy and painless. Lenard was by turns in an agony of worry about her, adoring when they placed his son into his arms, thrilled at being a father, on his knees worshiping the woman who had given him this great gift.

Even while she let her mind construct all this happiness that was to be hers, she was well aware of what she was doing. She was escaping from the reality of carrying inside her a bastard child, rejecting the knowledge that its father would be one of two men. At times the dreams turned sour and she looked ahead, with mounting panic, to the time when her condition would become evident. Already the Easter Sunday dress was becoming tight. Her shawl was inadequate for purposes of concealment, and the weather had grown too warm for her cloak.

She was wearing the green merino dress on the afternoon she went to see her sister. It took her many days of indecision before she set out for the O'Flynns' apartment. She was nervous about Annie's learning of her pregnancy, for there was no closeness between them now. On the few occasions Megeen had visited the dreary rooms on B Street, Annie had been distracted and inattentive.

But they were sisters. Megeen kept reminding herself of that. Annie could not turn her away or refuse to help her. There had been all those years of growing up together. Marm had taught them to be loyal to each other. Regardless of any quarrels they might have in the family, the Ahearns stood side by side when they faced the world.

But it turned out to be, that day, Megeen who did the comforting instead of the other way around.

Why her sister needed comforting she learned only after long silences, awkward and meaningless exchanges of words, glances that did not meet.

Megeen had plenty of time to study the other girl. She saw the red-rimmed eyes, the blotches left by recent spells of weeping, and the restless hands that picked at the ruffle on her apron.

Annie did not notice the dress the Megeen was wearing. She did not even seem to realize that Megeen had kept her shawl over her shoulders in this airless room under a flat roof baked by a brilliant sun.

Megeen said finally, "I had something to tell you, but it seems, Annie darling, that you're in no condition to be listening to my troubles. You would like to tell me what is wrong with you?"

There was an explosion of tears and weeping. Annie put

her untidy head on her arms, which were resting on the table. Her shoulders rose and fell. The crying drifted away into whispering gasps. To Megeen that seemed sadder than if the weeping had gone on filling the room with its sound.

She went to the stove, where a brown china pot of tea was filled and ready. Somehow, that seemed to bring her closer to the unhappy girl, who was still hiding her face. In every Irish household she had ever visited, she had not failed to see on the back of the stove a generous-sized teapot. And always the tea had been strong and black—could have walked by itself Megeen often joked. There was nothing so bad—grief or worry or discouragement—that was not better for a cup of the strong brew.

But Annie was not interested in the steaming liquid. She lifted her head and pushed the cup aside. Her eyes were full of pain as she whispered, "Oh, Maggie, I don't know what to do!"

"What is wrong then? Come, tell your sister. Do you have a pain somewhere? Surely Tom has not lost his job? You have not quarreled with him? All young couples do, I suppose, until they get used to each other."

Annie's hair came tumbling down, freed from its pins as she shook her head. "Not exactly a quarrel, though I wish that was all. But when he comes home and I have to tell him . . ." She drew a shuddering breath. "But the monthly period began right after he left this noon."

"And you are in pain as you always were on the first day. The cramps and all."

Annie cried out impatiently, "It is not that. But we want children and he will be even more angry this time, for I was three days late and we hoped . . . he hoped . . ."

"But you're not married much more than six months!"

"He thinks it long. He feels . . . well, shamed. For some of his cronies do make fun of him and taunt him by asking if he has nothing to give his wife. One of their wives conceived on the very night she was married, and only a month after she gave birth, she was caught again and this time it was twins. Envious of that, Tom was. And he fears his friends will think of him as something less than a man if I don't get that way soon.

"And now there's the three days," she said, her voice rising in anguish. "When he can't have anything to do with me because of the period, he gets . . . oh, irritable and loses his temper over the least little thing. He's not an easy person to live with when his pleasure is denied him."

Megeen reached across the table, but Annie pulled her hand away. A small, frail hope was taking shape.

"If you and Tom want a child, Annie dear, there must be many who are without father and mother. Marm told us how it was during the potato famine—little tots found by the wayside in the arms of their dead mothers. The orphanages and workhouses were filled with them. Here, too, there must be hundreds of them without homes and families. You could have your pick of them, I'd think, and think how pleasing you'd be in God's sight in taking as your own one of His little ones. Or it could be the baby of someone you know."

The fragile little hope died an instant death. In one swift movement, Annie sprang from her chair, her face bleached white and disbelieving.

"You don't mean that Tom and I could take in someone else's child! It would never be the same—never! I know all too well how he'd feel and what he'd say if ever I were to speak of a thing like that to him. It would shame him all the more. His friends would know that he'd given up trying to make a baby. He's got his pride, has Tom O'Flynn, and something like that," she finished on a flat note, "would all but destroy him."

"Annie, I'm sorry!"

"Then spare me any more foolish ideas. And much as I do not like sounding rude, it would be better for you to run along now, Meggie. For he'll be coming home soon, being on the early shift today. It will be the very first question he'll be asking me. When he finds out—well, 'twill be worse if there's an outsider here."

An outsider. One for whom Annie had not a loving word, whose finery had not been noticed, who had not been asked the contents of their mother's last letter.

Annie was consumed by her dread. She was facing in the other direction when Megeen picked up her shawl and her purse. She paid no attention when the final attempt was made.

"Surely it cannot help matters for you to remain in these rooms all the time. There's much to do in the city. The stores—have you been to R. H. White's or Houghton and Dutton's? Mr. Vickery himself owns a store on Washington Street. And there's the Common, with all its trees, and they're laying out the new Public Garden. Sometimes I walk over that way. It might do you good, Annie, to go with me. Make you forget your troubles."

Annie had heard at least part of what she had been saying, for her voice grew scornful.

"Why should I waste my time when I have everything I want right here? Besides, Tom wouldn't like it at all if I were out gallivanting and not here waiting for him when he comes through that door."

Megeen could think of nothing more to say. Her heart felt cold and heavy when she went downstairs. Outside the dark and ill-smelling hall, the lowering sun was shedding its last hot brilliance of the day and the gentle breezes were kindly.

She knew the way home now, but she was tired and lethargic. It was as though she carried a heavy burden inside her that slowed her feet and made each step an effort.

As she reached the first crossing, a carriage pulled up beside her. She looked away quickly, for she was always conscious of the vulnerability of a woman walking alone in the city. But then she heard someone calling her name. She turned and looked up into the face of the driver.

"Miss Ahearn! I take it you do not remember me."

She stepped closer to the curbstone and recognized immediately the man who had called to her. He was the neat, quiet friend of Tom O'Flynn's whom she had met in her brother-in-law's tenement on the night of her arrival in the new country.

Martin Mulcahy. His name had come back to her, too, before he had jumped down to help her into his carriage.

"This is indeed an unexpected pleasure. You must allow me to drive you home."

She was on the point of refusing. Indeed, she told herself, she was in no mood for company. She did not feel that she could keep up a polite conversation, with so much sadness in her heart, when this man was a stranger whom she had met only once.

"Come," he said, stretching out a hand. "It will not take long. Mrs. O'Flynn told me where you are working and I shall have you there in no time at all."

At the time she did not think it odd that he had spoken of her to her sister. She was merely grateful that he had spared her a long walk on this warm spring afternoon.

Chapter Nine

They did not talk very much on that journey through the crowded streets. When she asked him how he happened to be abroad at this time of day, he answered, "Business."

She did not want to know any more. She hated to know that she was riding in a rig paid for by the poor wretches who spilled their wages on the bar at Mulcahy's Irish Saloon. And thus, no doubt, left their wives and little ones hungry and ill-cared-for.

She loathed the Destroyer with deep passion, although the man beside her seemed not to fit at all the role of destroyer of bodies and souls. She sensed in him a depth of kindliness, and despite his silence, she felt comfortable with him.

When they had reached the Vickery house, he made a few false starts but finally managed to ask, "Will you walk out with me some evening, Miss Ahearn?"

She felt a painful stab of regret. "I do not walk out with anyone sir." Her head hung forward and she gripped her reticule with tight fingers. "I thank you just the same."

An instant later she heard the slap of reins against the horse's rump. The harness jingled and then came the fading sound of hooves clattering, growing fainter until she could no longer hear them. The street fell into lonely silence.

She would never walk out with a man, she realized. Never would she be courted, for she belonged, in an odious but unmistakable way, to the man who had put a baby inside her.

That man had become faceless during the passing months. Try as she might to remember something about him that would identify him as Lenard Vickery, she could not truly match the self-absorbed, somewhat dandified young master of the house with the brutal, beastly creature who had made her pregnant. As for his father . . . unthinkable. Megeen saw in Alexander Vickery everything that was kind and compassionate. She refused to believe that his nature would have

51

changed to such a degree, even by overwhelming lust and drunkenness.

If she pleaded with him, revealed her condition, he would, she was sure, make arrangements for her care. He would send her away with money in her pocket, for at least pride would not allow a child of a Vickery man to be born in the workhouse.

The shadow of the workhouse loomed larger and darker as the heat spread, like a brassy dome, over the city. This place, which she had not yet seen, became almost as real to Megeen as the kitchen of the Vickery house, her airless room, and the flourishing garden where only the faintest of breezes made the evenings bearable.

She did not walk very far on those blisteringly hot summer afternoons. Although she was only in her fourth month, her condition was becoming evident. Slender and small-boned, she did not carry her child gracefully.

Humiliation darkened all her hours. When she was in church, she was conscious of the person on her left who might notice her ringless hand, although she prayed fervently against the sin of distraction. Both Tessie and Mrs. Callahan made a few pointed remarks, but somehow they seemed strangely without malice.

The dispositions of all of them were affected by a long, unbroken spell of hot weather; a word or even a sniff or a sharp word would have torn apart nerves that were already stretched and frayed.

The kitchen seemed no cooler than a baking oven. The big, old wood stove had to be kept going for cooking purposes. Tessie grumbled that it was a sin and a shame to have to work in a place that was hotter than the deepest pit of hell.

"Over at the Loverings', they've got a new kind of stove—run by gas, it is. It practically don't throw no heat at all."

Tim Hanley, in his livery, which he complained was heavier than a blanket, was the one from whom Megeen learned more and more about the Vickery men and their neighbors.

The master, said Tim, should not be spending the summer in the city in all this heat. Megeen thus learned that her employer's health was not robust.

"Weak lungs he's got. Had 'em since he was a kid. That's why it was funny—well, I do not mean comical—that the missus went off afore him. He ain't gonna have old bones, that's sure enough. Maybe that's why he don't push hisself. He's got someone to run the store down on Washington Street and an overseer down at the mill. And he ain't what you might call an ordinary lawyer, don't do nothin' about court cases, that is. More like he was"—he frowned, searching in his mind for a word that did not come to him—"well, it's more like takin' care of rich people's business. Wills and estates is what he does."

Megeen was hearing for the first time about the source of the Vickery fortune. She had not known about the paper mill situated in a small town named Fairbridge, ten miles to the north of the city, or what went on in the State Street office.

All of it seemed remote from her own life. A nightmarish experience in the spring had locked her into a dark place of shadows where she was always frightened, often sad, and sometimes desolate.

She slept badly. Even breathing was difficult in the small room off the kitchen, and she would go out to the areaway, climb the steps, and stand looking across the park.

There were lights filtering through the leaves of the trees and resembling a swarm of fireflies. Now and then she heard music, faint strains on the summer night air. She guessed that Lenard was over there at the Loverings', courting the young lady of his choice, for Tessie had told her that Mrs. Lovering was under the care of a Boston doctor for some vague ailment known as "nerves." The Loverings had not moved to their summer home as they usually did each June because Dorothea's mother did not want to be too far away from her physician.

Megeen's mind would fill to overflowing with pictures of Lenard's leaning over the piano while Dorothea played prettily the sentimental tunes that tinkled through the open windows.

Sometimes anger would strike her with the force of a sudden blow of a weapon. She would feel the tightening of her scalp and her eyes would become fiery. Then she would reach out and grip the first thing that came to hand, an iron picket or a corner of a step of the outside staircase.

She prayed for control, but when the pain of the blow had subsided and the fire burned itself out, she was weak and unsteady on her feet.

Even her favorite saints seemed to have deserted her, but she went on praying doggedly. And moving from one statue to another in the cathedral. One morning, she came upon that of St. Joseph, the guardian of the Virgin, stepfather of Jesus, patron saint of families.

She prayed for a miracle, but in the end it was a mundane thing, a tin bucket, that put into motion the happenings that affected her whole life.

The rain had come at last. The heat wave was shattered by the lancing of lightning, the crashing of thunder, and the opening of the skies with a downpour. After the storm was over, the east wind swept up from the ocean, sending the thermometers plunging downward, cooling the burning side-walks and the sweltering roofs.

When the sun came out again, it slid bars of brightness without pity into the dirtiest parts of the house. The wind had whipped out of the fireplaces' fine dustings of ashes. A leak in the roof left a smear of wetness in some of the upstairs rooms. The foyer beyond the front hall wore grimy footprints on its tessellated floor.

Mrs. Callahan argued against Megeen's scrubbing that floor. "Near on to mealtime and ye've done a full day's work and more. No sense in killin' yerself, for ye'll get no thanks, my girl, from either of those two. One of 'em's too wrapped up in mournin' his dead wife still and the other's off gallivant-in' all the time."

Megeen could have told her that she had no wish to impress the two men. She welcomed the weariness, for, if she became exhausted enough, she was able to sleep through the long nights.

She was secretly pleased that the house had come to look so well since she had taken upon herself the chores of clean-ing it. The mirrors in the drawing room glittered and the sur-faces of the furniture gleamed when struck by the sunlight. Staircase banisters were polished to a high gloss. Even the crystal doorknobs threw off colored splinters of light.

Ignoring the cook's carping, she took her pail of hot water, a scrubbing brush, harsh yellow soap, and clean rags upstairs. She was on her knees, half of the mosaic tiles scoured so that their intricate design had been restored, when Lenard Vickery came down the stairs. He did not see the small figure crouched there as he crossed the hall—not, at least, Megeen realized, as a human being like himself. She had known for some time that she and the other servants were to him only background figures, like the furniture and other inanimate objects.

He was whistling softly, and he did not break his stride or look down.

She called out a warning and reached for the pail of water, to slide it out of his path. But she was not quite in time. His foot struck against the pail and tip-tilted it. A flood of water poured over the floor and he skirted it deftly.

"Sorry!"

The front door opened and then closed behind him. He did not even look back.

Megeen crawled through the spilled water until she reached the clothes rack, which stood against the wall on one side of the foyer. She had always considered it an ugly thing, with its bristling pegs and shaped as it was like a tall, narrow chair with a long mirror forming its back. It did not at all match the other lovely pieces of furniture in the house, but now she was glad that it was there. She used it to pull herself up from the wet and slippery floor.

She had only one brief glimpse of herself in the mirror. She did not recognize her image. That girl wearing a drenched apron, her red hair flying every which way, freckles stark against the pallor of anger of her skin, blue eyes shooting sharp, bright darts—this was a stranger.

But a determined one. Her feet were steady and firm as she went down the hall. She did not knock politely on Mr. Vickery's door, but with her hand clenched into a fist, she pounded loudly.

When a tired voice said, "Come in!" she slapped open the door. Then, because she wanted to keep her hands off the sodden mess of her skirt and apron, she folded her arms across her chest.

That she looked formidable she could guess well enough. She was not swayed by the bewildered expression of her employer. He was sitting on a straight-backed chair drawn up to a small table with a chess set upon it. Megeen felt one faint and brief throb of pity for him. There was something pathetic about a man like him: rich, influential, surrounded by beautiful and probably priceless objects, and he had nothing to do but play, in solitude, a game that called for an opponent.

But the scene in the foyer had not lost its sting. She raised her voice so that he would hear every word she said to him.

"Sir, I wish to be married!"

Chapter Ten

She had all his attention now. He got to his feet slowly, as though by great effort. He motioned to the chair at the other side of the chessboard. She hesitated, a little daunted by his courtesy, but when he came around the table to pull out the chair for her, her face returned to its grimness.

"Perhaps you would be more comfortable somewhere else?"

There was nothing in his voice except solicitude but, she refused to let that affect her, too. She looked directly into his eyes and said stonily, "You see, I must. Get married, I mean."

He did not appear in the least shocked, or even surprised. He said quietly, "Megeen, the days of slavery are in the past. I don't know why you feel you must have my permission to leave my employ. That's what you came to tell me, isn't it? I shall be sorry to see you go, but I'll accept your notice or, if you wish to leave at once, you may do so, of course."

"That is not what I meant, sir. Not at all."

Her gaze did not falter. She had not allowed herself to be thrown off balance by his misunderstanding—or pretending to—the meaning of her statement.

"It was not for that, sir. You see, I am—" At that point she was daunted. She could not decide how to say it, after all. "That way," was too indefinite. "In trouble" would make her sound like some poor creature of the streets. "Carrying" would call too much attention to the ugly bulge that lifted her apron out of place.

"You are going to have a baby?"

She threw him a glance of gratitude because he spoke so quietly and with nothing, not condemnation or even surprise, in his voice.

"You knew!"

"Yes, Megeen. At least I guessed," he said, pretending not to have seen that obvious mound below her waist. "I am not an ignorant boy, you know. I was a very young father, scarcely twenty when Lenard was born. However, all that is of no importance now. We must talk about what you are to do."

"That is why I am here, Mr. Vickery. Your son is going to have to give my baby a name. I will not give birth to a bastard. He is its father, and little as he will be pleased about taking the consequences of his sin, he will have to accept them. That night in my room—"

"Ah, yes!" His hands played disconsolately with the chess pieces. "It was then it happened? And you have blamed your condition on my son?"

"I have indeed. For there were but the two of you. Sir," she said earnestly, "there was no one who came inside from anywhere else. And it would not have been you. I decided that long ago. Not at your age."

His lips moved in a wry twist. "Too old by far, you think? That I am fit only to sit and play this game in solitude while the young bucks dash about scattering their seed?"

Again a little puff of sympathy blew into her mind. It softened her voice. "And there is your health. The servants have told me that it is not of the best."

"You may tell them from me in turn that that's supposed to be the last thing of a man's body that dies."

Color flashed into her cheeks. She began to stutter, but he waved her silent.

"And so you have explained to me that you intend to force my son to marry you. Will you now reveal how that is to be accomplished?"

Her spine felt stiff against the back of the chair. She met his gaze with her own unwavering one. "I shall appeal to his better nature."

His eyebrows rose. "Lenard's better nature?"

"Indeed, each man must be ruled by his conscience. And it would not mean much to him, if so he wished it. We could be married without anyone knowing. Then I would gladly go away if he would give me a little money for his child. Enough so that I would not have to go to the workhouse to be confined."

"A wise plan." Mr. Vickery nodded. "But how will you persuade my son to agree to it? Suppose he refuses?"

"That he will not dare to do. For I'm sure he wants no scandal attached to his name. It is said that he is courting

Miss Lovering from across the park. How could he ask for her hand in marriage when he had got another woman in the family way? How could he refuse to do the honorable thing?"

"How, indeed? I vow, Megeen, that all this resembles one of the dramas one may see at the Boston Theater!"

"I know nothing of playacting," she said coldly, "never having set foot in a theater."

"Indeed! But tell me, suppose my son refuses to do the honorable thing? What will you do then?"

He was watching her closely, his hands still now. There were droplets of sweat along the edge of his hair.

"I shall visit that fine house of the Loverings. I shall appeal to Miss Dorothea for help in persuading him to marry me." She threw back her head defiantly. "You see, I will have no other choice."

Mr. Vickery asked her several questions. Did she not know that there was an ugly word for what she was planning? And was not she, too, possessed of a conscience? By what reasoning could she justify the destruction of the happiness of two young people?

"And even more," Megeen said, wringing her apron between her hands. "For Tessie McNamara does say that Mrs. Lovering is an ill woman and 'tis doubtful that she could endure a bad shock to her nerves. It would be a sorry day in that house if the truth was to be learned. How miserable they would all be! What is their religion, may I ask?"

He told her that they were Episcopalians and that they attended services at the Church of the Advent on Brimmer Street.

"Not even the comfort of the true faith," Megeen said sadly. "But then not everyone is lucky enough to be born a Catholic."

"No, indeed." She thought she detected a wry note in his voice, although his expression was solemn. "We must not condemn them for that."

"That I do not! The truth is, I feel sorry for them all. Should I have a daughter, I would suffer as much as she, should I learn that the man she intended to marry was not worthy of her. Miss Dorothea, from the glimpse I had of her, looks a little frail. I fear that she might take to her bed and never leave it, like the lady in one of Mr. Dickens' books."

A moment later she cried out, "It would be a dreadful thing to do!" in such a loud voice that he winced. She went on with her one-sided argument, allowing him no opportunity to speak. "It would be better for me to have my baby in the workhouse than perhaps cause the decline of health of that poor, innocent young woman! To say nothing of her mother!"

She stood up and glared down at him so fiercely that he began to apologize in a bewildered manner, as though he did not know why he was begging for forgiveness.

"We will say no more on the subject," she told him in a voice that sounded kindly. "I shall manage somehow, you know. The saints will come to my aid."

She started toward the door but stopped when he called her back. "How old are you, Megeen?"

She could not guess at the reason for the question, which seemed meaningless to her. But she answered him politely. "Eighteen, Sir."

"And I am a bit over forty. Decrepit and weighted down by years though I may seem to you, I am not quite ready for the grave. I beg you to consider that before you give me an answer to the question I am about to ask you.

"Would you consider marrying me?"

Stunned, she experienced the feeling that everything had left her: wits, the power of speech and movement. There was a long, strange silence, and then, her eyes examining his face, she said hoarsely, "You are joking, of course, sir. I think it is a poor joke. And I find it a cruel one."

"Megeen!" He moved slowly to her side, as though she were some small, frightened animal that might dart away at any moment. He cautiously picked up her trembling and icy hand. "Do you think I would distress you in that manner? You are right, it would be cruel. I am in earnest. You would have married my son as a matter of convenience. That is all this marriage would be. Not a true one by any means. So how can my age matter?"

"It is not only that, sir. My baby should be acknowledged and provided for by his true father."

He interrupted her, speaking rapidly and earnestly. "But Lenard is not, you see. He was not the one who violated you. That night . . . well, it is difficult for me to speak of it, for never was I in such a drunken condition before then, or afterward, you may be sure. In fact, there were many days when I did not even remember what happened that night."

He dropped her hand abruptly and went to a window and

pulled back its draperies. The room was at the back of the house and she knew that he was looking out over the garden where the bright fall flowers she had planted were coming into bloom, and probably not seeing them. He was, she guessed, too ashamed to let her see his face.

His voice was strained when he resumed speaking. "If you will consent, we can carry out the plan with only one change, a different bridegroom from the one you intended. We can be married quietly. No one need know. Then we will find some-place for you to go until you give birth to your—or rather our—child."

He let the drapery fall into place. When he turned back to her, there was little color in his face.

Poor man, he did not look well, she thought. And now she was touched by a new feeling for him. She longed to be able to spare him from the shame that was undoubtedly plaguing him and to find a way of helping him relieve his conscience.

"If you were to marry me, sir, if it were to be found out, think what your friends and the people here in the park would say!"

"Yes, indeed!" His lips twitched faintly. "There would be a great hullabaloo, wouldn't there? But it really concerns no one except us."

He grew sober again and said softly, "Every man is enti-tled to do one decent thing in his lifetime and, alas, I have not had the opportunity yet. Perhaps it will soon be too late."

"I do not understand you, sir." But that, she added quickly, was not in any way his fault. "There must be sense in your words, but I feel myself to be in some sort of dream. Not a bad one. Not a nightmare by any means. What it is, you see, is that none of this seems to be real. Are we really to be-come man and wife? If so, I shall make no claims upon you. Not ever. You need never acknowledge us, and if I must take a little money from you, I shall consider it only a loan. And one day I shall be able to pay it back to you."

He nodded. "Fine! I shall be looking forward to that day."

She did not know why he was smiling now or what she had said to amuse him. But his eyes were grave when he glanced down over her water-blotched apron and limp uniform.

"The occasion, I think, calls for a new gown. If you will tell me what it will cost—"

She interrupted him, her chin thrust forward and her gaze hard with pride. "I shall take from you only as much money as is needful for other purposes. For my debt to you will be large enough without fripperies."

"Then there is no more to be said except to set the date."

The coldness inside her was beginning to melt. The dazed feeling was being replaced by a glow of relief and happiness.

"It cannot be for three weeks or more, for it will be necessary for us to have the banns called from the altar on three Sundays. Not from the cathedral," she hastened to assure him as she saw his face change. "For that is where the servants from the neighboring houses attend Mass. When I was walking about the city one day, I came upon a church on one of the side streets. St. Dominic's it was. Perhaps the priest there would consent to marry us and even allow our names to be called only once. Or in South Boston, which is where my sister lives, there are St. Augustine's or St. Peter and Paul's. . . ."

She stopped speaking because his eyes seemed to have lost their color and were filmed with hardness.

"Do you really believe," he asked, spacing each word slowly and deliberately, "that I would consent to stand before a Papist clergyman and let him say his mumbo jumbo over me?"

"You are speaking of the holy sacrament of matrimony!" she cried in outraged protest.

"Call it what you will. No, Megeen, that is asking too much of me. I am willing to go with you to City Hall and obtain a license. I am acquainted with two or three judges, discreet fellows, all of them. Or there are justices of the peace outside the city whose silence can be bought with a few dollars. But I will have no part of a Romanish ceremony."

"There can be no other kind." A sudden gushing of tears that she would not let herself shed scraped her throat and made it ache. Disappointment and affront shook her voice. "I will thank you not to speak about the Church in that manner. For it is of the greatest importance in my life. And to be married in the way you describe would be no marriage at all in the sight of God, and a grievous sin besides. It would even mean excommunication, which is death to the soul!"

She drew herself up taller and lifted her chin. "And so, sir, we must forget the whole matter. Now there is work to be done before the evening meal."

Chapter Eleven

It was like a small war that neither side had much heart in waging. There were mild skirmishes, but no real victories. There were periods of truce and an offer of compromise that was summarily rejected.

Mr. Vickery, explaining that Tessie McNamara made him nervous with her fluttering about him at meals, requested that Megeen do the serving. Thus they were often alone together in the dining room, for Lenard usually had other things to do and places to be at dinnertime.

As Megeen was removing his soup plate one evening in early fall, he seized her wrist and forced her to face him.

"You'll never give in, will you? I know that much about you now. So how would this be? If you insist upon a clergyman marrying us, we might have the Reverend Parker of the Methodist church perform the ceremony. We would both be compromising, for I have no liking for any religion and you are letting blind superstition rule you."

Her lips mouthed a small cry of surprise and affront. "If you truly believe that I will stand before a Protestant minister to say the vows, you are much mistaken, for that would be the worst, the greatest sin."

On another afternoon when she went into the drawing room to pull together the draperies so that the lowering sun would not fade the carpet, he was standing in front of the fireplace with his hands clasped behind him as he stared up at the portrait of his dead wife. He turned as Megeen drew closer, and she saw a faraway, sorrowful glaze across his eyes.

"Her greatest disappointment was that we had only the one child—Lenard. For she loved all youngsters but especially the babies. She was looking forward to Lenard's getting married and being a father. They say most ladies dislike the idea of becoming a grandmother, but she was eager for it."

Although he was speaking aloud, he seemed to be talking

only to himself. "I shall never know why she was the first to die. Delicate as she looked, she had a strong constitution. Many were the times she nursed me when I had spells of ill health."

It was a potent weapon, but Megeen would not let the thrust of sympathy defeat her. Her armor grew thicker with the aid of novenas, vigil lights burning at the base of the statues in the cathedral, special prayers and penances.

There were partisans in the little war. Now they all knew about her condition, Mrs. Callahan, Tessie, and Tim Hanley. By using the dumbwaiter as a listening post, all three had heard enough of what went on between the master of the house and his scullery maid.

Poorly educated but gifted with a certain native shrewdness, none of the three could have failed to see what was in front of their eyes. And the two women, with a deeply embedded loyalty to their sex and station, ranged themselves stubbornly, if silently, on the side of the victim of the passion of a common enemy—man.

Tim Hanley fell back into his taciturn ways on the night he offered one sentence of weak defense for his employer and was fiercely set upon by Tessie, who, it seemed, would have talked him to death, and Mrs. Callahan, who happened to be rolling out pie dough and began to brandish the rolling pin like a weapon.

In spite of the fact that kindness came with difficulty from the two women, Megeen knew that they were her friends. The knowledge warmed her during those bleak days when the sense of aloneness grew deeper and thoughts of the future constantly threw their dark shadows over everything she did.

The war ended on a warm evening in October. Indian summer had come; the trees in the park flamed into color as though to hide the fact that all about them flowers and plants were in the first throes of death.

Mr. Vickery came into the garden, where Megeen was sitting with a shawl around her shoulders. Always, when she could, she kept her condition hidden. Now as she moved along the bench to make room for him on it, she felt awkward, her body cumbersome, even the slight exertion sending trickles of perspiration down her side.

He spoke of the unseasonable weather and she answered him politely. He said that he hoped she was not working too hard these days. She was not to do any heavy chores, he told

her; he would speak to Mrs. Callahan himself and see that his
orders were carried out.

"What then," she asked, "am I to do with myself? When I
have time off, I walk a fair piece. And there is the sewing. I
have been to your store a few times to purchase cloth and
yarn for the little garments. And speaking of the store . . ."

She was about to say more but then shook her head. "It is
not my place to talk to you about the store. What I was
meaning to say is that even with those things to do, my days
are not filled. If I did not clean and help with the laundry
and the serving of the meals, how would I fill up my time?"

He picked up her hand and pressed it between his two
long-fingered ones. "You work too hard," he insisted. "The
house was not this well taken care of, not even when Flora
was alive. Poor kindhearted girl, she was too easy with the
servants. But enough of that!"

He thought for a few minutes and then said, "There are
plenty of ways for you to pass the time. The books in my
study are at your disposal. You have a lively mind, my dear,
which is something not possessed by everyone. I'm sure you'd
enjoy learning much about many things."

The compliment and the term of endearment startled her,
and all she was able to murmur was, "I thank you kindly,
sir."

"On nice days such as this one has been," he suggested,
"you might take a book and go over to the park and read."

"The park!"

She lifted her head and turned her face toward him. The
shadows were kind to him, and in that moment he had taken
on a look of youth. He seemed as young as his son and the
resemblance between them was strong. She felt a sudden striking of pain and her heartbeats grew stronger and swifter. If
only it were Lenard who sat beside her in the fragrant twi-
light!

After a short spell of silence she was able to control her
voice and ask, "What park are you speaking of, sir?"

"The one across the street, of course. There are benches
there and sometimes babies in their prams tended by their
nannies. Or small children playing on the grass. On days
when I come home early from my office I have seen them."

"But I would not be allowed in."

There was no bitterness in her voice. She did not sound either resigned or resentful, but the pressure of his hands grew

stronger and the color in his eyes deepened and became brighter.

"For I am an outsider, and so am not entitled to use the park. You must know that to be true. There is a sign on the fence that makes it clear enough. I believe that it says—"

He stood up abruptly and dropped her hands and thrust his own into the pockets of his trousers. "It is not necessary for you to quote it word for word. I was one of those who drew up that rule. We felt that if we did not prohibit its use to outsiders, we would have the city's riffraff swarming over the grass, leaving debris all over the place. That was why we built our houses here, to escape the worst features of the city.

"But it was never meant to exclude members of our families!"

"But I am not a member of your family, only of your household," she explained patiently. "As are the others, Mrs. Callahan and Tessie. As for Tim—well, I cannot believe that he would care for passing the hours that way. I have never seen the servants of the surrounding houses sitting out there, except when caring for the little ones.

"Please," she urged, "do not distress yourself about the matter, for that is just the way things are and there is naught anything anybody can do about it."

He was pacing up and down a narrow strip of path between the shadowy bushes and the beds of flowers that were almost swallowed up by the darkness. She could not see his face clearly, only the steady movement of his body, but she knew that his jaw was rigid, for, when he stopped in front of her and spoke, the words seemed to be forced from between clenched teeth.

He said, "We will be married at the first possible moment, Megeen. In whatever manner you wish. It is not important, I suppose, who performs the ceremony."

She got to her feet with some effort. "By the priest, then? You are willing that it be so? Oh, you are a good man, Mr. Vickery! I shall pray for you every night for the rest of my life!"

Whenever she thought back to the night of his capitulation, she felt vaguely that the park, from which she had been barred, had had something to do with his surrender, but she never knew just how or why.

Chapter Twelve

It was the simplest of weddings. There were no flowers or music or well-wishers to shower the bridal couple with rice; nor were there ribald jokes to bring blushes to the cheeks of the bride. Megeen refused to let the lack of any or all of those things sadden the day. She was not even nervous, for her heart was too full of relief and gratitude because Alexander Vickery was making her his wife.

But Father Brendan Corrigan, outraged by the fact that he must unite in holy matrimony one of the true flock with a Protestant, was not disposed to make it easy for the couple. He asked questions with cunning, as though hoping to unearth some good reason why the ceremony should not take place, probed into matters like birth certificates, baptismal records, dates of Megeen's first communion and confirmation.

He had a thick brogue, which seemed to grow thicker with each question. He spoke of dispensation, the calling of banns, the promises that the bridegroom must make concerning the bringing up of the children of the union as Catholics.

In spite of her fear that Mr. Vickery would stalk out of the rectory in outrage and refuse to take part in a begrudged ceremony, Megeen could sympathize with Father Corrigan. He believed he was shepherding his flock and in danger of losing one of his lambs. The Church tried to discourage mixed marriages, fearing the loss of souls.

Megeen had given in to Mr. Vickery's urgings and purchased a new cloak. Pearl gray, it was soft and warm and concealing. In the sparsely furnished room of the rectory, while the priest's sermon went on and on, she held the garment together with her crossed arms until Mr. Vickery motioned her to drop them.

It was strange, she thought, that she would feel no shame at a moment like this. Father Corrigan had let his voice drift away as his eyes touched her swollen body. There was no emotion in them; they merely looked pouched and tired. His face was haggard.

Once more she felt a throb of pity for him. No doubt he had listened to so many stories of woe and sin that he had taken on some of their effects and would be forever marked by them.

"As you see," Alexander Vickery said, "the lady is with child. Haste is necessary."

"That is true." The priest looked very worn at that moment, old and worn and agonizingly burdened. "It happens too often and we must help those who fall by the wayside and put them back on the paths of righteousness. Christ tells us we must not cast the first stone at sinners."

He did not look as though he believed that last phrase and went quickly on in a more businesslike tone. He said that he would perform the ceremony only on the bridegroom's promise that the child would be baptized in the true Church. Mr. Vickery, whose mouth was flattened against his teeth, looked as though he would promise anything, meet any and all conditions, in order to escape from the dreary little room. Walls, furniture, even the worn carpet were the same drab shade of brown. Nothing had been spared the cheerlessness.

Father Corrigan was speaking to Megeen now, telling her that he was going against his conscience in joining her in matrimony with a disbeliever, reminding her of her duty to bring up her child a "good Catholic" and to exert all possible efforts to open her husband's eyes to the "true faith" by her prayers and womanly conduct.

And so they were married. The words were said and the begrudged blessing given in the same room, for only when both parties were Catholics were they allowed to be married in the church itself.

Witnesses were a housekeeper, who kept glancing over her shoulder in the direction of the back of the house, as though fearing something in her oven would burn, and a very young curate, who had evidently been reading his office and was using his forefinger as a bookmark for his breviary.

It was cold that night. The chill of autumn was in the air, and while Mr. and Mrs. Vickery were riding home, there was a brief, heavy shower. Megeen tried not to think that it was an evil sign. She was only a little superstitious but could not help believing that that was a bad omen and the only bride who would be happy in her marriage was she upon whom the sun shone.

The rain was having a more serious consequence and she immediately forgot her own wandering thoughts. The man beside her—she found it difficult to think of him as her husband—sneezed twice in loud explosions. His breathing became labored, and when she turned in his direction, she saw that the shoulders of his coat and his fine, low-crowned derby were drenched.

"Sir, you are not too uncomfortable, I hope? It is but a short way home, but if you care to take shelter somewhere . . ."

His hands were so tight around the reins that their knuckles had turned white. "I am all right," he said impatiently. "What annoys me is your form of address. I am no longer 'sir' to you. I have never favored the custom of wives calling their husbands 'mister,' followed by a surname. You will please me by speaking to me as Alec."

It was difficult indeed for her to visualize herself using not only his given name but its shortened form. And she would never know a more difficult moment than when they walked down into the kitchen of 17 Nightingale Park and faced the people with whom she had worked as a servant.

She saw the shine of curiosity in the eyes of all three. They had known, of course, why she had gone off with the master two hours before, but they listened politely while he made his brief speech.

"You will take your orders from Mrs. Vickery from now on. She will be in complete charge of the household. I hope there will be as little comment as possible on the subject of our marriage."

He looked directly into Tessie's face. Plainly his words were intended for her. "The news of the marriage will doubtlessly be known before long. That is to be expected. I hope that you have prepared a room for Mrs. Vickery upstairs?"

She bobbed her head. Her smile was edged with slyness. "The blue guest room across the hall from yours, sir. Being as Mr. Lenard sleeps at the other end of the corridor, it seemed you would have more privacy."

His eyebrows lifted and she became confused and babbling. "Megeen—that is, Mrs. Vickery is who I mean."

He turned then to Mrs. Callahan. "I'll be back after I

change to dry clothing. Mrs. Vickery will probably wish to do the same. You may prepare something for us all to eat. Hanley can fetch a couple of bottles of champagne from the cellar."

That, then, was her wedding supper. Five persons at the servants' dining table; cold chicken, which Megeen could not force herself to eat after the excitement of the day; wine in the second-best goblets; an awkward toast by Tim Hanley.

Conversation was stilted and difficult. It was plain that the other servants felt strange with the new shift in relationship. What would they think, Megeen wondered, if she were to reveal the fact that her plans could not include being the mistress of the house for very long? Certainly they all must be aware it was what Mr. Vickery—Alec—called a marriage of convenience.

He was a kind man, Alec Vickery. Megeen had only to glance down the table and see him with his head bent in Tessie's direction when she lost her awe of him and chattered on as though her tongue was possessed of a life of its own and was completely uncontrollable.

Most of her monologue was concerned with their neighbors, the people who lived in the other houses around the park. While Tessie spoke, Megeen could see in her mind the high-nosed dowagers, the hearty men in their rich clothing, the girls her own age with their beaux and parties and fashionable frocks.

A drifting of sadness touched her. These people were doubtlessly Alec's friends, or had been. No doubt some of the friendships had started in childhood. And she feared that the scandal of his marriage to a servant girl would seriously threaten and even destroy those friendships.

For she could not be received in any of those luxurious drawing rooms. She wished that she could tell all those people with their proud family backgrounds that the marriage had been merely an alliance between a decent man and a desperate girl, a temporary thing. And that soon she would be going away and her presence would no longer affront them.

Mr. Vickery—well then, Alec—was giving her this pleasant memory to carry with her. When she remembered her wedding day, it would be this scene that would stick in her mind: Aggie Callahan's face breaking into smiles after her third glass of champagne; Tessie, singing a wordless song;

Tim Hanley, keeping time to it by beating on his glass with a spoon.

Alec's face, Megeen saw, looked flushed, and she knew that it was foolhardy for him to be sitting in the cold, damp kitchen when he had been so recently drenched by the rain. She fretted silently, remembering that he suffered from something described as "weak lungs," and wished that she had the courage to suggest a hot toddy and his bed, with its warm blankets tucked around him.

But in spite of the fact that she was to be called "Mrs. Vickery" and could speak to him by his nickname, she was not actually his wife and so could offer no wifely advice.

Finally the wedding celebration was over. The last toast was offered, hands were clasped and shaken, Tim said that he would take care of the locking up. Megeen and Alec walked upstairs together. At the door of the room across the hall from his own, he bent and kissed her cheek, which flamed at once with color.

"Sleep well," he said.

She did not believe that she would even be able to close her eyes. She was sure that she would lie awake for hours in this large and beautiful room. The bed, on a low platform, had a tester of blue ruffles. There were two chairs upholstered in pastel brocade, an ivory-colored highboy decorated with gold tracings, a deep carpet that matched in color the deep-blue satin draperies. And a fireplace—how luxurious that must be to have a fire burning in one's bedroom on a chilly morning!

She did sleep, in spite of her fears. It was a swift, sudden plunge into oblivion, but when she awakened during the darkest hour of the night, she did so just as quickly and completely.

She had been awakened by the sound of voices. They came from somewhere down the hall, and though she could not make out the words that were being shouted, she knew that Alec and his son were in the midst of a bitter, furious quarrel.

She guessed that she was the cause of it. Alec must have waited up for his son and announced that he had married their scullery maid. She was able to picture how the young man's face had looked when the shocking news had been broken to him; his first thoughts, of course, would have been for the girl he was engaged to and the members of her proud Yankee family.

Megeen felt torn, in sympathy both for Lenard, who would have been stunned by surprise and outrage that a servant girl had been put in his mother's place, and for the older man— no matter what angry things he was shouting—who had never given her anything but kindness.

Was he explaining to his son why he had taken Megeen as his bride? She wanted desperately to join the two in that room down the hall. She might have assured Lenard that it was not a true marriage at all and that soon she would be going out of both their lives.

But then the voices grew quieter and finally died away. She heard Alec come along the hall and his door open and shut. The house became silent and she was not sorry that what she would eventually have to say to Lenard when they met face to face would be postponed.

She slept again. And she dreamed. She was back in the rectory parlor and she was saying the words of promise— love, honor, and obey. She turned to look into her bridegroom's face and it was not Alec who stood beside her and vowed to cherish her always; it was his son.

And so on her wedding night, alone in her comfortable, clean, sweet-smelling bed, she yearned for the arms and the lips of a man other than the one she had married.

Chapter Thirteen

Annie O'Flynn's eyes were an unusual color, a strange shade that was like the green of stormy seawater. And changeable. But instead of becoming blue by reflecting the tints of the draperies and carpet as they should have, they were like tiny mirrors throwing off images of ugly, disagreeable thoughts.

Envy: Megeen knew that her sister had been struck by the green-eyed monster from the moment they had come into this lovely, tranquil room. Envy: because of her sister's possessions, but most of all of what was growing in Megeen's womb.

There had never been any jealousy between them when they had been growing up together. For Annie had always been the prettier, the most admired, the one the boys had trailed after from the time she was fourteen. Megeen had never resented that fact. God had given Annie certain gifts. To have begrudged her them would have been questioning His wisdom.

Annie's scowl and stormy eyes marred the flowerlike face today. This had been her first visit to the Vickery house; and when she had knocked on the basement door and been told that her sister was now the mistress of the house, she had been jolted into shrewishness.

"Fine thing! Not even telling your own sister! Letting me find out from that mean-faced old woman!"

"Annie, I'm sorry. There just wasn't enough time to tell you. And the way things were, right up until the last minute."

"No doubt you had a battle on your hands to get him to marry you?"

She did not feel like talking to Annie while she was in this mood. When she spoke of that cheerless ceremony in the priests' house, it sounded furtive and twisted by disgrace.

"You are not to tell Marm yet," she warned. "I shall write to her myself when I can think of the right words to use."

It was plain that Annie was not interested in anything concerning places and people beyond her own small world. She walked around the room, touching a chair here, a drapery there. She pulled out the drawers of the highboy and frowned because they were empty.

"You've got all else," she said with a sneer in her voice. "How does it happen you've so little clothing? Well, that will come, I suppose. Mrs. Alexander Vickery will be decked out in furs and diamonds, no doubt."

Megeen, watching her sister with pitying eyes, said, "It is not to be like that, Annie dear. You see, Alec and I were married only to give this baby a name. I shall be going away soon, when he has made arrangements for a place for me to stay."

"More fool, you!" She threw Megeen a scornful look. "You know nothing about men. You can make him do anything you please. If you ask at the right time, that is. When you are in bed and he is half-crazed with wanting, then you hold off until he promises to give you what you are asking for."

"Annie!"

"Never mind the pious looks. Although," she said, bitterness coarsening her voice, "you may well tell me that I'm not the one to be advising you how to go on. For the way it is with my own marriage . . ."

Her head drooped and Megeen realized with sadness in her heart how much Annie had changed. There was nothing left of the high-spirited, care-for-naught girl of their growing-up years. It was as though she had died and her ghost had returned as this misery-locked woman.

"Things are no better for you and Tom?"

"How could they be when I am not yet with child."

Megeen pushed herself out of her chair by the aid of her hands on its arms. "I will have someone bring up a fresh pot of tea."

"Not for me." Annie was beginning to look uneasy. "For I must go. Tom would be angry indeed did he reach home and not find me there. I came only because, as you said, one can go loony staying indoors all the time. I decided to take your advice."

There was no spirit at all in the way she spoke. "His is crazily jealous, you see. Because it is hard for me now to be wanting of his body, he is sure that there is some other man making me excited. He thinks no one can live without it and he will not allow any man to come into the house—not even Marty Mulcahy, who does not have his eye on me but comes to ask about you."

She rubbed the upper part of her arm, stroking it from shoulder to elbow. In her distracted frame of mind she seemed unaware of her hand's motion.

"Annie," Megeen asked gently, "he does not—does not strike you?"

"Oh, well, when he is in drink, he does not know what he is doing. And when he is all worked up and all I can do is lie there with my legs apart, he does things—does things that he expects will excite me. It is no use." Her hand dropped and touched her stomach. "I am always hoping so hard that someday this will grow with a child."

She picked up her cloak, which she had thrown over a chair where its shabbiness was even more marked against the rich brocade. She glanced about her once more, sighed, and said, "Do not forget that you have a sister, Meggie, even though you've come up in the world."

Megeen was about to reply when she heard the sounds of commotion from outside the street. Both she and Annie hurried to the window and looked out. The voices grew in volume as the quarrel became more furious. Annie, her face bleached, clung to the drapery and moaned, "It is him! I told him this morning that I wanted to come here to see you and he forbade it. Now he must have come home early and tricked Marty into driving him here."

She swept her eyes around in terror. "He will kill me! I must get out of here!"

The voices broke off and now there were footsteps pounding on the front staircase. Annie, looking as though she might faint at any moment, staggered to the door and, in blind panic, raced down the hall where a narrower flight of steps led down to the kitchen. Megeen could hear the rush of her sister's feet as they grew faster and fainter.

Tom O'Flynn heard them, too. When he reached the second floor, he stopped for a moment and then followed their sound. His face crazed with fury, he pushed Megeen aside with a rough hand and she tottered and clutched at the banister to hold her balance.

Praying that Annie had found a way to escape through the kitchen and the areaway, Megeen lowered herself down the front staircase carefully. Martin Mulcahy, who had unsuccessfully been trying to catch up with the other man, rushed forward to guide her downward.

"He will kill her!" Megeen cried with the image of that twisted face and burning eyes terrifyingly clear in her mind. "We must stop him!"

"They are outside by now," the man said in a voice meant to be reassuring. "Perhaps that is better, for he will not beat her in a public place."

He was mistaken. Even before they reached the sidewalk, Megeen could hear the awful sound of bone cracking against flesh.

Annie was on her knees, trying to protect her face with her hands. Tom was not only bent over her, pounding at her with his fists; his foot was in motion, and each time a kick landed on a tender spot, Annie's muffled screams rang out on the quiet street. He backed away for a moment and reached up to the carriage, which was drawn up in front of the house, and he snatched from it a driver's whip.

Now there came a new sound. The lash of the whip whistled above his head and then hissed as it descended on the fallen figure of his wife. Annie's shrieks became gasps as he raised his arm again. Martin Mulcahy threw himself on the taller man and grabbed at the moving arm.

"Tom! Tom! For God's sake, man, are you trying to kill the lass?" He was finally able to push Tom a few steps away. He said sternly and in anger, "When you asked the favor, I took it that all you wanted was for us to drive your wife home from a visit with her sister."

Tom began to struggle, but although he towered over his friend, he seemed to be on the edge of drunkenness and he could not throw off the strong, restraining arms. He swayed on the balls of his feet as he tried to break loose, and the two men moved back and forth as though performing a grotesque sort of dance.

Finally it ended and Martin said, panting, "Nothing can be solved in this manner. To strike a woman for any reason is the work of a beast."

Tom O'Flynn, his great chest heaving, gasped, "But she is my wife! When she does wrong, it is my duty to punish her."

A voice behind Megeen spoke. "And this is MY wife!"

She had not noticed that another carriage had drawn up. Tim Hanley sat on its box, his body twisted around so that he could look down at the scene with its enlarging group of spectators. Mrs. Callahan and Tessie, round-eyed, stood on the top step of the areaway. Passersby, on their way to the houses at the other ends of the street, slowed down their gait in order to miss nothing of what was taking place.

Lenard Vickery, his face dark with outrage, had followed his father out of the carriage. He seemed to be on the point of bursting out in temper, but Alec waved him silent and took charge of the situation.

"If we hadn't arrived home from work at the time we have, I don't like to think what might have happened. What matters most is that my wife was forced to listen to and witness such a scene as this. There will be no more of it."

Lenard's mouth worked, but no words came from it. He pushed his way to the front stairs, muttering under his breath so that Megeen was able to hear only part of what he was saying.

". . . riffraff" and "disgraceful marriage."

Martin Mulcahy helped Annie to her feet. Tom, his face sullen, opened his big hand and let the whip drop from it. Then with a last glare of hatred at Alec, he climbed into Martin's carriage without a glance in the direction of his weeping wife.

"You may put away the rig," Alec told Hanley. "We won't be needing it again today."

Mrs. Callahan and Tessie moved slowly down the areaway steps, seeming reluctant to leave the place where they had watched the diverting spectacle. Even before they were lost to view, Alec had his hand around Megeen's arm. He walked at her pace, matching his footsteps with hers.

When they reached the front hall, she drew away from him. She lifted the hem of her apron and began to make little pleats in it so that there was a ruffle around its edge.

"Sir, I am deeply distressed about what went on. I'm afraid that my sister's husband—"

"I am not at all interested in pursuing that subject, Megeen. And I thought it was agreed upon that you were to call me by my name."

He sounded displeased, and it was the first time he had spoken to her in a reprimanding voice. "Kindly keep your hands still. You are not a frightened slave waiting to be punished."

She was still feeling sickened by remorse and shame and self-reproach, knowing that she was the cause—even though an innocent one—that the whole wretched episode had taken place.

"I would not have had it happen for the world!" she cried. "But she is my sister, you see, and troubled as she is, she came to me."

They were talking at cross purposes. He had not heard her outburst of regret and self-blame. His mind was occupied by what he had been saying. "Megeen, I beg of you to keep your hands still. There is no reason at all for you to be wearing that apron anyway. You are no longer a servant. I know there is much to do, but we will hire another girl to take your place. You may take care of that."

She heard only a little of what he had said. "Your friends!" she wailed. "And the people who are your neighbors! This will provide gossip for the dinner tables this night and for many to come. Alec, I would not have chosen to hurt you at all, and I have!"

"Nonsense!" He sounded testy and impatient. "None of that is of any importance."

Then his face began to soften and there seemed to be a twinkle in his eyes. "You are right, though, in one respect. We have given them something to talk about."

Her hands were clasped tightly together and she stared at him as earnestly as though she were at prayer. "Though they look down at me now, it will not always be so. Someday I shall be like them. I will be able to talk about the things they talk about and wear fashionable clothes and have my own carriage. No one will dare to ignore me or cross me for I shall be a great lady!"

"And how," Alec asked mildly, "will you accomplish that?"

"I do not know yet. But it will be so. And I'll be able to go into the park any time I please. If not this one out front, then some other like it."

"My dear!" He took her arm to lead her up the staircase. "I cannot help believing that you will do all those things."

Chapter Fourteen

The first frost of the year came early in November. It silvered the grass in the park until, in midmorning, the sunlight turned it soggy. The trees were gradually becoming bare, their leaves turned brown and crisp and lay like discarded things along the narrow paths.

For Megeen, the days seemed to become longer and quieter. She shortened her walks on fine afternoons, for she would not take the risk of being jostled in the busy, crowded streets.

Alec told her that never had Boston been this thronged, so full of activity. There were new stores opening and tenements being built for the workmen and their families. People who had fled from the devastation of the South and emigrants from European countries were pouring into the city.

None of the noise or bustle reached Nightingale Park. The nights were especially quiet in the Vickery household. Sometimes Megeen would sit gazing across the chessboard at the man who was teaching her to play the game; and she would marvel at what had happened to her. She was married—if only in a legal sense—to a man who was the age her father would have been had he lived.

She began to forget that she did not belong there. Then the truth would suddenly strike her like a dash of cold water in her face when Alec would call her, always in a light tone, "Mrs. Vickery."

Startled, she would remember who she was.

She had not cared to learn to play chess. It seemed to her a silly game and not worth the time and concentration that had to be given to it. But it pleased Alec to have a partner, and for his sake she pretended enthusiasm and accepted the lessons with great attention. She owed him that much. She was always conscious of how deeply she was in his debt. And she was grateful for the other things he taught her, naming the objects in the various rooms.

Already touched by their beauty, she liked knowing what they were called and where they had come from.

She could now recognize the work of Chippendale in a graceful chair with curving legs, and a writing desk that had been made by Thomas Sheraton. A set of ruby-red goblets with fine tracings of gold lines was Bohemian glass. A strange piece of furniture on slender legs was a Chinese box, and Alec demonstrated to her the intricatries of hidden panels and secret compartments.

Patiently he named for her the figurines of cloisonné in a curved-front cabinet. He taught her to recognize jade even if its color was not always the same shade of green. There was a dinner service of Limoges and one of Spode. The silverware was stamped "Sheffield."

These bits of knowledge she treasured, and the lovely things around her became more precious because soon she would be going away and leaving them behind.

Each night she waited for Alec to speak of her going. Absorbed as he might become in the ivory chess pieces, she knew that there would come a night when he would look up and say that it was time for them to make plans for her future and her baby's.

Then she would tell him, proudly and firmly, that he need

not trouble his head about her, that he had done enough by giving her his name.

What then? Well, she would pack her things and go quietly out of his life. And, since she would have no other place to go, she would have to become an inmate of the workhouse until her baby was born and she was able to work again.

Several times lately she had walked past the building that housed the impoverished elderly, the unmarried mothers, those so deeply in debt that, a century ago, they would have been sentenced to prison. Little by little, from Tim Hanley and Mrs. Callahan and Tessie, Megeen had picked up these small bits of information about the workhouse.

Fascinated even though repelled, she kept returning to the street where the stark, unpainted building stood. Although the sight of it sickened her with dread, she found herself moving past it slowly day after day until she could count every uncurtained window and curling shingle in her mind.

It dominated her dreams at night. And soon she could not enjoy the quiet hours in Alec's study. Try as she might, she could not broach the subject to him; and she suspected that he, this kindly, gentle man, was waiting for her to speak of it first.

Finally she began to feel that the actual fact could be no worse than the anticipation. After dinner, on an evening when a bitter, wind-lashed rainstorm rattled the windowpanes, she went upstairs to her room. There she fell upon her knees beside a chair, and with her head in her hands, she prayed long and earnestly for courage and self-control. For this was the night when the dreaded words must be said, the plans made, the matter settled once and for all.

She walked downstairs with a hand clinging to the banister. Her head was held high as she rehearsed in her mind what she would say. When she reached the study, she stopped at the threshold, feeling a little dashed because Alec was not in his accustomed place at the chessboard.

There was no fire in the grate and a damp chill hung in the air. Clutching her shawl more closely around her, Megeen went in search of Alec. The entire downstairs area of the house, she discovered, was cold; and she wondered why Hanley, whose duty it was to keep the fires burning, had not performed it on this raw, stormy night.

She found Alec in the drawing room. He was standing in

front of the cold and empty grate gazing at the portrait of his dead wife.

Shadows from the lamp streaked his face and he looked as though he were talking silently to the lady in the portrait. Megeen saw that his lips were moving but then realized that it was trembling that was putting them in motion.

Slowly and then with a terrible relentlessness, he began to shiver. His whole body—arms, which he threw about himself, legs, face, shoulders—all seemed to be racked by a fit of shuddering.

"Sir! Oh, Alec!"

Megeen hurried across the room and wrapped her shawl around him. But the shivering did not stop. The sound of his chattering teeth almost drowned out her voice.

"Best you should get upstairs to your bed. Come with me, do! We shall have you warm in no time."

He looked at her blankly and her heart fell. She was aware that Alexander Vickery was not a robust man, but she had never before seen anyone as sick as he seemed to be. She was frightened by the chalky pallor of his skin. When his hands began to flutter in helpless gestures, she caught at one of them and it felt like a chunk of ice in her grasp.

He did not resist when she led him across the room, but at the foot of the staircase he looked up the long expanse of steps and shook his head.

"You can do it! Oh, dear sir, you must try hard. Lean on me if you will and hang onto the banister."

They reached the first landing before she spoke again, and then, panting with the weight of his body on her shoulder, she said angrily, "Hanley has not taken care of the fires this night. Alec, you must reprimand him, for he has left us in a fine pickle."

When they went into Alec's bedroom, she found that there, too, the grate was empty. The room was even colder than the ones on the first floor, for there were two windows facing to the north and those overlooking the unbroken expanse of the garden. The roaring of the wind and the assault of the rain on the windowpanes sounded louder here.

Megeen helped him to lower himself to the edge of the bed and then went to the velvet rope that rang a bell in the servants' quarters. Mrs. Callahan and Tessie should still be in the kitchen finishing their cleaning-up chores. It was the first time she had summoned them in that fashion, but she did not want to leave Alec alone, sick as he seemed to be.

They came after a long wait. Megeen had removed Alec's coat and was struggling with his boots when the two women, their eyes bright with curiosity, edged into the bedroom. Megeen, on her knees, turned to look up at them and she spoke to them in a sharp voice.

"Where is that wretched man? Why is it that we've no fires burning on a night like this? Find him and send him here first, for Mr. Vickery is ill and has taken a chill that is very bad, very bad indeed."

Mrs. Callahan and Tessie exchanged uneasy glances. Then the older woman drew a long breath and said, "He is nowhere about, ma'am. How it is with Hanley, may God forgive him, he has his little holidays, if you know what I mean."

"Holidays, is it?"

Anger clogged Megeen's throat so that she could scarcely speak. It was all too plain to her where Hanley was at this moment and where he would be all night and on the following day and perhaps for days after that. In a ramshackle saloon where bottle after bottle would be emptied until his money was gone. Then there would be a period of recovery before he returned to his duties, weak and shamefaced.

She knew this because that was the pattern Clement Ahearn had followed time after time. Also a slave to the Destroyer, her father had neglected his duties, turned his back on his family's needs, and, finally, the strong drink had killed him.

"Tessie, run and find more blankets! Take them from my bed if you must, but hurry! Quilts, counterpanes—anything you can find. Then bring up wood and paper. Surely Hanley has chopped enough firewood for this room at least. Mrs. Callahan, you can help me to undress him."

They both wore sullen expressions. But she did not care what they thought about her. Not now. For a short time she had considered them her friends. With her marriage to the master of the house, that had changed. Behind those blank stares and the occasional false smiles was resentment. They would not, she was certain, mourn her when she went away. Within hours of her leaving they would revert to their old careless ways and let the house return to its sorry, neglected state. Of this she was sure.

"Put him down carefully," she said to Mrs. Callahan, who was hovering ineffectually over the bed. "Then you can help me to remove—to remove his trousers."

Alec's hand went out then and groped for Megeen's. The cold, bony fingers wrapped themselves around hers, and he said in a weak whisper, "Stay with me, Megeen! Please stay with me."

"That I will, sir. And soon you'll be warm. We will have you better in no time at all."

Gritting her teeth, she pulled her hand free and then began to unbutton his waistcoat. Mrs. Callahan, with her strong arms, lifted his body so that Megeen could take off that garment. Her cheeks burned with embarrassment as she unfastened the buttons of his trousers. She pretended not to see the sly smile on the cook's face.

Megeen went on undressing the man who had sunk back on his pillow. For one brief instant her hand touched the strip of bare flesh below his navel and she drew back as though she had been burned. Without looking up, she said, "There must be a hot-water bottle somewhere about. Find it and fill it with boiling water. When you have done that, you and Tessie can bring up what is needed to make a fire."

"For just this room?" Mrs. Callahan asked in a bland and innocent-sounding voice. "Or will ye be spendin' the night in your room?"

"It matters not to you where I shall sleep this night!"

Never before, Megeen was sure, had she ever spoken to another human being in that tone of voice. But worry was sharpening her anger, for even under the covers of his bed Alec was still shivering. His teeth continued to fill the room with the sound of chattering. His face had not lost its look of white transparency.

The hot-water bottle, wrapped in a heavy towel, was put at his feet. Blankets were piled upon him. When the grate was stuffed with papers and logs and the fire began to burn, the room became warmer, but the spasms of shivering went on.

Mrs. Callahan, edging toward the door, said, "He'll be fine and dandy now. The girl and I had best go to bed now. Else we'll have no strength for the morn' were we to miss our sleep."

"Have you no thought for anyone but yourself?"

Megeen rubbed a hand across her forehead, which drummed with pain. She did not know what more to do for the sick man in the bed. Panic was making her own hands unsteady.

"One of you must go for the doctor, for I have done all I could."

Tessie and Mrs. Callahan moved closer together, as though forming an alliance of resistance.

"On a night like this? You cannot mean that, ma'am! For ye need only to listen to the storm outside and know that a person could not walk a few yards in it without bein' soaked to the skin and maybe catch the worse of colds. No, ma'am, I'll not go beyond the doors this night. Nor will Tessie, I'm thinkin', for all she's younger and healthier than me. Ye cannot send her anywhere in this storm."

The girl beside her nodded vigorously. "What she's sayin' is the truth, Megeen." She clapped a hand over her mouth. "I beg pardon—Mrs. Vickery. Without Hanley here to do the errand, I don't know how you'll manage. But then you always do—manage, I mean."

In desolate silence, she watched them leave the room; it would do no good, she realized, to argue or plead. There was no one to give her the help she so badly needed.

"Megeen, come here!"

Alec was crying out to her in such a weak voice that she scarcely heard him. When she reached his side, he pulled his hand out from under the bedclothes again and she took it into hers.

"Stay with me, Megeen! Please!"

"I will indeed. And somehow I will get you warm, poor man! However it is to be."

She hesitated, thinning her lips, and then she lowered herself to the edge of the bed. She drew back a corner of the bedclothes and eased herself in beside him. When he turned to her, she put out her arms and gathered him into them.

The bulge of her stomach kept her from drawing him up against her closely, but when she threw one leg across his body, she was able to mount him and put some of her weight on her hands, which were pressed against the mattress on either side of him.

She lowered herself slowly until his face was lying in the hollow of her neck. After a few moments she realized that she was not helping him as much as she had hoped. So she slid off him and wriggled out of her clothing. She moved her body around so that she could force its warmth into the cold flesh of his; she rubbed against him in slow, steady rhythm. The roughness of his underwear chafed her sensitive skin, but she went on stroking him up and down, across his chest, even his thighs and knees. Her hand suddenly became still, for she felt, with astonishment, a tide of warm feeling rising from inside her. She had carefully kept her hand away from his private parts, but now it crept slowly toward his groin.

And was snatched away when his voice came weakly from his lips, which were resting on her bare breast.

"You will not go away? You will not leave me, dear wife? I wish for you to stay here always."

He did not know what he was saying. The sickness was putting him off his head, and she could put no faith in the ravings of a sick man. Temptation came crawling into her mind and was quickly banished. She had remembered what Annie said about a woman having the best chance to get what she wanted by using the most deadly of female weapons. In bed was the best place to extract promises and ask for favors.

Megeen thought, What if I were to take him seriously? Suppose tomorrow, when he has recovered, I tell him what he said. He will not remember, and so will be unable to deny it. And he is too fine a gentleman to go back on something he said, even though he did not know he was saying it.

The chill was beginning to leave his body gradually. The stiffness was drawing out of his legs. The chattering of his teeth grew fainter and slower, and the skin of the bony face lying in the hollow between her breasts was becoming softer and warmer.

She raised herself on an elbow to look down upon him. He appeared peaceful now, almost to the point of drowsiness. The fire still burned in the grate and the crashing of a falling log with its shower of sparks startled her. An instant later she started up again for the bedroom door had opened.

Lenard stood in the doorway, remained there motionless for a long moment, and then came striding across the room. Megeen could not see his face clearly, for the light was at his back. But she knew from the stiffness of his shoulders and the set of his head that he was in the grip of some strong emotion.

He seemed to be speaking with a clenched jaw when he said, "So this is the way you get what you want, isn't it? Congratulations! They are belated, I fear, but now I see that I must call you 'Mama.' "

He sounded as though the word had choked him, but when Megeen stuttered, "He has been sick, poor man," Lenard honked a derisive laugh. "But not so sick, it seems, that he could not enjoy a roll on the mattress. Well, why not? If he is to be manipulated by a common servant, surely he is entitled to get some fun out of it."

"Lenard, listen to me!"

He turned away and started for the door. He turned back, not to give her the opportunity to speak but because he had more to say.

"You are a liar and a cheat, Mrs. Vickery. You have pulled the wool over my father's eyes with your wild tale about being forced to submit to someone in this house. And you have caused estrangement between him and myself. Tonight I thought to heal the breach. I came to this room hoping to find him still awake so that I might apologize for my part in the quarrels. Dorothea said—"

He broke off and, as he went out, flung over his shoulder, "But how could you understand what a decent, chaste young lady would say or feel?"

Chapter Fifteen

From the night Lenard had found her in his father's bed, his manner toward Megeen changed. Before that he had treated her with supreme indifference, seeming to look through her as though she were unaware of her existence.

Now, on the rare occasions they found themselves together, his eyes sometimes rested briefly on her face. They were of a strange color, gray like the shade of burned-out ashes and yet as though fire smoldered behind them.

There was no more dense silence, for he muttered snatches of ugly phrases that he never spoke loudly enough for her to completely understand them.

She wished she was able to, so that she could fling the words back into his face. She wished he would give her the opportunity to explain why she had been covering Alec's body with her naked one.

Let him jeer, accuse her of lying, even call her names. Anything was better than the glares full of hatred and the ugly, mumbled words.

Only once was she given the chance to defend herself. Alec, three days after his chill, was unable to come downstairs for his meals, and she and Lenard were alone at the dinner table.

At one end of the long table and with Lenard at the other, Megeen did not try to hear what he was murmuring, but in the silence that had stretched between them a few moments before, her ears seemed to have become sharper.

"Money! No doubt you thought it was a fair chance to put your hands on the old man's money."

She sprang to her feet. She was trembling as she moved slowly past the empty chairs and stopped beside him, her hands on her hips.

"God forgive you!" she cried in a rising voice. "It was not that at all! The sinful thought has been nowhere but in your evil mind. All the money in the world could not buy what your father has given me. He has made me respectable by marrying me. He has given my child a name, little matter where it is born. Do not worry yourself at all, sir! I shall soon be gone and you need not worry about your fortune. For I'll make no claims on that good man!"

She sounded, she knew, like a brawling fishwife, but rather than be disgusted, as might have been expected, Lenard threw back his head and roared with laughter. Megeen had seldom heard him laugh, and she was silenced, drawing back when he would have taken her hand. She did not understand it at all. Why should her anger affect him in this strange way: set his eyes on fire, bring color to his face, shorten his breath?

Disturbed and somehow frightened, she backed away even farther. She put her hands behind her out of his reach, and that for some reason seemed to amuse him even more. His laughter had notes of wildness in it now and she fled from the room as quickly as she could with the cumbersome burden inside her.

Alec was sitting in front of the fireplace when she went into his room. He smiled and put out his hand, his face warm with pleasure. He was still recovering from his illness, and when he would have arisen, she gestured to him to remain seated.

It was a spacious room and its furnishings were designed for a man's comfort. High-backed chairs flanked the fireplace. A tall mahogany chifforobe matched a lowboy. The big bed, as she had noticed the night she had lain on it, could have held an entire family without much crowding.

She gave Alec her hand absentmindedly, her thoughts still on that monstrous bed. She was wondering if his wife had been in the habit of occupying the bed with him or if their noctural couplings had taken place in her room.

Megeen did not deliberately try to bring into her mind a picture of Alec and his wife; it came unbidden, and she saw them moving and wriggling, arms and legs entwined. She felt hot color stain her cheeks and was unaware that Alec was speaking until he gave her hand a shake.

"I'm sorry. I didn't hear what you said."

"Megeen, what troubles you, my dear? You're not usually given to daydreams. I said that I hoped my illness has not placed more work upon your shoulders. Up and down stairs a dozen times a day, that must be difficult in your condition. Could you not have let one of the others . . . ?"

"Take care of you?" Her voice was almost fierce, although she could no longer see him, for his face swam in a sudden surge of tears. "It was no more than just, dear man, for there is so much you have done for me! And I shall always remember your kindness, even when I leave this lovely house."

"Leave?"

"As I must, of course. It was the agreement. You were only to have given me your name. Which you did. God bless you for that!"

He drew her closer to him. "And where do you intend to go? How do you plan to support yourself and a child?"

"They will take me in at the workhouse, will they not? And then later I can find a job. One that will allow me to keep the little one with me."

His voice grew firmer and fuller. "The workhouse indeed! Where, may I ask, did you get an idea like that? Haven't you been happy here with me? If I remember correctly, it was only three nights ago when you promised you would not leave me. Do you intend to go back on your word, Mrs. Vickery?"

He sounded stern, and she wiped hastily at her tears with

her free hand. "But you knew not what you were saying, Alec. It was the illness."

"I was not in delirium. And, besides, the subject of the workhouse never arose. I do not understand," he said in a way that sounded peevish, "why you want to go away at any rate."

She freed her hand and pressed its palm tightly against her other one. "It is not fair that you should give up so much for me!" she cried. "No friend of yours has come into this house since the day we were married. There has not been one single visitor. The little statue in the front hall—Tessie calls it a blackamoor. You know the one I mean?"

She scarcely waited for him to nod and then her voice raced on.

"There he stands, that little black boy with his hand outstretched holding a card tray. Tessie explained that to me, too. When friends and visitors come, they leave a card on the tray. It is a sort of . . . language. When the left-hand corner of the card is turned down, it means that a return visit is requested. Turning down both corners means the caller will come again."

"I know," Alec said with an impatient wave of his hand. "Am I to let my life be ruled by what lies or does not lie on a tray that is part of a statue? I have never liked the blackamoor at any rate. I shall have Hanley get rid of it."

"Not for my sake! I was using that as an example to prove to you that I cannot go on being the cause of your loss of friends."

He put in dryly, "No doubt they will think a great deal more of me if I send my wife to the workhouse."

"Then perhaps somewhere else? If I were to move away and you would loan me money, I could repay it to you when I was able to work again."

"Megeen, it so happens that I am not a moneylender. Now let's talk no more about this boring subject. It seems that you have forgotten that the child will be mine, too. You will both remain here." His tone had grown softer. "Can't you see how much I need you, my dear wife? This house has been different since you have been in it. There now, why are there tears at this point?"

She did not know how to tell him. There was no easy way to explain. The bruising pain that had tormented her for so long had been washed away by his good, kind, generous regard for her. Too much gratitude would, she was sure, embarrass him. After all, he was a dyed-in-the-wool Yankee. So she would say nothing and try to repay him by long sessions on her knees asking every saint she knew of to shower him with favors.

What was it he was saying now?

"On one condition . . ." She began to listen carefully. "And that is that you find another servant girl. We have always had a staff of four, counting Hanley. I want you to hire someone to do the sort of work you did when you first came here. Will you promise me that?"

She would have promised him, at that moment, the most extravagant, improbable thing ever known to man. As she lowered herself to the ottoman beside his chair, she thought again of what a strange turn her life had taken. Only a few months ago she had arrived in this new country—a greenhorn with scarcely a coin to bless herself with. She had to come seeking a job in someone else's kitchen; now she was a mistress in charge of a household and was to hire a girl to do the menial work.

Impulsively, she picked up Alec's hand and pressed it against her cheek.

Chapter Sixteen

She had not the slightest idea of how to go about hiring a servant and was too proud to ask. Tessie would find it a huge joke that the mistress of the house did not know a simple little thing like that.

Tessie's manner, when Alec was not around, bordered on insolence. Both she and Aggie Callahan made it plain that they considered her no better than themselves in spite of her elevated position. Tim Hanley had been more surly than usual since the night he had been away on his "holiday," seeming to blame her for the sharp reprimand he had received from the master.

For the sake of the child she carried, Megeen did her utmost to remain calm and even-dispositioned. She knew that if she did not allow herself to get upset or unhappy, she would have a happy and contented child, although Alec laughed at her for her belief in what he called old wives' tales. He brought home a magazine one night and read to her an article that claimed that prenatal influences only slightly affected an unborn child.

Megeen refused to believe that, for had she not seen with her own eyes the marks on little bodies signifying that the mother had been frightened by a beast or a reptile before the birth or denied some article of food for which there had been an unfulfilled craving?

The article had also stated, against everything that all people believed to be true, that the mother-to-be should eat sparingly; and there were other theories—a regime outlined that Megeen knew to be harmful—in contradiction of all she had heard and known.

"Do they wish for the little ones to starve to death even before they come into the world?" she asked Alec indignantly. "And as for this part here, about how women should take even more exercise than they were accustomed to.

"And kill us all? Is that the intention? For if it were not necessary for me to go looking for a new girl each day, I would be most happy to sit by the fire and rest as all mothers carrying children should."

She did not enjoy the hunting for a servant girl. Often she went down to the center of the city where a group of men lingered in front of a ramshackle building. A sign above its entrance read: NO IRISH OR COLORED NEED APPLY.

The men waited with dogged patience. It seemed to Megeen, each time she passed the job office, that the same men she had seen last week and the week before were still standing idle. But perhaps it was their facial expressions, for upon their features was stamped the look of the unemployed male—something compounded of worry, shame, and less evident, the smoldering of anger that threatened to flare up at any moment.

She knew that somewhere in the city there must be a job office for women. But she never happened to find it and on an unseasonably warm day in November, she decided to search in another direction, a part of the city she had never been in before.

During that long voyage across the Atlantic, there had

been several other young girls, all with the same purpose in mind: to obtain work in this land where there were no famines, where money was plentiful and could be sent to the people left behind.

Surely Patrick Gilligan was not able to take all the new arrivals under his larcenous wing. There must be some who would find themselves adrift in an unfamiliar place. She had only to go down to the wharves and undoubtedly she would find a frightened, willing girl whom she could train to be a good housemaid.

She had picked a fortunate day indeed. For when she came to the waterfront, she found herself in the midst of burgeoning crowds, all hurrying in the direction of the wharves. Their eager, quick gait told her one thing. A ship was docking that day, and even the curious, who would know no passenger, were excited by the arrival of the ship, which was already far into the harbor.

Megeen walked slowly, managing to avoid careless outthrusts of elbows. Thus, by the time she reached the waterfront, the ship had already docked.

It was a proud ship, with its sails like huge wings. She knew that steam was used to drive packets across the ocean, and this boat, with its figurehead of a goddesslike woman on its prow, had come from some distant, unknown place.

When she drew close enough to read its name and sailing point, she saw the words SCOTIA and, in smaller letters, HALIFAX.

The passengers began to move down the gangplank and she studied each one carefully. She knew little about the land to the north of the United States, only that it was said to be a wild country and part of the British Empire.

Her thoughts slid automatically to Alec. He had a fondness for books about places he had never visited, and she knew that he would listen with interest when she described to him the *Scotia*, which had come from a coastal city far to the north.

He was not getting around much these days. He seemed to be spending more and more time at home, letting Lenard take care of the business at their State Street office and conducting affairs at the paper mill by correspondence and special messenger.

As for the store on Washington Street . . . well, someday she would tell Alec what she thought of that rackety place where goods were not displayed to best advantage and prices were shockingly higher than in other stores.

At the sound of a bellowing voice, she turned to look at a man in uniform who was calling out instructions to the passengers through a horn; his nasal voice had notes in it which Megeen had never heard before and she understood scarcely a word he was crying.

The steerage and lower-class passengers streamed down the gangplank as he was calling out. Megeen recognized them for what they were by the bulky packages they carried, flimsy boxes that seemed about to fall apart at any minute, and the bundles wrapped in bed sheets and tablecloths. Her heart went out to them in sympathy, for she remembered the panic, almost like an assault of sickness, that had slowed her own footsteps as she had walked down that other gangplank and found herself on the soil of a new, terrifying, bewildering country.

Someone behind her, a girl from the sound of the high-pitched titter, was laughing at the odd clothing of the new-comers. Megeen turned about sharply to glare at the woman who was finding amusement in watching the disembarkation. Her glance never reached its destination. Megeen's eyes went no farther than the figure of the slender young man who stood a few yards away.

Lenard Vickery towered over the people around him. He was bareheaded and his hair had turned golden in the sun-light.

She shrank farther back into the crowd, for she did not want to be seen by her stepson at that moment. Her pride—she was willing to admit that it was vanity—made abhorrent the idea of his recognizing her like this: her hair blowing every which way, her belly bulging, her fair skin reddened.

She need not have worried. Lenard was not looking in her direction, and the expression on his young, handsome face showed her that he might not have realized who she was at any rate, even if their eyes had met.

He was staring up at the ship, gazing with a look she had never seen in anyone's eyes. It was pain. It was yearning. She followed that gaze with her own eyes and decided that she must have imagined something that was not there. For there was nothing on deck to cause him anguish. The passengers had all left. No one remained up there except a burly sailor who was stripped to the waist and carried upon his sweat-slicked shoulders a pair of bulging carpetbags.

Within the next ten minutes, Megeen had found Ruth Tilton, hired her, and was on her way back to Nightingale Park.

"And if I'd had the sense of a rabbit," she told Alec a few days later, "I'd have left her where she was, but how was I to know what she was like and that she'd come to be a trouble-maker?"

What she was like could not be neatly explained or precisely pigeonholed. Ruth Tilton was uncomfortably outspoken and conscientious, arrogant and scrupulously honest, domineering and hardworking.

Megeen had found her standing in the doorway of an old building beyond the wharf. She was a big woman, more than a head taller than Megeen. Everything about her—hands, feet, features, shoulders—was larger than those of any woman Megeen had ever met.

It was difficult to guess her age. She would have been old at twenty, still have the look of vigor and strength about her at fifty. She was, she eventually told Megeen, thirty-five.

She was staring down at a slip of paper in her hand, a scowl wrinkling her wide forehead. Still fresh in Megeen's memory were her own first bewildering moments in the new land, and she stopped and spoke to the woman.

"Do you have someone to meet you?"

"No, indeed!" She seemed to grow in height as she glanced down at the smaller woman. "I have friends about somewhere, and when I have got my bearings, I shall have no trouble finding them."

At her feet were two packing boxes tied with rope. In them, Megeen guessed, were all that she possessed in the world. She knew nothing at all about this strange city, but there was no flicker of uneasiness on that strong face. Her attention became centered upon Megeen and her sharp eyes traveled up and down the swollen body.

"Ma'am, you should not be on the streets in your condition," she scolded. "Two months to go, haven't you? Oh, you need not blush! My marm gave birth almost as often as old Bessie, our cow. Seventeen of us there were. And me the second oldest. Well, there was just me left unmarried and it did not suit me to be alone, so I decided to make a little money and get some pleasure out of life."

The long speech had not left her out of breath and she went on, "None can say I'm not a fine housekeeper and a good cook. Ruth Tilton's my name, ma'am. I do suppose you've all the servants you need, but if you're knowing of some of your fashionable friends needing a servant, I'll be looking for a job."

So Megeen took Ruth Tilton home with her and brought her down into the kitchen. There Tessie and Mrs. Callahan sat with a pot of tea in front of them and a lurid magazine being shared.

Ruth Tilton paid little attention to the introductions. She looked around with keen and critical eyes, and she wrinkled her nose in disapproval.

She glanced in turn at the unwashed luncheon dishes in the sink, the unpolished surface of the stove, the damp, dirty mop standing in a corner.

"You were right, ma'am. You do indeed need someone to see to things here. I've been in cleaner pigpens than this here place!"

Megeen said hastily, "Ruth will be helping out in the kitchen. Mrs. Callahan, I am depending on you to show her what to do."

"I need no showing! For it's plain enough what's to be done. The swill there." She pointed to an overflowing tin bucket. "It should be taken out and buried at least once a day."

She went to the stove and picked up a teakettle, shook it, and frowned when she found it empty. She upended it and gazed at the blackened underside.

"Some elbow grease is what's needed. But have no fear, ma'am." Megeen saw her smile for the first time. It was a frightening experience for Megeen, for the woman's teeth were wide and shiny and looked as though they might jump out of her mouth at any moment. "I'll take care of everything."

She allowed Megeen to show her the small room off the other side of the kitchen, and when she had surveyed it without enthusiasm, she said, "It will do for now. But later on when you are nearer to your time, you must find something closer to you. For you never know. First one, isn't it? It could come early or late."

Aggie Callahan and Tessie McNamara were on their feet when Megeen came out of the small room alone. Their baleful glances were on its door and they were breathing heavily.

Pitying them at that moment, Megeen said soothingly, "It will be all right when she gets used to us and our ways. She just got in today from Nova Scotia and everything is strange for her. We must make allowances."

They did not answer her and it wasn't until she was climbing the stairs that she heard the chattering begin.

"Nova Scotia, is it?" Mrs. Callahan's voice was hoarse with loathing. "A herrin' choker! And not, I'll bet me boots, one of our own kind!"

Chapter Seventeen

It turned out to be even worse than the two women had feared. Not only was there a Protestant in their midst but one who felt herself to be as good as they were and had not the slightest feeling of shame about her religion.

Indeed, she did not at all mind talking about it and the holy picture on the wall of the little bedroom had been taken down and placed into Mrs. Callahan's hands.

"For I do not pray to statues and pictures and other Romanish trappings," Ruth said cheerfully. "That is for those who know no better."

Aggie Callahan's face began to swell as though all the shocked words were trapped in her cheeks. She was continually muttering to herself these days, rehearsing the phrases she would use when giving her employer her notice.

The worst day of the week was Sunday. Then Ruth would dress herself in her respectable best—well-brushed coat, hat with a feather soaring above the crown, clean cotton gloves—and leave to attend services in the Old West Methodist Church on Cambridge Street. Not only did she go to the morning service but, unless the weather was too severe, returned there for the service at night.

If it had only been the churchgoing at the wrong church, Tessie and Mrs. Callahan might have forgiven her, even though grudgingly. But, as Tessie pointed out to the cook, nobody could like a bully.

Somehow there had formed in Ruth Tilton's mind the idea that she and she alone was in charge of running the household. She badgered the other two to take more pains with their work. She was critical of the cooking. The floors had to be scrubbed and polished more often, bed linen was changed twice a week, the front steps and the areaway must be swept each morning.

For Megeen she had only the tenderest of care. She took the privileges of her self-appointed role as nurse and ordered her patient about gently and scolded when it seemed necessary.

"You're to get as much rest as possible. For it's necessary for you to save your strength. You're a mite small there, you know, scarcely any hips at all, and that could mean trouble. But you're not to worry, ma'am, for I shall be with you and take care of everything."

And give birth to the baby herself, if that were possible, Megeen thought wryly. Yet, in spite of her domineering manner, Ruth was a comfort. Having moved a cot into the small room next to Megeen's, she was always on hand should anything unexpected arise. And she had good, strong, skillful hands for rubbing a back that ached at the end of a day.

There was a lull in the hostilities between the servants that lasted only a short time. Christmas, the time of season of goodwill and peace, brought on almost unsurmountable problems. The three who had been born in Ireland made preparations to observe the holiday as they had in the old country. Strips of holly, having what significance they did not know, were to be hung across the windowpanes, thus darkening all the rooms by closing out the thin winter sunlight.

On each windowsill was a candle to signify that the Babe would be welcome in this household and not denied a birthplace as He had been nineteen hundred years ago.

Ruth declared stoutly that there would be no such Romanish twaddle in any house she lived in. She pointed out the dangers of fire, for, when the holly grew dry, the candle flames would leap up and set a fire. They might be all burned to death in their beds.

Alec's patience almost reached the breaking point before Christmas Eve finally arrived. He forced upon the servants a sort of compromise: the candles were to be lighted for a few hours but extinguished before all members of the household retired for the night. His presents to the servants had been gold pieces, how many Megeen did not know, but she suspected that he had been overgenerous this year.

Life beyond her bedroom door was growing less real and important to Megeen. She had hoped that her child would be born on Christmas Day, for surely a baby who shared His birthday would be blessed with special favors.

It was not until the seventh day of January that she felt the first unmistakable pains that she welcomed with a sense of relief, happy that the waiting was now over and that she would be soon holding her infant in her arms.

If she could have found strength enough to laugh during the next horrible, agonizing hours, she would have done so over her ignorance and belief that she would deliver as easily as her Marm had done during her last two confinements, which Megeen had witnessed.

Two days of raw, torturing pain when it seemed that her body was being torn apart. She knew nothing, only the pain, and when it released her for a few blessed, breath-catching minutes now and then, she knew that it lurked there waiting to send its worst assaults upon her exhausted and helpless body.

Ruth was at her side all during those agony-filled hours. It seemed to Megeen that only Ruth was in charge of the horror chamber, her voice soothing, coaxing Megeen to sip at a cup of tea held at her dried lips, offering her big hand to be squeezed, wiping the sweat-drenched face with a clean towel.

Alec came into the room from time to time. She saw his face, bent over hers, and the anguished look on it made her want to comfort him, but the screams that had made her throat raw had robbed her of her voice.

Annie—was she truly seeing her sister? The thought that she was close to death streaked into her mind. Had Alec sent for Annie, his wife's next of kin in this country? Could he have decided that the presence of her sister would bring her some peace while she was on her deathbed?

But Annie did not look at all like the girl Megeen had loved and admired. The beautiful, dark-red hair had the appearance of neglect and was in need of washing. The face was pinched and pale, and the features drooped like those of a discontented woman. Megeen was having a lucid period, free of the pain for a few minutes, and when Annie leaned over the bed, Megeen could smell the stench of whiskey. Oh, not Annie! Not her darling Annie!

Annie said in a slurred voice, "Marty Mulcahy drove me over. He's out in the hall. You know how it is with us. I'd a notion all day something was happening to you. It wouldn't let me be. I couldn't stay away."

Her face had grown sullen. "So this is what it's like! Maybe it's just as well it didn't happen to me. No man is worth going through this for."

Megeen wanted to ask her questions, but when she opened her mouth, no sound came. Where was Tom O'Flynn? Why had he not driven his wife to the bedside of her sister? Surely at a time like this a man would forget his petty grudges and grievances. If not, why had Annie run the risk of being beaten and horsewhipped by going against his wishes?

The questions fled from her mind as she tried to stifle a scream. And then Annie was gone and the battle to release her child resumed.

The doctor came at last and put over her mouth and nose a piece of cloth saturated with some sweet-smelling liquid, and after that came the final wrenching agony. Only seconds later she heard the lusty, wailing cry; it sounded as though the baby, too, had fought its own torturous battle for birth.

"A boy." The doctor leaned over and wiped her face. "A mean one, that he is. No need to spank his voice into coming out. A fourteen-pounder, I guess. And his fists already clenched. You're going to have your hands full with this one."

Over and over, in the months to come, Megeen had to admit that the doctor had been right. Mean—that was a good word to describe the Vickery child. There was no question of his being spoiled. He did not wait for that. From the day of his birth he knew how to get his own way.

He was a small tyrant, shrieking and bawling for what he wanted. He was a contrary child, sleeping through much of the day and keeping the whole household awake during the nights. He was always hungry, so that Megeen's nipples were sore with his strong gums constantly sucking at them.

Only Alec was enchanted with him. He hung over the cradle, fascinated by the small, determined face; the eyes, which he was sure were seeing what went on around him; the flailing fists.

At night, when Ruth and Megeen were weak with exhaustion from walking and rocking and patting, Alec would come into the room and take the stiff, squalling body into his arms, and by some miracle—or so it seemed—the baby would become quiet within a few minutes.

Two weeks after her son was born, Megeen sent him to St. Dominic's to be baptized. She had expected an argument with Alec when she announced that the child must not live any longer without the sacrament.

She had sensed a slight coolness when she had first broached the subject, but when she attempted to explain how it was necessary for her son to be properly christened, Alec had said only, "I gave my word. All I ask is that you do not expect me to accompany him. The choice of a name I have left to you. May I ask what you have decided?"

Her face became very serious. "Matthew, if you've no objections. St. Matthew, before he followed our Lord, was a tax collector. I've always felt sorry for him. The other apostles were loved—Luke, the doctor; John, who stood by the cross; Mark, the journalist. Well, there was a time when Matthew was thought to be a scoundrel.

"I should like Jude for Matthew's middle name. He was a relative of Christ's, but he bore the same name of the traitor who betrayed Him. And he is one of the finest of saints," she said earnestly. "When all other prayers fail, 'tis said that he can accomplish the impossible."

She reached out and touched Alec's hand. "But if this does not please you, dear sir, you may choose other names. I would not ask you to give him your name because—"

She could not say it. She could not tell him that far back in her mind was always the tiny doubt about his actually being the child's father. Search that small face as she would, she could see no resemblance to Alec. Nor, for that matter, to Lenard either.

Lenard had not shown the slightest interest in the infant. He was away much of the time, and when Megeen asked about that, Alec said that Lenard was fond of visiting friends, some of whom lived far away, and that things at the office were in a sad muddle because of his absence.

She worried about that because Alec was tiring himself out with the full burden of the office work during the day and the sessions with the baby at night. But his vigor had returned on the day that Hanley, the godfather, and Tessie, strutting with importance because she had been chosen as godmother, came back after the christening. He marked the occasion with some of his rarest vintage wine for them all.

Only Ruth was grumpy and refused to toast the newly named child. "If it's all that important," she said to Megeen, "I'd have thought you'd be there, too."

"It's not the custom for the mother to attend. Nor to go out in public until she's been churched."

Ruth threw her hands over her ears. "I want to hear no more. You Irish! Next thing you'll be talking the master into going to Mass with you."

Megeen's lips twitched in a secret smile. That was exactly what she intended to do.

Chapter Eighteen

As the stingingly cold winter wore on, snowdrifts sometimes as high as the windows of the first floor, Megeen found herself worrying more about Alec's physical condition than the state of his soul.

He was never warm, even when fires burned in all the grates. He dressed almost as heavily when he was in the house as when he was outdoors.

Megeen coaxed him to send for a doctor, but he merely smiled and said, "He could do nothing. The blood is thin, Megeen. Too much intermarrying perhaps. Well, our son has a chance of missing that curse. Do not worry about me. I shall perk up when the fine weather comes."

There was something else that nagged at her mind. She was a wife and never yet had she been asked to perform her wifely duties. It was two months since she had given birth to Matthew; yet since the night she had held Alec in her arms and warmed his body with the heat of her own, she had never entered his bed or welcomed him into hers.

Was she not attractive to him in that way? Was he hesitating because she was nursing Matthew and feared that making love would upset her and so affect the child, who still bawled for her breasts every three hours?

Could it be that he was waiting for her to signify that she was willing to receive him?

She asked him finally. It was on a night when Matthew, after a long session of screaming and tossing his body around, had finally fallen into deep sleep. He looked like a small angel, she thought, gazing down at him as she held him in her arms. An illusion, of course. If only Matthew would only act the way he looked!

Alec arose and took the baby from her. He moved carefully as he placed the child in the cradle. Then he remained there, seeming lost in thought.

Seeing him like that, his face soft with love, she felt the growing of something sweet and warm inside her, an affection that had been strengthening with each passing month. She went to him and placed a hand on his shoulder.

"Dear sir," she said softly, "it is almost as though we are a real family."

Startled, he turned his head to look up at her. "And are we not? That is the way I think of you and my son. What more could any man want?"

"A wife in the true sense of the word," she said stoutly. "A woman in his bed when he wishes her to be. Dear Alec, you are the least-demanding man in the world, I'm sure. You have asked nothing from me, yet you have given me so much."

"I have never been good at bartering." He arose to his feet slowly. "Nor have I ever wanted an unwilling partner. You owe me nothing except what you care to give."

She grasped his hand and drew him in the direction of his bedroom. "I think, my dear," she told him, "that you had best get into bed right away, for it is too cold for you to undress anywhere except under the blankets."

She got in beside him, first unfastening her own clothing and then helping him with his buttons. They both raised their bodies from the mattress to shed their outer garments at the same time; and it suddenly struck her as funny, the two of them bouncing and wriggling about. When each was stripped to a single garment, they turned and with entwined arms and legs, shook the bed with their laughter.

It was a gentle union, as she had somehow believed that it would be. On that other night she had been in Alec's bed, she had felt the stirring of desire. If only she could feel that hot, throbbing urge again, she knew that this time their union would be easier and more pleasant for them both.

He seemed to know it, too. He did not hurry her. There was no swift, ugly taking of her body that had shamed her and debased her on the night Matthew was conceived.

He touched her in places where no other hand had ever been. When her gasps and cries grew louder, he put his hand in hers and let her guide it to the sensitive places that gave her the most delight.

"There!" she panted. "Oh, no, my darling, that is better! Are you liking it as much as me? Can you wait, for it is so wonderful I do not want it to end!"

It was like hearing the voice of someone else. She could not be saying these wanton things with her own hands busy, every pulse in her body throbbing.

Now she knew why her sister had cried out in pleas for the only thing that could satisfy this overwhelming want. But Alec had none of Tom O'Flynn's cruelty. He did not tease her or make her beg. Only when her frenzy had mounted to mindlessness did he enter her, and if there was pain as he pushed his organ into her, she was too driven and filled with bliss to be aware of it.

They were swept up to the highest peak of ecstasy together, called out at the same moment. After the slow descent they lay quietly in each other's arms. Drowsy and sliding into sleep, she heard Alec murmur, "Thank you, my darling."

This was to be the pattern of their coupling for the weeks to come. Alec never invited her into his room, but on nights when the baby was quiet and illness and worry about his business enterprises were not plaguing him, she would go quietly to his bed and slip in beside him.

He was a tender lover. His nature was less fiery than her own and his control was the greater. There were nights when Alec could make her climax come swiftly and others when he could prolong sensations for long, wonderful stretches of time. He never failed to please her; she was never left unsatisfied or disappointed.

Even in the most frantic moments of their lovemaking, he never demanded that she utter fervent phrases. Never once did he ask if she loved him. Nor did she say it of her own accord.

In spite of her lively conscience, it did not seem to her that it was wrong to enjoy her marital relations even though she and her husband were no more than affectionate friends.

The thing that bothered her most of all was Alec's being deprived, because of her, the friendship of his neighbors and those he had known before his marriage.

She had hoped that with the arrival of the baby there would be callers who were to come only from curiosity. She had allowed herself to dream a little about the future. Matthew would go to Harvard as Alec had done. He would marry into a fine old Boston family. There were already signs in his character that would assure him great success: stubbornness, the ability to get what he wanted, a certain charm when he was in the mood to favor his family with his first sweet smiles.

When he was old enough, he would manage all the Vickery interests, which Megeen suspected were being neglected now because of Alec's uncertain health and Lenard's sulking in the home of a friend somewhere.

She had no idea of the size of the Vickery fortune. There were entire evenings when Alec sat frowning over his papers and ledgers. Yet he was always openhanded about money to run the household and was constantly urging her to buy new clothing, seeming to have taken a dislike to the garments she had worn before Matthew's birth. In this matter she acceded to his wishes, for she knew that being a Vickery placed upon her the obligation of looking as much like a lady of fashion as possible.

She was glad on that mild, sunny morning when she had taken Matthew out for an airing that she was wearing the sealskin tippet Alec had given her for Christmas, the maroon serge coat with the silken frogs from throat to hem, the boat-shaped hat with its tiny feathers.

For when she was passing the house next door, proudly wheeling the perambulator, an old lady was coming down the front steps, leaning on the arm of her coachman. Stiff-spined and with a look of great dignity, she was dressed all in black. But she looked far from drab because, as she moved out into the sunlight, the rings on her fingers and the diamond brooch at her throat danced with glitter. A hat, no bigger than a child's, was set squarely on her white hair and tied under her chin with a large bow.

Megeen waited beside the steps to allow the old lady and

her coachman to pass. The dried-apple face turned in Megeen's direction. The pale lips opened briefly.

"Good afternoon," the old woman said.

Only two words and yet Megeen felt a great surge of triumph. It was as though she had achieved a victory that was so long in coming that it was doubly sweet. She could scarcely wait for Alec to come home so that they could rejoice together. The waiting seemed long, but she filled the hours with plans for the future.

Alec was to go next door and leave his card and his wife's—she must have them quickly printed—on the receiving tray there. Then they would extend an invitation to dinner to the entire family in the neighboring house, whoever and how many there might be.

She would work hard to have everything exactly right and proper for that important dinner party. For she was certain that that little old woman, despite her out-of-date clothing and vulgar display of jewels, was someone of great influence among the people Megeen wanted to know for Alec's sake and, eventually, her son's.

She cared nothing for the fashionable crowd, the lively young ladies in their bustles and ball gowns, and the young gallants who fluttered around them. The ones she wanted to establish friendships with were the solid people, whose names and money were both old, those she had heard of but never seen.

When Alec came home that afternoon, she dashed down over the stairs and threw herself into his arms. She could not wait for him to take off his driving coat but pulled him into the music room at one side of the hall.

"The finest thing has happened, dear sir! You will be so happy for me—for both of us. Now you see, I'm sure, that the things you want will come to you if you just have faith and do not give up praying even when it seems to be doing no good."

And then she told him. She described the little old lady in her unfashionable gown and small, jet-trimmed hat who had spoken—and of her own accord and not in reply to anything, mind you—to her young neighbor.

"Well, to be sure, it was not very much, Alec," she admitted, for it did sound so when spoken of aloud. "But a start. Now that she has recognized me, others will be following her lead and soon all your friends will be back and they will accept me as your wife."

She looked into his face anxiously. "She is indeed important, is she not? Someone—what is the word? Influential? You know who she is, of course?"

He said quietly, "Yes, I do know, my dear. She is Carina Lyman. She is the last of a line of a very rich and socially distinguished family. And, of course, she is what you said—extremely influential. She has ancestors who arrived here in the *Mayflower* and others who were heroes in the Revolutionary War."

Megeen's eyes were shining with joy. "Even though she merely greeted me, it is a start, is it not? Imagine me having a friend like that! It will make a great difference to all of us. I do not expect miracles at first, dear man. . . ."

Her voice trailed away, for his face had become closed and there was a look of sadness in his eyes. He drew a long breath, and when he spoke, the words seemed to come with difficulty, as though he hated having to say to her what he must.

"What is it, Alec? What makes you unhappy at a moment when you should be . . . well, not overcome by joy, perhaps, but at least a little pleased."

He took her hand in his and held it gently while he went on talking.

"I cannot let you be carried away by false hopes, dear child. That Carina Lyman spoke two words to you means nothing at all. You see, she is almost blind. She would not have known who you were. She saw a face, a figure. It might have belonged to one of her friends—or to Tessie or Mrs. Callahan. Anyone. Not, however, to Hanley perhaps."

He smiled at his own weak attempt at humor and then drew her close to him in an effort to soothe her disappointment.

Chapter Nineteen

March was the hardest, longest, most disagreeable month of all. Megeen did not spend much time brooding over her disappointment and discouragement. She was too busy and work-worn, and she marveled that one small child could cause so much upheaval and so many additional chores. Even with Ruth to help her, it seemed that there was constant turmoil.

Matthew's wakeful periods became more frequent and longer until he was sleeping only a few hours each day. He wailed for attention, and when Megeen developed a cold and was forced to wean him, he cried almost continually. The entire household was affected by the sleepless nights and tempers grew short.

He was healthy—there was that at least. She did not worry in that respect as she did about Alec. It was as though the baby, becoming more sturdy and self-willed every day, was drawing off the strength of the man, whose health was in a state of deterioration.

Again Alec refused to see a doctor. He repeated what he had said before. When spring came and the sun rose higher and warmer, he would then feel better. He could sit outdoors and let the sunshine heal all his pains and illnesses.

"Sit out where?" Megeen asked. Nerve-ridden and exhausted, she did not care that she was saying a hurtful thing. "Across the street in the park? Then you must go alone, for I would not be welcome there."

"And I would go nowhere without you."

She felt a swift pang of self-reproach. No words could take back her cruel and unfair ones. She told her sin in confession. ("For he is as near a saint as a man can be outside the true Church, Father, and much do I owe him, which makes it all the worse.") It did not ease the nagging of her conscience, and even her prayers and little acts of reparation were not enough.

But she tried. She nursed him through his bouts of illness and lethargy as though there were no other hands to feed him, to pour out his medicine, to change his nightshirt and bed linen each morning.

Then on the last day of the month there came the opportunity to repay him, at least in part, for all his many kindnesses to her.

A man came riding on horseback, and that in itself was something odd, for she had not seen many mounted men in the center of Boston. The rider was arguing with Ruth in the front hall when Megeen went downstairs. She could not see his face clearly, he had not removed his hat, which was pulled far down on his forehead. He had about him a look of nervousness and haste. And she was almost certain that he was bringing bad news.

"Ma'am, it's Mr. Vickery he wants," Ruth said peevishly, "and he insists he must, although I've tried my best to make him understand that the master is not well enough to see anyone."

Megeen motioned him to follow her into the music room. "Now what have you come to tell my husband? And I think you had best tell me who you are."

"Albert Swanburn, ma'am. I'm in charge of the mill when Mr. Vickery is not around. Well, it's been a time since he's been to the mill and my letters to him haven't been answered.

"Now I'm at the end of my rope, you might say. Things are happening that only the owner of the mill can solve. I've come to urge him to go back with me to Fairbridge."

He was a tall man and she had to tilt back her head to look at him. He had a long, solemn face and a hard jaw. His eyes were too small for the rest of his features, but they were gravely concerned. She felt herself trusting him at once.

She tried to explain the nature of Alec's illness and how it would be impossible for him to go out into the bitter-cold weather.

Biting her lip and rubbing her hands over each other, she asked, "What is the emergency that brings you here, sir? What is it that needs so desperately my husband's presence?"

It was some of the men, Mr. Swanburn explained. "They've been asking for more money. Troublemakers is what they are. It is not in my power to grant them raises in pay; Mr. Vickery alone can do that. Not all of them have walked off their jobs. Those of them that are still working are being badgered by those who are calling for a strike. It's real trouble, ma'am, and can be taken care of only by the man who can meet their demands."

She made up her mind swiftly and nodded in a decisive manner. "Since Mr. Vickery cannot be there today, I shall have our coachman drive me to Fairbridge. You may go ahead and I shall be there as soon as possible."

"You?" His mouth had fallen open. "Beggin' your pardon, but what do you think you can do with a crowd of unruly men?"

"I shall talk to them and make them listen to me. Then I shall relay any messages they may give me to my husband. It is necessary, I think, that one of us be interested in their welfare."

She stood with her arms folded across her chest. She had not lost all the weight she had gained during her pregnancy, and being short of stature, she carried it badly. Her hair, although fashionably arranged, had never seemed redder, for the sunlight coming in through the fanlit door was polishing it to a brighter color. A stubborn, outthrust chin and tightened mouth added no beauty to her appearance.

"The mill is no place for a lady." Then he sighed. "But you'll do as you like, I'm thinking. As a favor I will ask that when Mr. Vickery hears of this he will be told I did my best to prevent it. It could cost me my job, you know."

"I shall make sure it does not."

There were other arguments. She could not persuade Hanley to drive her to Fairbridge until she threatened to hire a public hack to make the journey.

The three women in the kitchen became, for a little while, united in purpose: to prevent their mistress from disgracing the household by a shockingly unladylike and perhaps dangerous foray into a situation such as she was contemplating.

Their grudges forgotten, the quarrels as much out of their minds as though they had never been, three voices were raised to sound like a Greek chorus.

The master, they prophesied, would no doubt suffer a fatal spell were he to know that his wife was acting like one of the females who—God forgive them!—were crying out for women's rights (whatever those might be) and trying to turn themselves into men.

"Then if there's no stopping you," Ruth pleaded, "let me go along with you, much as I despise the idea."

"You will stay here," Megeen said stonily, "and take care of Matthew. And if Mr. Vickery should awaken and ask for me, you are to make up some sort of story."

She looked at each of them in turn. "Should he find out the truth, the one with the busy tongue will find herself turned out without a reference."

In her heaviest clothes—her woolen cloak, the hat she had crocheted before leaving Ireland, and knit mittens—she was still cold. The rug over her knees seemed to give her no warmth. Even inside the carriage her breath puffed out like white smoke.

Hanley said not a word during the long, bone-chilling trip. His back was stiff with disapproval, but his hands were sure and skillful on the reins.

He kept the horses at a gallop, and there were times when their hooves slid on patches of ice, and she feared that the rig would overturn and that they would be thrown into a ditch.

"Holy Mother, watch over us," she prayed silently. "I cannot think that it is a wrong thing that I am doing. How can it be anything bad when I want so much to help my husband? Alec, that is. Many times I have told you of him when I was saying the rosary."

Megeen did not have any formal routine when she prayed. "For when I speak to the saints each night," she had once told Alec, "we get to be friends."

That day she called upon many of them: St. Christopher, the protector of travelers; St. Patrick, the patron of her homeland, St. Francis of Assisi, who loved and watched over all God's creatures.

Try as she might, she could not stifle her fears while they were on the slippery roads, and she drew long sighs of relief when the carriage drew into the little town of Fairbridge. She was seeing it for the first time and she pressed her face against the window of the carriage, trying to see everything within her range of vision.

Rows of small houses, appearing to be newly built with their raw shingles and curtainless windows, stood in rows and were flush to the street. These were workmen's houses, she was sure, and there was not a single thing of beauty or grace about them.

Little knots of women were gathered on small flights of steps. They became motionless and silent as the Vickery carriage approached. Then, when it had passed them, they began to talk again. Looking back, Megeen could see the rapidly moving mouths and extravagant gestures. There could be only one topic of conversation—herself.

It was natural, it was to be expected, and it did not perturb her. Not until the mill came in sight did she feel a cold blast of fear.

Hanley spoke for the first time since they had left the park. He pointed with his whip. "That's it, ma'am."

The dirt road ended where there was a cluster of wooden buildings. The sign over the main entrance read: VICKERY PAPER COMPANY. EST. 1845.

"Not too late to turn back," Hanley said, pulling on the reins. "Seems that would be a good idea, for there's a fair number hanging around. Ugly customers they look to be, too."

"I have come this far and may as well go on." Her voice sounded squeaky, and because she refused to let Hanley suspect how frightened she was of the men who milled around the main building, she tried to divert him with another subject.

"What is that horrible stench? I think I have never smelled anything so disgusting." She lifted a handkerchief to her nose. "Must the people who live hereabouts have that dreadful odor in their nostrils all the time?"

" 'Tis the pulp," he told her. "Stinkin' stuff that it is. From the pulp comes the paper. And it's the wood of the trees sent down the river that makes the pulp. The river has a stink of its own. Do ye not know anything at all about the mill and where the paper comes from?"

She did not answer him, for now they were pulling into the cinder path that led to the entrance. Men who had been moving about changing positions stopped for one long, stupefied moment. Then, as if they had had orders to do so, they walked together to the carriage, and soon it was surrounded.

One of the men leaped to grab the whip from Hanley's hand, but he misjudged the distance and went sprawling on the ground. As though his fall was some sort of signal, the others began to form a human chain. Arms entwined, they stretched across the path of the carriage. Hanley, with the reins held tightly in his hands, called down to Megeen, "Now what are we to do, ma'am? I cannot let them be trampled under the hooves of the horses."

"I am sure they will let us through." There was only a

slight quaver in her voice. "I will tell them why I am here— to help them solve their troubles."

"Missus, I beg of you . . ."

But she had already opened the carriage door and climbed down. She stretched out a hand to the man who was standing closest to her, and after a bewildered glance around, he helped her to alight.

"We will leave the rig here and I shall walk the rest of the way. So please step aside, gentlemen, I am sure there is none among you who would try to stop me from entering the mill when my purpose in being here is to help you."

A jeering voice called out from somewhere at the back of the mob. "Help is it indeed, mavourneen? And how, may the saints deliver us, is that to be done?"

He was mocking her brogue, which came into her speech in times of stress and anxiety. She had worked hard to conquer it for Alec's sake, so that he would not have a wife who sounded like a greenhorn. Now she wondered how these disgruntled men saw her. And decided that she did not care if they guessed at her humble beginnings. It might be to her advantage.

"Do not be afraid that I could do you any harm. I myself was a working girl, a kitchen maid. So my sympathies must be with you. But I cannot do anything until I know what it is you want, why you walked off your jobs. You!"

She beckoned to a man who hastily snatched off his hat. "You! Come forward and tell me where the trouble lies."

He was short and cocky, and when he spread his legs apart and gestured with closed fists, he was a formidable figure.

"I'll tell you, lady, sure enough. We works from dawn to dusk, never see a bit of sunlight except through the windows. The pay is small and our children must work if there is to be food upon our tables. Ever been hungry, ma'am? Thought not. It's our sweat that puts money in the pockets of the rich men who owns the factories and the mills."

He stopped and looked around as though asking for confirmation and support. It came in loud cheers and cries of encouragement. "Alexander Vickery," he went on stoutly, "makes his money off us and our families, yet he cares so little for working conditions here that we do not see him from one end of the year to another."

"My husband is not a well man." She managed to keep her

voice from quavering and her eyes from blinking nervously. "I have come in his stead."

There were hoots of derision and jeers and catcalls. They called out phrases that made her shrivel inside. "Come in his stead, she did!"

"When a female can take the place of a man, Gawd help us!"

"Suppose she can take his place in bed? And that Papa stays home and does the cookin'?"

She held up a hand and gradually the voices drifted away.

"You are having trouble here and it will gain no one anything at all if you lose your day's pay for being idle. If you will let me pass and enter the building, I can see what is going on here and tell him what I have seen and heard. Then he will be able to correct what needs to be taken care of. Move to one side, please."

It seemed that they were not to do what she asked. They exchanged sullen glances. They muttered to one another. There were a few more catcalls. Then, finally, the man she had been talking to stepped back and gestured to the men that they were to make a path for her.

Inside, there was a loud grinding noise that made it nearly impossible for Megeen to hear what Tim Hanley was saying. He was speaking about the pulp being rolled out and becoming paper. When there was a lull, she heard him say, "Aye, it is not such a bad place, ma'am. I have been in other mills and like hellholes they were. At least, the windows are clean here, one of them even bein' open."

She did not answer, for Mr. Swanburn had hurried out of his cubbyhole of an office and it was plain that he was perturbed by her presence.

"I did not really think you would come," he said frankly. "As I told you, it is no place for a lady. I've tried my best, Mrs. Vickery, to get the strikers back to work, but, as you can see, I am badly shorthanded."

"I am sure you did your best."

He repeated what he had said in the hall of the Vickerys' house: that it was important for Alec to come and talk to them about wages and hours; the striking workers would at least feel that he was interested in their welfare. And that he, even though superintendent of the mill, could promise them nothing.

She kept nodding her head in a distracted manner as she

walked down the aisle between rows of machines. Her footsteps grew slower as a sick sort of horror spread coldness through her veins.

Standing on boxes were small children. The boxes were necessary, for they were not tall enough to reach the parts of the machines they were working on in any other way.

They were small in every way there was: skinny little bodies, baby faces grown old too soon, knobby knees and pipestem legs. Valiantly they stood at their places, pushing and pulling and snatching, doing work that would be arduous and monotonous even for grown people.

Megeen turned and said fiercely to the man beside her, "How do you allow this? They are no more than babies! I demand that you send these children home at once!"

"That I cannot do, ma'am. I am sorry if it displeases you, but this is the way it is in every mill in this country. The children come in with their mothers in the morning. Otherwise the women would not be able to work, for there would be no one to care for them during the day."

"In the morning," Megeen said on a cracked tone. "And they are here until dark?"

"So that they may eat," Mr. Swanburn said shortly. "It is just as well for them to learn early that life is hard for people like us."

She murmured, "Oh, my God, it is not to be endured! Something must be done."

A few feet away from them, a tiny girl, no more than six years old, had her small hands wrapped around the handle of a huge, bladed instrument. A stretch of paper came rolling down from a machine far above her head, and when it reached the point at which she was standing, she brought the knife down upon it.

She was cutting sheets of stationery, Mr. Swanburn explained to Megeen over the whirring and grinding noises. He slid a piece of paper from the cardboard box into which it had fallen after being cut to size and held it up to the light. She could see the watermark, a shield with the name VICKERY stamped upon it.

"Our finest product," he said with pride in his voice. "There's no finer paper made anywhere in the world."

"But, oh, dear God, at what a price!"

She could not take her eyes off the little girl who stood on her box holding the handle of the big, wicked-looking knife.

Of all the children Megeen could see, this was the smallest, the frailest, the one in the most danger.

Her hair was matted, as though it had never felt the bristles of a brush. If washed, it would be the very pale, almost the white color of the tiny eyebrows. Her mouth was a baby's, small and soft and sweet.

Megeen, the horror being replaced by anger, cried, "Poor little thing! Each morning to be pulled from her bed, too tired to get her eyes open, I've no doubt, and set to work like a beast in the fields. This cannot be allowed."

As though realizing that she was being talked about, the little girl turned, seeming to forget the knife in her hand. Then, with a faint and almost inaudible sigh, her knees collapsed and she fell forward.

Megeen lunged forward and snatched the child out of the path of the knife, which was descending slowly. She cried, "Help me!" and Mr. Swanburn threw an arm around each of them and dragged them backward a few feet. He took the limp form from Megeen and carried it to the open window.

The danger past, Megeen could give vent to her rage against the people who allowed small children to be used in this despicable manner.

"Who is she? Where are her parents? Do they not care anything about her at all?"

Mr. Swanburn frowned. "She has none, I believe. She has a home with a family who are able to take care of her only if she earns her own way. She is nobody's child."

"Indeed! That is the saddest thing I have heard for many a long day. Now, sir, you will oblige me by turning off the power."

She held up her hand as he started to protest.

"Those are my orders, if you please. I shall tell my husband what is going on down here. No doubt he will wish to shut the mill down for a few days. That will give tempers a chance to cool."

As she looked down at the colorless little face, she saw the pale eyelids begin to flicker.

"I shall not wait for heaven to take a hand in this," Megeen said firmly. "There are times when a person must do what is necessary herself."

Chapter Twenty

The woman looked frail and workworn. No more than five years older than herself, Megeen guessed, but aged by too many pregnancies, too much worry, and, possibly, too little to eat.

The pale face was stiffened by defiance. "I did the best I could for her. Her mama left her with me. Threw her away, she did. Just up and walked off after I'd given the two of them shelter, as I thought, for just a day or so. Walked off and never been seen since. I don't know nothing about her pa. Nor does anybody else."

Megeen looked down at the little girl with concern. But there were no signs that she had heard. There was no expression on the small face, and the eyes, a pretty shade of blue, were clear and clean and empty.

"I dunno what more I could have done," the woman said in her flat, uninflected voice. "My children, none of 'em older than this one—they got jobs here. She gotta work like the rest, Ellie does. Lest she wouldn't be able to live.

"Ma'am, I been as good to her as I could. Believe me, that's the truth. Mornin's when she's too tired to walk over from the house, I've carried her. Still sound asleep in my arms, she couldn't of got here by herself. A couple of my own hangin' onto my skirts and this one ... well, she ain't as strong and quick as the others. I done my best. Not easy, I can tell you with my man sick at home most of the time with lung disease."

The little girl's name was Ellen Cosgrove. As far as the woman knew, she had no kinfolk. Megeen had only to hear that. She beckoned to Hanley, who was slouched against the door that led to the outdoors.

"We will take her home with us. If anyone speaks of her, asks where she is, I am easily found."

She looked directly into the woman's face as she spoke, a face that sagged a little with relief. Megeen could almost read the thoughts behind that brightening of features. One less mouth to feed. One less body in an overcrowded bed. No more carrying the burden of a child escaping, for a few more minutes of sleep, the cruelty of her world.

Megeen spoke sharply to Hanley. "Am I speaking some strange language that you did not understand what I said? The little one is going home with us. Lift her gently and carry her to the rig."

Still he hesitated. "Ma'am, ye cannot act in this highhanded way. Givin' orders to shut down the mill. Takin' off with a child ye've never seen before, like she was a stray dog or somethin'. It's himself should be givin' orders like that if there is to be orders."

She placed her hands on her hips and looked into his eyes. There had been a time when she had been a little in awe of Hanley. His size and gruffness and his weakness for the bottle had made him, in her eyes, a formidable figure.

She was not afraid of him now. Nor was she intimidated by the others, who edged closer to the little group. She scarcely heard their muttering as the news was passed along that the mill was to close and would not reopen until the owner was able to appear and solve the workers' problems.

All Megeen was aware of was the little girl, who gazed up at her, still as a wax doll. She lowered herself to her knees and picked up an icy hand. She said soothingly, "Ellen, you are coming home with me. Do not be afraid, dear. I promise you this—you'll never again work in this place. Nor will they."

She arose and gestured toward the children, who had edged their way up through the aisles between the machines. They stood staring with puzzled eyes at the coachman as he lifted the pitifully thin body from the floor.

Mr. Swanburn followed Megeen to the door. "I shall get in trouble for closing down, Mrs. Vickery. It could be worth my job. May I point out to you that the orders should come from your husband?"

"And when he is unable to give them, then I must. Now you are to send all these people home. I have no more to say."

After she had climbed into the carriage, Hanley put the little girl on her lap. There had not yet been a sound coming through the lips tucked tightly against the small teeth. What was she thinking? Megeen wondered. Did she realize that never again would she be carried, too sleepy to walk, to the daily hell of her dawn-to-dusk job?

She neither moved nor spoke. Throughout the long ride she lay as motionless as a corpse. It was not until they had almost reached the park that Megeen felt pinching in her wrist. She looked down and saw that Ellen's fingernails were digging deep into the flesh that her mittens did not quite cover.

There was a slight, stinging pain, but Megeen did not draw her hand away. And she kept silent; nor did she reveal in any way that she was aware of the terror of the unknown that Ellen was feeling.

Ellen did not speak for two days. Once they had put aside their resentment at additional housework caused by another person in the household, Mrs. Callahan and Tessie took turns trying to coax the little girl out from behind the wall of silence she had built around herself.

Ruth, who was now in charge of the market shopping, bought special tasty items to tempt the child to eat. Clothing became a problem because on the morning Megeen planned to take Ellen to the shops and outfit her, the child showed an emotion for the first time. She ran and cowered in a corner, rigid with fear.

"Most likely thinks you're taking her back to that awful place. Ma'am, it'd be better if you stayed with her," Ruth suggested. "If you go off and leave her now, she's going to think you'll not come back. Let me go and buy some material and all of us can pitch in and make her some dresses and underwear and nightclothes. Her shoes are good enough for now. And don't worry, ma'am, she'll get over it soon."

But it was not the prospect of new clothing that brought Ellen out from behind the wall. On the first two nights in her new home, she slept through the night on a pallet that Megeen had set up in her own room. During the middle of the third night, awakened by the whistling of the wind, Megeen arose, lighted her gas lamp, and went to the corner where Ellen had been sleeping. The little girl was not in the makeshift bed.

There was a moment of heart-stopping panic, and then as the wind took a respite from its noisy assault, she heard a faint sound from the next room. A voice was singing tunelessly. She tiptoed as far as the threshold. In the light from her lamp she saw Ellen kneeling beside Matthew's cradle.

The baby was awake and, for once, he was not crying or

thrashing about from side to side. His tiny hand was curled around Ellen's finger.

Megeen went back to bed quietly. She pretended not to know that Ellen spent the rest of the night on the floor at the baby's side. Like a good dog, faithful and devoted, Ellen was never far from Matthew in the days that followed.

At first she spoke to no one but him. And he, the strong-willed tyrant, the unmanageable ruler of the household who had learned to scream and wail for his own purposes, became sweet-tempered when Ellen soothed him and crooned to him.

During her first days with her new family, she held herself from the others. The shadow of fear still clouded her eyes, and when the doorbell buzzed or tradesmen came to the area-way, she ran and hid like some hunted thing. It was impossible to get her to leave the household without tears. When Megeen insisted on taking her to church, Ellen whimpered all the way, but was awed to silent wonder by the choir, the beauty of the inside of the cathedral, and the pageantry of the Mass.

She became so firmly a part of the household that it seemed to Megeen that she had always been there. But, in spite of the fact that she was beginning to love the quiet, gentle girl more each day, she could not feel completely easy. She had only to look at Ellen to remember that there were hundreds—perhaps thousands of children no older than Ellen who were slaves to a system that robbed little ones, scarcely out of the cradle, of their childhood.

It was Ellen, innocent and unknowing, who caused the first quarrel between Megeen and Alec. Out of consideration for his illness, she postponed for a few days telling him of the little girl she had brought home to live with them.

"And, oh, dear Alec, I'm sure you could not have known what was going on in the mill. Those poor little things never to know daylight! I told the man in charge—Mr. Swanburn, that is—to close down the mill until all the men were satisfied with their wages. In the meantime, we can send food to them so they will not be hungry. I know that we can't take all the children from their jobs right away, but little by little. . . ."

Her voice drifted away and her lips became unsteady as Alec threw his legs over the edge of the bed and reached for a dressing robe. She had never seen his face so stiff and pale with anger.

"You had no right! It was none of your concern! You have shamed me in the eyes of those who are supposed to be following my orders. A fine figure of fun I must be to them now that my wife had a notion to take my place!

"And how did you get there? Hanley drive you? I shall have his skin for this!"

"No, Alec, do not be angry with him." Tears sprang into her eyes, so hot that they seemed to scald them. "I persuaded him. As for Ellen, I did not think you would object to my bringing her home. Even in this short time she has been so good with Matthew. But she is but one. Don't you see that all those other children should not be used for such a dreadful purpose?"

He moved to the highboy at the other side of the room. There was something vulnerable about the way he looked—his thin legs bare, his faded hair unbrushed. He set his shaving mirror at a different angle, but although he stood looking into it, she knew that he was not seeing his image.

"There is nothing I can do," he said flatly. "It is the same in all mills and factories. Operating costs must be kept down, else there would be no work for anyone. These people . . ." His voice fumbled, as though he could not force himself to say the word "children." He drew a long breath. "What is the alternative, starvation?

"This is the way they must live in order to exist. You cannot change it by one visit to one mill. As for this little girl you brought here, you may have done others a great disservice. No doubt there will be dozens of them down there who will be dissatisfied now, wanting what she has or expecting that a Lady Bountiful or a fairy godmother will come along change everything for them, too."

He was taking a clean, folded shirt from one of the drawers of the highboy. She saw him cling to the knob of a closet door; she took a few steps in his direction, but he waved her away.

"You have erred twice, Megeen, and I am very much perturbed. You meddled in my business affairs and so diminished me in the eyes of my employees. You high-handedly brought into this house a child about whom you know nothing. Did it never occur to you that there might be unpleasantness about that at some future time?"

She stared at him silently, too wretched to try to think up an answer.

"Consider this," he said coldly. "After having this child for a while, you would, naturally, become fond of her. And then a parent shows up to claim her and threatens to take her away unless you pay for her. My dear Megeen, life is cheap where those people are concerned. To buy and sell a child is not an unheard-of thing."

"But they are not all like that!"

She was thinking of the woman who had taken Ellen into her household. The woman whose name she had never learned, the work-worn, very young woman who had carried Ellen to the mill when she was too sleepy to walk, the woman who would have been a little girl for a very short time.

Then, when Alec took down his driving coat and threw it across a chair, she ran to him and grasped his arm.

"Oh, no, dear sir! You mustn't think of going out. The wind is much too sharp. Perhaps tomorrow will be more pleasant. Another day in bed, it will not matter."

He threw off her hand. "You have made it necessary for me to try to repair the damage you have done. There is much you have to learn, my wife. One cannot keep a household running without money. And of that there is not an unlimited supply. So I must straighten things out at the mill, which is our main source of income."

It was the first time she had heard him speak of money in that fashion. She had taken for granted the fact that her husband was extremely wealthy. The house was full of beautiful, costly things. Had he not urged her to buy only the most expensive clothing for herself and their son?

"The store?" she asked diffidently. "And your law practice? Surely those must—"

She barely heard his faint sigh. "The store has been losing money for the past year, yet I do not wish to close it down, for it was one of my father's favorite enterprises. As for the law practice . . . well, you would not approve of my clients, for they are those you are learning to despise: the Howards, the Allertons, the Crawfords—millowners all. And, yes, employers of small children like myself. I may lose these people at any rate, for I have been forced to neglect the business. And Lenard . . ."

There was that strange little squeezing of her heart when Alec spoke his son's name.

"Yes, what of him?" She turned away lest he see on her

face a reflection of that peculiar excitement. "Does he not share in the businesses, do some of the work?"

"He is supposed to."

The sigh was louder this time, and she felt a sudden twisting of pity for Alec was struggling into his heavy coat. She took a step forward to help him and then thought better of it. She had wounded his pride, perhaps irreparably, and she could think of no way to undo the harm she had done.

"Lenard is of little help."

His son, he told her, had gone to Canada with some friends. She frowned over that piece of information. Lenard's place was here, at his father's side, when he was needed. She was about to say that aloud, but Alec spoke first.

"If you are so interested in my business affairs, perhaps you would like to look over the records."

He gestured toward the rosewood desk in a corner of the room. It was a lovely, graceful thing and Megeen guessed that it was of great value. But now it was cluttered, ledger books in untidy piles, papers spilling out of pigeon holes.

After Alec had left, stalking off without saying good-bye, Megeen drew up the desk chair and sat looking at what was in front of her. She did not know where to start. The larger heap of papers was made up of bills. The smaller one contained receipts. It took her hours to sort out everything, and when she had finished, she knew that Alec Vickery's financial affairs were in very poor condition.

The bills for food, fuel, and servants' wages were all high, and some of the indebtednesses had not been paid for months. She discovered that the servants' wages had been owing for weeks, and she became indignant that these people who worked hard for their wages were forced to wait for them. She made little notations on the debit side of the ledger that Hanley and Ruth and Tessie and Mrs. Callahan were to receive their money before any other expenditures were made.

When Alec returned home later that afternoon, he refused all Megeen's efforts to make him comfortable. He wanted no hot tea, no warm bed, no change of clothing.

That night there was no chess game. Alec ate only little from the tray Megeen carried to his room. Then he spent the evening reading, or pretending to. He retired early after having spoken only a few words for the past two hours.

Megeen waited until she was sure that he was in his bed

before, in nightdress and robe, she went quietly into his room. She slid out of her garments and slipped in beside him.

It was not pity that had sent her there, or remorse, or compunction. She had hoped that he would share with her his feelings about what he had seen that day at the mill.

She suspected that he had never taken much note of his employees, never really been aware of the small children who stood on stools and boxes and crates in order to reach the machinery. She had made him see them and now she must erase that picture from his mind. She felt impelled to comfort him in the only way she knew how.

But there was no comfort for him. His body was stiff when she reached out to him. He made no response when her arms went around him.

"Alec! Alec!" she whispered hoarsely. "Do not be angry with me!"

But she knew he was not angry. He was broken and unhappy, and she was not doing anything to lighten his spirits. When she put her hands on either side of his face and kissed him, his response was mechanical, without ardor. She rubbed his ankle with the sole of her foot and then let her toes slide upward and rest upon his thigh. She spread herself across him, but even her naked body moving slowly atop his did not arouse him.

On another night he would have put his hand into hers and let her guide it to the places where his touch gave her the most pleasure, but tonight his hand was cold and unwilling.

She went on trying for a long time, with her lips and hands and warm legs twisted around him. She stopped only when she feared that she was exciting herself too much, that she would reach the high peak of ecstasy alone. She slid off him and dropped into an inviting posture, legs apart, her impatient hands ready to caress him.

He turned and shifted. He ran his fingers over her hard nipples. And then, with a deep sigh that shook his whole body, he rolled away from her. He lay staring at the wall beside his bed, seeing nothing in the darkness, she knew, except his own dark thoughts.

"Do not feel bad, my dear. It was not your fault, I know."

"Whose, then?" She could hear the desolate note in his voice. And then he said something in which she could find no meaning. "So that is what it's like! I never believed that I would find out!"

She only knew that he was heavyhearted with shame and she said soothingly, "It doesn't matter. There will be other nights, better ones. If there is any blame, it is mine."

Lying there beside him, she longed to be able to explain her guilt. Having insulted his manhood by interfering in his business affairs, she might have robbed him of his important function as a man.

She left the bed as quietly as she had slipped into it. She found her robe and put it on, and she went back to her room with slow, heavy steps. Her shoulders sagged as though she carried upon them a great burden.

There arose in her mind all the things she must do: to bring back joy to Alec and make him glad she was his wife; to put in motion the legal procedure that would make Ellen Cosgrove actually their daughter; to find a way to pay the overdue bills and straighten out the financial tangle, which seemed a monstrous chore.

She felt desolately alone in spite of the fact that there were two children in the next room, three servant girls asleep in their small rooms, her husband in the bed she had just left.

If only Lenard would come home! she thought with longing that was almost a physical pain. He would share with her the responsibilities and worries. He had been away now for a long time and she saw him with the faulty vision of memory.

He did come home a week later, but his arrival helped nothing and no one. It made things worse.

Chapter Twenty-one

It was not that Lenard used his voice to make his presence felt. Sometimes he did not speak throughout the serving and eating of a meal, ignoring the enigmatic dialogue that went on between his father and his stepmother.

There would be a grim sort of silence, and then Megeen would blurt, "Twelve!"

The answer to that was always a shake of Alec's head. At first Lenard would look up and his glance moved from one to the other in puzzlement and curiosity. It was as though the two were playing some sort of game that did not include him and that he did not understand.

Later the word was "ten." By that time the tone of Megeen's voice had changed. There were more urgent, pleading notes in it. Gradually Lenard saw that she and his father were engaged in some sort of bargaining duel.

"If you would just raise the age limit, dear sir. Can you truly look at our own little Ellie and not think of those children who may not live to reach the age of ten?"

Lenard remained outside the argument, bored and indifferent. But Megeen was always conscious of him. If the baby cried during the night, she worried for fear he was disturbing Lenard. Ellen was warned that she must keep out of the area on the second floor where Lenard's bedroom door was always shut against the ordinary household noises. He paid no attention to the children and seemed annoyed when his path happened to cross theirs.

Megeen had hoped that with Lenard's return much of the burden of financial worry would be shared and so lightened. But when she tried to bring up the subject of the paper mill, the dwindling law practice and the slovenly run dry-goods store, he did not even bother to listen to what she was saying.

On one occasion, when she tried to speak to him of those things, he slid a sly smile across his lips, and she knew that he suspected that she had manufactured an opportunity to be alone with him.

He must know that she found him attractive: whenever they were alone, her body warmed and she flustered. An urgent need rose from deep in her stomach and her throat became sealed so that she could do little except stare mutely at him and press her hands together lest their trembling betray her.

Sometimes, all too aware of her confusion and battle for self-control, he laughed aloud. He taunted her with his smile, touching her shoulder lightly or letting his hand rest, for the briefest moment, on her breast. He made it seem accidental, but she knew that he was playing his own type of game, robbing her of her breath and making the sweat spring out on her forehead. Perhaps, she thought, he did not realize that there was cruelty in his little game.

For she wanted him badly. Each time she looked into his face, a hot flood ran in her veins. She longed to throw herself against him and be lost in that dark, steamy world that she glimpsed behind Lenard's knowing smile.

She prayed. She tried to make sacrifices, self-imposed penances. Sunday Mass was not enough to fortify her against her forbidden thoughts, and she began to attend benediction on Friday nights, walking over to St. Dominic's, where she and Alec had been married. She felt that she could reaffirm her vows more easily where they had been said than in the cathedral, with its distractions of stained-glass windows and the thundering notes of the organ.

Too, the long walk wearied her and she could fall asleep more easily and not lie awake, as she usually did, for hour after hour, even after Alec's lovemaking ended in contentment and lethargy.

At the end of a few weeks, Megeen noticed that the same faithful people were in attendance at benediction, the same people in the same pews. She came to recognize them by sight if not by name. In front of her, her fingers slipping over the beads of a silver rosary, there was a young woman of about her own age who became a familiar figure.

One night she spoke to Megeen. They had reached the vestibule of the church at the same time. Their hands dipped into the holy-water font at the same moment. They smiled, walked through the door together.

" 'Tis a foolish thing for us to see each other time and time again and not speak a greeting."

She had a sweet and lilting voice, and she did not try to disguise or hide its brogue. It sounded like music to Megeen's ears and she knew in that moment, with the mysticism that sometimes touched her with its magic, that she and Martha Laverty were to share something important in the future.

"Martha! A fine name for an Irish lass, would ye say? I know not why I was given it. At home—Donegal, that is— no other bore a name like that."

In spite of her fine clothes, she had the look of a washerwoman: a sturdy body, flushed cheeks, a prim little mouth. Her eyes were merry and dancing. Her ginger-colored hair under the fashionable hat was lighter than Megeen's but more unruly. Even its side combs, of tortoise shell studded with colored stones, did not keep it in place.

Martha Laverty talked all the way to the corner where the two women would part. Even there she lingered on, speaking mostly of herself. She was twenty-one years old, had come to America six years ago, was married for four, had a two-year-old baby and a husband fifteen years older than herself. He did most of his work in the big hospital at the bottom of Beacon Hill and had his offices in the front rooms of their house on Pinckney Street.

"The only Irish on the hill," she said with a little sigh. "Only for the scarcity of doctors in Boston and that Ambrose is needed, we couldn't have bought a toolshed up there. My brother—God bless him!—must live in Roxbury. He's a merchant and been here fifteen years and well-to-do at that, but bein' Irish the doors are shut in his face when he looks to find a place to house his family. Roxbury is nice enough, to be sure, but away out almost in the country, it's lonely for him and his family."

She pulled the collar of her coat up farther around her neck against the chill of the night breezes. "It's me other brother ye'll be hearin' about and seein' his name. Coleman Sheehy—he'll be runnin' for alderman in the fall and I doubt not that he'll win the office, for there are many of us in the city now and as Colie says, we're deservin' of recognition."

She paused only to draw a deep breath. "What I'd like to do is start a club for people like you and me. Well, it could be religious, couldn't it, but a way to pass a social evening, too. 'Twill do no harm to speak to Father Corrigan about it and that I will do on the morrow. Let us hang together, as the sayin' goes, and we will accomplish much in the way of helpin' them less fortunate than ourselves. Now, dear lady, I've about talked your ear off. Ye've been the soul of patience. But I noticed when I spoke of helpin' others there was something troubled in your face. Is there anything botherin' ye, lass?"

That pleasing voice and the lively blue eyes had something compelling about them. Megeen found it easy to speak of Ellen Cosgrove and the little children who toiled from dawn to sundown in the mills and factories.

"Indeed, yes." Mrs. Laverty's face had grown sad. "I've heard of such. There seems to be little we can do now, but with Coleman elected and women like us workin' for a common purpose, perhaps we can make some changes. I'll point that out to Father and no doubt we can get started right away."

But Father Corrigan would lend no assistance and was bitterly opposed to the whole idea.

"An excuse to be gallivantin' about the streets!" he said in his stern, Sunday-sermon voice. "A woman's place is at home, takin' care of her husband and children. 'Tis in the Scriptures, and are ye plannin' to fly in the face of the Lord's teachin's? Ye'll have no support from me. The next thing ye'll be wantin' to vote, God help us! At times I fear the whole world is goin' crazy. 'Tis a silly whim, madam, and ye'll have forgotten it within the month!"

But Father Corrigan had little insight into the true nature of the stubborn Irish-American women of Boston. The doors of Yankee society might be closed against them; they might be ignored and snubbed, their children refused admittance to certain private schools. But there was a degree of iron in their souls and they were determined that the next generation would have a part in the governing of the city. They were planning on forming their own society. Proud and with shrewdness not easily discerned behind the turned-up noses, the freckles, the ready smiles, the blue-green, thick-lashed eyes, they gathered together for strength, each bringing with her the doggedness of the Irish and the firm purpose they all shared.

Martha Laverty, her stubbornness hardened after her futile appeal to Father Corrigan, opened her house to women bearing the names of Clougherty, McKinney, Lyons, Linnehan, Farrell, O'Neil.

All had been Irish-born. Before their marriages they had been cooks and chambermaids, scrubwomen, laundresses, housemaids. A few had come as picture brides and had not laid eyes on their bridegrooms until they met at the altar for the wedding ceremony.

They had one thing in common: their husbands had prospered, money was not a problem, and their ambitions for their children ran high.

Only Megeen, who helped Mrs. Laverty to form the Martha Guild, had married into an old New England family. It set her apart from the others at first, and except for Martha Laverty, she had no real friend among the other women.

She had, too, a sense of guilt. Money was dispensed freely, well-spent but putting a drain on her pocketbook. Mrs. Laverty was constantly discovering a family in need of food, a young man wanting to go into the priesthood but deterred by lack of funds, a sick and destitute old woman in her husband's hospital whose last days she felt impelled to brighten.

Martha spent the money freely, collecting contributions from the members and insisting on high dues in order to keep the treasury full. Megeen was certain that she was the only one who felt the pinch and she was always conscious that it was Alec's money she was spending.

She felt traitorous because one of the proposals high on the Martha Guild list was the reform of child labor. Names were passed out and there was a mill or a factory for each member to investigate and write a report upon. Megeen was both relieved and embarrassed. The feelings were sharpened because she had no one with whom to talk the matter over. Certainly not Alec, the dear man whose money she was spending in an unacknowledged war against him.

In spite of the still-fresh memories of the agony of Matthew's birth, she was delighted when she discovered that she was pregnant once more. Somehow it seemed that all problems would be solved, all differences disappear, with the birth of this new child.

There would be no doubt about the male parent of this baby. She felt that she would be giving to Alec the gift of his self-esteem. And engrossed with the preparations for the delivery, sewing new small garments, trying to figure out where they would put one more member of the crowded household, she felt certain that Lenard and the guilt-ridden longing she had for him would disappear, too.

Chapter Twenty-two

Ellen went to school that fall. She could not have been anything except studious, docile, and self-effacing, for the months she had spent in the Vickery household had not lightened her sober manners.

There were no childish games or outbursts of gaiety. All her waking hours, until that crisp and crystal-clear September morning when she walked out of the house with Megeen, had been spent with Matthew. At night he would not sleep if she were not lying on a mattress at his side.

From the first day of school and for weeks after that, life became horror. Each member of the household, except Lenard, took a turn at trying to quiet the wailing baby. The strain on his vocal cords seemed too great to be borne, and during the short periods of respite when, exhausted, he fell asleep, hiccups rose in his throat and his little fists remained clenched.

He was nine months old and already iron-willed and mean-dispositioned. Even Megeen, who, as a mother, was supposed to have God-like patience, found there were times when she could no longer stand that relentless sound of anger and bad temper. She would have to put on her coat and walk around the block several times, cravenly taking peeks at her watch, hoping that its hands were flying and that Ellen would soon appear carrying her satchel of schoolbooks.

It was on one of those flights from the nursery that she saw Carina Lyman coming down the steps of the house next door, as she had seen her on another day months ago. Megeen, remembering Alec's cynical remarks about the old lady and his warning that there was no hope of gaining her friendship, hung back for a moment.

If she were indeed blind, Megeen thought, it did not necessarily follow that she had lost possession of all her senses. The past few weeks had been unseasonably warm. Open windows must have brought the sounds of Matthew's tantrums into the house next door. There was a shared wall through which the screams must penetrate. And the old were said to be sensitive to certain noises. Megeen hoped fervently that her stubborn, unhappy son was not causing distress among the members of yet another household.

She moved forward as the old lady, on the arm of her coachman, reached the bottom step. She had no selfish purpose now in speaking to Carina Lyman. Her apology was as sincere as it sounded. She was genuinely sorry for what annoyance her bad-tempered son was causing the neighbors.

"And there is nothing we can do for him until his sister comes home from school. I regret that the crying may be disturbing. Perhaps soon he will get over being so unhappy when she is out of his sight."

Mrs. Lyman thrust her head forward, and the old-fashioned bonnet she was wearing wobbled on her sparse hair. Her eyes were faded and wore over them a film of near-blindness, and there was a web of wrinkles crisscrossing her cheeks. But there was pride in the way she stood and her features—hawklike nose, strong mouth, wide brow—gave her a look of invincibility.

The briefest of smiles touched her lips and transformed her face so that Megeen was able to see the woman there had been until the years had wrecked her beauty and sparkle.

"I have heard babies cry before," she said dryly. "Though I confess that if he were mine, he would feel the palm of my hand on his little bottom. I would let him know who is the boss!"

She peered forward farther and gazed intently into Megeen's face. "It is not easy raising children these days, I imagine." Then she said abruptly, "Come to tea tomorrow. At four or thereabouts. I've no doubt it would do you good to be away from that house for a little while. Irish, are you? Then you'll be wanting the tea strong and hot. I'll mention that to Mrs. Coulter. My housekeeper, that is."

It was the first of many visits Megeen made to the Lyman house that fall and winter. What had started as an act of kindness by one turned out to be reciprocal, with the other giving the gift of her presence. Carina Lyman seemed pathetically glad whenever Megeen took the time to call upon her. It was apparent that the old woman was spending the last, lonely years of her life with only bittersweet memories to keep her company.

She had outlived her husband and her children. Most of her friends were dead; the few who remained were as incapacitated as she was.

It was plain that she had never known anyone like Megeen, who had married her employer after working for him as a kitchen maid for a short time. She had never imagined, in her young, autocratic years, that she would find herself entertaining one of the despised upstarts in her own drawing room.

In that room, and in the others Megeen glimpsed, there were awesome treasures, even older and more precious than those belonging to the Vickerys. A French clock smuggled out of Paris, Mrs. Lyman told Megeen, during the Revolution there. Desks and chairs and love seats and divans made by

English masters, which Megeen could identify because Alec had taught her well. Priceless Persian rugs, tapestries depicting France's bloody history. Satin wallpaper, faded now. Intricately carved silver tea things.

Megeen paid for the quiet hours among beautiful surroundings with the coin of news about her own family. Mrs. Lyman heard about the lack of sufficient bedrooms now that Matthew was growing older and should be moved into a room of his own. And about Ellen, who had been absorbed into the family as though she had been born into it. Mrs. Lyman listened to the story of one child being rescued from the slavery of the paper mill, and by the time it was finished, her jaw had settled into grimness.

"This I have known for a long time," she sighed. "And it was even worse twenty or so years ago. It was the reason why, when my husband died, I sold the textile mill. It was not of much use, my refusing to carry on a business—if I had been able—that exploited small children. Except that it kept my conscience quiet. You say your women's club is trying to improve conditions for those poor little souls? How are you paying your expenses? I should be happy to make a contribution if it is needed."

Megeen was careful not to speak a single word that would be unfavorable to Alec. She avoided the subject of his floundering law practice, the fact that there seemed always to be trouble at the mill, the drain on his finances because the drygoods store was consistently losing money.

The Vickery summer residence had been sold. Megeen learned that only when she had suggested, at the end of June, that the children might enjoy the country for a few weeks. He had told her, almost casually, that he could not afford to maintain two houses, but she never knew whether the money realized on the sale had lightened his financial situation or whether overdue bills had swallowed it all up. He had removed all the papers and ledgers from the rosewood desk and she had felt the unspoken reproof. Only the slightest flare of dismay had leaped into his eyes when she told him that she was expecting another baby.

"Not another Matthew!" He had drawn her into his arms. "Surely we've had our share and more of difficult babies! Megeen, my dear, this time it will be different in other ways, too. It seems that ladies go into the hospital now to deliver.

I've heard that there is an entire ward in the hospital on the Charles River just for that purpose."

"It is here in my own home that my child shall come into the world." She spoke firmly with an up-and-down motion of her head. "I wish Marm could hear of this! I will write about it in my next letter to her. A hospital indeed!"

The baby inside her was quiet, unmoving for so many long periods of time that she was fearful. With only Matthew as a basis of comparison, it seemed that his new brother or sister would be delicate, provided it survived at all. Matthew had made his presence felt by strong kicks and turns. The life in her womb now was gentle.

She was determined that this new baby should be treated with as much loving welcome as her firstborn. She would not use as a layette the garments Matthew had worn. A new set of clothing was the right of every newborn infant, and she went shopping at the dry-goods store her husband owned. Not willingly. Not without some dread, for she had formed a strong dislike for Henry Broderick, the manager of Alec's store and its only salesperson.

He was a man with little meat on his bones; she compared him in her mind with a scarecrow. His face was long and it had a rubbery look, as though it had somehow become stretched during the middle years of his life. His muttonchop whiskers were full enough, but there was little hair atop his head. His eyes looked buried in that grayish flesh. There was upon that somehow repulsive face a look of impatience when, long after the bell above the door jangled, he came out of the back room.

While waiting for him, Megeen had taken a critical look around the store. She thought she could understand why the place was losing money. Everything was in a jumble. Bolts of cloth were thrown carelessly on the shelves. In one of the display cases, fine netting was caught in a package of common pins. Ladies' purses and reticules were thrown in a heap so that their quality and fashion did not show up to advantage.

And over everything there were signs of neglect. The showcases needed to be cleaned. Dust hung in the air, and the floor was badly in need of sweeping.

As Henry Broderick came into the store proper from the room behind it, Megeen heard a burst of masculine laughter. In that second she knew why the condition of the place was a matter of indifference to the man who was supposed to be its manager. For there was a new sound now: that of poker chips clicking.

"What do ye want, ma'am?"

He had given her only a careless glance, but now, his eyes sharpening, he recognized her. There was a change in his expression. He gave a quick look over his shoulder and his face became distorted with his effort to smile.

"Well, Mrs. Vickery, what can I do for you? Something in the way of flannel for those young 'uns of yours? Cool enough for warmer nightclothes?"

She stared directly into his face until he was forced to bring his quickly moving gaze back to her.

"Before anything else, Mr. Broderick, you will send those men back there home. We are not running a gaming club, you see. Or a saloon."

The unmistakable reek of liquor was beginning to fill the airless store. She sniffed in distaste but kept her eyes on the sullen-faced man until he began to edge his way out from behind the counter.

"Yer husband has no objections to me havin' me friends here when things are dull. Right tiresome it gets hour after hour when there's no customers."

"My husband has not seen the state this place is in. Nor has he looked at your account books lately."

It had been said at random. She hadn't meant to accuse him of anything; but when his face grew even grayer and hot, and naked hatred shot out of his eyes, she grew a little frightened.

He turned abruptly and went through the curtained doorway to the back room, where, evidently, there was a door leading to the alley behind the store, for she heard the scuffling of feet and then the dwindling of voices.

The man returned, fear and hostility plain on his face. "Decide what ye want?"

"Several yards of cambric and some Val lace, the narrow kind. But none that you have on display now." She pointed at a bolt of cloth on a low shelf. "That is soiled. And the lace should be in a better position, for it should be easy to sell with so many uses for it."

And then she added, in a voice as casual as she could make it, "While you are finding what I want, I will be taking a look at your daily account records, if you please." He would have argued if she had not waved him silent. "They have not been checked for too long a time, sir, and I intend to examine them carefully now."

His face had changed color again. A dull and angry red tide rose under his skin. His voice had thickened when he said, "No need for that, ma'am. I'm the one that's in charge of the bookkeeping and have been since the old Mr. Vickery hired me."

"Then there's no harm in my seeing how things stand, I think you will agree."

She spoke calmly enough, but some of his nervousness seemed to be infecting her. Loosening her arms from the sleeves of her cloak, she settled down at the desk on the other side of the curtain with a purposefulness she did not feel.

He hovered around her, peering over her shoulder and clearing his throat until she lost her patience and ordered him to find other things to do.

The accounts were in a sad jumble and it took her a full hour to complete her task. The desk, by that time, was littered with scraps of paper covered with her figures and notations.

She arose stiffly and went into the main part of the store. The bell above the door had not rung once since it had sounded at her entrance. But at that moment lack of customers was not her main concern.

She still held the current ledger in her hand when she looked steadily into Henry Broderick's face and asked, "Why are the bank deposits—all of them dating back for years—so much smaller than the receipts? I find that that is so over and over again. Even taking into consideration your salary and the expenses of heat and light, there is a large difference." She tapped the book with a finger. "You have evidently found a way to put in the bank only a portion of the money that belongs there. The rest, I've no doubt, has gone into your pocket."

It was a daring thing to say, alone as she was in a store that might not have another customer for the remainder of the day, with a man facing ruination. She saw his long hands clench and unclench rapidly and steadily, as though they were pieces of machinery driven by some hidden power. His face looked murderous.

"Are you accusing me . . . ?"

"Of nothing yet, sir. There will have to be a closer check. Then my husband will have to decide what to do about you.

Do not waste your time or breath." Again she interrupted him, her hand raised and her face stony. "I could not understand why this store was steadily losing money. Now I do. Mr. Vickery trusted you to take care of the receipts and the ordering of stock. That I have not looked into as carefully as is necessary, the purchasing, I mean. But I can guess that there was cheating there, too."

He growled deep in his throat, "Ye've no call to name me a thief and a cheat. I shall lay my side of the story for yer husband to see."

"In the meantime," Megeen said, holding out her hand, "you will oblige me by giving me the keys. This place will be locked up for now and you may consider yourself fired. And without a reference. But consider yourself lucky that you do not land in jail."

Her voice betrayed her in the end by breaking, for Henry Broderick was staring down at her from a great height, it seemed, and there was hatred and evil in the depths of his eyes. And she knew that as long as this man lived he would carry with him those feelings and a sickness that could be cured only by revenge.

Chapter Twenty-three

She received no praise from Alec when she recounted to him what had happened in the dry-goods store. She had not expected him to be wholeheartedly approving, but she was shocked by his reprimand.

"Good God, woman, how could you have dared to face a character like Broderick in that way? He was hired by my father because of what he is."

"What he is?"

"At the time of the draft riots at the beginning of the war, there was looting. Washington Street was like a battlefield. Some of the stores were stripped of their stock and never reopened again. Broderick came in from the west, toting a gun and knowing how to use it. The store might not be standing now if he were not the rough character he is."

"But he was robbing you!" Megeen unfolded her hand and showed him the key that lay on her palm. "I have discharged him," she said calmly. "It was foolish to let him go on putting his hand in the till. Oh, Alec, I am sorry if this upsets you. . . ."

"What upsets me is that my wife takes these high-handed actions without my knowing about them until it is too late. And that she has put herself in danger as well as our unborn child."

"I meant only to help." She could feel the trembling of her lower lip and bit on it hastily. "Everything you say is true, I know. But when I see things that you do not . . . that you are not able to do. . . ."

Her voice went drifting away, but he was aware of what she had caught herself from saying. "You must think me a poor fellow, dear wife, unable to conduct my own business affairs. Well, perhaps you are right."

She could hear the bitter note, and she grasped his hand in an impulsive gesture of apology. "Not at all. You cannot be every place at the same time. Nor has your health been of the best."

That, too, had been tactless; he turned from her and went to the chessboard. He played with the little ivory pieces in a preoccupied manner, seemingly busy with his thoughts.

She waited for him to speak. The silence was a long one, and finally he said, "And what do you suggest I do about the store now, dear wife?"

"I do have a plan. If you approve, that is," she added hastily. "It would be foolish to just abandon it. The location is fine. There are bigger stores in the city—Houghton and Dutton's, Shepard-Norwell, R. H. White's. But ladies like to shop, too, in smaller places where the customer is treated more—more personally, I think you would say."

She was leaning forward, her face grown lively and her eyes sparkling with enthusiasm. "If we stocked a special kind of lace, a finer type of linen than the other stores have, trimmings and feathers more fashionable than those to be found anywhere else, we would prosper. I know that we could."

She squeezed his hand tightly. "It would need a certain type of person to run it as it should be. Somebody honest— that goes without saying—and with a good head for business.

And imagination, Alec, for that is most important. And smart enough to remember the customers' names, for that is flattering."

His mouth moved in a faint smile. "But there is only one of you, my dear wife. Of course you are describing yourself. A pity! You cannot turn yourself into a shopkeeper; you are needed here and soon your condition will become evident."

"Not me! Oh, Alec, I should so enjoy it, but as you say, my duty lies here. But walking home this afternoon, I did think about the problem. And what I have is a fine idea!"

"I shudder to think what it might be." The wry note was still in his voice. "You had best tell me gently, for I am not sure I can stand up under another of your ideas."

She burst out, "Ruth!"

His forehead wrinkled, he repeated the name. Then he asked slowly, "Our Ruth? Our servant girl? Surely you cannot mean what I think you are saying. Dealing with the public when she cannot, evidently, spend five minutes with the other two women without irritating them. And a woman to manage a store?"

"But that is just it," Megeen said eagerly. "She wants things just so and it bothers her that the work is not done right. Oh, Alec, she is very smart! She reads and writes very well, and if she had something to do other than tiresome household chores, I'm sure she'd be very good at it."

"But a woman! We should be the laughingstock of the city!"

"Then perhaps people would come out of curiosity."

Something about the set of her jaw and the steady shine of her eyes seemed to tell him that she did not intend to relinquish her purpose without long, wearying quarrels.

And so on the following morning, Ruth Tilton put on her good black serge dress with its stiffly starched white collar and cuffs, her well-brushed coat, and her Sunday hat, and went forth to Vickery's store with her head full of plans and ideas.

Megeen, assailed by curiosity though she was, waited for an entire week before she visited the shop. Then, her presence having been announced by a healthy ringing of the repaired bell over the door, she stood stunned into silence as she looked around.

She could not figure out how Ruth had accomplished so much in so short a time. Every glass display case had been washed and polished. The bolts of cloth were neatly piled on their shelves. The walls had been painted a soft leaf green. Somewhere Ruth had found a pair of Windsor chairs and needlepoint cushions for their seats so that ladies could sit and rest while deciding on their purchases. There had already been a satisfactory number of customers, Ruth said with a touch of pride.

Alec had to admit finally that no one could have done a better job than Ruth, no one more conscientious about her work and certainly no one more honest.

Every week she carried the receipts to the bank, keeping out only enough for her own modest salary. Profits were very small at first because she was gradually getting rid of the old stock and replacing it with newer, more fashionable merchandise.

The store was not yet able to support an entire family. Megeen tried valiantly to cut down expenses, but when one hole in family spending was plugged up, another seemed to appear.

At the end of a month Ruth moved out of her room and went to live in the North End. She had a tiny flat where she could come and go, disturbing no one if she worked late at night, cooking her meals on her own time. Too, she was able to walk to and from work and thus saved the expense of the horsecar fares.

"It will give you a little more room, ma'am," she said to Megeen. "And that is needful. Do not fret about my leaving. I shall be seeing you once a week at least, when I come to make reports to the mister. While I shall miss the young ones, we must take the sorrows along with the joys."

She had scarcely moved out when Megeen found herself with someone else who needed shelter under her roof.

Dark had come early that Sunday evening when the gloom of low clouds pushed its way into the shadowy rooms of the Vickery house. Despite the lighted lamps and the fires crackling in all the hearths, Megeen felt a strange sort of darkness in her soul. She was not unhappy for any definite reason. A premonition that she could not shake brought with it malaise. Something seemed to be hanging over her, like a threatening, darkening cloud.

She feared that she might, as Marm had said, have the "gift," might be aware of things before they happened. She tried to shake off the feeling, but when, at ten o'clock, she was preparing for bed, she heard the clatter of horses' hooves on the cobblestones outside. With the whirring of the front-door buzzer, she knew that she had not been mistaken. Disaster was upon this house, although she did not know what form it would take.

She tightened her wrapper around her swollen waist. In the corridor she met Alec, who was muttering about being disturbed. But a few minutes later he was the one who gave the orders in a shocked voice that quickly turned into a furiously angry one.

He led the way into the drawing room and gestured for Martin Mulcahy to lower Annie Flynn onto the sofa. Megeen, too stunned to speak or move when she saw what Martin was carrying, lost her vision in a flood of boiling tears.

Every inch of Annie's body that could be seen was red and raw. Wounds were still bleeding. The bodice of her dress had been torn away, and from her neck to her bared breasts loose hunks of flesh had been ripped away from the bones.

Her face, the lovely features that had made her the prettiest girl in all of Kerry, was battered almost beyond recognition. One of her eyeballs had been pushed back into its socket. Clumps of hair had been pulled from her scalp. She moaned like an animal mortally wounded, seeming conscious of nothing and no one around her, only the pain that was turning her into a whimpering, mindless thing.

There was fierceness in Megeen's voice when she finally managed to ask, "Who did this? Him?"

"O'Flynn, yes. With the whip and his fists. He locked the door so that I could not get to them. He beat her as long as he was able to stand."

In Martin Mulcahy's eyes there was deep anguish. For a moment Megeen saw in her mind the picture of a pair of fists pounding on a locked door, heard the pleas that were drowned out by a woman's agonized cries.

"I am part to blame. I should have sent her home. She came only for a growler. A can of beer, that is. But he happened in and he saw her chatting with me at the bar. The names—I cannot repeat what he said. He dragged her home by her hair and that is why—"

Megeen raised her hand to silence him. Then she dropped it hastily. He must talk, she knew. He must say it all or else it would flourish inside him like a poisonous plant that would infect all his feelings and emotions.

In spite of her own incredulous horror, the numbness that held her in its nightmarish grip, she could feel concern and pity for this man, whose own gentle nature must shrink from even the thought of violence and evil.

Tessie, standing on the threshold, began to whimper. Megeen whirled on her. "Do not stop there like a witless fool!" In her agitation Megeen was slipping back into the old ways of speaking. She had no thought now for the brogue she had tried so hard to eliminate from her speech. "Bring me a basin of hot water right away. Then ye'll run for the doctor at once. Haste, girl!"

She drew a long breath, and staring straight ahead, she uttered the lie that she was going to force them to accept and so draw them into the conspiracy of falsity she was already planning.

"She was set upon by a dog." She said the words in a clear, ringing voice. "She was attacked by a mad beast."

True in part at least, and to be sure no great sin, that deliberate lie. There was no one to contradict her. "And if so much as a word to the contrary you are saying outside this house, ye'll find yerself out upon the streets," she said fiercely to Tessie when the girl returned with clean washcloths and a basin full of hot water.

She kept repeating the statement until it would have been easy enough for her to believe it. She said it loudly when Lenard came into the room and peered curiously over her shoulder. Turning, she had only a glimpse of his face, saw the color drain from it, and thought for a moment that he would collapse where he stood or vomit all over the poor creature on the sofa.

Most loudly and firmly of all she said it for the benefit of the doctor, whose distant, professional manner was suddenly shattered with the first glimpse of the beaten woman. He had treated members of the family for colds; he had delivered Matthew; Megeen visited him because there was some newfangled program called "prenatal care" that Alec insisted that she try; he had treated Tessie when she had scalded a hand. He was a member of an old Boston family and Megeen recognized a common trait shared by the Irish-Americans and people like him. They did not hang out their dirty wash for everyone to see.

He would, of course, speak no word of what had brought him to 17 Nightingale Park. When he ordered Annie to be brought to a hospital and came up against her sister's unshakable refusal to permit such a course of action, he did not argue. He stitched the worst of the wounds and forced through the swollen lips medicine to relieve the pain. He became a daily visitor for two weeks.

Annie had been carried up to Megeen's bedroom, there was none other for her to occupy, for Megeen did not want her in the small cell that had been Ruth's room.

Alec, who had controlled well his distaste of the whole situation, moved his wife's things into his own bedroom, which they were to share until the baby was born.

Sometimes in the new intimacy of Alec's room he would give her pleasure with his hands, careful always of the mound of her belly. It was not as pleasing as when he could lie atop her and put himself in her, but it relieved them both and she was warm and comfortable when, their passion spent, they lay with their naked bodies pressed together and sometimes fell asleep that way.

Joseph Brendan Vickery came into the world easily and with only a minimum of pain for his mother. Quiet as he had been in her womb, he was a good, gentle baby when he emerged from it.

But there was to be, for Megeen, an edge of sadness in her memories of his birth. And it was to last for a long time. For Carina Lyman, her friend—in fact, her only friend in Nightingale Park—died on the night that Joseph Vickery was born.

Chapter Twenty-four

Alec told Megeen that she was not to grieve. "For she lived a long life and a good one. She was a great belle, you know. And she made what is known as a good marriage. Her husband was rich and, as far as anyone knows, faithful."

"But she died without the sacraments." There was a mourning note in her voice, and although he started to say something, he thought better of it and shrugged.

He changed the subject to one that would not lead to one

of her dissertations on the Church and its dogmas. He spoke about Ruth Tilton, who was still spending her Sundays in the Vickery house. Now, he said, she was the best advertisement for the shop, for she had changed her drab, servant's clothing for stylish garments and was an imposing figure.

She made her weekly visit for the purpose of making her report to Alec, but Megeen suspected that that was but part of it. With no other friends in the city, she undoubtedly had pangs of loneliness. There was something else, too, and she told Megeen and Alec about it at teatime one Sunday.

"That Henry Broderick!" Her eyes seemed to be saying more than her voice. "Much as I dislike alarming you, I think it's best that you know I have seen him several times since he was discharged. Once across the street from the store. Another time he was standing on the sidewalk near the door. When I passed him, he mumbled something about 'the children.' I could smell the liquor on him, and I found it frightening. Well, I do not mean to scare you, Mrs. Vickery, but I fear he means business—bad business."

Now Alec was trying to reassure Megeen, to chase from her mind any fears she might have for the safety of the children. "I do not want you worried, especially since you may not have recovered yet from having Joseph."

She found herself trying to put his apprehensions at rest instead of the other way around. "We are all seeing bogeymen, my dear. There was a night just this past week when I looked from the front window and thought I saw someone standing by the fence in the park and staring up here."

When he whirled and began to stride from the room, she laughed. "Oh, Alec, of course there is no one out there now! It was dark. No doubt I was seeing a shadow. If you are putting stock in Ruth's stories, you are worrying without need. Henry Broderick would not come all this distance just to stand outside and look at the house!"

"Nor Tom O'Flynn?"

A cold prickling sped up her spine when he spoke the name. They had not talked of Annie at any great length since the night of her beating. Her wounds had healed slowly and there were scars that might remain on her face for the rest of her life.

That she seemed to care nothing for her appearance was, to Megeen, the saddest part of it all. Annie sat for hours with her hands in her lap looking across the park where another spring was showing its new awakening in a lacy tracing of leaf buds on the old trees. She did not leave her room at all except to go to the water closet across the hall. Her hair remained uncombed for days. She washed sketchily; her meals were served to her in her room.

Annie seemed to have nothing to do at all with the servants, but she managed to lay her hands on a bottle of liquor every time she felt the necessity to drink herself into oblivion.

The burden of worry grew even heavier for Megeen. Although Alec tried to keep the news from her, she learned that there was trouble at the mill. The men had walked off their jobs in a demand for higher pay and fewer working hours.

There was less money with which to run the household, even though its numbers had increased. Annie needed help, although Megeen did not know how to give it to her. Matthew, far from being jealous of the new baby as she had feared, ignored him completely. Only Ellen could control the willful, harsh-tempered little boy. When she was not there, he went on long rampages of tantrums, destroying what he could find to rip up, tear, and shatter.

And all through this, Alec seemed to be concerned only with her recovery from childbirth and the fact that she had not regained all her strength.

"If it would make you feel better, love, we can hire a watchman. I could see to it that Hanley was around all day, and if we have someone at night . . ."

She said firmly, "We cannot afford it."

When she blurted out things like that, she was immediately repentant, for Alec's face seemed to lengthen with embarrassment. "We will manage," she added hastily. "It just seems that you carry a heavy burden for one man."

"But when your inheritance comes through, we shall undoubtedly have no more worries."

He was making an effort to speak lightly, to make a joke of the subject as he had been doing ever since Carina Lyman's death. For a week after the old lady died a sober-faced lawyer dressed in dark, subdued clothing had called upon Megeen and announced that Mrs. Lyman had left her young friend a legacy. He was duty-bound to discover if there were any of her relatives still alive to make a claim on her property. If he found distant kinfolk who would feel impelled to contest the will, Megeen might find herself involved in a long, expensive lawsuit.

"She probably left me some small trinket," Megeen guessed. "Or a piece of fur no doubt long out of fashion. No matter. I am happy that she thought enough of me to remember me."

Mr. Thurston, the lawyer, said that a complete inventory must be made and the value of each piece of furnishing, down to the last piece of bric-a-brac, listed.

So there was nothing to get excited about, Megeen told Alec. It had been merely a kindly act by the woman she had come to love and admire.

Most of all, Alec worried and fretted about her health. "For with Ruth gone, many of the tasks are falling upon you. Isn't it possible for you to hire another woman at least part of the time?"

Never once did he point out that there was an ablebodied woman drinking and dreaming her life away in the comfortable room that had been Megeen's. On the rare occasions that he and Annie met face to face, he was unfailingly polite, although he must have abhorred the thing she had become.

"Now I will not have you treating me as though I were at death's door," Megeen admonished him. "By the time summer comes I shall be as strong as I have ever been. Stronger, in fact. Yes, you are right in one respect. I must not try to do too much in the months to come, for my days will be even busier come autumn."

He lifted his eyebrows in a suspicious manner.

"I meant to tell you, Alec dear, but I did not know how you would take it. What has happened is that I have been elected president of the Catholic Women's Club. . . ."

He said shortly, "I have never heard of it."

"I know. We started out as the Martha Guild, the name given out of respect for Martha Laverty, who started it along with me. But Martha had twins just after Christmas and she's lost interest some."

"So they picked you! They chose my wife to head a club of Catholic women, which is plain enough by the name." He added sourly, "To gossip and drink tea, I suppose. To show off new hats and boast about their husbands and children."

"Oh, no, Alec! We have grown too big for that. Do you know that at the last meeting there were three hundred women! The ballroom of the American House, where we have decided to meet, was scarcely large enough for all of us.

"As for gossiping and such, it is not that at all. What we

are doing is drawing up plans for getting Coleman Sheehy—Martha's brother, that is—elected as alderman. And using our numbers to make improvements in the city—and even the state."

His face had grown colder. "By shutting down mills and factories because you disapprove of the age of the people working in them."

"Little children only, Alec. Yes, we will do that. And I have another idea in mind."

He muttered, "I am sure you do."

She went on as though she had not heard him. "I have found that visiting the doctor before Joseph was born helped me greatly. I am sure that was why it was easier this time. Now why should there not be something like that for all women expecting babies? Even if they are not able to pay a doctor's fee?

"Prenatal care is what it's called, and though I did not take to the idea at first, now I am convinced it is of great benefit. The poor women, who cannot pay for this, should be given it free. Then they would, I'm sure, be giving birth to healthier children and help themselves as well."

He looked at her as though he was convinced that she had lost her senses. He shook his head in wonder and changed the subject.

He did not mention it again or speak of Carina Lyman until Mr. Thurston paid Megeen another visit.

This time he brought with him the news that shocked them all. Instead of his client having left to Megeen some small, valueless token, her entire estate—exclusive of generous bequests to servants in her employ then and in the past—had been left to Megeen Ahearn Vickery, her "dear friend" and next-door neighbor.

Chapter Twenty-five

"Now if we were to have the workmen cut through the wall at this point, it would be like having one big house instead of two."

Megeen's hands reached up and outlined the shape of a door on the wall that separated No. 17 Nightingale Park from No. 19.

"And perhaps we can sell one of the dear woman's paintings, so, dear sir, this will mean no added expense to you."

Alec stared at her with disbelief in his eyes. "There is not the slightest need for that. She didn't leave as much money as I'd have expected; no doubt the fortune shrank during the years of the war. But sixty thousand dollars is a fair enough sum. Don't you realize that it would not be necessary for you to raise money on anything? You can pay for having the wall cut through many times over."

"I do not think of the money as belonging to me," she said calmly. "It is for the children, mostly. For I spent many an hour talking to dear Mrs. Lyman and telling her about Ellen and Matthew. She was lonely, you see, and if it hadn't been for my stories about the little ones, perhaps she wouldn't have enjoyed my visits so much."

"And why should our children need a sum of money of that amount?"

"For their education, to be sure. Matthew, of course, will go to Harvard and take over your businesses when he has graduated. Ellie, I think, will make a brilliant match, for she is bonny and sweet-tempered. As for Joseph . . ."

When she or anyone else spoke of her younger son, it was in the same sort of soft, pleased voice. For Joseph, from the day of his birth, was a charmer. Long before the age when babies were supposed to smile, he was smiling. To please his visitors he would grasp at a finger offered to him and cling to it as long as anyone wished to play the game.

146

He was a handsome child, with his hair as soft as black velvet, his Irish-blue eyes, and his rosebud mouth. Joseph, Megeen declared, was going to be a great statesman. She did not hear Alec when he muttered, "Another Irish politician is all we need in this city!"

It was autumn before Megeen could engage workmen to begin the making of the two houses into one. That summer there were so many activities and so much building in progress that laborers were busy with other work.

Grandstands had to be built for the parade that took place on the Fourth of July. All the storefront windows were polished to their highest sheen for the holiday. Streets were cleaned, the Common's paths were swept, the grass cut and raked.

Independence Day was a swelteringly hot day with the temperature reaching to the mid-90s. But Megeen, who had brought her family out to celebrate, scarcely noticed the heat. She was too awed by an inventor who inflated his airship with an audience of seventy-five thousand Bostonians and those who had come in from the outlying districts. She did not even mind the waiting until six o'clock that evening when the "Buffalo," Professor King's balloon, took flight and sailed up over Beacon Hill.

After dark, she and Alec and the servant girls watched a display of fireworks. She had much to write about in her next letter to her mother.

Alec was not enthusiastic about her plans for breaking down the wall and throwing the two houses together. It would mean more work for her and the housemaids. There would be two kitchens to keep clean, double sets of stairs for them to climb, and at first at least, more confusion.

Too, they would have to keep the children out of certain rooms of the Lyman house. He pointed out to her the William Morris wallpaper, the entire set (not a single piece chipped or missing) of the delft china, the French clocks, the Sheraton dining-room set. He said that the little ones must be trained to keep away from the precious heirlooms.

But finally it was settled. Lenard would keep his regular room. Annie was to remain in the one she was now occupying, which had been Megeen's. Tessie and Aggie might move into the rooms on the second floor of the Vickery house while

Megeen and her husband and children took quarters in the bedrooms of what had been the Lyman house.

At first she felt as though she were living on the other side of a mirror. Everything was opposite to the way it was in the house next door. She had to learn to turn to the left at the head of the staircase instead of to the right as she was used to doing. Her clothes hung in closets that did not seem to be in the right places. The upstairs corridors ran along in the same direction, but on the wrong side.

It never occurred to her to wonder what Alec's feelings were about being uprooted from the house where he had lived for years and to which he had brought his bride. With only token arguments, which were nothing more than lively discussions, he gave in to all Megeen's arrangements.

She had not given a thought, either, to the effect of the cutting through the wall might be on his health. For an entire week there seemed to be a cloud of snowlike substance hanging over both houses. No one could take a deep breath without inhaling the plaster residue into the lungs. The carpets became gritty and white footsteps were tracked upstairs and down. Megeen managed to keep the children closed in their own nursery. It was only their father who suffered.

He and Megeen no longer shared the same bedroom now that there was no crowding and lack of sleeping quarters. So it was a week before she realized how shallow his breathing was and how congested his lungs sounded.

When she realized these things, she went into his bedroom nagged by a sense of worry and guilt. It had been a long time since she and Alec had made love. He had refrained from making demands on her, she guessed, because he suspected that she was tired out from the new arrangements, or that she had too many things on her mind to give herself wholeheartedly to her marital duties, or that she feared another pregnancy so soon.

He must be waiting for her to make the first move.

She had scarcely reached the bed when he was overtaken by a wracking spasm of coughing. She went to him and held his body upright, and she could feel, even covered as they were by his nightshirt, the sharp bones of his shoulder blades. In the light of the gas lamp beside the bed, his pallor was frightening. He looked, in that moment, like an old man. His hair had been shaken loose by his coughing and it had grown grayer and thinner than it had been when she had seen him for the first time.

She slid into the bed beside him, and when he had lowered himself down carefully on the heaped-up pillows, she took his hand and placed it against her throat. Then she untied the ribbons that ran through the bodice of her nightgown and squirmed about until her breasts were bare.

He pulled away from her. "No, Megeen," he said in a thin, breaking voice, "I cannot tonight. Nor can I even try. Forgive me!"

"There is nothing to forgive, my dear love."

She covered her nakedness, and so that he would not feel too humiliated, she said, "It was not for this I came. When I saw you looking so poorly this evening, I thought perhaps to comfort you."

Her breath was ragged, for there was a strange and urgent feeling that warmed the place where he had entered her on other more joyous nights. She clung to her self-control tightly lest her rising passion make itself evident in a tremor of her voice or a rush of heat to her face. She squeezed her legs together in an effort to discipline that part of her body that longed for the caress of a man's hand.

This she must do, for Alec, having taught her to share his urgings, was now denying her the pleasure of his manhood. She had not realized how much joy and excitement he had given her. Now must she live without those satisfactions.

"Why did you come then, my wife?"

She seized eagerly on a subject that had been in her mind for weeks. "As soon as we are completely settled, and that should be soon now, do you think we might invite some of the neighbors in for . . . well, maybe just for tea? For some of them still have their tea each afternoon as they do in England. So Tessie tells me. Friends of dear Mrs. Lyman, they would be. And this, after all, was her home."

In the meager light of the lamp she could see his eyes, and they were soft with pity. "I know how much you wish this, Megeen, but Carina had no friends after my parents died."

He did not add that if there had been anyone who cared enough for the old lady to come and look at the place where she had spent her last years, he or she would be horrified at what had been done to it. Babies in the bedrooms, which had been painted bright colors. Many of the precious art objects packed away in the attic because Megeen had decided that they made too much work for the housemaids. Dust covers removed from the drawing-room furniture so that delicate fabrics were left exposed to the sunlight.

She did not argue. She was still shaken by the intensity of her feelings. Only the faintest sigh escaped from her lips, which had suddenly become dry. The heat of men's desire, she was sure, must cool when they reached Alec's age.

It was a cruel trick of nature that she was only just reaching her place as a wife and woman when Alec's lustiest period was passing. She could not expect much more time when their relations would be wildly joyous. Soon she would be living in a sort of sterile limbo until her husband should die.

Until her husband should die . . .

It was the first time the thought had come to her mind in definite outlines. And it struck her with all the force of a physical blow.

If Alec should die . . .

She was stunned by the evil that must have been lurking inside her, unsuspected. Try as she might to tell herself that she did not want her husband dead, the image of him lying in his coffin must have been there. And could not the picture of his son, which came quickly and then disappeared, been conjured up by wishful yearnings?

God forgive me! she cried silently. Oh, dear saints, one and all, pray for me!

Day after day she walked to the cathedral and knelt and murmured the words that were always close to her lips now. She asked for penance; she prayed that no punishment would befall her through her children. Or Alec.

But that form of punishment came.

It was during the first blustery days of December that Alec fell ill. He had been in bed for almost a week before he would allow Megeen to summon a doctor. His fever was high and he was in no condition to argue; and then, his wife was certain, he was unaware of the man who came to his bedside and examined him gravely.

The diagnosis was double pneumonia, and it struck terror into Megeen's heart. His first spells of delirium stunned her with fear. Days and nights ran in together, but she refused to leave his bedside.

Time and time again she sent Hanley out to find the iceman, who had to be tracked down as he drove his cart up and down the streets. Large chunks of ice were packed around Alec's body when she could do nothing more for him and his labored breathing filled the room where he lay.

A basin of water with chunks of ice in it was always within arm's reach. For endless hours she sat there, soaking towels in the cold water and sponging him with them until her hands felt frostbitten. She was dazed from lack of sleep, but she refused to let anyone else nurse him, not the professional nurse the doctor suggested, or Tessie, or Aggie, or Annie, who, surprisingly, came out of her isolation to offer to take her turn at the side of her brother-in-law. Who was dying. Who had always been kind to her. Who had given her shelter and asked nothing from her in return.

Megeen insisted that she had to do it all herself. Only by keeping alive this man whose death she had thought about—if only for the briefest of moments—was she able to atone for her sin.

No outsiders except Martin Mulcahy came to inquire about Alec's condition. A basket of fruit came with Dorothea Lovering's card attached to it. But that, Megeen was sure, was a gesture for Lenard's attention, for the two had evidently broken off their romance and perhaps she was hoping for a reconciliation.

Mr. Mulcahy, so unobtrusive that Megeen did not notice when he was in the house, kept Annie company for hours at a time. He helped care for the children, ran errands for the servants, came into the sickroom to try to persuade Megeen to take short periods of rest.

It was during one of those brief respites that, coming into her own bedroom, she found Lenard there.

Chapter Twenty-six

He had been standing at the bedroom window, looking out at the dismal, late-autumn dusk with its obliterating shadows and the trees that were becoming swallowed up in them.

There was little light in the room, but she recognized in an instant the fine, tall figure.

"What are you doing here?"

He whirled to face her and she saw in his eyes a strange expression. She had never known him to wear uncertainty like an unfamiliar mask over his features. He was in his shirt-sleeves and his hair was tumbled, as though he had run his fingers through it many times.

He did not answer her and she was forced to ask the question again. "Why are you here? What do you want?"

"Because my father is ill, of course. He is my father, after all. I suppose I belong near him at a time like this."

"He is not going to die," she said fiercely, "if that is what you are thinking. What brings you here in my bedroom?"

"Perhaps because I can do nothing for him and it occurred to me that I might join you in saying prayers for him."

He mocked himself with his smile. "You know, make a bargain with God. If my father is allowed to live, I will be a good boy."

"Lenard, that is blasphemy. I will have no part in it." But, her conscience told her, it is no different from what you are thinking and doing. So that none of that would show on her face she said testily, "Please, I am tired. I cannot talk to you now. If you really feel that way about your father, then you should be with him."

She stood aside to make clear a path to the door, but he remained where he was and for some reason the uncertainty was gone and the arrogance had returned. His smile had a cat-and-mouse quality. His voice was soft and persuasive; and she almost was able to believe in what he was saying.

"That saloon keeper is in his room now. I dislike him intensely. And the only other place where I feel close to my father is here. For this is where he comes, isn't it, for some of his happiest times?"

She could not look at him. She felt suddenly faint and grasped at the back of a chair. The weakness seemed to be spreading throughout her body and there was a churning of nausea in her stomach. She had lost track of her monthly periods since Alec had fallen ill, but she knew that there was a possibility that she might be pregnant again. There had been a night several weeks ago when she had coaxed Alec and tantalized him, using her hands and her lips to send him into uncontrollable frenzy, and she might be carrying the seed of that union now.

Her face was flaming as she remembered, but she could not avoid looking into Lenard's face because he had put his hand firmly around her chin and he was forcing it upward.

"How delightfully you do that! Blushing, I mean. But you must answer me, dear stepmother. Here in the dark hours of the night—"

She interrupted him savagely. "That is not true! He never comes here!"

She wished that she might have bitten off her tongue before she spoke the words. For she was giving to Lenard the opportunity he wanted to embarrass her and render her tongue-tied.

"Then you go to him. What a lovely picture! The wife sneaking down a dark hall, crawling into a bed she had not been invited to share. How times have changed!" he mourned with a mock sigh. "I fear that the women who try to take over the duties of men might win out at last."

"It isn't like that at all!"

He moved his hand and placed it around her throat, and it seemed to be burning into her flesh.

"Then tell me, darling Megeen, what is it like? I should like to be able to imagine you and my beloved father sweating and groaning and climbing upon each other. Have you ever amused yourself, sweetheart, by picturing unlikely couples in the act of copulation? It's drollest when the woman is a snobbish bitch or the man looks as though he has nothing at all in his pantaloons."

"You are horrible!" The words choked her and she feared that she could not keep the nausea down now, and how humiliating it would be if she were to spill it all over his highly polished boots! She pulled away from him. "Lenard, please go! I cannot endure another moment of your lunatic talk. I am tired, so very tired!"

She reached out her hand for the chair back again, but Lenard grasped it and pulled her up against him. "Then let us lie down together on the bed. It's such a waste if my father does not use it. Someone should."

She twisted her head to one side so that she would not have to look into his face. There were wild clamorings in the vulnerable parts of her body, and there were throbbing pulses everywhere. She dropped her eyes and put both hands on his chest and pushed him away.

"You are doing it again, my lovely Megeen," and he chuckled. "You are staring with longing at what may be called forbidden fruit. Don't think I haven't noticed that whenever we meet you can't take your eyes off my body."

"Oh, my God!"

It was only a whisper, but he heard it. And this time he laughed aloud. "Forget the prayers! They are scant comfort on a cold night, I should think. There are better things to do. Here! You shall have the treat that you have been wanting."

He took her hand and pressed her fingers against his groin. She cried out as though she had been burned and he laughed even louder. "Perhaps you would like it better if there was nothing covering it. Come," he said in a harder voice, "you know you're craving it. Don't pretend with me. The bed looks comfortable. You won't refuse to let me put it to good use even though my father is too old or stupid to take advantage of it—and you."

His arm slid around her waist and he tried to pull her toward the bed. She moaned softly, "Lenard, no! Please let me go!"

"You need more coaxing? Come, I'll make you want it as you never have before. No hurry, my darling Megeen. We can play for a while. You'd like that, wouldn't you?"

He swung her about suddenly. She almost lost her balance, but his arms were around her in a strong circle. He bent and his mouth found her lips and then her tongue. She made no effort to pull away now. She was imprisoned not only by his arms but by her own urgent need. All the lonely nights she lay in yearning solitude that had built up inside her were erupting now.

Her mouth was against Lenard's, as demanding as his. Her hands, so controlled and useful until that moment, began to stroke and explore his body. Now she was the one who moved toward the bed, inching backward and drawing him with her.

And then she heard the scream from the nursery. Even from two rooms away, it struck her with such force that she could feel a physical pain. It came again while she was trying to push Lenard away. And then the crying began, noisy waves of it rising and falling as though a small heart were breaking with grief.

"Joseph!" she cried, terrified.

Joseph, who never opened his mouth except to gurgle happily or smile. He never cried except when he was in pain. Joseph, her good baby of whom Aggie was in the habit of saying "was scarce a bit of trouble at all, like a little angel was Joseph."

Now the little angel was wailing as though to bring the house down. Megeen pushed herself out of Lenard's arms and hit at them when he did not release her quickly enough.

"Leave me be! I must go to the baby!"

"Now? You want to stop now? To hell with the child. Somebody'll take care of him. You deserve your bit of fun, my dear Megeen."

My bit of fun. My "playing," as he called it, while my child is probably hurt or in pain. And my husband lies dying.

She could not look into Lenard's face. Her shame was almost paralyzing her, and there she was nothing she could see there that would waft it away.

She backed toward the door, and then, her skirts lifted in her hands, she turned and ran down the corridor as though a crowd of demons were at her heels.

Ellen was trying to comfort the baby when Megeen raced into the room. Joseph's face was wet and red, and the rocking of the cradle was not soothing him.

Matthew was crouched in a corner playing with a toy train, his two-year-old face wearing a look of innocence, and his eyes, when he smiled at his mother, so clear and sympathetic that she could easily have been deceived. But she was not. Young as he was, Matthew knew the tricks of pretense.

He lisped, "Poor baby crying, feels sad."

"What happened?" Megeen spoke to Ellen, who would not, at first, look up from the cradle. "Did Matthew hurt him in any way?"

The little girl nodded. It was agony, Megeen knew, for her to tattle on the child she adored. There were tears flooding her cheeks and eyes, as though she were the one who had already received the punishment she feared was coming to Matthew.

"What did he do, Ellen?"

The answer came out slowly, one choked word at a time. "He pinched the baby. But, oh, please, ma'am, he did not mean to be bad! It is just that—just that he is afraid that I love Joey more than I do him. I was singing to the baby to try to put him to sleep. You will not hurt Matthew—you will not—"

Her voice had risen to a scream. The look of her face was pure agony. She gasped when Megeen yanked the little boy to his feet and lifted the skirt of his dress. Crouching, Megeen tore his pants from his bottom and threw him over her knee.

All the anger she felt at herself for having come so close to committing the grievous sin of adultery, the disappointment of her body, which had been offered and then denied what it clamored for, overwhelmed her. Her arm rose and fell, rose and fell. The sound of her palm against the flesh was lost under his outraged shrieks.

In chorus with each shriek was Ellen's protesting scream. She kept her head turned steadfastly away, unable, it seemed, to bear the sight of Matthew's punishment. As the vigorous spanking slowed to a few more light taps, Ellen edged her way across the room with her hands outstretched, ready to comfort the sobbing boy.

"He must know that he cannot do such things." Megeen was breathless, too. She got to her feet with difficulty. "Suppose it had been something else. Suppose he had actually hurt Joseph!"

"But he would not!" Ellen said fiercely. "He did not know what he was doing. There, sweetheart, there! You must not cry anymore."

She stopped down and took him into her arms and pressed him against her. His little tearstained face loomed over her shoulder. When he glared up into his mother's eyes, his eyes contained no repentance, only defiance and something that chilled her to her bones.

It was hatred, naked and undisguised. She could not believe that a child that age would feel such violent emotion. Her son hated her—and that was a dreadful thing indeed. But no worse than the knowledge that was eating at her insides like some evil disease.

Shame was possessing her, for she knew that if there had not been a baby's cry within hearing, she might at this very minute be tossing and tumbling in her bed, condemning her soul to hell by the forbidden act with her stepson.

Chapter Twenty-seven

Alec's convalescence was slow. When he was able to leave his bed, he spent most of his hours in front of the fireplace with a book in his hand, his knees warmly covered by a quilt. No matter how lively the fire was, he was never quite warm enough.

It was a bitter winter, with vicious storms and blizzards every few days. Megeen was restless when she was confined to the house for long periods of time. Even Christmas brought little joy except to the children. The older people had no enthusiasm for the holiday, and on the Nativity Megeen could not even go to Mass, for snowdrifts barred the way down the front steps and temperatures remained well below zero all day long.

There was no one to do the shoveling, for Hanley had disappeared on one of his own "holidays" and Lenard, as soon as his father had passed the crisis, went off on an unspecified journey. It did no good to ask Alec where his son had gone. He merely shrugged, and shook his head.

"I know no more than you, dear wife."

She did not ask again. Speaking of Lenard made her self-conscious. It was all too easy to let her mind become flooded with pictures of that wild, rapturous few minutes when Lenard's lips and tongue and hands had aroused her to a pitch she had never reached before.

No task was too arduous for her during the following weeks. She sought out hard things to do. She welcomed every pain and ache during the early days of her pregnancy, offering them all up for the removal of sin from her soul.

She was patient when the servants grumbled. Now and then she went down to the kitchen at night and listened to their complaints, most of them having to do with the fact that they were imprisoned indoors by the weather.

"Though maybe there's one good side of it," Aggie admitted. "That wretched man who's been hangin' around across

157

the street and lookin' up at our windows all the time. Well, he's not been about lately. Easy enough to understand—the villain! He'd be as frozen as an icicle were he to stand there in this weather for more than a few minutes."

Megeen's head rose sharply. "Has he come back? Sometime ago, when he was last in view, Mr. Vickery spoke of hiring a guard. I have not thought of it since," she confessed. "I thought it was just someone loitering because he had nothing else to do."

"Scarcely that, ma'am. For when I chanced to be walkin' on that side of the street, he took himself away, quicklike, seemin' not to wish to have his face seen, for he pulled down his hat and turned his head."

How could she have forgotten that loiterer? Megeen asked herself in wonder. Was she so besotted with sinful thoughts that even her own children and their safety had been pushed out of her mind? Why hadn't she remembered Henry Broderick, who, when discharged from the Vickery store, had been sullen and vengeful?

Now she was carrying another child, keeping the fact from everyone as though it were a shameful secret. She had wanted to keep the knowledge from Alec lest he worry about her and, because of his age, find being a father again a heavy responsibility.

She told him on the night of the disturbing conversation with Aggie. "God had blessed us once more, dear sir. Surely there is room in our hearts for another little one! Perhaps then Matthew will not be . . . well, so hard to get along with. If he sees that Joseph gets but a small share of the attention."

"Matthew," Alec said firmly, "will not turn into a sweet, gentle child regardless of any reason. He is not going to share Ellen with anyone. However, if you are glad about this, then I must be, too. When you are saying those prayers you believe to be so effective, why not pray that the baby comes to us more like Joseph than his older brother?"

Lawrence Anthony Vickery was born on the first day of June and what his father had hoped for came to pass. It was somewhat of a miracle, Megeen thought, for if Joseph had been a quiet, happy baby, his new brother was even more so.

"Look, Alec," Megeen would say as they bent over the cradle, "how sober he is. He will not smile as easily as does

Joseph. He seems always to be deep in thought and you would wonder what goes on in that dear little head."

"Maybe he's thinking of how he will make his first million dollars. Or he may become a great scholar and is sharpening his brain with mathematical equations."

Megeen smiled at his joke, but there came into her mind for the first time—but far from the last—her dream for Lawrence. He would be a priest. For did not a mother who gave a son to God's service earn for herself in that way a place in heaven? She could almost see at this moment her tall young son at the altar, murmuring the familiar Latin phrases and, in his cassock and Roman collar, dropping in to visit his family and bringing special blessings by his presence.

It must be Lawrence whose vocation would save them all. Not Matthew. God forbid! His disposition was growing worse and heaven knew that there were enough cantankerous priests around as it was. Nor Joey, their smiling, good-natured boy whom they must share with the public. And these three were the only children she would have, for the doctor had told her that she would never conceive again. It was a saddening fact, but God knew best. Perhaps He was giving her only as many as she could care for properly.

No mother was ever more conscientious about caring for her children. In spite of her club work, which took many hours of her time, the children always took precedence over any other duty. She never thought of her life as anything other than the kind led by thousands of other women and she was unable to understand why two articles appeared about her in the newspapers only a few months of each other.

The journalist from *The Boston Globe* might have been a guest she was entertaining in her drawing room. He was soft-spoken and made it seem as though their conversation was merely pleasant chatting. She was appalled when the article appeared. Her hopes for the improvement in education for city children were made to sound like plans. She emerged as a reformer, strong-minded and bent on forcing the cessation of child labor, and the neglect of those whose brains had not developed or were hopelessly insane.

She had espoused the latter cause when, passing the work-house one afternoon, she had felt impelled to discover what the inside of it was like. There had been a time when the workhouse had monopolized all her thoughts. It would not hurt, she decided, to see what God had spared her from.

When she came out, she was pale and shaken. Not only were small children in various stages of retardation kept in the building but grown people as well, all of them locked in little rooms on the top floor.

The second article in the *Globe* described her as a "dedicated wife and mother who finds time to give long hours of service to the people of her adopted country."

She hated reading about herself, especially since Alec's name was mentioned only in passing. But the stories accomplished one thing that lifted her spirits. The barriers against her, raised by her neighbors and those who had been her husband's friends, seemed to be about to crumble.

A young lady who looked vaguely familiar to Megeen was passing her on the sidewalk near the park and stopped and asked hesitantly, "Aren't you Mrs. Vickery?"

She had a long, rather pale face and the military-style suit she wore, the latest in fashions that season, did not become her. She looked as though she had lost weight since its purchase and her shoulders drooped unattractively.

"Why, yes." Megeen had no smile to go with the words. The young lady was too deep in her own unhappiness, it seemed, to respond in kind. "I am sorry. I'm afraid I don't remember. . . ."

"Dorothea Lovering. I was Lenard's . . . well, we were close friends at one time."

"Now I do remember!"

Megeen put her hand out impulsively and touched those in their soft leather gloves. "I should have known you!"

"No reason why you should."

Miss Lovering's eyes were not on the woman she was talking to but upon the Vickery house a few hundred yards away. She said with a faint stutter, "It was some time ago. That I saw Lenard."

Her gaze came back to Megeen, who did not have a single word to offer for comfort. She did not know where Lenard was. She had never heard him speak lovingly of this young woman and so she had nothing cheering to repeat.

Miss Lovering freed her hand and her spine stiffened. "It is not of Lenard I wish to speak. We—my mother and I—have read the newspaper articles about you. I may say that I admire your purposefulness—yours and the ladies' of your club.

"We have little groups, too, formed for the purpose of high thoughts and good deeds. Small clubs, that is. We do try to bring about improvements in the lives of women and children." Her voice took on a bitter note. "It seems that I shall never marry. If spinsterhood is to be my lot in life, I shall devote myself to helping others. I told my mother that no matter who . . ." She faltered, apologized and went on. "Any woman with a conscience must agree with what you are doing. We cannot ignore what is all around us. So, Mrs. Vickery, I should like you to speak at our Wednesday Afternoon Guild, which will be meeting at our house this week. Perhaps you will tell us about your progress and plans."

So that was how it was to come about. Megeen was mute for perhaps half a minute. Her brain whirled. And she who was always so quick with words could not think of the right thing to say.

That Miss Lovering's purpose was not entirely innocent was more a certainty than surmise in Megeen's mind. For the young woman could not keep her glance from roaming toward the Vickery house. What she hoped for, obviously some means of re-forming the tie with Lenard, was all too evident in her yearning gaze.

"And it matters not a bit to me," Megeen told Alec when she was recounting to him the meeting with Miss Lovering and its result. "For now, at least, I shall accomplish something. I'll have a chance to know the wives, and no doubt some of their daughters, of some of your friends. A small group is best in a case like this, do you not think? It will make everything more cozy, is what I mean."

He did not answer and she said hastily, "But it is not merely to establish friendships that I hope for. I am sure that if we meet on common grounds and agree on certain things, we may be able to accomplish much."

"Like shutting down the mills and factories owned by their husbands and fathers?" he asked dryly.

She scarcely heard him. She was too busy with her thoughts.

"I must prepare a fine speech, one that will make them sit up and take notice. And I must make an impressive appearance. Oh, Alec, what do you think I should wear?"

Chapter Twenty-eight

Alec said that Bostonian women did not put a great store on appearance, that it was considered vulgar to dress in too smart a fashion.

The entire family was drawn into the discussion of her clothing for this important occasion, Aggie, Tessie, and even Ruth when she made her regular Sunday-afternoon visit. Annie emerged from her room long enough to riffle through Megeen's closet and shrug. If Annie could pick out a costume for her sister, she would have decked her out in bright satins or velvets, a hat that would have made the good ladies gasp, and an eye-dazzling array of jewelry.

In the end Megeen made her own selections. A dove-gray tailleur trimmed with black braid, a lacy jabot cascading between its lapels, a boat-shaped hat with a cargo of delicately colored flowers.

She began to bathe and dress early in the afternoon, although the meeting would not open until three o'clock. The house was quiet and calm, because everyone in it seemed to sense Megeen's nervousness and determined that there would be nothing to upset or annoy her.

Joseph and Lawrence were in the nursery under the watchful eyes of both Tessie and Annie. Ellen had taken Matthew out for a walk around noontime, and although she did not usually keep him out for very long, they were gone from the house for quite some time.

Megeen could imagine how it had been. Matthew, although he was more than three years old, still loved to be pushed through the streets in his rattan baby buggy with the sunshade above his head. He would whine until Ellen gave in and took him out. He had probably screamed and kicked when she turned the buggy around in the direction of home. And so she had given in to him, as she always did, forgetting time limits in her eagerness to please him.

He was not an appealing child and Megeen's conscience

bothered her because she did not love him as much as she did her other two boys. And she was guilty of the feeling of relief because the responsibility of keeping him happy was Ellen's.

At two o'clock came the first thrust of fright. The two had not had luncheon before they set out, and that in itself should have brought them home long ago. Ellen, even after three years of being fed nourishing and plentiful food, acted as though it might be snatched away from her at any minute. And Matthew was a greedy little boy, ill-tempered when his meals were late for any reason.

"I will have to send Hanley out to look for them," Megeen told Alec, who was watching in silence while she lay out the garments she would wear. "They have never been out as long as this."

He said things that were supposed to reassure her. "They'll be along at any minute. Ellen is a sensible child, and dependable. In lots of ways she's older than her nine years."

"Then why are they still out?" She paced the length of the room, and then, with a fearful look at the clock on the fireplace mantel, she said, "Unless something's happened to them and they can't get back."

"Megeen, what are you thinking?" He put his hand around her arm as she passed him. "Don't get any crazy ideas. In a little more than thirty minutes you're going to have to face those women at the Loverings'. You'll want to be calm."

She twisted her elbow to free it from Alec's grip. "Do you think I care about that now? Do you suppose I could walk into that house and forget that my children are missing?"

She was beginning to slip back to the brogue that was scarcely more than a lilt in her voice. "Call it foolish if you will, Alec. But it was not so long ago that we saw that figure hanging about across the street. 'Twas that villain Henry Broderick. It could be he kidnapped my two. Or it might be that Ellen did have a relative—an unknown father or uncle—who has come to claim her or wants money to let us keep her."

"And waited all this time to make himself known?" He shook his head as though realizing the hopelessness of logical arguments. "Now finish your dressing, my love, so that you'll be ready to leave the minute the children are home."

Then he said with a pitying glance at the face stiff with pain and fear, "If you like I will walk across the street with you. There is no reason why you should not deliver your speech. It shouldn't take long and when it's over the children will undoubtedly be here and you will wonder why you spent so much time worrying about them."

Since she could not find any other outlet for her nervousness and had to keep moving, she changed into her gray tailleur and pinned upon her hair the hat with its garden of flowers. She kept running to the window to pull aside the drapery and look out. There was nothing to see except the park, with its empty benches, and beyond that, carriages pulling up in front of the Lovering house.

She had glanced at the clock a dozen times and now she gave it another pleading look as though it could halt its tiny golden hands and push time back to where there was no worry about two missing children.

"It's already three o'clock," Alec said in a voice that was almost as quiet as the ticking.

"You think I do not know that?" She whirled upon him with a hot and angry glare. Then, almost immediately, she was sorry. She ran to him and threw her arms around him. "Forgive me, Alec! It is wrong of me to take out on you what I am feeling. But what shall we do? Send Hanley for the police?"

He took her hand in both of his and kissed it. "Not Hanley. I shall go myself."

"Oh, no, there is a raw wind today. You might become chilled. Stay here and I shall go downstairs."

And then, hearing sounds that seemed to come from a long way off, she got to her feet slowly. At first she thought they were only in her imagination, something she wanted so badly to hear that her mind was playing tricks on her.

But that was surely Matthew's voice. She could not have failed to recognize his protesting whine. She ran to the head of the stairs and from there could make out Ellen's soothing tones.

Hot with anger, the carefully selected clothing already feeling too warm, Megeen raced down to where the little girl held tightly to Matthew's hand. When he saw his mother rushing toward him, he slid behind Ellen and peeked out from behind her skirts.

But it was not her son at whom Megeen's rage was directed. It was not his fault that he had been kept out on the streets for three hours and caused her to miss an opportunity that might have meant a great deal to all of them.

"Where have you been, you wretched girl?"

"Oh, Mother, I am so sorry!" Tears were beginning to roll in large, swift drops down the delicate little face. "I know it was wrong to stay out so long, but we went to the Common." She gulped as though something was sticking in her throat. "And there were children playing there and Matthew wanted to watch them. They were playing games, hide-and-seek and catch-me-quick. And they had hoops and Matthew wanted to try to roll one. A little boy let him try his, but he couldn't do it—Matthew, I mean. That's why we were so long."

Yes, Megeen thought, seeing the picture very clearly. Matthew, with his flinty stubbornness, would have insisted upon persevering until he had mastered the trick of hoop-rolling. Ellen, who could deny him nothing that was within her power to give him, had been torn in two directions, poor child. She had made the choice: letting him have his own way although she must have known that she was causing their parents unnecessary worry.

"You know the wrong you have done," Megeen said severely. "I shall have to punish you."

Matthew began to howl, but was quickly silenced when his father scooped him up and gave him into the care of Annie, who had followed them down the stairs.

"I don't want you to ever do a thing like that again," Megeen said in a cracking voice. "You are not to be wandering around the city, either alone or with Matthew. There are all sorts of dangers. You are nine years old now. There are men, bad men. . . ."

"But I would not let them speak to me," Ellen interrupted. "Aunt Annie has told me not to. She says you should not speak to people you don't know, for they may be strangers."

Megeen and Alec exchanged glances, hers with a what-am-I-to-do expression and his with concealed laughter that seemed about to escape at any minute.

"Your mother will deal with you later. Run along now and have your lunch." He turned to Megeen. "Come along, I will see you across the street."

When she looked at him blankly, as though she did not understand a word he had said, he took her arm and turned her around in the direction of the door.

"It's no more than ten past the hour. A few minutes' tardiness cannot matter. Perhaps they will be expecting that. Society, so they say, arrives late."

"But, Alec, I cannot." Her voice was little more than a

whisper. "I am sure they will look upon it as rudeness. They will dislike me at first sight. I do not know any of them, or they me, except Miss Lovering."

Panic was causing her voice to shake, but he held her arm tightly, led her out the door, down the steps, and across the street to where two dozen women waited to hear what a former kitchen maid had to say to them.

Chapter Twenty-nine

Actually there were twenty-seven women present. Dorothea Lovering, a smile of relief lightening her face, told that to Megeen as they walked to the first-floor powder room. The opportunity to give a last critical look at herself in the mirror and tuck back a few wisps of vagrant hair was much appreciated by Megeen, and she found that the fluttering in her stomach was somewhat eased.

Dorothea looked quite pretty. Bustles were going out of style and she had a slender, graceful figure that lent itself better to straight, flowing lines and simple trimmings.

Today she wore a delft-blue afternoon gown, its loose panels moving gently as she walked. Its bodice was cut modestly, revealing her long throat, and the sleeves were full and caught with bands of velvet at her wrists. Her hair was arranged in a shining Psyche knot at the back of her head; she seemed to be aware that she was looking her best, for she had more poise and self-confidence than Megeen had yet seen her display.

"I am much encouraged," she told Megeen as they moved along the wide hall in the direction of the drawing room. "This is the largest gathering we have had so far. Perhaps it's the nice weather that has brought them all out."

No, Megeen thought, it is not the weather this time. It is curiosity. They had come to look and listen to a girl not quite twenty-two years old, a greenhorn who had come into their midst as a servant girl and married one of their own number.

They would regard her as an interloper or one of the freaks in Mr. Barnum's circus.

They were all there in the drawing room, all twenty-seven of them, their heads turned in her direction as she and Dorothy came through the archway leading from the hall.

She knew Dorothea's mother by sight, but every other face was that of a stranger.

What was she to say to these women, who broke off their conversations at the sight of her? They sat very straight and silent on the gilt chairs that had been arranged to form a semicircle around a cleared space at the farther end of the big room.

All the carefully prepared words she had rehearsed were gone as completely as though she had never thought of them. She was aware of Dorothea's holding up her hand unnecessarily for silence and what she was saying. The introduction was brief, not long enough for Megeen to regain her composure. When Dorothea stepped aside, Megeen stood awkwardly, mute. The applause was sparse. Only a few pairs of gloved hands slapped against each other.

She knew that she must say something. It was ridiculous to be standing there, staring into space. So she said the first thing that came into her mind. She apologized for having been fifteen minutes late in arriving.

"I am sorry that I kept you waiting. But something came up which seemed, at the time, to be a great crisis but which—thank God!—turned out to be nothing of great importance."

She told them of her worry over her missing children. And she could see that she had captured their interest. Some of them leaned forward in their chairs. One or two nodded agreement when she pointed out the dangers that the city held for small children. Among them, undoubtedly, were mothers who could sympathize with her fear and panic when the children did not come home when they were expected; and those who were grandmothers remembered their own apprehensions.

"I felt that my daughter must be warned not to speak to anyone who might approach her, perhaps offer her candy. Her reply, I must say, was not what I expected."

She repeated the phrase that had made it difficult for Alec to maintain his sternness. She heard the little wave of laughter that spread through her audience. It was well-bred laughter, but something more than politeness. Some of the older women seemed to have trouble with their mouths and teeth, as though they had not laughed for a long time. One old lady in the first row of chairs evidently had trouble hearing, and Dorothea, who was sitting beside her, repeated slowly and loudly what Megeen had said.

"The little girl told her that she shouldn't speak to people she didn't know because they might be strangers."

There was a fresh outburst of tittering, but that was the last time that afternoon that they found anything amusing in Megeen's speech. She went on talking about Ellen, recounting the circumstances under which she had found the little girl. And how long it had been before the child stopped cowering and shivering at the sound of a knock on the front door or the ringing of its bell.

"Because, you see, she was terrified that someone had come to take her back to that old life."

She had their complete attention. Mothers and grandmothers and perhaps a few unmarried ladies—all were gazing at her intently. It was no longer difficult to speak to them. In spite of the unmistakable Yankee look about them (a certain way of holding their proud, long faces, their high-bridged noses, their pale eyes, and their finely made clothing somewhat out-of-date), she saw them only as women.

"Ellen was only one of a great many," she said with a note of sadness in her voice. "There were others her age, boys and girls both. I have no figures, but it would stand to reason that these children do not have a very long life span."

A hand was raised. "And what can people like us do about it, Mrs. Vickery?"

"There must be new laws. We—I am speaking about my own club—have helped to elect a certain alderman. His name is Coleman Sheehy."

When she heard a faint rustling of whispering, she smiled and shook her head. "We like him no better than any other candidate for office. But he has promised to work diligently for new laws. If he does not keep his campaign promises, then he will find a great many indignant women making his life miserable."

She anticipated the next remark and said, "Not having the vote ourselves, our only hope is to influence our husbands to elect candidates who will correct these evils."

The second part of her speech was not so well-received. It

became plain that the women who had been so attentive before were not interested in learning what she called "the deplorable conditions" in the workhouse.

They seemed uneasy when she spoke of her visit there and how appalled she had been when she learned that poor mindless creatures were isolated and, in a few cases, chained to walls. The faces of the women became closed, and Megeen guessed that they were already aware of what she was describing. Their lack of sympathy might be caused, of course, by the fact that such treatment of the insane was common knowledge.

No doubt there was insanity in some of their own families, and even all the money they possessed could not cure what they accepted as incurable.

Megeen tried to tell them of an article published in one of Alec's magazines. It was concerned with a new treatment for the deranged that was being used with some success in Germany.

She lost them completely then. They began to glance at the watches on their chests and move slightly in the manner of people who are bored but try politely to conceal their boredom.

But it had been, on the whole, a fairly successful afternoon. She knew that she had made an impression on them, and while tea was being served by two uniformed maids, a little group gathered around Megeen and expressed their interest in her efforts to raise the age limit of children who worked in the mills and factories.

"My husband has already forbidden children younger than ten years old to be employed in his mill. I am sure there will be others who will do the same without being forced by law to do so."

When she returned home that afternoon, she recounted every conversation to Alec. "Oh, Alec, there were two or three who said they'd like to hear more about the mills. And they invited me to come to tea at their houses," she said triumphantly. "Imagine that! It was what I hoped for all this long time!"

He asked, "Were they definite invitations? Did they say on what date they wanted you to come?"

"Well, no," she admitted reluctantly. "But I'm sure the invitations will not be long in coming. Do you think they will arrive by mail or delivered by servants?"

They did not come at all. Everything she had worked for and hoped for seemed to have been swept away only a few days later when a dead body was discovered in the gutter outside the house at 17 Nightingale Park.

Chapter Thirty

It was a manservant from a house a few doors down the street who found the corpse. Megeen was to hear that dreadful word several times during the next twenty-four hours. It was spoken by a policeman. The undertaker used it. The man-of-all-work who had made the gruesome discovery took his cue from them as he described, for the other servants in the neighborhood, his shocking discovery.

"There I was, sweeping off the walk, and what I seen was him—the corpse—lying in the gutter. Well, I thought, it was naught but some old derelict what had wandered too far from a saloon and gone unconscious. But when I went to see, meaning to make him take himself off, I seen the blood all over him. And his face—oh, my Gawd!"

He had to shudder away from his memory that destroyed face. As did all the others who saw it that morning. So badly battered was it that there was not a single feature left intact. The broken jaw hung open. The nose was unrecognizable as such. The mouth had been torn apart. Blood had seeped into the wide-open eyes and turned them into rust-colored objects that resembled a child's marbles.

Megeen first heard the shrilling of a police whistle and then the clattering of horses' hooves on the cobblestones. She went to the window and looked down at the closed wagon with the letters POLICE painted on it; and she saw the little knot of people gathered around it, mostly servants, although there were a few who looked like householders.

It was early in the morning and she was still in her dressing gown. There was not time, she decided, for careful grooming. She put on clothing, only that she might be decently covered. When she went along the hall, she stopped at

Alec's room, put her head through the door, and said, "There is something going on outside. Pray don't get up, for I fear that it is something unfortunate. An accident, perhaps."

Tessie, as was to be expected, was already coming up from the kitchen. Megeen repeated what she had said to Alec and added, "You are to make sure that the children do not leave the house while whatever it is goes on."

Tessie grew sulky and perhaps would remain so all day. But Megeen paid her little heed. She went up the areaway steps and saw that there were more people gathered in front of the house now. She did not look to see any she recognized, but edged her way to the gutter, where the manservant, still clinging to his broom, was telling his story to a policeman.

The police officer looked beyond him to Megeen and then motioned to the others to make a path for her. He seemed to believe that she, too, was a servant and he used the same tone of voice he had used while speaking to the man-of-all-work. It was not exactly gruff but much less than civil.

"Ye from the house there?" His long arm rose and fell. "This anyone belongin' to you?"

She had her first look then at the dead body. It was a brief one. She turned away quickly at the sight of bloodstained clothing and the face that was not a face at all but like something seen in a butcher shop.

"No, no!" Her voice rose and cracked. "May God rest his soul in heaven! No, he would not be one of us."

Then she lifted herself to her full height and said sternly, "Whoever he may be, must he be left there like a dog who has died and cannot tell who his master is? And has none of you thought to call a priest; even though he may have died some time ago, he may still be given last rites."

The policeman shoved back his helmet and scratched his head. He looked confused and puzzled, and she felt a little sorry for him. She was looking and acting like a little Irish shrew, and yet he must suspect that she was much more than that. And could not figure out how to treat her.

He was pulling his helmet back into place when Megeen felt herself jostled from behind. She turned to see the face of her sister, bleached as white as snow, hair tumbling about her shoulders, her tongue licking her dry lips as though she were in agony for the want of her cure-all—the friendly, obliterating bottle.

"No, Annie, do not look at it!"

Megeen tried to grasp the thin, shapeless arm, but Annie pushed her away. For a long, silent moment she stood staring down at the destruction of what had once been a human being. Then, when the policeman touched her shoulder, she said in a hollow voice, "You need ask no more about him. He is my husband—was, that is."

And then she collapsed in Megeen's arms, her head hanging over her sister's shoulder, and she wept so loudly that the sound seemed to fill the street.

Annie O'Flynn, whose left eye had never seemed to match her other one since the day her husband had almost poked it out with his fist, who still wore the scar of that beating on her cheek, cried as though her heart would break.

But perhaps, Megeen thought as she hugged and patted and murmured, Annie was not crying for the man himself but for the days and nights of their youth when they had not been able to get enough of each other's bodies. And for the new areas of lovemaking. And for the dreams of a future with handsome sons and sweet, lovely daughters around them.

Gone now were dreams of any sort. There was only this mangled, dead thing and what consolation Annie could find in her precious cure-all.

Thomas Patrick O'Flynn was waked in the drawing room of the Vickery house. Annie had mumbled, "But he was nothing to you, Alec, so why should you want him here?"

"He was my wife's brother-in-law," he said quietly. "And so, I think, part of my family. There is nothing you can do for him, Annie, except give him a decent burial. If it is a question of money . . ."

She said that it was not. There had been an insurance policy that she had paid for at five cents a week to a man who had come to collect these past few years. She would be able to pay for a modest casket, the requiem Mass, and the grave.

Megeen did not think that many people would come to the wake, but there were even fewer than she expected. Tom's friends would have been those he drank with in a favorite saloon, but none of them came. Martin Mulcahy was there on both nights, and because the big room was empty for long periods of time, Megeen often found herself in conversation with him.

He told her that he had sold his interest in the saloon he

had owned. "It seemed a sinful way to make a living, feeding on men's weakness."

"But what will you do now?"

He did not know, he said, but he would be looking around for some other type of business to invest in. "I've no need to worry about money for a while."

The professional keeners came. Three old women, dressed in rusty black and with forced tears in their eyes, knelt down beside the casket and lifted their voices in shrill, piercing cries.

Gasping and sobbing, they began to enumerate the virtues of the man they had never seen, and although they called him by name, they were describing someone who had never existed.

Alec went to them and silenced them. "I don't think you are doing anything to comfort the bereaved. Please leave us alone."

One of the three got to her feet with difficulty. "Ye will let the lad go to the gates of heaven without a voice raised in sorrow?" she demanded in outrage.

Then she looked uncertainly at the casket, with its lid closed because the undertaker had not been able to perform miracles upon the battered face.

She asked, "It is a lad, isn't it?"

Megeen went to her husband's side and whispered into his ear. He took out some money from an inside pocket and handed a bank note to each of them. They did not bother to thank him, but moved away quickly, chattering like huge, black birds on the hunt for new prey.

Aggie had argued for the clay pipes and bowls of tobacco that were always to be found at an Irish wake. But she admitted finally that they would have been a shameful waste.

"For there were none that would have noticed the lack. And what the parents of himself would have said to all this I cannot think. Here in their own house—the crucifix above the box and the candles and all! And you, ma'am, sayin' the rosary each night even though there's but Hanley and Tessie and me to make the responses!"

It was Megeen who persuaded Father Corrigan, after some harsh words, to allow Tom O'Flynn to be buried with a requiem Mass and to be laid to rest in hallowed ground.

Facing him in the drab little room of the rectory, she asked, "How can you know that he did not receive the sacraments within the past year? And that he did not say an act of contrition when he was dying?"

"I am sure that he did not. For was he not sodden in drink when he met his death?"

Priest or not, he angered her by his uncharitable words. "Jesus Christ did not come to earth to save saints but sinners. He loved and forgave!"

The ruddy face took on even more color. He would not be swayed by argument or persistence, she knew. She opened her reticule, pretended to search for a handkerchief, and allowed a few bank notes to fall to the floor. She retrieved them casually and put them on a nearby table. She said in an offhand manner, "There is no chance then that you will say the Mass? You must obey your conscience, Father, I understand that. So we will say no more on the subject."

Then, as though a sudden thought had occurred to her, she said, "Martha Laverty, who is one of your parishioners, told me you had trouble heating the church last winter, for the collections for coal were not large enough to pay the bills. And that you're wanting a stained-glass window for behind the altar, never having been able to afford one."

He opened his mouth and then closed it after a hurried glance at the bills she had left on the table. He gulped and said, "Since we know so little about the death of this man, perhaps we can assume that he died in the state of grace. We can set the Mass for ten o'clock tomorrow, and if a hack is provided for me, I will say the prayers at the grave."

It was a very small cortege, merely two closed hacks—in addition to the one for the priest—that jolted their way to Calvary Cemetery. Megeen and Alec rode in the first one with Annie and Martin Mulcahy. The servants and Ruth Tilton were in the one behind them.

Annie's face was hidden behind the long, thick veil Mrs. Callahan had insisted that she wear. Annie would be criticized, said the cook, if she did not show this sign of respect.

Megeen could not think of anyone who would criticize except Aggie Callahan herself. She seemed determined to make of Tom O'Flynn's last rituals an occasion of respectability and propriety. She prepared breakfast for them all after the funeral and it was then that they speculated, for the first time, on what or who had caused the beating that had led to his death.

"Handy with his fists, no doubt. Got into a barroom brawl,

got walloped real bad, and come to where his wife was livin' and fell into the gutter before he got to the house."

Mrs. Callahan seemed quite pleased with her theory and it was a less frightening one than Megeen's, which was that Tom had been watching the house—as he might have done in the past—hoping to waylay his wife. And then he had been set upon by a thug bent on robbing him, put up a fight, and been mercilessly beaten.

She did not reveal those thoughts to anyone else. Now that she knew Annie was safe from the threat of more violence from her husband, she tried to coax her sister out of her isolation, to live in pride and usefulness again.

Martin Mulcahy seemed to be bent on the same goal. After Tom's funeral he fell into the habit of calling on Annie two or three evenings a week. Sometimes they would sit in the morning room quietly, talking only now and then. When the weather was fine, Martin would insist upon taking her for a long walk, over the bridge to the Public Garden, up Tremont Street so that she could look in the shopwindows, once or twice to the Boston Theater when there was something light and humorous playing there. On Sundays he would come in his carriage and take her for a drive.

Now she was wearing her hair in an arrangement that hid most of the scar on her cheek. She began to wear spectacles so that the mismatching of her eyes was not noticeable. She was still a fine-looking woman, tall and straight and graceful. And Megeen found herself weaving little dreams in which Annie became a wife once more and perhaps a mother.

One night she broached the subject of Martin Mulcahy to her sister. "He's a fine man, darling, and he'd make you a good husband. The year is nearly up and none could criticize you for marrying in, say, another few weeks."

Annie threw back her head and her voice rang out in a rich peal of laughter. When she caught her breath, she cried, "Meggie, you ninny! Can't you see what is right there before your eyes? I'm not the one Marty wants—it's you! The poor man has been in love with you since the first day he laid eyes on you!"

Chapter Thirty-one

On her thirtieth birthday, Megeen looked long and intently into her mirror. She was not in the habit of studying her reflection. She had never been vain, feeling that she had little to be vain about. This lingering in front of her looking glass was for assessment purposes.

Thirty had seemed a long way off when, at eighteen, she had arrived in Boston, a green girl with little except determination and pride to sustain her. And the saints to protect her.

There were few traces of that girl now. Her hair had not faded; it was still rusty red. Her eyes were a calmer blue and her face had taken on an expression of self-assurance. Her clothing made most of the difference. She had learned what colors became her best, what fashions she should not wear, regardless of their popularity among other women.

Because she was small and slender, she looked younger than her years, not old enough surely to be the mother of a boy of twelve, a great, husky boy, bigger than most boys his age. Ellen, of course, did not count, for she had come to them at six, but Megeen often lost sight of that fact and had to stop and think for a moment before she remembered that Ellie was not her natural child, and at any rate she could not have given birth at twelve.

She was proud of Ellen, who was in her last year of convent school. She was not much taller than Matthew, and she was graceful while he was lumbering, soft-spoken while he bellowed and roared, just as when he had been a baby and denied something he wanted.

Ellen was an extremely pretty girl with her loops of pale-gold hair swept about her ears, her deeply blue eyes, and small, even features.

"She should have a beau." Megeen sometimes fretted when there was only Alec to hear her. "At eighteen she should have the boys flocking around her."

She was thinking of a certain type of man as a suitor for their daughter, the kind of young man she sometimes caught glimpses of when there were parties or Sunday-afternoon teas in the houses around the park. Young men with the faint, unconscious arrogance of those whose social background is impeccable, wealth taken for granted, good manners instinctive.

"When the daughters of the friends you had, Alec, reach Ellen's age, they are introduced to society with balls and such formal affairs. Coming out is what they are called, isn't it?"

"But impossible for our Ellie."

It was one of the few times that Alec had denied her anything. She did not understand it. The double houses would have been ideal for Ellen's coming-out party. The older people would be in the rooms on one side, the young ones could have the whole of the other for dancing and flirting and conversing in cozy corners.

It was not a question of money. For the Vickery fortunes were on the rise. The little store that Ruth Tilton managed had now a sales force of three, the other two a pair of girls she had hired after their graduation from convent school and trained them in her own way. Two years ago Alec had purchased for her the shop next door to his; now it was twice as large as the original one and the customers were more comfortable while being served.

Ruth had even gone to Europe to purchase certain articles not to be found in any other Boston store, an unheard-of adventure for a woman even of Ruth's years.

"How lucky we are to have Ruth!"

Megeen repeated that sincerely meant sentence often, usually after Ruth had brought the records of her bank deposits and beautifully kept ledgers for his inspection.

Alec seldom went to his office these days. At fifty-two he was already old. His hair had faded to a uniform gray, his movements were slow and his energy seemed to have drained away. Nor did he make the long journey to the Vickery mill more than once every several months.

Megeen's embarrassment over Annie's statement about where Martin Mulcahy's affections lay had died very quickly. She did not believe, and never had, that Martin desired anything more than her friendship, lonely man that he was after he had sold his saloon.

There was trouble at the mill shortly after Megeen reached thirty. It was a dreary day, and the clouds threatened to drop their burden of rain at any minute. Martin and Annie were playing a listless game of cards in the morning room. Megeen knew that these small amusements were Martin's method of keeping Annie's mind off the bottle. And she was deeply grateful.

The man who came with the message for Alec was loud-voiced. He demanded to see "the boss, though a poor one he is," and became quarrelsome when Megeen refused to rouse Alec from his nap when she was not able to judge just how important the man's message was.

"I'll tell him that and no one else, ma'am, so I advise you to awaken him. If you do not, the trouble will worsen."

Martin and Annie, attracted to the hall by the loud voice, stood silently for a moment or two, and then Marty said, "You will not quarrel with the lady, my lad. I am much surprised that you have not been thrown out on your ear." He turned to Megeen, his face stern. "Hanley is not about?"

She shook her head and his face split in a grin. "Then it shall be my pleasure. I'll be only too glad to show you what we did with ugly customers when I was the owner of a saloon."

"No!" Megeen shook her head. "Let him remain. I must know what it is he came to say. Sir?"

He muttered that the workers had walked off their jobs and were threatening to destroy the mill.

"For what reason?" Martin asked the question, and when there was no answer, he cried impatiently, "Well, come on then! What are the complaints?"

"Two men have been turned off their jobs. For there is a new machine that rolls paper flat without a human hand touching it. So it will be with all of us. Soon the machines will be doing all the work and where will we be then?"

He sniffled through one nostril, and without looking directly at anyone, he said, "It's not like it was when you was there them years ago, ma'am. Now they're threatening to burn the mill down. The super talks of calling in the police, and if that is done, well, we will all suffer."

Megeen turned to Annie and said, "Will you run to my room and fetch my coat? We cannot disturb Alec and I shall have to go to the mill."

Martin and Annie and the messenger were in accord in

one respect. None wanted her to take the long journey to find herself in a troublesome situation. She listened to no one.

When she had put on her heaviest coat, a shawl about her head, and knit mittens, Martin stepped to her side.

"You do not plan to——"

"But indeed I do. Annie will watch the little ones, so you need have no fear there."

It was true that Annie was good with the children. When she was thus occupied or busy with mending, cleaning her bedroom, or doing small chores around the house, she did not give a thought to the destroyer in the bottle. And when she knew that Martin would call, she took some pains with her appearance.

Many times Megeen had blessed him silently and now he was insisting upon accompanying her to the mill; and although they said little on the long drive, she felt safe with him and unafraid of what they would find at the end of the journey.

What they found were crowds around the main building, larger crowds than those she had forced her way through on that other occasion. One of the men held a lighted torch over his head. Others carried weapons, heavy sticks and large stones. One was brandishing a big, old-fashioned pistol.

"Wait here!"

Martin pulled up his horse when the crowd surged toward the carriage and there was no way for it to proceed farther. He jumped down from the seat and shouted to make his voice heard over the mutterings and the angry roars.

Megeen did not hear what he said to them. She sat huddled in the corner of the carriage, her arms about herself as though she could, that way, melt the iciness of fear that was beginning to chill her. Martin came back finally and helped her down from the carriage. A path was made for them as they walked to the entrance of the building, and she saw that inside were only empty spaces and idle machines.

Mr. Swanburn, older and grayer and more work-worn, came out of his cubbyhole and invited them into it. But it was to Martin that he spoke, quoting attendance records and salaries, giving him messages to take back to the owner of the mill.

He did not speak to Megeen at all, except to say condescendingly, "It is not the sort of thing that should concern a woman. Mr. Mulcahy here has enough information to carry back to your husband and there is no reason why you should bother your head about any of this."

She had to bite her lips to keep from crying out. Women were not all delicate, doll-like creatures. They did not need to be shielded from the unpleasantnesses of life. She wished that she might point out that Ruth Tilton was making a success of a business through her good sense, astuteness, and hard work.

Things were changing, did he not see that? The women of Boston were making their influence felt in the governing of the city. The lot of small children and the unfortunate witless ones was showing great improvement.

"Thick Irish!"

She did not let him hear the words. And later she would have been willing to take them back, for all that he and Martin discussed that afternoon—much of which she did not understand—was for the benefit of the workers and designed to make their lives less slavelike and easier.

She heard it all again that evening when he repeated to Alec what had been said and promised to the millworkers. She heard about pay raises and shorter hours and the fears of men who could imagine the fate of the working man when the hated machines robbed them of their jobs.

"I would say," Alec sighed, "that you know more about running the mill than I do, Martin."

"Business is business, whether a saloon or factory. I have been looking around for something that will interest me since I sold the place."

Before he went home that evening, Martin Mulcahy became a sort of manager of the Vickery Paper Company. "A sort" it was because Mr. Swanburn was to be kept on as supervisor. What Martin was to be, as far as Megeen could make out, was Alec's lieutenant, the guiding force from whom the workers and the management were to take their orders and voice their dissatisfactions.

The arrangement was successful. Martin earned the salary he protested about taking and was forced to do so by Alec.

There were changes, all for the better. There were the girls, for instance. Annie, in a teasing mood, called them *his* girls, those strong, rosy-cheeked young women whom he recruited from Haverhill and Pittsfield and even as far away as Maine. In addition to putting them to work, he found living quarters for them, guarded their spiritual and physical welfare, and said good-bye reluctantly when they left to be married. As they all did.

They were a new breed, these daughters of respectable small-town people. No women of their class had held jobs before. They worked long enough to fill their dower chests with blankets and sheets and petticoats and nightgowns and bath towels. They did embroidery during the lunch period that Martin had instituted.

All over New England girls of marriageable age were beginning to leave their homes and earn their dowries. In Lynn, Lowell, in Holyoke and Taunton, they were replacing the children whose age would soon make them unemployable. Many were attracted to the Vickery mill because of the higher wages and the modern toilet facilities—and Martin Mulcahy's strict rules of behavior between them and the workmen, who had to learn to keep their hands away from tempting buttocks and breasts.

Megeen was well aware of the difference Martin made in all their lives. And she wished fervently that he and Annie would see each other in a different light.

Chapter Thirty-two

Annie! Would she ever get over her astonishment about Annie?

After years of keeping herself locked away in her bedroom, coming out only occasionally and reluctant to leave the house, she had, early one morning, dressed without being urged to do so, brushed her hair into something resembling its former beauty, and gone out.

She refused to say where she was going, and Megeen spent a long morning wondering where her sister had gone and worrying about her.

When she returned at lunchtime, Megeen's visions of sleazy bars and men bent on seduction disappeared. For Annie's face was lighted by the sort of brightness that made her look very much pleased with herself.

"I have found me a job. I am to be a daily."

Megeen could not grasp it at first. She stared mutely at her sister, who now appeared to be overcome by a fit of giggling.

"That's what I am called—a daily. For I would not take a live-in position, wishing rather to still make this my home." She ignored Megeen's attempts to speak. "Now you know I have a knack for housework. I can cook and clean and I could sew and mend better than any girl in school back home. The nuns themselves admitted that. I do not," she said, growing sober, "wish to be a burden to Alec any longer. I need not take money from him now."

"But you have not been. And if you felt that you must work, there were other jobs he might have found for you. At the store, for instance, or perhaps in an office like his own."

Annie shook her head. "There are little ones in the family. With none of my own, the next best thing is helping to take care of someone else's."

It was with some anxiety that Megeen broke to Alec the news that Annie would be working for a rich family on Beacon Hill.

"Lillecutt, their name is. Perhaps you know them. She will be coming home each night. But, oh, dear sir, how will you feel to have your sister-in-law a daily maid?"

He looked back at her calmly. "Is that worse than having a wife who was a domestic?"

She had asked him to step into her bedroom to listen to what she had to tell him about Annie. It was a lovely, elegant room. Shortly after taking possession of Mrs. Lyman's house, Megeen had had it done over. The walls had been painted a pale yellow. The tester bed had a new canopy, stiff, yellow-sprigged material with wide flounces. The carpet was grass-green and as soft as a well-kept lawn. There were some of Mrs. Lyman's objets d'art on the fireplace mantel. And because there were no holy pictures or religious statues anywhere, she had gone out and, feeling slightly guilty, bought an expensive print of Botticelli's *Madonna and Child* and hung it in a prominent place.

"I think we must let her do this without argument, Alec. It is the first time she has done anything for herself. I hope it does not upset you." She placed an affectionate hand on his arm. "Because it was you who have kept her alive, my dear, and I shall never forget that—never!"

He looked a little uncomfortable. And she knew that they

were thinking of the same thing: that little scene when she had come across Alec in the dining room and he had been watering the whiskey that was kept in an unlocked cabinet. He had looked embarrassed then. He had muttered something about not wanting Annie to go into the streets to find a saloon or a store where she could exchange what little bit of money she possessed for a bottle of cheap liquor.

"On the other hand," he had said, "she could destroy herself with full-strength whiskey, and that would be a tragedy."

Megeen wondered if Alec had, at any time, been able to glimpse the darkness in Annie's soul. Sometimes she felt it, too, that dense shadow of loneliness in spite of all she had to do and all the people around her.

Megeen could not explain this. Not to Alec or even to herself. Perhaps, she thought, this was part of the punishment of being sent out of Paradise. Perhaps this was universal, that all human creatures felt this yearning for something they could not give a name to.

At night it was worse for Megeen and, she suspected, for Annie as well. A bed occupied by only one person was a lonely place indeed.

How much torment did Annie suffer, she wondered, now that she was denied the pleasures she had known with Tom O'Flynn during the early months of their marriage? A man carrying upon him the agony of want could find easily enough the means to relieve it. He need only go forth from his house and cover a few short blocks and the hapless dowds would be there, bartering their bodies for a sum of money.

There were, too, Annie had told her, houses which looked respectable enough but in which a man could have a woman for a sum of money.

But what was someone like Annie to do? Megeen was sure that nothing like that was between her sister and Martin. And now Annie was letting herself be coaxed into attending Mass on Sundays, sometimes in the company of the man. A few times he had driven her to confession on a Saturday night.

Megeen's sympathy for Annie took seed and grew from her own tormenting need. A word, a phrase, a snatch of music, Alec's hand upon her shoulder—any of those things could send a hot thrust between her legs, rob her of her breath, make her hands, her voice, her lips tremble with the longing to have a man inside her.

She could no longer slide into her husband's bed with an

easy mind and a body already warm with anticipation. For she would do nothing that would endanger his health.

Several months ago, during one of Alec's frequent illnesses, the doctor had warned her in oblique but understandable language of the danger of too much excitement or activity. The heart, he said, touching the front of his own coat, was tired. He was surprised that Alec had lived even this long. In order to keep him alive, she must keep him quiet.

She was so lost in thought that she started when Alec spoke to her now.

"You must be happy for Annie that she has found something to do that will make her happy. She needs more than we can give her, even the children. I wish that she might marry again, but this, it seems, is the next best thing."

But a poor second, Megeen said silently, pitying all the mateless women in the world. How sad that they were taught to enjoy the tantalizing, the being lifted up to a peak of pure bliss until the body was mindless, and then have it all snatched away.

She became aware that Alec was regarding her intently and color flamed in her cheeks. Could he have been reading her thoughts? He moved closer to her and put an arm around her waist.

"Come, dearest Megeen, I should like to take you to bed."

She could only stare at him mutely. She gulped down a lump in her throat, but still the words would not come.

"Must I demand my marital rights in harsher terms?"

She thought that he must be joking, that this was only a bit of Alec's wry humor, which came to the surface now and then.

She choked finally and said weakly, "Surely you are only funning. Alec, it is the middle of the afternoon."

"There are laws prohibiting a man from enjoying his wife's favors just because the sun is shining? Come, my dearest wife"—and his hand went to her throat, his touch as light as a butterfly's wing—"no one will disturb us, for I shall lock the door."

Still in a daze, she heard the click of the latch. Then Alec was at her side again and began to stroke her once more, his hand moving from her neck to the mounds of her breasts.

The flame inside her leaped up until her entire body seemed to be on fire. But she held herself stiffly, her fists clasped behind her in an effort at self-control.

He asked softly, "Are you worrying about what the doctor said?"

"He told you?" She could hear the thickness in her voice, as strange as though it belonged to someone else.

"To be sure he did. When you were out of the room. But it does not matter, my darling. I should prefer to die than to lose what you give me—more closeness than I have ever known with any other human being. I want you, Megeen my love. I need you."

He led her over to the bed. Perched on the edge of the mattress with his knees apart, he drew her in against him. Now she could feel the rising and hardening of his maleness. While he was unbuttoning her clothing, her hands were busy. She let them have their way, pulling his shirt out of his pantaloons, stroking the naked flesh of his back and chest.

He put his hands on her hips and moved her from side to side until she was ready to cry. Then with one last frenzied movement against her, he fell back onto the bed with her on top of him. He was forced to roll her off him while he undressed, but the wildness of desire was not lost and he thrust himself into her on the silken coverlet while the sunshine poured across them in golden bars.

She had been crying all through the spasms of the climax, "Make it last! Oh, my darling, I want it to go on forever!"

But she had not been any more able to slow that sweeping tide than he had been. When it was over and he had rolled off her, she lay trying to catch her breath.

She turned to him and snuggled into his arms. "Alec, are you sure you have not taken chances with your health?"

"Megeen!" She heard the note of distress in his voice. "What sort of man would I be if I worried about becoming ill because I enjoyed—a pale word, that!—the act of love with the wife I have sorely missed these past weeks?"

An act of love. It had been that indeed. She fell asleep in his arms, and when she awakened, the sunlight was gone and they lay in the soft and kindly light of dusk.

His hand was on her thigh and it moved slowly as she opened her eyes and looked into his, which were so close. Neither of them spoke but drowsily touched the parts of each other's body that had leaped into wild flames in the rapturous encounter of a few hours ago.

This time the touching was slower and gentler. The kisses weren't so frantic. An act of love: the phrase repeated itself in Megeen's brain as Alec's lips explored her breasts, her navel, her thighs. This time she could not have cried out for him to make it last longer, for she was lost in a euphoric daze, knowing that she could bring him inside her at any moment but postponing that moment because she did not want this wonderful feeling to be lost.

Finally the playing and the teasing ended abruptly and they grew frenzied at the same moment. But it was different this time. There were no whimpers or frantic thrashings. Alec seemed to hold himself in complete control, trying only to please her, making it in truth an act of love.

She dozed again and stayed there alone until dinnertime, stretching out on the bed like a luxury-loving kitten. The feeling of well-being sweetened her senses. And she thought of her sister with pity, for Annie would perhaps never know again the lovely surrender of her body to a man.

Poor Annie! How their fortunes had changed and how bitter was the contrast!

Annie had been the pretty one, the high-spirited, ever-smiling girl, and now she was to waste what was left of her youth and beauty as a servant in someone else's household. Megeen had expected that the good things in life would be showered upon her sister as a reward for charm, a bonny face, and a merry heart.

Now Annie was where Megeen had been when she had landed on American soil. And Megeen did not understand it.

Chapter Thirty-three

During those years while the children were growing up, Megeen saw little of Lenard. Sometimes she heard his voice, late at night, coming from his father's bedroom. Their arguments were conducted in low tones, out of consideration, she guessed, for the members of the household who were sleeping.

She could not hear very much of what was being said, but she suspected that Lenard returned home only when he needed money. Once she heard the subject mentioned. Her door and that of her husband were open and Lenard's words were clear enough.

"I suppose you'll be leaving everything to that scheming Irish bitch and her brood. God, it's downright indecent—you with a string of children at your age! All I ask is that you remember the night my mother died. She told you to see that I never wanted anything. And there was money—some of it hers. That was what she meant."

Megeen did not hear Alec's reply, for she moved away from the door and went to sit down on the edge of her bed. The bitter notes in Lenard's voice seemed to ring in her ears. Yet her tears were not because he hated her or because of the epithets he had used. She was crying because, in spite of how contemptuously he had spoken of her, she could not tear from her heart the longing to see him.

It was madness, but she had never forgotten him. She had loved him since she first looked upon his face, and she feared that she would love him until her eyes were closed in death.

This was one of the temptations Satan himself had put in her way. Praying did not help. She had told her sin to the priest in the confessional so many times that she knew what the response would be before the words were said.

"Your secret thoughts are seen by the Lord. They are stains on your soul. I can give you absolution only if you promise God that you will never think of this man in that light again."

She had promised. She had said her penance. She had gone about the church lighting candles in front of the statues. But the sinfulness of wanting her husband's son seeped back slowly.

One morning, after having quarreled with his father the night before, Lenard did not appear for breakfast. He had left as quietly as he had come, and it was weeks before he returned.

On that day he ate one meal in the house and it was a wretched affair. Annie was in the habit of eating dinner with them if she came home from work in time. Ruth Tilton joined them, too, as she sometimes did. Ellen and Matthew were there, for she was too old to eat in the nursery and Matthew would fly into a tantrum and upset them all if he were not allowed to come to the dinner table while she was there.

It was not a festive occasion, although Megeen had tried to make it so. She was always happiest when in the midst of her family; and having Lenard there should have added something special to the occasion, not only for her own sake but for Alec's. Seldom did he look across the table and see his eldest son there. Despite their quarrels they must be fond of each other, for above all they were father and son, bound together by memories and a shared love for a woman who was now dead.

It was too much, she supposed, to expect Lenard to be a congenial participant in that meal. By the time they had finished their first course, she would have preferred silence. For Lenard was at his most disagreeable, his tongue at its sharpest. His mood was a dark one indeed.

Megeen was used to what was called "black Irish doldrums." For all the men in her family had had their fits of low spirits. The spells did not last very long and were confusing to their womenfolk, who were never sure of when a temper might flame or a silence might last for weeks.

But when Lenard's dark mood lightened, his jovial air was laced with sour humor. Matthew was the target for most of his jibes.

"Well, young sir, how do you like being surrounded by housemaids?"

Matthew slid an uncertain glance at Ellen. "Housemaids?"

Alec put in, "Lenard, get off that subject. You are confusing the child. Don't ask him questions that have no answers."

Lenard's chuckle had a jeering sound. "Surely he's old enough to know what's what. It was a simple enough question. Unless, of course, you have never told him how his mother happens to be just that."

He turned his head in the direction of the mute, glowering boy. "You have never been told the pretty, romantic tale of the king and the beggar maid?"

Seeming to realize that he had gone too far, Lenard kept his glance away from his father. He smiled a coaxing smile and his voice took on a lilting cadence.

"How does the nursery rhyme go? The one about maids all in a row? For that is what we have here. Your mother, your aunt, and dear Miss Tilton, too. Two of them have managed to pull themselves up a notch, but poor Auntie is still slaving in the kitchens of the rich. So we must be kind to her, do you not agree?"

He pulled his face down, and Megeen could scarcely keep from jumping up from her chair and going around the table and letting him feel the sting of her hand on his cheek.

"That's enough," Alec growled. "More than enough. You have a wicked tongue—for a man. Anyone hearing only your voice would suppose you to be a spiteful woman."

Lenard did not move for more than an entire minute. Then his movements—turning slowly, lifting his chin, transferring his gaze from Matthew to his father—were as slow and precise as though he were a statue coming to life.

When he spoke again, it was in a weak and unnatural voice. "I thought to do a kind thing, and that was the thanks I got for it." He drew up a long, false sigh. "I'm sure that the young man does not want his aunt to be unhappy. What I meant was that he should offer her his services for running errands and such. Well, if she should happen to feel the desire for a little drink and there was nothing in the house to take care of her thirst—"

Alec's chair went clattering to the floor. On his feet, his eyes blazing, he was angrier than Megeen had ever seen him.

He said with clenched teeth, "You will leave my table! I will not have the members of my household insulted for any reason!"

Lenard rose leisurely and said, "You forget, dear Father, that it happens to be my table, too."

He walked around the table and paused when he came to Matthew. He dropped his hand on the boy's shoulder and squeezed it.

"No matter," he said silkily, "we shall find other times to become acquainted. How old are you now—twelve? Strange, your body is more developed than other boys your age. One of these days I shall take you to meet friends of mine. They will be very happy to get to know you."

He left then, but the aura of something evil and unhealthy remained.

After a long, unpleasant silence, Matthew burst out, "Is it true what he said? Were you all servant girls—you, Mama, and Auntie Annie and Ruth? He was only funning, wasn't he?"

Alec's voice was not quite back to its normal tones when he said, "There is no disgrace in honest work. There is nothing in the background of these *ladies* that you or they need to be ashamed of."

"What I don't understand," Matthew said, thrusting out his lip in a familiar fashion, "is why it is like that in our house. The kids I go to school with don't have mothers who used to work in kitchens. I guess they are all richer than us, too."

"You are not to say one more word on that subject," Alec said sternly. Then turning to Megeen, "I think, my dear, that it is time to take our son out of St. Boniface's and send him to public school. I do not care for what he is learning in that expensive academy."

For a long time after the others had left the dining room, Megeen sat among the platters of unfinished food and the remains of half-eaten meals. She remained there, her head resting in her hands, until Mary Donovan, after peeking in at her mistress several times, would wait no longer to clear the table. She came in with heavy, determined footsteps and banged the dishes about as though she had some bitter grudge against them.

Tessie McNamara had been the first to leave. After walking out with the driver of a brewery wagon for a few months, she achieved what she had secretly hoped for and what had brought her to America. She had met a man who cared not that she had no physical beauty. That when she opened her mouth it was as though she had suddenly become drunk and could not stem the flow of words that poured out. Who had enough money saved so that he could rent a tenement a few blocks away from the park on Dorchester Heights and furnish it with good, substantial pieces.

Now Tessie, too, came back to visit, wheeling her twins in their huge, expensive perambulator. She loved to be on the streets and to have people stop and stare into the carriage and marvel that she could tell Stephen and Sean apart.

Aggie Callahan, for all her complaints about Tessie, found that she could not go through the trouble of training another green girl. When she had taken the sock in which she kept her savings out from under her mattress and counted her bank notes, she discovered that she had enough for passage home to the Green Isle and some to spare.

Enough, at least, to impress her sisters and brothers and their young ones and the children of the young ones. Never had she let anyone know how homesick she had always been and how she wished to be buried in the soil of her homeland when the Lord called her.

So it had been Megeen's chore to find and train new housemaids, and when she came upon the Donovans, she thought that she was lucky indeed.

She found them through a system that she and a few other members of her club had instituted. Now it was no longer necessary for a girl seeking work to be swindled by shady characters like Patrick Gilligan. Nor to apply for work at dark little "job agencies" that demanded payment even before the position was obtained.

Martha Laverty, who had an army of relatives still in Ireland, had written to some of them asking to be notified of any young girls who were known to be coming to America in the hopes of finding work. At the end of the long journey, the green girls were met by Megeen or anyone wishing to take a turn at the service.

Sometimes a job would be waiting, for although the old-family ladies of the Back Bay and Beacon Hill did not mingle with the women of the Catholic Club, they were glad to know where to obtain a hardworking, docile, poorly paid green girl when they needed one.

The Donovan sisters were neither subservient nor underpaid. They made their own rules, which Megeen was obliged to accept. It was not difficult, for she could remember what it had been like when she had come to a strange house in a strange land to work for strangers.

Mary and Catherine Donovan refused to be separated. If she hired one, she must hire the other. She was impressed by their sisterly devotion until it was plain that there was no affection between them at all.

There were other stipulations. They must be allowed time off on the same days, which confused Megeen because they derived no pleasure in being together.

Sometimes the whole family—even Alec occasionally—attended the same Sunday Mass. Megeen found it a strange sight to see Catherine and Mary Donovan march up the aisle together, kneel side by side at the altar rail, and then walk home in the familiar angry silence.

But they were good workers. The house shone as it never had before, even when Megeen had been doing the menial work. Megeen included the Donovan sisters when she counted her blessings.

She had a long list of those. She was the wife of a man who saw that she wanted for nothing. She was the mother of three fine sons. True, Matthew had always been a handful to manage, but there was always Ellen to control him. Joseph and Lawrence were growing up to be exactly as she had expected. Joseph could charm the fish from the sea and he was the best-looking of the three, with his wavy black hair and bright blue eyes and his ready smiles.

Lawrence was the scholar. Even when Alec insisted that his sons be removed from St. Boniface's, the Catholic day school, because he feared they were becoming young snobs, Lawrence conducted himself in the public school exactly as he had in the other. It was Lawrence whose catechism lessons Megeen heard every week. She often started conversations with him by saying, "When you are a priest . . ."

And Ellen, dear Ellen, with her soft, sweet voice and her impeccable manners and gentle ways. Megeen mourned for the rich young man who had not yet come to carry Ellen away and make her a loved and pampered wife. She deserved no less, but even when she reached her twentieth birthday, no suitors appeared. Already she was an old maid, although anyone else who suggested such a thing to Megeen would have received the edge of her tongue.

When she told Alec that it might be a good idea to send the girl to Europe in hopes that she would meet someone who would fall in love with her, he threw back his head and laughed.

"Twenty, is she? Looks no more than sixteen. Why the haste? Don't you and your club women friends claim it is no longer a disgrace to be unmarried at twenty?" he asked slyly. "Besides, she seems to like her work. Perhaps that's all she needs to satisfy her."

Ellen, ever since she had graduated from convent school, had been working at an unpaid position in an institution for blind children. It was far outside the city and she had a long trolley ride each morning and afternoon, but she claimed she did not find it tiring. She talked sometimes about the children without sight, but never in Annie's presence. She realized that Annie's sensibilities were even more easily bruised than her own.

In that decade between her thirtieth and fortieth birthdays, Megeen knew not only happiness but contentment as well. And she was able to distinguish between them.

She had become an influential figure in the city. Often, usually in the last days of summer or the early weeks of au-

tumn, men flocked to her door, hats in hand, asking her to
try to persuade the women of Boston to help them to be
elected to one office or another.

She did not let herself be swayed by promises of favors or
by oratory. If she believed in a candidate's integrity and good
character and qualifications, she would call a special meeting
of her club and discuss the coming election with knowledgea-
bility, earnestness, and quiet good sense.

Boston had its first Irish mayor. She marveled at that, certain that even ten years ago no man bearing the name of
Hugh O'Brien could ever have hoped to be elected to the
city's highest office.

And if there was a nagging little pain in her heart now and
then, she ignored it. It usually came when she heard Lenard's
name spoken. This was the only thing she could not share
with her husband. Lenard would return someday, she knew.
He would arrive with his jaunty step, his selfish demands, and
those wise and mocking eyes.

And he did come, on a day when the heavens dropped
down a curtain of cold, mean drizzle. And he brought a wife
with him.

Chapter Thirty-four

Her name had been Millicent Lapierre before her marriage to
Lenard—or so she said. Megeen did not believe in that outlandish name; it seemed as false as the two round dabs of
color on the woman's cheeks.

When she had recovered from the shock of being introduced to Lenard's wife, Megeen was able to recognize the
whole facade of deceit: the twittering voice with its accents,
which were supposed to sound "refined"; the girlish mannerisms, which were ridiculous, for she had left her girlhood behind her many years ago; the casual glances around her, as
though she felt that she must display no awe or admiration
but was used to surroundings of luxury.

"My wife," Lenard said, his own smile dishonest. "I've told you about Megeen, Millie—my stepmother."

The woman looked from Megeen to Lenard, and the china-blue eyes, which resembled those of a doll, began to look uncertain. "Pleased to meet you," she trilled. "I hope you won't hold it against me that we kept our little secret till now. Lenard here"—and she tittered up into his face—"swept me off my feet, you might say."

Lenard left them alone for a few minutes. While he was outside overseeing the unloading of her trunk and suitcases from a hired hack, Megeen had an opportunity to recover her wits.

The announcement of the marriage had stunned her for a few moments. There was no reason, of course, why Lenard should not have taken a wife. He was thirty-eight years old, two years older than his stepmother. But to have brought home a bride like Millicent Lapierre—or whatever her real name was—when his good looks, his money, and the eminence of his ancestors should have given him a wide choice.

Megeen had never before been this close to a woman who painted her face and her lips. Nor worn such outrageous, vulgar clothing.

Even though it was bedraggled and damp, the bride's skirt was much too short and showed an immodest amount of lower leg. Her coat was too tight and its buttons strained against big, melon-shaped breasts. When she removed it, there came into view a great many limp ruffles on either side of a deeply cut neckline.

Her hat sagged and its oversupply of artificial cabbage roses were drenched. Her jewelry—rings and brooches and a string of colored beads—was cheap and flashy.

When Lenard returned with the luggage, the hired driver staggering under the weight of the trunk, he motioned to his new wife to follow him up the stairs.

"Dinner will be at seven," Megeen called weakly after them.

She was glad that it would take them some time to unpack, bathe, and change clothing. It would give her an opportunity to tell Alec and the others about the arrival of their new relative. The children were merely curious, but Alec lost his temper, as he seldom did.

"To have done a thing like this without consulting me! When he cannot put his hand on a dollar unless I release it to him. His mother knew him better than I, and everything she left to him is in trust with me. What is she like, this creature he married? What sort of woman would assent to a hole-in-corner ceremony? If, indeed, there was one?"

He was to discover that there had been one. They had been married by a justice of the law, which, to Megeen, meant that they were living in sin. For she suspected that under that false name and the theatrical mannerisms there was a woman who had been a child of the true faith, no doubt baptized in it and taught its precepts by poor and hardworking parents.

It had been easy to guess, too, that Millicent was not what she claimed to be: an actress in a respectable play that had been presented at the Boston Theater a few weeks ago. The trunk that the driver had carried upstairs had been pockmarked with stickers from many different cities, names unfamiliar to Megeen. But she was sure that Millicent's contribution to the stage had been a part in one of those sleazy, cheap musical shows of which Megeen had heard but had never, of course, witnessed.

On her first night in the Vickery house, Millicent came down to dinner in a gown of shiny crimson with fringes of bugle beads that moved and tinkled faintly with each step she took. Everyone else, even Lenard, was in subdued clothing and their moods had the same element. Only Millicent's voice was heard during that awkward, miserable hour. She said all the wrong things. She called her father-in-law "Al," which outraged him so that he seemed to have difficulty unclenching his teeth long enough to eat. She recounted some of her experiences on the stage, making her "career," as she called it, sound like a great, exciting adventure.

But when Megeen met Millicent's eyes across the table, she saw that there was a sort of desperation in them. How out of place and uncomfortable this unlikely bride must be feeling! Megeen resolved to try to make Lenard's wife welcome in this house in spite of her own nagging pain.

If it had been Dorothea Lovering whom he had brought home as his wife, Megeen's pain would not have been so sharp, she was sure. Dorothea was someone she knew. There was no real friendship between them, but Dorothea belonged in Lenard's world. She was not someone he had picked up backstage in a dismal theater or in one of the bawdy houses Annie had spoken about.

Annie had learned much (some of which Megeen wished she hadn't) since she had gone to work on Beacon Hill. The other servants were a gossipy lot, she said cheerfully, privy to the secrets and scandals of the families they worked for. She was not at all surprised by the union of Lenard and the raucous-voiced Millicent.

Alec had said angrily that Lenard's wife had married him for his money. "As for him, I can only call it blackmail."

For Lenard had pressed for the money he believed was due him. Had Alec given him a large enough sum, he would have taken his bride out of his father's house and, probably, sent her on her way. "But I shall not do it. He will get nothing until I am ready to give it to him. She does not upset you, Megeen?"

He asked her the same question several times during the next few days. She did not tell him the truth, that she had come to dread mealtimes, especially those at which Millicent appeared in her outlandish clothing, her frizzed hair, and her imitation jewelry tinkling on her arms and around her throat.

For Millicent flirted desperately with the men. She was all coyness when Martin Mulcahy joined them at dinner, as he sometimes did. With Lenard, who responded by growling. And even with eighteen-year-old Matthew, who despised all women and girls except Ellen. Millicent seemed to sense that Alec would never succumb to her charms and so did not try to use them on him.

Megeen could pity both Millicent and Lenard, the woman most of all, for sometimes looking into those eyes, which seemed strangely old, she could see in them the hardness of pain.

It startled her, and she could not imagine why Millicent was suffering. She now had everything she could wish for: a husband, luxurious surroundings, a lazy life that allowed her to sleep the daylight hours away. No more drafty theaters, night journeys on dusty steam trains, the worry about the ravages of time on her person and fears for the future.

Millicent gradually became quieter. When Megeen pointed that out to her sister, Annie said, "Sure, she's quiet enough when she's around you people, but she and Len sure are noisy at night."

The bride and groom had been living in the house only two weeks when Annie moved into the other side of it.

"I don't care if I have the smallest of bedrooms. I'll move in with Ellen, if need be, but they keep me awake, those two, and I need my rest if I am to go to work in the morning."

Her words brought a faint, memory-filled smile to Megeen's lips. Into Annie's cheeks came a sudden bright flush. They were both thinking of the same thing: the early nights of Annie's marriage when the sounds of wild lovemaking had seeped through the thin walls.

Megeen could almost hear again her sister's frantic cries.

Annie's face was still rosy and her voice was thick and low. "It's not like that with them. It's the quarreling that keeps me awake."

The marriage lasted exactly forty-seven days. Lenard left the house on a wet, stormy night when the weather seemed to lend itself to stealth. He said no good-byes to anyone. It was not an unfamiliar leave-taking. All his comings and goings had been unannounced, but this time he left a wife behind him.

Megeen and Millicent kept up the pretense that he had been obliged to leave to attend to something important, but after two weeks his bride called a halt to the charade.

"He ain't gonna show up again," Millicent said in a resigned voice. "He's gone for good, as far as I'm concerned anyhow. I can't say I'm sorry. If he didn't walk out on me, I woulda left him."

They were in the bedroom she and her husband had shared for so brief a time. It was untidy now. Underwear and small articles of clothing were thrown over the backs of chairs and hung on doorknobs. The smell of cheap perfume was heavily sweet on the air. A paintpot was in plain sight on the lowboy. The bed looked as though it had not been made properly for a long time.

A straw suitcase was open on the bed and Millicent was throwing the contents of a gaping drawer into it.

"But where will you go?" Megeen asked. "Do you have any friends who will help you?"

Millicent laughed shortly. "I been takin' care of myself since I was twelve years old. Some of the ways I done that you wouldn't wanna hear about. This is maybe the craziest thing I ever done—getting hitched to that——that—"

She turned away quickly as though there was something on her face that she didn't want anyone to see.

"My own fault!" she muttered. "How it was, I figured I'd be on easy street gettin' hitched up with someone like Lenard. He kept tellin' me how rich his father was. That was at first. Then he owns up that the old man won't come across with the money he said belonged to him.

"You're wonderin' why Lenny married me," she said harshly. "It was spite. He wanted you all to hate me and havin' me here. He was sore at you and his father especially, and that was how he got even with you."

Megeen could hear a faint sniffling and she crossed the room and put an arm around Millicent's waist. "He couldn't be as cruel as that. You're a person. I can't believe that Lenard would do such a thing."

Millicent stared into Megeen's eyes. "You don't think so? Gawd, you don't know him very well, do you? But then you got a sneaky feeling for him, I guess. Oh, don't say it ain't so!" Her voice rose as Megeen tried to speak. "He told me that himself. He said that though you'd married his father, you wished it coulda been him. Lemme tell you this, Meggie, you got the best of the deal."

She looked around the room as though searching for things she might have forgotten and didn't want to leave behind. She threw a few more things into the suitcase and closed it.

"Aw, to hell with him! I'll be better off alone. Look, you can have your coachman help me with the luggage if you wanna. Say, cheer up! I'll come back to see you someday. Maybe I'll be with a rich husband. A *real* man this time." And she threw back her head and bellowed a wave of coarse, bitter laughter. "Well, this ain't no good. I'll be on my way," she said, drying her eyes. "It was just a bust, that's all."

"Not yet!" Megeen put herself in the woman's path. "You must tell me what you mean!"

Millicent looked away. Her face was bleak and the stamp of her years and mode of living was on it.

"Just that he can't do it with a woman. Christ, the time I had with him! I never run up against nothin' like that in all the times. Well, never mind. A woman like you wouldn't know about things such as that. I tried. Gawd knows I did. All them nights we was in bed together and I did everything I could think of to make him hard."

She broke off as she turned and saw Megeen's expression.

"He shouldn't never have got married. Because he can't get it up!"

Chapter Thirty-five

All that day Megeen felt as though she were lost in a spinning world. Some force she could not control seemed to be whirling her about, sickening her, nauseating her.

When she realized that she was not in any fit condition to take care of the things that needed her attention, she locked herself in her bedroom. Knocks sounded on the door from time to time, but she ignored them. Then, as worried voices called to her, she answered them wearily.

"Go away! Let me alone, let me rest!"

There was no rest for her. As though they had been crouched in a corner of her mind awaiting just such an opportunity, the wretched thoughts came crashing into it. And they seemed to be poisoning her entire body.

Deliberately and stubbornly, she had not let her imagination conjure up pictures of Lenard and Millicent while they had been occupying his bedroom in the other part of the house. She had refused to let herself think of them rolling and tossing with their legs and arms twisted about each other.

That battle she had won. But she had lost the one that was raging now. Nor did she have the strength to fight. What Lenard and Millicent had actually been doing during those long, dark nights was so pitiful and, according to Millicent's own admission, so futile that Megeen could almost feel a sharing pain in her own body.

A belief that she had clung to was being ripped out of her. In spite of what Alec had said, she had been sure that it was Lenard who had come into her cell-like room on that night so long ago and impregnated her. She had not thought about it for many years, not consciously, and Matthew had always been one of her children, no different from the others. All of them had been Alec's in her regard and treatment.

But he was not Alec's son, she would have thought if she had let the subject come into her mind. Now facing the truth, she was forced to face the fact that it was not Lenard who had violated her on her first night in the Vickery house. And the pain deepened and spread.

She would never see Lenard again; a strong premonition told her that. Perhaps Alec had given him money, worn down by the arguments and pleading. And no doubt he had known that Millicent would pour the shameful truth about him into the first sympathetic ear she found. He could have had no hope that his secret would be kept.

He would be exposed as a fraud, his dashing air and his brazen, suggestive glances recognized for what they were— means of hiding the fact that he was not the man he worked so hard to portray.

Of course Alec must know. How could he have helped knowing? There was a tiny Roman candle of anger against Alec exploding inside her where the pain was the sharpest. And then reason came back. Alec had never lied to her. He had acknowledged the baby as his. Her doubts had distorted everything, given her faulty vision.

She was not able to remain in bed for very long. She had things to do. She must make sure that Alec took his medicine. Dinner was always late if she did not prod the Donovan sisters into moving with greater speed. Ellen was attending a reunion of her high-school class that evening and Megeen had promised to press the ruffles on her best dress.

Little things. Small things that were woven into the fabric of her life. The things God gave her to do; now she was grateful for them. She could banish Lenard and her yearning for him.

She could give her feelings one last thought, weighing them and deciding that the scales were far from being in his favor. She would never think of him again—never. It had been like a sickness she had suddenly recovered from, the tears and the pain and the nausea gone.

But when she went into Alec's room, there was one more moment when the tide threatened to rise again. They looked into each other's eyes, his sober and sympathetic, hers with shame reflected in them. Silently he stretched out his arms, and she walked across the room to the bed and let herself be folded into his embrace. She rested her head against his shoulder.

Dear Alec! How could she have lived without him all these years? He was her gentle friend, her strength. Past now were the nights of frenzied lovemaking. Seldom did he give her the previous pleasures of his body. When he came into her bed, it was after some minor household crisis or disappointment, and his arms were offered for comfort and to warm whatever coldness lingered in her.

She raised her head and looked into his eyes. He did not speak of Lenard, but that mocking, smiling face seemed to hang between them. It was easy to exorcise it. She had only to put her lips on her husband's mouth. "I have missed you, dear sir," she said honestly and without guile.

Then she stood up and shook out her skirts. "When you are feeling stronger, my love . . ."

Her voice cracked. For it was as though a cold wind had swept into the room—a chilling, icy blast that threatened her with some dreadful sort of evil. Or sorrow.

Sorrow, certainly that. For she knew in that moment, someway she knew, that Alec would never again be strong enough for the strenuous, exhausting act of copulation and that that phase of their marriage had ended.

She was sad, not so much for her own sake but for Alec's. She was thirty-six and she did not believe that women's passions continued on much longer after forty. But for him it must be a bitter realization that now, at the early age of fifty-eight, he would no longer be able to keep up the pretense of vigor and potency.

She went back to the bed and kissed him once more. They did not speak, but there was no need for words. She saw the tenderness and love in that good, kind face, the gratitude because she had not made demands upon him and thus unearthed his shame.

Now that he knew she expected nothing from him, she would be able to come more often to his bed. They smiled at each other in friendliness, and she prayed silently that she might be able to keep up the pretense about him recovering.

Megeen celebrated her fortieth birthday in exactly the manner she would have arranged if Ellen had not taken it upon herself to plan it all. The girl (Megeen could not think of her in any other way even though she was almost twenty-eight) had grown even more quiet and shy during the past few years. But on that night when she moved from kitchen to dining-room helping to set the table and giving soft-voiced orders to Catherine and Mary, there was an unmistakable glow in her face.

She had placed a low centerpiece of tea roses and daisies on the long table, which was covered by Megeen's finest Irish-lace cloth. The silverware glistened. The candles at either end of the table streaked patches of brightness on the Spode dishes. At Megeen's place there was a mound of presents in colorful tissue paper and bright satin ribbons.

It was a Saturday night. Megeen was always to remember that. Somebody had spoken of going to confession and Megeen had reminded him (her?) that he (she?) would have to hurry away as soon as the meal had ended.

It was decided that one more week wouldn't matter and the plan of going to church was dropped. That was one of the things that would stick in Megeen's mind. There were others. But what she was to remember longest and most vividly was the pride she had felt as she looked around the table.

Alec had come downstairs to take his place at the other end of the expanse of fine lace. He was impeccably dressed; in the candlelight his hair shone brilliantly and it was impossible to see that it was almost completely white and not the pale gold it had been.

The sight of her three handsome lads there lifted her heart to great heights. Matthew's face had lost its habitual glowering expression, and she began to hope that he would soon begin to follow the road that she had dreamed of for him.

At twenty-two he was still without purpose, having spurned his father's offer to find him some sort of employment that would suit his tastes.

He had refused curtly the suggestion that he learn the paper-manufacturing business. Under Martin Mulcahy's guidance he might have started at a lowly job and worked his way up to taking over the family business. The law practice, which was being conducted by a smart young graduate from the Harvard law school, did not appeal to him. Matthew, according to his own surly admission, wanted only to be a writer. Megeen had thought at first that it was merely some sort of whim, born of his discontentment. She had expected long ago that he would tire of the drudgery, but he was still locking himself in his bedroom each day to cover sheet after sheet of paper, and he had begun to wear his hair long and to affect flowing neckerchiefs.

Matthew's present to his mother was a locket with a picture of him on one side and one of Ellen on the other; Ruth Tilton had brought the latest in colored silk stockings and a pair of ruffled garters that made Megeen blush. From Martin there were fine handkerchiefs, from Ellen a new prayerbook, and from Annie a French fan.

Lawrence, in his quiet way but with his face bright with pleasure (for he loved parties and all gatherings in spite of his reserve), had done his own purchasing; the reticule of softest leather pleased her for both its quality and the fact that he had gone forth into female territory to buy it.

Dear Lawrence! He would graduate from high school in the spring. And while he had said nothing about entering a novitiate to begin his studies for the priesthood, she was sure that it would be only a matter of time before he confided to her that he intended to spend his life in God's service.

When all the gift opening was finished, Joseph handed her a stiff white envelope that she accepted with a puzzled frown.

Inside, there was an invitation, and when she had finished reading it, she was speechless.

"Senator and Mrs. Nathaniel Woodward Howard request the pleasure of your company at a reception to be held on April 23rd, in the ballroom of their home at 55 Marlborough Street, Boston, Massachusetts, at eight o'clock."

When she could make any sound at all, she whispered, "Oh, Joey, how wonderful!"

Her eyes were full of tears as she lifted her face to her grinning son. "It is a wonderful gift! But how in the world did you manage it?"

He put a finger to his lips and shook his head. "Ask me no questions. There are ways of getting everything you want if you know the right people."

She had been troubled at times over this merry young man with his ready smiles and honeyed words. She did not know exactly how he spent the hours of his day. She knew only that he had "friends" who were on the political scene. He seemed to have an unlimited amount of spending money. He was never at a loss for new clothing to wear to the parties and balls and "nights out with the fellows" that kept him busy every evening.

She did not like the fact that he found nothing wrong in seeking out and making friends with people who could do him the most good. Megeen had dreamed of him becoming a great statesman. His ambition, it seemed, was to be an influential politician.

Now everything was brushed out of her mind by the anticipation of attending a reception for one of the leading figures of the state. She did not even notice the long, velvet jeweler's box until Ellen slid it into her hand. When she opened the lid, a string of perfectly matched pearls glowed in warm and soft beauty.

"How lovely!" she breathed. "Oh, Alec! I shall treasure these always!"

"I am glad you have them now," he said with a thin smile. "For you will wish to wear them to the reception."

She reached up to kiss him. "There will not be much joy in that if you are not with me! I do hope you will go, too."

They were still playing their little game of pretense. Even though he never left the house these days, they pretended that it was through his own choice and not because of the seeping away of his strength.

"Joseph will escort you, I'm sure. It will be well if you begin immediately to have a gown made. I'm afraid that Ruth won't have any material suitable for a formal affair like that, but do consult with her. She will know the best places to shop."

They were moving slowly up the staircase. That, too, was one of their pretending games. With one arm around his waist, she clung to the banister with her free hand, and she puffed and sighed just as though she were the only one who found the climb arduous.

He seemed to be finding the ascent even more difficult than usual tonight. His footsteps were shaky and Megeen was annoyed to find that the second-floor corridor was only dimly lit, and thus a source of danger for him.

"I can't seem to get those girls to put in fresh gas mantles when the others begin to fade and crumble."

She stopped speaking because, when she looked down the corridor, there seemed to be a figure half-lost in the gloom there. Her eyes finally grew accustomed to the feeble light and she realized that it was not a single figure she was looking at but two. A man and a woman had been in a close embrace, body pressed against body, arms circling and locked, mouths lost in each other.

As Megeen cried out, they sprang apart and turned in her direction. It was not to be believed. She must be seeing things. Or they had concocted this silly joke merely to tease her.

But it was not a joke. Neither Matthew nor Ellen were

given to pranks. And she had only to look at the girl's face, flushed and shimmering, to know the truth.

As she moved woodenly closer to the two, Megeen saw that Ellen's eyes held sadness in them, a shadow that dulled their brilliance. Everything about Matthew seemed exaggerated. His scowl had never been so deep, his face so defiant, his jaw so rigid. He slid his arm about Ellen's waist and made the gesture look like deliberate insolence.

Megeen felt as though she were in a cold vacuum of some sort and her voice sounded hollow and echoing. "I would like to know exactly what this means. But not here. I would not **like** anyone to hear what must be said."

She took a few steps toward her bedroom, but Alec grasped her arm firmly and steered her in the direction of his room. The numbness was melting, leaving pain in its wake, and she was able to realize what he was doing. The next few minutes were going to be shattering for the four of them. He did not want her to remember, every time she walked into her bedroom, the scene that inevitably would take place.

They stood there, all four of them, stiff and silent, like actors in a play who were waiting to be given their lines. Megeen was the first to speak.

She said thickly, "Very well, Matthew, let us hear it. How is it that we find you kissing your sister in such a manner?"

Ellen had been standing with her head dropped forward. Now she lifted it and said in an agonized voice, "But I am not! I have not loved him in that way for a very long time. And I am not ashamed of what we are to each other. We are to be married next week!"

Megeen's head began to throb and she pressed her hands against her forehead. She stared incredulously at the girl. What had happened to that shy, gentle voice and the sweetly serene face?

But was it strange, after all? Ellen had spent her girlhood protecting and defending Matthew. Now he wore an ugly scowl and she was doing the explaining and the pleading for understanding.

"We were to have told you tomorrow. I didn't want your birthday to be spoiled. If you are wondering why we didn't say anything about intending to be married, we were forced to wait, for I could not give the priest my baptismal certificate, not knowing where I was born or in which church baptized. We were forced to wait for the dispensation."

The words buzzed around in Megeen's brain like a swarm of bees suddenly released: ". . . intending to be married . . . what we are to each other . . . dispensation. . . ."

"Oh, Mother!"

Ellen crossed the room and tried to take a pair of icy hands into her clasp, but Megeen snatched them away. She felt ill with chagrin and disappointment. She was bitter when she remembered certain little things, little signposts that, if she had paid any attention to them, would have revealed the truth to her.

She should have guessed why Ellen had never been interested in another man. She should have been able to sense the difference between a brother-sister attachment and that of a passionate man and the woman who adored him.

The talking, the arguments, the pleading and outbursts of anger went on far into the night, exhausting them all. Nothing was accomplished, nothing changed. Ellen and Matthew were not to be shaken from their purpose: their determination to become man and wife.

Chapter Thirty-six

Nothing that either Megeen or Alec could say would sway them. Ellen was the elder of the two by six years, but that did not matter to either of them. Matthew had no means of supporting them; Ellen said that she would find a job that paid a salary until he was recognized as the great writer she knew him to be.

What would their friends say? They would find themselves laughingstocks, for the conventions ruled that the husband must be older than his wife and that it was he who earned the money to support them.

With her face growing pale and weary, Ellen said that they had no friends. And that even if they had, neither she nor Matthew would have been influenced by their opinions.

When Megeen tried to put delicately a certain question, Matthew sprang to his feet with his hands clenched. He shouted, "If you're hinting that I've been there already, you can have another guess. God knows I've wanted to often enough. But we both wished to save it for after we're married."

Ellen nodded and the golden knob atop her head wobbled. "It's true, Mother. We didn't want anything shabby like Lenard and Millicent had, either. We're to be married in the rectory on next Saturday evening, the twenty-third. I hope with all my heart that we may have our father and mother there."

They could both call her "Mother" and yet they were aching to be man and wife. She could see the want in their faces: Matthew's strained and flushed, that of his beloved seemed to be only a pair of enormous, suffering eyes.

Alec asked, "On Saturday? The twenty-third, that is?"

Megeen started to say something and stopped, and they all turned to look at her.

He went on, "That's the night of the reception, isn't it? The invitation . . . Joey's birthday present?"

Ellen's drawn-in breath sounded overloud. Matthew's groan, Megeen thought bitterly, was not one of distress for anyone but himself. He feared that there might be a delay or snarling of his own plans. It had been this way always; he would be the same until the day he died.

Megeen spoke firmly. "I shall not be going to the reception. Whether or not I shall be a witness to your marriage, I do not know at this time."

Ellen's little cry sounded as though something had pierced her heart and a rushing flood of tears glazed her cheeks.

"Oh, no! We shall not be responsible for your missing that! Matthew, darling, we can postpone, can't we? For a week, perhaps, or we could make it some evening sooner."

He had no chance to reply, for his mother said, "You will do no such thing. I have no intention of going to the senator's reception. I should not, even if things were different. Because there seems to be some evil spirit perching on my shoulder at times so that I am not fated to gain the things I want."

Alec's mouth had fallen open. He stared at his wife in astonishment and then moved to her side and put his arm around her.

"You can't know what you're saying, dearest wife. Malicious fate! Evil spirit! I know how you are feeling, my love, how disappointed you are. But it cannot be the end of the world. If you do not go to the reception, you can send re-grets. There will be other chances. As for you two . . ."

They moved closer together, hands entwined.

"Let there be no more talk about who will support whom. You had best stay in this house until your are financially able to set up your own home."

He squeezed Megeen's hand so tightly that she winced. "You would not want our children living in some shabby room, would you? It need not be so different. They will still be part of the household. Come, think how unhappy they would be if you were not at their wedding!"

She answered with a sour twist of her lips. "Indeed, I'm sure their hearts would be broken!"

Then she walked out of the room with her shoulders stiff and her spine straight. She walked alone and in silence, and that was to be her manner for weeks ahead.

Alec was her only friend. She felt as though she lived in a nest of traitors. He could not have known what was going on between his son and his foster daughter. He seldom left his room these days, and so he, too, had been unaware of what was happening.

The others had known. She could see the guilt in their eyes in that instant before she turned away from theirs. They had kept the secret well and so the shock was all the greater.

It did no good for Martin Mulcahy to plead their cause.

"They were merely trying to spare you, lass. They believed they were being kind. So it is all out in the open now. For-give them, that's what you should do. Their hearts will be sore indeed if you go on refusing to speak to them so much as a word!"

She paid no attention to his words. Nor to Annie, who, with Ellen's help, was trying to run the household smoothly without quite succeeding.

Annie said, "You are making us all unhappy as Da did when we were small girls. Sometimes weeks would go by and he would not open his mouth except to eat. The black mood was upon him as it often happened with the men of our family. Uncle Dennie and the Geohegan cousins. Those were dark days for their womenfolk."

The coaxing failed. The arms that reached out to comfort her were pushed away. You knew! Megeen cried silently. You all knew and you saw fit to deceive me.

Ellen and Matthew were married on the twenty-third of April as they had planned. The bride wore a suit of ivory serge with black silk rickrack trimming and a small black straw hat that rode far down on her forehead. A long, slender feather rose back from the point, and the whole effect was one of fashion and good taste. She had never looked so beautiful.

Megeen, from her pew facing the side altar where the ceremony was performed, was appalled by the hat's trimming. Black was unlucky for a bride on her wedding day; so was a feather. But it was none of her business, she remembered. If Ellen wanted to fly in the face of fate, let her take her chances.

Alec was at her side, kneeling when she knelt, standing when she stood. He was responsible for her being there. Even the night before, she had been undecided about coming.

"I have no wish to be sanctioning it. It is wrong and so I shall believe to my dying day."

"So you wish to share that opinion with those who might snigger over it? It has never mattered to me what people say or how they gossip over what goes on in this house. But it has for you, always. Where's your pride, my girl?"

She was forced to admit, slowly and grudgingly, that everything Alec said was true. When this strange marriage became known to all, at least it must be said that the mother of the groom—and of the bride in all senses but one—had been there in the front pew with her husband beside her at the nuptial Mass.

She had selected her own costume with unusual care. Her pale-green silk coat was cut with wide shoulders and a high collar. Her bonnet-shaped hat was rather old-fashioned but suitable for a woman of forty years.

The droned words had no meaning for her. "For this cause a man shall leave his mother and father and cleave to his wife; and the two shall become one flesh."

They had been said when Megeen and Alec had been married in the cold, clean room of the rectory. She did not know who had decided that the Mass should be said in the church proper, even if at one of the smaller altars. She did not care. She was saying her own wretched litany: the deceit of her children, her sister, and the two who were supposed to be her friends—Ruth Tilton and Martin Mulcahy.

They all returned to the dining room in the Vickery part of

the house after the final blessing was over. The Donovan sisters had prepared for them a wedding feast and Alec had brought up from cellar a few bottles of vintage wine, but Megeen slipped out of the room before the toast could be given and did not return until it had been drunk.

Her face was cold with lack of response when Ellen kissed her good-bye. The bride and groom were taking a short honeymoon to New York on the steam trains. That did not stir Megeen's interest, nor did she run to the door with handfuls of rice as the others did to send the couple on their way.

For the little shards of pain inside her had festered and spurted poison into everything she felt and did. She clung to Alec as she had never done before, spending most of her waking hours in his bedroom, her skin bleaching for lack of fresh air and sunshine and her eyes bleak with the hurt that did not soften.

She was standing at the window of Alec's bedroom one bright and showy spring day when she saw Tessie, their former maid, wheeling her twins in their enormous baby buggy. Tessie, although she had a home of her own now, still kept up her friendships with the servants in the houses around the park. When she visited at the Vickery's, it was for the purpose of collecting gossip or distributing it.

Megeen, seeing the carriage begin to slow down, raced out of the room with no explanation and reached the areaway just as Tessie was trying to pick up both her sons at the same time. When she caught sight of her former mistress, she gave a gusty sigh of relief. She had one of the little boys in her arms and thrust him toward Megeen. "Here, you can carry him down for me. There's times when two of 'em's too much for me."

Megeen felt her heart soften as the baby smiled at her. No one who was not a mother, she thought with a pang of sadness, could know how much you missed the baby smells, the toothless grins, the soft-as-velvet skin against your face.

"Not down that way," she said. "We'll go into the drawing room. We can talk more quietly there."

With the babies crawling about on the carpet and Tessie posed in a ladylike attitude on a Chippendale chair, Megeen went directly to the subject that had been out of her mind for only a few minutes.

"I suppose they're all talking about us. About Matthew and Ellen getting married, I mean. Was there much talk?"

Tessie, with her fingers stroking the arm of the chair, looked around the room with lively eyes. She was savoring this, Megeen knew. Here she was as a guest in the room that had felt the sweeping of her broom, the rubbing of her dust-cloth, and the scouring of a clean cloth on its windows.

Megeen said impatiently, "Tell me what is being said!"

This, too, Tessie was relishing. Her tongue raced over her lips as though she were tasting something pleasant.

"Well, ma'am, it's true there's been talk but perhaps I shouldn't repeat it. I fear it would upset you. That being the case—"

Megeen cried in a stern voice, "No more of this shilly-shal-lying. Speak up, girl!"

Tessie admitted that the Vickerys had been the sole topic of conversation at all the dinner tables in Nightingale Park, Rutland Square, and Beacon Hill. And at tea parties in Louisburg Square, Marlborough Street, and Bay Village. And in the servants' quarters in the houses of the rich and fashion-able.

Tessie had friends and friends of friends in many of those places. Being as she was, she could not have helped hearing what went on in most of them.

"What they said, Mrs. V., is that Matthew and Ellie com-mitted—" Her forehead crinkled in a frown as she searched for a certain word in her mind and did not find it. "It's like somethin' in church. You know. At benediction when the priest wears the fancy robes and swings that gold thing back and forth. And the smoke and the smell come from what he's burning in it."

Megeen's face twisted. "Are they saying it's incest?"

"That's it! That's the word!"

Tessie's high spirits returned now that the word had been found. "Incense! It's supposed to mean something bad, is that right? And it's a crime, too, ain't it? I mean, they could go to jail for that."

"They could not! For they have not done anything wrong."

Megeen got up stiffly from her chair and walked to the fireplace and stared down at the empty grate.

"They had forgotten the circumstances," she said as though talking to herself. "Ellen came into our family so long ago that people have forgotten that she is not Matthew's sister at all. That is what has been overlooked."

Megeen's thoughts came back from their journey and she

sighed. "I suppose I must thank you, Tessie. It was necessary for me to know all this. Now if you would like to go downstairs, I'm sure Catherine and Mary will give you tea. I believe they baked this morning. There should be fresh Irish bread."

Thus was Tessie paid for services rendered. Tell me something that will break my heart and I will reward you with a cup of tea and a slice of Irish bread.

Chapter Thirty-seven

She did not tell Alec anything of what she had learned that day. She could see no reason to distress him. He seemed to be growing weaker during that spring and summer of his sixty-third year. He spent most of his time reading, for even a game of chess wearied him.

Megeen watched his decline with deep sorrow. She no longer allowed Ruth or Martin to discuss business matters with him but checked their figures herself. There was no pleasure for her in the business details she was forced to oversee, but she knew that she must spare Alec as much as she could.

She was still holding herself as aloof as possible not only from them but from all members of the household as well. Her manner toward them was cold and curt. It was like living among strangers; only Annie had the courage to speak out frankly.

"Isn't it about time that you got over the sulks?"

A freezing stare was the only answer. Megeen turned on her heel thinking that things would never be the same between her and any of them and she did not try to pretend that they would be.

Lawrence graduated from high school that June. He was the oldest pupil in his class, not far from twenty, for he had lost a year when he was ill with measles, chicken pox, mumps, and whooping cough all within six months' time. He seemed older because of his quiet, scholarly ways and tall, stocky body. Of the three boys, Lawrence was the one who most resembled his father; not in height or stature, but his hair was as blond as Alec's had once been and his features were as well-arranged and attractive.

There was no celebration to mark his graduation. He asked that there not be and Megeen was relieved that this was his wish. Weeks had passed since the wedding of Matthew and Ellen, but the shadow of pain was still darkening her spirits. She wanted no part of any festivity. Besides, Lawrence would soon be leaving to study for the priesthood, she was sure. And that would be the time for a party.

She realized that it was quite some time since that subject had arisen. How long had it been since she had sent for information about a certain order of priests? Lawrence had thanked her, she remembered now, and put the letter in his Latin book and not mentioned it to her again.

Uneasy, although she could not have said why, she called Lawrence into the music room, where they could talk undisturbed, on the night after graduation. The gift she gave him was a chamois bag filled with gold coins.

"You will find use for a little extra money," she said, the darkness gone from her soul as she gazed up at her tall, handsome son. "You might as well get the best of everything, Lawrence. Cassock, surplice, and your other garments will be used much. It will pay in the long run to buy them of the best material."

He turned his face away for a brief moment. He drew a deep breath into his lungs. Then he faced her again.

"Mother, I shall not need those things. I have decided on what I wish to do with my life. If I can spend a couple of more years studying and going to college, I can become a schoolmaster. And that is what I've always wanted to be."

"No!" She laughed a little at this idea. "You've planned, since you were knee-high, to become a priest."

"That was your dream, Mother." He spoke gently, but his jaw was like marble. "Perhaps I should have told you before this that I knew I had no calling."

The pain came in agonizing thrusts, lancing all parts of her body. She winced with each fresh stab.

"It cannot be true! You did, you had the true vocation. The holy pictures in your room—"

"It was you who hung them there, Mother."

She was gasping now. "Oh, my dearest son, God will punish you if you turn your back on Him and don't answer when He calls you!"

She took a shuddering breath. Then something came into her mind, sent there by God in His everlasting wisdom, she knew.

"Lawrence, darling boy!" She threw her arms around him in a burst of great joy. "There is no reason why you cannot teach school if that's what you want. Many of the orders have schools. You can be a priest and a teacher both, if that's your wish. Perhaps you would like to be a missionary and teach the heathens. I can see you in some faraway country . . ."

She had no doubt but that he would release that stubborn jaw and smile that small-boy grin that transformed his face. Lawrence had never been one to argue. When the boys had had their squabbles, he had surrendered first and let his brothers have their way.

"Don't you think that's a fine idea?" she coaxed. "We could buy the finest of linens. Ruth would select it for us. Your aunt Annie is a first-rate seamstress and in every stitch she'd put her love, and that, they say, adds to a priest's glory. You four children have always meant a great deal to her, for it was her sad lot not to have any of her own."

When he began to turn away, she grasped his sleeve. "Do not close your ears to me! It breaks my heart that I have failed! I beg you not to make me the cause of a spoiled priest!"

He put his arm around her and hugged her tightly, as though he could press the unhappiness out of her body and into his own. She freed herself and stood away from him, her face drooping in lines of anguish. Now she realized at last that nothing she could say would change his mind.

"You will be sorry!" That, too, was futile and heaped even more pain on the pile of it inside her.

During the following months she would not allow her hopes to die completely. One of these days, she was certain, Lawrence would come to her and admit that he had been wrong. He would say that he did indeed have the true vocation and would be leaving soon to enter a seminary.

It did not happen. Annie grew concerned about her sister's listlessness and apathy. Megeen seldom left the house, claiming that the hot weather drained her energy and that she found the crowded streets irksome.

"But you never complained before. You haven't been outside, luv, for ages."

"Well, of course, Alec needs me."

"Not every hour of the day and night. I hate to see you going about like this, Megeen. Maybe it would be well for you to see a doctor. You could be starting the change."

Her features tightened in affront, Megeen cried, "I am too young! I am not yet forty-one . . ." Her voice drifted away on a sigh. The brief outburst was over. "Still, some women begin it at my age."

When she said no more, Annie sighed, too. "I am glad you snapped at me and showed a little spirit. Even a tiny bit. There's something else I must say. You were always the pious one in the family. How can you hold a grudge in your heart and still be sinless in the sight of God? Do you never think 'Thy will be done'?"

"That is my own affair."

She spoke sharply, although she knew, deep in her heart, that every time she said, "Forgive us our trespasses as we forgive those who trespass against us," she was making a mockery of the prayer. But the bitterness was flourishing. For Ellen was unmistakably pregnant, busy with baby clothes and polishing the cradle that had held her husband and his brothers.

She felt drowned in the blackness of her unhappiness when she learned that Lawrence was keeping company with a girl his mother had never seen. The knowledge would not have been so shattering, she was sure, if the girl had been a neighbor or one of Ellen's friends who infrequently came to the house.

Megeen told herself—and managed to believe it, by some method of twisted reasoning—that this girl was the cause of Lawrence's refusing to follow his calling. Annie's words were wasted when she tried to point out that Lawrence had known Stacia only a few weeks and could not have been influenced by someone she had not yet met.

Stacia: what sort of name was that? Megeen asked Alec. Had he ever heard of a saint called Stacia? And what sort of girl could she be to have come between the Lord and one of His servants?

"But, my dear," Alec said mildly, "you will have to receive

her. She is Lawrence's friend, and if you cast any slurs upon her, you may lose his love."

The whole disagreeable truth forced itself upon her. On the rare occasions that she went downstairs for dinner, she heard the good-natured teasing directed at Lawrence by his brothers. She wanted to believe that's all it was, lighthearted raillery, but then Lawrence came into her room one night and told her quietly that he would like to bring home a guest some evening.

"She is very important to me, Mother, and I wish to have her meet the family."

Quick to take offense these days, she thrust out her chin and asked testily, "Have I not always made the friends of my children welcome in this house? Why do you look like a scared rabbit? You need not even have asked my permission."

She realized her mistake. There was no way now to avoid meeting this girl, who had lured Lawrence from the place God wanted him to be. Even though she might not have been known to Lawrence when he made his decision, there could have been a chance that he'd have seen the light during the past weeks. If only this Stacia person had not come along and bewitched him.

A stiffening purpose made Megeen drop her eyes so that her son would not guess what she was thinking, that this girl was not going to walk away with the spoils of the battle that easily. Oh, indeed, she intended to wage war, a holy war, for the soul of the future Father Lawrence Vickery. And to do so she must be armed. She must know all there was to know about her opponent: her weak spots, her lacks.

"Where did you meet this young . . . lady?"

Lawrence gave no sign that he had heard the note of hesitation. He was too bemused by his infatuation to notice much of anything. "At a meeting of the whist club. One of my classmates invited me to go and I did. She was there that night. Ma, I wish you could have seen her! When we were introduced, she blushed rosy red; it was as though we had been waiting for each other to come along. And we knew that we had found what we'd been looking for."

There was nothing there that his mother could store away in her memory and use for ammunition later.

"And where was this, dear?" Her voice sounded cool and sweet. "The whist-club meeting, I mean?"

"Hanover Street. Not far from where Stacia lives. In the North End, that is."

There was nothing she could find to criticize in that. She knew that part of the city from long walks taken in the past, and she knew it to be a neighborhood of respectable people living in respectable, well-kept houses.

She said aloud, "It is not as nice a place as it used to be, though. They do say it is becoming overrun with foreigners. Italians, mostly. Soon they will be crowding out the ones who belong there."

She looked up into his face and knew, appalled, what she had done. "Her last name?" She faltered.

"Minuetti. Do you want her whole dossier? Her parents are Salvatore and Secondina Minuetti. They came to America twenty years ago, so Stacia, who is eighteen, was born here. They own a small store on Prince Street, and Stacia helps out in it sometimes. Anything else?"

He spoke without a quaver in his voice, but he was angrier than she had ever seen him before. There were white lines at the corners of his mouth and his eyes blazed.

"It did not take you long to forget, Ma. It was not so very long ago that we were the ones in front of the dogs. I never saw the signs myself, but I have heard that they were on almost every gate of every factory and mill, including Father's. 'NO IRISH NEED APPLY.' You don't remember that?"

She had heard it said that the anger of quiet, even-tempered people was a terrible thing when it was aroused. She was seeing its eruption now and she wrapped her arms around herself to try to melt the coldness—half-fear and half-distress—that poured into her veins and froze her lips. She struggled with her voice, feeling the need to justify herself so that her son would look at her with love again.

"But they are different—"

He raised his voice over hers. "As our people were different not so long ago. Stacia's parents came here not much later than you, Ma. When there is a different cast of features, a foreign language, a different culture—well, those are the things that cause suspicion and lack of understanding."

"You need not talk to me as though you were lecturing a class," she cried resentfully. "I will not be spoken to like that! Everything I have done, Lawrence, has been for only one purpose: the welfare of my children. As for this Stacia Minuetti, it is only natural that I do not take kindly to your association with her. But for her, you would be in a seminary now preparing to do God's work on earth!"

"Jesus!"

There was a sharp little prickling sensation when she heard the word. Never before had she heard him or any of the others in this house take the name of the Lord in vain. She was about to reprimand him, but he gave her no chance.

"You know that's a lie! If I had let you talk me into joining an order, I'd have been a rotten priest. You keep hanging on to that idea, and now you blame Stacia that I had sense enough to realize that the priesthood is not where I belong at all!"

He took a step toward her and gazed into her face. He shook his head.

"I hate to say this to you, Ma, but you are thick Irish. Get something into your head and you keep it there forever. Nobody can blast it out."

He turned to leave the room, but she caught at his sleeve.

"Bring her here then by all means! Invite her to dinner some night next week. If you feel this way about her, then I will have to get to know her."

He put his hand on her chin and lifted it. He looked deeply and intently into her eyes. What he searched for, she knew, were any traces of planned trickery or remnants of resentment toward Stacia Minuetti.

Her blue eyes were bland, innocent, and without guile.

He said, "We'll plan it for Wednesday night then."

Chapter Thirty-eight

The cherished dinnerware—the delicate Limoges dishes and plates—was set upon the table on Wednesday night. The Waterford crystal glasses and the Sheffield silver sparkled under the light of the freshly washed and polished chandelier.

The table had never looked so beautiful. Ellen had cut from the garden, which Megeen was no longer interested in, a great bouquet of asters and marigolds and gladioli. Arranged beautifully though it was, the long stalks of the pink and yellow and orange gladiolus in full bloom formed a shield so that Megeen could not see the face of Stacia Minuetti, who sat at Alec's right.

Only Megeen knew how much effort had been necessary for Alec to bathe and dress and come down to this dinner party, which meant so much to his youngest son.

Megeen was at the foot of the table. She kept craning to see her husband, afraid that he might soon be tiring, concerned that he eat enough, for his appetite had fallen off to an alarming extent lately.

Nor could she hear his voice, for the others seated on either side of the table were engaged in lively conversation frequently interrupted by bursts of laughter.

Ruth Tilton, Martin Mulcahy, Annie, Joseph, Ellen, and even Matthew—all of them had gathered around this table many times, but never had Megeen seen them so high-spirited and—yes, happy. But there was something in their manner that did not admit her into that circle of shared jokes and good-natured teasing. For too long, she realized with a deep sigh inside her, she had refused to speak to them except when necessity demanded it. She felt like someone who had left a comfortable, dearly loved home and could not find her way back into it.

But she could not have taken each of them aside and said, "I'm sorry," for she was justified in feeling injured, she knew, when they kept from her Lawrence's secret. Having the right on her side was cold comfort when she could not share in the laughter and the raillery. She sat at her own table and felt like an outsider, a stranger.

It was not much consolation, either, that the table had never looked so beautiful with its glitter and its sparkle. If there had been a stealthy, small hope that Stacia Minuetti would be overawed by the splendor of her surroundings, and so realize that the Vickerys were far above her station in life, it died before the first course was served.

That very young lady whose parents were shopkeepers was at home here, as though she had spent all her life among luxury. Three forks beside her plate, Mary and Catherine in their uniforms, the richness of the table settings—if all or any of those things daunted her, she gave no sign.

All the others seemed to be enchanted by her, even the formidable Matthew, who had no fondness for strangers and would, had he acted in his usual brusque manner, rejected any overtures at friendliness. Had he done so, it would have been like being cruel to a child.

That was Stacia's charm, Megeen saw, while she was the silent, uncomfortable one. Stacia had a trustful way, as though she expected only kindliness from everyone. She was eager to love and be loved, and there was a warmth about her that seemed to be stirring the same sort of response from the people she had only lately met.

There was no denying that she was as pretty as any girl Megeen had even seen. Even Annie, before her lush young beauty had been ruined by a man in a spasm of rage. And even Ellen, the serene, fair-skinned young woman (wearing a radiant glow now that she carried a baby inside her) was overshadowed by Stacia's black-velvet eyes, warm ivory skin, a swirl of midnight-black hair hanging loose, and a soft, lovely mouth that any man would ache to kiss.

She was dressed as primly as any daughter of the strait-laced Beacon Hill families. Her flounced skirt hid all but her toes. The bodice of her pearl-colored peau-de-soie gown was modestly high. She wore no jewelry except a chain of fine gold links looped around her throat.

And what, Megeen asked herself sourly, was I expecting? A folk-dancing costume of some sort—swirling skirts, sturdy boots, and a headdress with long ribbons hanging down from it?

At the other side of the centerpiece, Alec's voice sounded strong and even. These days even a short conversation seemed to tire him, and Megeen knew that he was making a special effort to put Lawrence's friend at ease, an effort that was evidently not needed. For as soon as he fell silent, there were the others eager to talk to her.

Ruth asked about her family. Martin discovered that they had a mutual fondness for Mr. Dickens. Lawrence awaited his turn to speak to her with proud and doting eyes that did not leave her face for very long.

It had been a successful evening. And with no thanks to me, Megeen admitted. She was the only one outside what was plainly a tender conspiracy to protect this enchanting girl from any touch of coldness and resentment.

"And that, indeed, is what hurt the most!"

They were back in Alec's room and she was helping him to

undress. It no longer embarrassed her to take his clothes off. His poor body seemed to be all bones.

"Do you think he will marry her? Things have not gone that far between them?"

"If he does, he will be extremely lucky."

"Oh, Alec, how can you say so?" Her voice had become a thin wail. "Lucky! Their ways are different. She sounded as though she is very close to her family. How will he fare with such in-laws?"

"Well, indeed, I should think. If they are like her, that is." He pulled on the nightcap that Megeen insisted that he wear to keep out the night drafts. "We were cheated by Matthew's quiet wedding. And no other family was involved. Our family did not expand."

When he was in bed, she pulled the blankets up over him. It had never occurred to her that there might be times when, in spite of the bustle and noise of a large family, he had moments of loneliness. In each person's soul was an area of darkness and not even the presence of other people could dispel it.

"We are born alone, we die alone."

As the words came into her mind, she grasped at his hand. A feeling of panic constricted her throat, for she knew that, no matter how tightly she held to him, she would not able to protect him from the angel of death when his allotted time on earth came to an end.

She lay down on the bed beside him. The sad thoughts she put resolutely out of her mind, but then the painful ones took their place. "They are not seriously attached to each other, do you think?"

"Yes, Megeen, I believe they are. If I read the signs correctly, he is courting her."

He turned and smiled into the face close to his own. "You are not acquainted with that one of our American folkways, are you? Well, it cannot be all that different than in other countries. Some, it seems, have stricter customs. Until a short time ago, a young man would be an outcast from society if he sought to press his suit without first getting permission from the young lady's father."

She began to say something, stopped, and then started again. She could have counted the times he had spoken to her of his first wife. He had had the portrait of the frail-appearing Flora Vickery removed from its place over the fireplace mantel in the drawing room so long ago that she could not remember when his tact and consideration had prompted its banishment.

Now she did not mind speaking the name of Lenard's mother, for that other marriage must now be like a faded memory that carried with it no pain.

"Was it like that when you fell in love with your first wife?"

"Indeed, yes. How young I was then! And how sick of seeing me on their doorstep the Lenards must have been! I pressed my suit with posies and bouquets of flowers and the little trinkets a young man was allowed to present to the lady he was courting."

There was music coming from the other side of the house. Young voices were raised to the accompaniment of the pianoforte, lively and joyful, but for Megeen the sound was painful. There was sadness in her heart, a wistfulness because she had never been courted; no man had ever appeared on her doorstep carrying flowers or small gifts.

She felt very old, as though it was her life that was coming to an end, and that barren spot of loneliness seemed to be spreading until she feared that it would consume her.

Alec said softly, "Come back to me, dearest."

She turned and moved closer to him, but he smiled and said, "Not just this way. I want that strong, brave, compassionate girl I married. She's been hiding too long behind the hurt and the stubbornness. And pride—the wrong kind. It's not so long now until Election Day. What's happened to that pet cause of yours, the law you hoped to have passed? Didn't you tell me that you were trying to force the authorities to provide education for all children under fourteen, even those with dim minds—the retarded, for as much as they could learn, and the ones not hopelessly deranged?"

Now the truth jolted her. She had turned her back on the need she had hoped to help fill. She had closed herself away from everything and everybody except Alec, refusing to answer the letters she had only glanced at, sulking because her young people had deceived her.

This was the greatest sin of all, the real reason why she had not been able to pray properly. She had allowed bitterness to destroy her love for God's unfortunate little ones and for this He was punishing her.

She pulled herself out of bed. "If only it is not too late!"

She sometimes talked like that to Alec, not really speaking to him but voicing her thoughts half-aloud. And he seemed always to understand as he did now.

"You had best get in touch with that friend of yours, Mrs. Laverty, isn't it? No doubt they have gone on with the campaign without you. No matter. Late though it may be, there is still time for you to pitch in and work."

The tea in honor of Michael Ignatius O'Flanagan was the largest gathering Megeen had yet held in the double houses. There were more than a hundred women who came to listen to Mr. O'Flanagan's promises to work, when he was elected, for improvements in the city's educational system. And they intended to see that those promises were kept. For they understood this type of man, a blowhard, a smooth-tongued orator—not quite a scoundrel, but close to it. Some of them were married to such a man. They were able to look below the rhetoric and the bombast and find out if there was sincerity there.

Ellen and Stacia helped to serve the cake and cookies and poured endless cups of tea, and Megeen shook hand after hand and was well pleased with the meeting. Mr. O'Flanagan had made a firm promise to shake up those do-nothings in City Hall and push, until he was successful, for more up-to-date and a wider scope of education for the city's children.

If he did not keep his word, he would find himself with dozens of irate women to contend with, and he was evidently shrewd enough to realize that.

As her guests filed out after the serving of refreshments, Megeen smiled into the faces of two women whom she did not recognize. But she knew immediately who they were when they introduced themselves. Their names were those of two of the oldest and most prominent of the old New England families.

"Mr. O'Flanagan has done my husband certain favors," the elder and dowdier of the women said. "He thought I should come and hear what the man had to say. Perhaps, Mrs. Vickery, you would be kind enough to come to tea someday and we will discuss Mr. O'Flanagan's candidacy at greater length."

"Yes, we should like that." Her friend nodded and the atrocious stuffed-bird figure on the brim of her hat wobbled and seemed to be about to fly away. "Do let us get to know each other better."

Megeen thought: But I have been through this before, and it led to the great disappointment of my life, up until then. How can I let myself be persuaded to once more battle to have my husband reinstated in his rightful place in society? And my children to be accepted by those who scorn them?

But she knew that she must try. Except for little knots of die-hards, people were crossing the lines. Here was undeniable proof. Mr. O'Flanagan had in his debt the husband of the tall, austere woman who had invited Megeen to call upon her. Perhaps this was the way it was to be done. Money and power could force down the barriers that had kept her and her family away from the place she had hoped for them.

So she was not beaten yet. The old dreams and hopes came back so strongly that it was almost like a physical thing that she felt. Her spine stiffened. She had money; she would be able to use what power she had possessed.

"Just let me know," she said with notes of friendliness in her voice. "I shall make a note of it and be glad to call upon you whenever it is convenient."

But this, too, was to be denied her. For a few nights later there came the horror, and everything else was wiped from her mind.

Chapter Thirty-nine

It was a cold night; the first chill of autumn came with a bleak, moaning wind. It awakened her, so she thought as she lay shivering in the mean, intrusive draft from the rattling windows.

But when she heard Alec's voice sounding unusually loud and clear from his bedroom, her first thought was that he was ill and perhaps had been trying to arouse her.

She snatched at her dressing gown and wrapped it around her, went on her knees to find her bed slippers, and was on her way to the door when she became aware that what she was hearing was not one voice but several, all deep and masculine, all with the same notes of gravity in them.

She could identify some of them as she reached the hall. Lawrence, Matthew, Joseph—all of them were there in Alec's room, for what reason she did not know. Fear made her stop in her tracks; she tried to compose her features, but her whole face seemed to have collapsed.

What had happened? Why were they all gathered at Alec's bedside?—deathbed? Now she recognized the light lilt in Martin Mulcahy's brogue. And she could scarcely hold her hand steady enough to turn the doorknob.

They were all there as she had guessed: her three sons and Martin, standing about in different places in the room. Alec was speaking and the others were too engrossed in what he was saying to notice that she was standing on the threshold. She heard only a few words and they were strange, fearsome ones.

". . . police . . ." and "How could he be so evil?" And "We must get him out before my wife . . ."

It was Lawrence who turned away and saw her there. He rushed across the room and took her arm.

"Ma, what are you doing poking around at this time of night? Come on, let me take you back to bed."

She yanked her elbow out of his grasp. "You'll do no such thing. As for what I'm doing here, I could ask you all the same question. Why are you robbing this poor man of his sleep, which he needs so badly?"

Matthew said in a gentle tone that she had never before heard him use, "Ma, Larry's right. This is no place for you. We are talking over—over some business."

"At almost one o'clock in the morning?" She snorted a derisive laugh. "Do you take me for a ninny?"

She wound her way among them until she reached the bed.

"Dear Alec, have we not had enough of secrets? Do you remember the harm they caused? Surely you will tell me what is happening! I shall imagine any number of things if you keep me in the dark, perhaps much worse things than you have been talking about."

Matthew shook his head. "There could be nothing worse," he groaned.

She was suddenly shivering, the shaking hand she put into Alec's as cold as the snow outside. The other hand went quickly to her throat, and she stroked the flesh there as though trying to ease an unbearable pain.

When Alec drew her closer to him, a pillow slid from behind his head and made a soft thud as it hit the floor. Lawrence picked it up and was about to put it behind his father's head, but Alec waved him back. He released Megeen's hand and threw back the bedclothes.

"This is ridiculous! I am not going to lie here like a helpless invalid. I can think better and speak to you all better on my feet!"

He reached for his bathrobe, and although Megeen wanted badly to help him with his thrusting of arms into sleeves, she knew that she must not. His face was troubled, but there was something else in it, too. She had never thought of him as proud in her own interpretation of the word. But now, in spite of his poor, scrawny legs and the nightcap and the growth of gray hair that was the beginning of a beard, there was a look of dignity about him.

Lawrence made one more attempt to send her back to her room, but Alec silenced him.

"She has a right to know. And we might have had to ask her for help at any rate. Disposing of art treasures and whatever else we decide to sell cannot be done in a few days. It would take time to find the right buyers unless we wanted to give them up to a pawnshop where we would get only a fraction of their worth—or do business with some shady individual who would cheat us."

Money. Pawnshop. Art treasures. Her brain was spinning. "Will you please—" she began in a sudden flare of temper.

Alec touched her lips with a gentle finger and said, "Yes, my dear, and I shall be the one to do it. It is Lenard."

The name seemed to echo there in the room; it had become so quiet that she could hear the breathing of the others. No one would meet her eyes except Alec.

"Lenard! What of him?"

Her voice sounded cold and brittle, like the breaking of a glass. "What has happened to him? Where is he?"

"In Charles Street Jail, my dearest."

She walked unsteadily to a Windsor chair in a far corner of the room and lowered herself slowly into it, her movements those of an old woman.

In jail. Not, at least, dead in some terrible accident. Whatever Lenard had done would be explained. Young men, she had heard, often engaged in high jinks and got themselves in scrapes that never caused great damage. They were easily recompensed for and quickly forgotten.

But Lenard was no longer a high-spirited boy who might have been caught in mischief. He was a man in his forties. And Alec would not be talking of selling art treasures unless the price he had to pay for his son's misdemeanor was very high indeed.

"What has he done, Alec? Why is he in jail?"

Alec went to a window and pushed aside its drapery and stared out at the darkness. Something of that darkness seemed to have seeped into his soul, for his face had turned a sickly gray color and his voice was bleak.

"He was arrested on Boston Common. There was a light snowfall this afternoon and there were children coasting for a little while before it melted. Some little boys—"

He turned and faced her, and she heard the agonized sigh.

"Lenard showed himself to them."

The effort to say the words had exhausted him. When Megeen sprang to her feet, took his arm, and led him back to bed, he made no resistance. He sank into it and let her lift his legs and cover them with a quilt.

Then she looked at each of her three sons in turn. Lawrence's face was as red as though fire burned under its skin. Matthew's forehead was deeply lined by a scowl. Joseph's easy smile was missing; she had never before seen such anguish on his face.

"I do not understand. And one of you boys must explain it to me. Your father has tired himself out too greatly, just by talking. You, Matthew?"

She turned to him because he stood nearest to her. She would have chosen him at any rate because of his bluntness and honesty. He would not hide the truth, or any part of it, with polite words. He could not have done so.

"It's what Father has told you. Late this afternoon Lenard was arrested for lewd and lascivious behavior. He unbuttoned his trousers and forced those little boys to—to look at his private parts."

She did not realize that she had moved until she felt Lawrence's arm around her waist. Nor did she know that her feet were unsteady and staggering until she felt herself being lowered back into the chair.

The hands that covered her face as she dropped her head

were icy cold. She was shivering; it was as though every part of her body was in motion. Between the chattering of her teeth she cried, "It is too awful! Too awful!"

"But you must listen to the rest of it."

Joseph put his fingers around her wrists and forced her hands away from her face. When she looked into his eyes, she saw that there was something besides shame in them. He was angry, for selfish reasons perhaps. Then she began to realize what Lenard had done to them all. He had poured his own filth over them. They would never be cleansed of it because this was not a secret that could be kept.

"What is to be done? Something, surely! When I came into this room, you were speaking of money and of selling things."

"Now you know why," Joseph said in a gritty voice. "Lenard was picked up through the description the little boys gave. A few hours after the episode he was arrested. The two charges weren't enough to guarantee a long sentence, but the booking officer evidently has a fierce hatred for people like him—like my dear half-brother. So he dug up an old law left over from the Pilgrim times that has lain on the books for a couple of hundred years. It's called 'Being abroad in the night without good cause.' It's still open, which means that Lenard can be tried whenever the judge desires and sentenced to a period of any length."

Megeen wailed, "But there must be something you can do! The money you spoke of . . . he cannot pay a fine or anything like that?"

"There doubtlessly could be that, too. I have been trying for hours to reach someone who will help us."

She did not ask him who there was among his acquaintances who could do what he sometimes referred to as "pulling strings." Or how it could be accomplished.

"I've been able to learn that he will be formally charged in the morning and that bail may be set as high as ten thousand dollars. For the judge, too, is a straitlaced character who has a drive to clean up the city. Now, at this hour of the night, there is no way to raise that amount of money, and this is what concerns us.

"If we had it, there would be one thing Lenard could do. He could forfeit the bond money and disappear. It would be the best thing for him and for the rest of us, too. True, we might never see him again, but I think we could all stand the loss," Joseph finished dryly.

"He is your father's son!" Megeen was on her feet, trying to fight down a rising tide of sickness. "Whatever he has done, there is no changing that."

She was trying desperately to control the nausea that squirmed and heaved inside her as the picture kept rising in her mind. The cold, crisp air of the late afternoon . . . the children pulling their sleds even though there was only a fine dusting of snow . . . Lenard approaching . . . She burst into hysterical laughter.

And when they all looked at her, shocked, she burst into tears.

She wept for the destruction of an old dream; and for Alec, who would be denied even a glimpse of his eldest son during his last years; and for Lenard himself, in whom they had not seen the signs of sickness and perversion until it was too late.

She swallowed her sobs and disciplined her voice. "If it is money that must be raised in a hurry, I shall be at the savings bank the first thing in the morning. There is that much and more, for I have touched only little of what dear Mrs. Lyman left me. The children's tuition at parochial school—I paid for that because it did not seem right, Alec, to ask you for that."

He said, a bit impatiently, "It was your money and you could—and can—spend it any way you like."

"Then I shall pay the bond and withdraw somewhat more than that amount. For Lenard will need money to live on, will he not?"

"Exactly! And he will need fare to where he is going." Joseph sounded almost happy in his relief. He had, his mother thought, the most to lose in this wretched business. "Perhaps he will opt for Canada, and we can send him money from time to time to stay there."

"How will he manage to reach Canada if he is—if he is a fugitive?"

"They will not know that he is gone until his case comes up in court, which may be weeks from now." Lawrence motioned with his head in Joseph's direction. "Joey, I'm sure, will be able to put the lid on the publicity that could flood us."

Megeen was learning fast. "And perhaps more money will be needed for that. Very well, it will be forthcoming."

Looking from Joseph to Lawrence, she was realizing, as she had never been before, the difference between these two sons of hers. If they had felt brotherly affection for each other, there had been few signs of it. And though their birthdays were little over a year apart, there had never been any real companionship between them.

Yet when the need arose, as it had now, they could be loyal to all members of the family in spite of personal feelings.

"I ask only one favor."

The eyes of all of them were on her, those of her three sons, her husband, and Martin Mulcahy, their good and faithful friend.

With her head erect and her spine stiff, she spoke in a quiet, determined voice. "You will say nothing of any of this to the ladies—Ellen and Ruth and my sister, and, yes, Stacia."

She put out her hand to Lawrence, and it was a gesture of surrender. "They will know soon enough, I fear. For Tessie, who used to work for us, will learn of this, I'm sure, and perform her usual, self-appointed duties as the town crier."

Her mouth twisted in a grimace and then, as her expression hardened again, she said, "Once that money is in your hands, I have no wish to know anything more. It will please me if you do not speak his name again in my presence. All this has shocked and disgusted me more than I can say."

She pressed her lips together, reflecting that she would never again lay eyes on the man who must be exiled to a far country that she had heard was a wild, uncivilized place, inhabited by Indians, loggers, and fugitives from the law.

It was the last thought she would give him. Lenard was out of her life. She was certain of that—out of her life at last and forever.

The next day, after his bond money had been paid, he returned home, only a little pale and subdued, but with not much of his jauntiness remaining.

Chapter Forty

She had been sitting at Alec's bedside, keeping watch until he fell asleep as she did so often now, even in the daytime, for he had frequent naps no matter what the hour was.

On that day, after she had made the large withdrawal from her savings account and given the money to Joseph, she felt especially weary. She was dozing when she felt the hand on her shoulder and came completely awake with a start. Her vision was sleep-blurred, and at first she did not recognize the face that hung over hers. When she did, she tried to leap to her feet.

A million needlelike thrusts in her toes and ankles made them useless. She staggered and fell into the arms of the tall man who caught her easily.

She had no trouble in recognizing him by that time. She did not speak his name even in that startled moment. She glanced worriedly at Alec, afraid that he would awake to see the son who had so little shame or even decency that he could face the people who, by his disgrace, were also disgraced.

She drew herself away from him, and he turned and walked to the bed on tiptoe. He remained there for a few minutes, gazing down at the ruined face of his father.

Afraid that Alec would awaken and find the cause of his heartbreak and humiliation bending over him, she whispered, "Come away," and Lenard followed her out into the hall. There she halted and asked, "Why are you here? What brings you?"

He did not answer but said, "I must talk to you. Where can we carry on a private conversation without being interrupted? Your bedroom?"

She had no desire to be in his presence at all. Everything about him—the defiant set of his head, his hands lying carelessly on her shoulders, the faint smell of whiskey on his breath—disgusted her. But he was Alec's son, and she supposed that he had the right to know of his father's deteriorating health.

But when she had showed him into a small sewing room on the second floor, she learned that he had not come home because of concern for or even interest in Alec's condition.

"I came back for my clothes. They're still over there in our own house. But most of all, I had to see you again."

There was only feeble light in the little room. The dressmaking form loomed like a headless ghost in one corner. Annie's sewing machine, which had been Megeen's present to her on her last birthday, had unfamiliar outlines.

"I think you had better get together what you are taking," Megeen said coldly. "And then be on your way quickly. If Alec knows you are in the house, it will upset him. So go, please, before anybody finds out you are here."

His face turned ugly. "So I am to take orders from our former scullery maid? I'm afraid you're forgetting that the other house is my home. You've bastardized it, but there's no help for that now."

She drew a weary sigh. "Lenard, let us not quarrel. I arose early this morning. Tomorrow I shall tell your father you are here—if you still are—and I will deliver any messages you might have for him."

He made a sudden lunge toward her. Because she could not sidestep quickly enough, she found herself in his arms. She struggled, but she could not get free of his embrace. In that faint light she could see that his face was becoming slick with sweat.

"Let me go!"

Her resistance seemed to rouse him to even more heat. His voice grew thick and his mouth burrowed into her neck and she was not able to understand the muffled words. Physically weary from the lack of sleep and her worry about Alec, she had little strength to fight off this man, for in spite of the shuddering of his body he continued to press himself against her and hold her captive.

She was suddenly afraid. But not so much of him as of herself. She could remember too well the long years when she had longed for just this: to be held this way, her lips against his, her body welcoming his maleness against her.

But he could not. . . . Millicent Lapierre, bluntly and harshly, had explained her reasons for leaving her husband. And now he was homeless, forced to find shelter in a strange country because of a despicable act among small boys. Her mind was whirling and she had no resistance when he lowered her to the floor.

"Just this once, Megeen!" He was tearing at her clothes, kissing her flesh as he exposed it. "Let me have you, Meggie."

His hand was under her skirt, feeling her thighs.

"God help me!"

She gasped the words aloud, praying that she would not be swept up into a mindless whirl. She cried out the only thing she could think of: "But you cannot do it with a woman!"

His hand became as still as though it was frozen. She heard him growl low in his throat.

"Only with you, darling. I could never do it with other women, till that night you came here, so many years ago. You were the only one. I want you again, I swear the other stuff will never come into our lives. We'll go away together."

He had begun to pant again. His threw his long leg over her and lifted her breast to his mouth. She was feeling faint, and his face wavered and blurred as he squeezed her nipple. Now it was all back again, everything that had happened in that little room off the kitchen. The weight of his body, the kneading hands, the moist and open mouth.

"Then you are Matthew's father! It wasn't Alec at all!"

He muttered, "Let's not concern ourselves with an old, old story. You've always wanted me, you couldn't hide that from me. Don't fight me. Take your hand and caress me!"

In his excitement he was stronger than she. She was not going to be able to squirm out from under him. And so she tried to trick him.

"Yes, my darling," she said, panting. "But not here, Lenard. Not on the floor like an animal. I want you in my bed."

She felt him stiffen and was afraid her little ruse had not worked. Then, driven by his want, he toppled off her, put his hot, dry hands on her waist, and lifted her up with him.

As they stood facing each other, he reached for her again. But she slipped under his arms and ran to the sewing table. A weapon came instantly to her hand. She grasped it firmly and pointed the blades of a large pair of shears at his stomach.

"If you touch me again," she said calmly, "I will run this through you."

He believed at first that she was joking. A titter, sounding girlish and silly, died abruptly. She saw the changing expression in his eyes; he looked uncertain, then frightened.

"Put that thing down, my silly darling. You wouldn't . . . you couldn't. . . . Good God, you want me as much as I do you." He took a step toward her, but she brandished the scissors and he fell back again.

"If it's what happened that night, forget it. My father is a fool. He figured I'd never marry you and he was right. Come away with me."

She had no voice. Not because she was tempted in the smallest degree, but because she was stunned by his effrontery. She always had been aware of his selfishness, but his callousness and cruelty had not come to the surface.

He was asking her to leave her husband, the man without whose loving care and concern she would have had to go out onto the streets with her baby and support them both in any possible way. Or find shelter in the workhouse or any other similar institution.

Lenard would have turned his back upon her and their child if she had ever made any demands on him. Now she was seeing him as he really was and always had been, this man she had been infatuated with for the past twenty-two years.

"You would ask me to do that!" She shook her head in something like wonder. "Your father needs me. Have you stopped to think that he may soon . . ."

She could not say the word and he supplied it. "Die? Of course I am aware of that. So that makes it easier to do what we want, doesn't it? Megeen, think! He can't live much longer. I could see that. So why should we wait? The sooner I get out of this city, the farther away I'll be when they start looking for me!"

She was gazing at him with loathing, but he did not notice. "If it's the money you're thinking about, I have enough to keep us going. I can even buy you a few pretties."

She came close to bursting out laughing. He was trying to tempt her with her own money. He had evidently not been told where the bond money had come from, or the extra cash in his pockets.

"It might be a good idea if you'd pack a few of the things that have some value and we can sell them if we have to. Paris! That's the place to go! We can come back after Father dies and it's a pretty sure bet he'll leave everything to you, regardless. He gave you everything you ever wanted, didn't he?

And I don't think he'll be mean enough to change his will, even though you've walked out on him."

She drew a long, deep breath. "You are despicable," she said slowly. "Nothing on earth would make me turn my back on Alec that way."

There came into her mind then a certain phrase he had spoken: "He gave you everything you ever wanted."

The shears trembled in her hands. It had not been an honest threat; she knew that she never could have plunged those sharp blades into Lenard's body. Even though he was a pitiless creature not fit to live.

She moved around him and reached the door. There she turned and said, "You will leave this house before dinnertime. Otherwise I will awaken my husband and have him give orders to Hanley to have you horsewhipped."

Then she walked away, and when she reached her bedroom, she fell into a chair, weeping soundlessly. She was crying for herself and in sorrow for the imminent death of the man who had been her strength, her bulwark, and ever her friend. And for the destruction of a dream that had turned into an ugly reality.

Chapter Forty-one

She said nothing to Alec about that scene in the sewing room. Under no circumstances would she have piled shame upon a spirit already burdened with it. If she had felt herself able to speak without emotion of the fact that Lenard had been there to collect his belongings, she might have brought up the subject. But Lenard had left upon her, too, the stigma of humiliation, and if she had begun to speak of him, she would have had to reveal the whole miserable business.

Much as she longed to tell Alec that now, finally, she knew the true identity of Matthew's father, she could not. Alec had guarded that secret all these years, taken upon himself the responsibilities of parenthood without complaint, acted toward

Matthew in exactly the same manner as he had toward the other children.

It was not the time to talk of anything that might upset or even faintly trouble him. Being silent on certain subjects was all she could do for him now. Fiercely trying to hold back the moment he would leave her, she stayed at his side throughout most of the daytime hours. Very rarely did she leave his bedroom before midnight, and never until he was lost in fitful sleep. Sometimes she dozed there and would come awake abruptly at the least little movement of his body and the faint creaking of the bedsprings.

On a night two weeks after Lenard's last visit, she awoke to see Alec moving about. She could not imagine why she had not heard him when he had left his bed and started the search for his clothing, which he was now putting on. In the faint light of the lamp she had left burning, she could see that he was bending over to pull on his trousers. When she cried, "Alec," he turned and smiled. And by some magic that she did not try to understand, he seemed to have become the young man she had never known—his face looking no more than twenty, his hair gleaming and golden as she had never seen it.

It was an illusion, of course, some trick of the lamplight. She shook her head quickly, and he came back into focus again, her elderly husband, her patient.

"Dear God, Alec, what are you doing?"

He let his trousers fall to the floor and stepped out of them. His movements were calm and steady as he crossed the room and took her into his arms.

"I did not want to awaken you, my love, but since I have . . ."

With his arm still around her, he led her to the bed. She was wearing only a nightdress and dressing robe, and those he stripped from her. As she lay naked, he began to make love to her slowly. He aroused her gradually, listening for the little gasps and murmurs when he touched a spot that gave her pleasure. His beard was soft, and when it tickled her and she gave a little giggle, he moved his head from place to place and stroked her bare flesh with his whiskers.

They were like a pair of lovesick young people, she thought with delight. She could not get enough of his kisses on her body. He kept stroking her in unexpected places, then taking his hand away. It was a game, a wonderful, lightheart-

ed game that they played until they were both mindless with
excitement. He did not need to force her legs apart when
they could wait no longer. She lay ready for him, and then
there was nothing in their world except the spasms of ecstasy
and the final crest of bliss, which they reached at the same
moment.

She stayed cuddled in his arms, exhausted, but her mind
was only on him.

"My darling, you have not—it was not too much for you?"

"What a question to put to your husband!" He spoke
lightly, but she could hear the notes of sadness underlying his
voice. And she knew, as he must know, that this would be
the last time.

A sudden thought made her loosen herself from his embrace. "Why were you dressing at this hour of the night?"

"It is almost dawn," he pointed out. "I thought to get an
early start, for I have many things to do today."

Sleepy and drowsy with contentment, she was unable to
continue the conversation and sleep pulled her down into
overpowering darkness before she could ask the next question.

She slept hours longer than was her habit. The sun threw
dancing dust motes across the tumbled bed and she knew,
without glancing at the clock, that the morning was well into
its middle hours. She sprang out of bed, worried because she
usually brought Alec's breakfast up from the kitchen as soon
as he was awake.

And where had he gone?

She went into her own room, dressed and washed hur-
riedly, and then began her search for him. She was weak with
relief when she found him in the second-floor bathroom,
combing his beard in front of a mirror.

Their eyes met in the mirror and she blushed as she
remembered the places on her body that had felt the softness
of that beard upon them.

Then everything else went out of her mind when she realized that he was fully dressed. There was no illusion of
youth now. He was once more a sixty-three-year-old man in frail
health. And what, she asked him in tones of bewilderment,
was the reason for his being dressed for the street when he
should have been in bed resting up—and she blushed
again—from the exertions of the night before.

He leaned forward to button his shirt. He went into his bedroom to select a neckerchief from the lowboy. When it was arranged to his satisfaction, he went to the wardrobe and took from it his fawn-colored driving coat, with its wide lapels, brass buttons, and long skirt. He had not worn it for a long time, or the matching square-crowned hat he held in his hand.

She went to a window and pulled back its drapery. The sky was a faded blue. Icicles, like bits of crystal jewelry, decorated the tree branches, and she knew that the sunlight was a fraud. It was bitterly cold out there; she felt the draft seeping in through the sill, and she could not allow him to go out into that freezing weather, even if he seemed bent on doing so.

But he was even more determined than she was. When she cried, "You must be daft to go out this morning, Alec," he went on with the buttoning of his coat.

"At least tell me," Megeen begged, "what can be important enough to take you from the house this morning. Has something happened? Is it Lenard?"

"No, my dearest." He turned to smile at her. "I just feel restless. I have spent enough time indoors. You have rejuvenated me, you see. After last night I am a new man."

"But before that!" She could not force her eyes to meet his. "You were getting ready to go out then. You said you had a long, busy day in front of you."

"Ah, yes. I should have known I could not fool you."

When she did not answer his smile, he took her into his arms. "I am sorry to worry you, dear wife, but this is something I must do. I am going to drive out to the mill. And I intend to visit my office. I wish to see what that young scamp there has been doing. I think it would be a good idea, too, to drop into the store. I will surprise Ruth."

"Oh, Alec, you cannot! Ruth will be here on Sunday if you wish to see her. And isn't this the day Martin reports to you? Can't you be satisfied with that?"

"I am sorry, Megeen."

He kissed her gently and then dropped his hands from her shoulders. "Now if you will have one of the girls find Hanley and have him bring the phaeton around."

Her face brightened with a faint touch of relief. At least he would not exhaust himself by driving the long distance. And she would give orders to the coachman to bring a closed carriage so that Alec would, at least, be sheltered from the cold blasts of wind.

He guessed too well what she was thinking. "The phaeton," he repeated in distinct accents. "And I do not intend to have Hanley drive me, only to have him bring the rig to the door."

She had never, in their long years together, had so much as a glimpse of this stubborn stranger. Slowly and with fear constricting her throat, she started down the staircase. She had reached only the third step when she saw Martin in the hall removing his hat and then beating his hands together.

She ran down the remaining steps with a little cry of gladness. She was realizing, this also for the first time, how much Martin had given to this household, how much she and Alec had come to depend upon him.

The quiet, taciturn man had been there in all the family crises. He had evidently been content to be at the edge of the Vickery circle, warming his own lonely spirit with the casual affection they were able to spare.

Since the day he had decided that his conscience would not allow him to be pandering to the thirst of weak men and had sold his saloon, he had served Alec Vickery well, taking from him the burden of running the mill. There had been other more personal things: presents for the children on their birthdays and Christmas, which he had always shared with them; tracking down Hanley when the man had been on one of his "holidays"; sitting at Alec's bedside now and then so that Megeen could snatch a few hours of rest.

He looked up as Megeen came running down to him. A greeting died on his lips when her face came into the light.

"What is wrong?"

She told him quickly of Alec's plan to make a three-stop journey. "And you know how cold it is outside, Martin, not at all the kind of weather for him to be out in, even if he were strong enough. Oh, dear friend, can't you persuade him to abandon this foolish idea? Perhaps if you speak to him, tell him he is not needed at the mill, he will listen to you."

But Alec was on his way downstairs at that moment. He was wearing the coat that she saw, with a sinking heart, hung loosely from his shoulders. He was drawing on his driving gloves and there was upon his face a tightened look. She turned to Martin with her distress and pleading in her eyes.

He spoke to Alec. "I have something to tell you. The men at the mill were about to strike yesterday, but I managed to hold that off until I had a chance to talk to you. I can, I think, satisfy them with a few-cents-an-hour raise, but I need your approval for that, of course."

"I will take care of everything."

Alec spoke in a calm, quiet voice, but Megeen heard in it the steely resolve against which she had battled futilely in their bedroom. Again she turned to Martin as he began to speak.

"I had intended to drive out there after I talked to you. My carriage is out front. If you insist upon going . . ."

"I do indeed." Alec smoothed the gloves on his hands. "I shall go alone, so there is no point in discussing it. I will not be driven by Hanley or by you, Martin. As a matter of fact, rather than wait for Hanley to be found, I shall walk over to Washington Street and have the phaeton hitched up myself."

Megeen ran to him and put her hands on his lapel. But she knew that she could not stop this determined man from what he had made up his mind to do, foolhardy as it might be. She dropped her head onto his shoulder in what she knew was a gesture of farewell, anguished and desolate.

"At least," she pleaded as she lifted her head, "please take a shawl if you are to be out in the cold for long."

She went to the hall closet and took from it the largest, heaviest knit shawl that hung there. When she tried to drape it around Alec's shoulders, he shrugged it off, but he did not refuse to take it with him. He was carrying it over his arm as he walked down the front steps alone.

Even after the door closed behind him, she remained standing there.

"Come." Martin touched her arm lightly. "It's drafty here. Wouldn't you like to go back to your bedroom and rest?"

Her lips moved in a twisted smile. "How much rest can there be for me when my husband is out on some foolish errand and may easily take lung fever and ruin his health?"

Martin allowed her to keep up her sad little charade when they both knew that it would make no difference in his condition if he tired himself out or caught a chill. His days on earth were numbered; he would leave them only a short time sooner.

When she kept repeating, "But why? What made him do this nonsensical thing?"

Martin merely shook his head. "Perhaps he felt he must."

He did not add, "For the last time," but she heard the words as clearly as though they had been said aloud.

They waited, all that long day, in Alec's study. There in that place where she had spent so many evenings with Alec, playing chess and discussing the books he had given her to read, she could pretend that soon he would come in to join her. Even though Martin spent those dragging hours in an armchair across the room, it was Alec's presence that she felt most strongly.

When people came tiptoeing into the room, she did not notice them. Ellen brought a tray with cups upon it and the strong black tea Megeen liked so well, but it lay there, ignored and cooling. Matthew, who usually spent the daytime hours in his room working on his novel, tried to tempt her with the raisin buns Mary Donovan had baked especially for her. She was not able to force a bit of the pastry past her lips.

They would have spoken to her as she sat locked in her silent fear, but Martin shook his head at each visitor and so she was let alone.

The long vigil ended at dusk. With the setting of the sun, the wind gained new strength, and with each of its blasts against the windowpanes, Megeen shivered and tightened her arms around herself.

The picture that had haunted her all day became even more vivid. In her mind she could see Alec up on the driver's seat of the carriage, the shawl wrapped across his shoulders too little protection against the bitter weather.

She was the first to hear the carriage stop at the door. She sprang from her chair and gathered her skirt in her hands. She heard Martin behind her, the distance between them widening as she sped down the hall.

Alec was coming in the door when she reached the bottom step of the staircase. In the light of the gaslight in the hall she saw his face, pinched and pale red from the cold, and his eyes that were glazed with exhaustion. His breath rose and fell, shallow and yet loud, and it filled the hall with its dreadful sound.

She stifled a cry and ran to him. As he put out his arms, the shawl fell from his shoulders and he tried to stoop to retrieve it, but he staggered and would have fallen if Matthew, leaping down over the last four steps, had not caught his father in his arms.

Like a tragic, solemn procession, they filed upstairs, Matthew carrying the half-unconsious man, Megeen behind them, Martin next in line, and then Ellen and the two servant girls.

Hanley trailed along a few steps behind the others, muttering, " 'Tweren't my fault. I nivir knew he was takin' out the rig."

Lawrence came in from his classes and Joseph arrived home from wherever it was he spent his days, and without being told what had happened in their absence, they went, as though by some strange intuition, directly to their father's bedroom.

The others were all there, gathered around the bed from which, every one of them knew, the man struggling for breath—now gray-faced and defeated—would never rise again.

Chapter Forty-two

She sat beside him all through the night. She guarded her place jealously, waving the others away when they came to urge her in whispers to get some rest. She could not give up her vigil, for she knew that these few hours would be his last.

Somewhere, a long time ago, she had learned that a dying person often had a period of clarity during which he could speak and hear with lucidity. She had much to say to Alec when he became fully conscious and she could not be absent when that period came. She must speak to him, and alone; what she said to him was only for his ears.

He awoke at three o'clock. When she saw the thin ridge of his body stirring under the bedclothes, she poured a glass of water from the bottle at the bedside and held it to his lips. They were so cracked and dry that she was sure he would not be able to speak even after he had sipped from the glass.

But he had strength enough to say, "Do not sit here with me, dear wife, for I don't wish to be the cause of your falling ill. And having you here will change nothing. We are born alone, we die alone."

She said in a hoarse, soothing voice, "You must not speak of dying, Alec darling. You will soon be well again."

"Let us be honest with each other, dear love. What sense is there in either of us pretending what is not so?"

She shifted her body and put her head on the pillow beside him. "Alec! Alec! I could not get on without you!"

"You have the boys—our sons. You gave me fine children, Megeen. And a little girl who grew up to be a true daughter. Between the four of them—"

She lifted her head and drew away from him. She wanted to look into his eyes while she was speaking. "I was convinced that Matthew was your son because Millicent told me that it was—it was impossible. . . . Now I know. Dear Alec, he might have been your own, for you treated him no different from the others."

Alec said nothing for a long time. Only the ticking of the clock on the mantel broke the silence.

Finally he said, "Then you know? Lenard told you?"

"I learned only a very short time ago," she said grimly, "the real truth. All these years he has allowed you to carry the burden of blame. He let you assume all the responsibilities and expenses of bringing up his son. Oh, Alec, why did you do it? Why didn't you tell me?"

The narrow shoulders rose and fell in a shrug. "Because he would not have owned up. Before his mother died, she made me promise that I would take care of him, as she phrased it. But it was not only that. I could not let you and your baby find shelter in the workhouse, which seemed to be your most dreadful nightmare."

He rested during a short silence and then she said, "From the day I came into this house, you gave me nothing except kindness."

"From the day you came into this house, I have loved you."

She dropped her head forward so that he could not see her face. She did not know whether the shameful feeling she'd had for this man's son had left its mark upon her.

"You delighted and amused me with your Irish ways," Alec told her. "I was glad to have an excuse for marrying you. I knew you could not love me in return, but no one ever had a better wife."

"Alec, stop! Please stop! I'm not worthy of your love and praise. I must tell you—"

She stopped on the point of blurting out the truth about Lenard. She knew that to do so would relieve her conscience, but by lifting the sin from her own soul by confessing she would be breaking his tired heart and making bitter his last few hours on earth.

She saw the softness of compassion in his eyes and she was almost sure that he did not need to be told. She stroked his warm face with a tender hand and said, "You have done so much for me. You gave me your name, shelter, whatever I needed. I gave you little in return. I robbed you of your place in society, your friends. I was no use to you at all."

"You were the only friend I ever needed. You gave me life. It is true," he said quickly, before she had a chance to speak. "Long ago I was told that I would never live to the age of fifty. Without you I could not have done so. Of no use you say!" A laugh stuck in his throat and he fell silent for a longer time.

Her grip on his bony hand was as strong as she could make it, afraid that if she let go he would slip away from her. When he could speak again, he whispered, "My dear one, do you believe that you have not been the best thing in my life? That of the others, too.

"Ask Ellen what her life would have been without you. And Ruth and Martin and your sister. It is your wonderful quality of caring. You warmed us all with your love and concern. And there are children we have never seen and never will who are alive now because of you, others who may learn to lead, perhaps, productive lives."

It had been a long speech for a man in his condition. Megeen murmured, "Rest now, dear man. I will be here when you wake up."

In that dimly lit room her vigil continued, and she had a long time to think about what he had said. There came into her mind the ending of an old prayer.

"I got nothing I asked for but everything I could have hoped for. I am the luckiest of mortals."

In the morning Alec asked to have a priest come to his bedside. "Because, dear Megeen, I am aware that we could not be buried together otherwise, and I wish us to be side by side through all eternity. I must not be denied a place in hallowed ground."

It was the last loving service he could offer her, and she

was so sickened by grief that she could not force herself to be in the room where Alec would receive the sacraments.

Not long after the priest left, Mary and Catherine lighting his way with holy candles, Alec left them as quietly and simply as he had lived. He died peacefully, with his wife, his three sons and daughter, his sister-in-law, and the two who loved him as a friend—Martin and Ruth—kneeling by his bed while Megeen said the five sorrowful mysteries of the rosary.

It rained on the day of Alec's funeral, not in gentle drops of short-lived showers. It was a vicious, wind-lashed storm, and Megeen's mourning veil was drenched by the time the cortege reached the door of the cathedral.

Everything around her was in blurred candlelight. She was able to walk the long aisle only because Joseph on one side of her and Lawrence on the other held her firmly by the arms and matched their footsteps to hers, which were slow and unsteady.

When the requiem Mass was ended, she refused their support and walked alone behind the casket. Now she was able to see those who stood in respect in the pews on either side of the aisle.

Dorothea Lovering was there between her parents, a handkerchief pressed against her mouth. Behind them were a few people whom Megeen recognized as neighbors. The lawyer who had kept Alec's law practice alive had come with his wife. Martha Laverty was there with several of her tall children. Ruth Tilton was flanked by her two assistants, for the store that bore the Vickery name was closed on this sad day. Ruth, usually so self-controlled, was slumped in an attitude of grief, weeping unashamedly.

There were three pews occupied by members of her club. Even Tessie was sober-faced and tearful. And Tim Hanley, who had not been seen since Alec's death, stood at the back of the church, pale and trembling, his hand lifting to wipe his lips.

There were others: Mr. Swanburn and a few of the men from the mill and the owner of the stable where the Vickery horses and carriages were kept.

Megeen could hear the steady, quiet footsteps behind her. They were those of Alec's sons and daughter, and Annie with her hand on Martin's arm.

At the grave site, the rain slashed down upon them and the wind snatched at women's hats and veils and whipped their skirts around their legs. She saw the movement of the priest's lips, but could not hear what he was saying.

Joseph touched her arm and said, "Mother?" and she started. The prayers had seemed short, and perhaps they had been as a concession to the weather.

As so it was time to part forever from the man who had been the other half of her life for twenty-three years, to leave him there beneath the rain-soaked sprays of flowers.

When she reached home, she went upstairs immediately. She discarded her wet clothing and, in fresh garments, walked into Alec's bedroom. She lay down on his bed and refused to leave it even when the members of her family came with offers of food or drink, merely waving them away with a tired gesture.

On the fourth day of her self-imposed seclusion, Martin Mulcahy came upstairs and found her sitting by the window, staring out at the bleak winter landscape.

"They tell me you have eaten practically nothing. You are being very foolish, Megeen—and selfish."

He had never, in all the years she had known him, spoken to her in that manner. Startled and indignant, she sat up straighter and clasped her hands together.

"What right have you to say a thing like that to me?"

"The right of an old friend who cannot bear to see you holding yourself away from those who love you. Have you given any thought at all to your young people? They have lost their father. It is sad that they are losing their mother, too, in a most unfair way. Your grieving adds to their grief." He held up his hand when she seemed about to speak. "I would never have said these things if it wasn't so needful. I am sorry."

She saw him take from his pocket a large envelope. Then he pulled up a chair so that he sat facing her and said, "I don't know whether or not you are aware that Alec made me executor of his will. It was drawn up not very long ago—"

"I don't wish to hear!" Her voice was thin and cracked. "Martin, please!"

"It is something I must do. The last thing I can do for Alec. You would not wish me to fail him in this?"

"But it can wait for some other time."

"It will be no easier then."

She had no strength to carry on the argument. She watched silently as he opened the envelope and slid out a few sheets of paper.

"It is a very simple document, Megeen. Alec left you everything he owned—the other house and all its contents. This one, of course, has always belonged to you. There is not a great deal of cash, but you are a rich woman in property, the valuable articles in both the houses, the mill, and the store. Alec turned over his law practice to the gentleman from Harvard. And there you have the essence of the will."

Now that her mind had become clearer, she had a question. "But what of the children?"

"There are small, token bequests, and even if one of them felt tempted to contest the will, he made sure the suit would be unsuccessful." He spread the sheets of paper on his knees and quickly found what he was looking for. " 'Knowing that my beloved wife will provide for them should it be necessary, I leave all my worldly possessions, except for such small bequests as noted, in her hands.' "

He gave her time to dab at the hot and bitter tears that boiled in her eyes, and then he said softly, "That is all there is to it, Megeen. Except for one thing."

He took a small, unmarked envelope from the larger one.

"He asked me to give you this, too."

Her eyes dried slowly and became bright with curiosity. She reached out a hand and took the envelope and opened it. She sat staring at the brass key that was all there was to be found in it.

"What is it for?"

She did not need to have him tell her. "It opens the lock to the park across the way? Martin, did he keep it all these years and never offer it to me? Why?"

"He was afraid you would be snubbed by the small-minded people you might meet there. But things are different now. He knew that the time would come when the silly barriers would come down."

She breathed a deep sigh. "But have they yet? Not that it matters to me now. I have only just begun to realize that I had something so much better than a place among people who, in rejecting me, turned their backs on a man whose shoes they were not fit to lace."

"Yes, but he knew you wanted your children to be accepted and perhaps they will be, and their children after that. Ellen, who will be a mother soon. And Lawrence and his Stacia."

He put out his hand. "Come, Megeen, let's see what will happen when you use the key Alec wanted you to have. Find a wrap and come with me across the street."

She hesitated for only one more moment. Then she put her hand in his outstretched one. The other she curled into a fist and held tightly to the key.

More Big Bestsellers from SIGNET

☐ **THE ROCKEFELLERS by Peter Collier and David Horowitz.**
(#E7451—$2.75)

☐ **THE WATSONS by Jane Austen and John Coates.**
(#J7522—$1.95)

☐ **SANDITON by Jane Austen and Another Lady.**
(#J6945—$1.95)

☐ **THE FIRES OF GLENLOCHY by Constance Heaven.**
(#E7452—$1.75)

☐ **A PLACE OF STONES by Constance Heaven.**
(#W7046—$1.50)

☐ **THE HAZARDS OF BEING MALE by Herb Goldberg.**
(#E7359—$1.75)

☐ **COME LIVE MY LIFE by Robert H. Rimmer.**
(#J7421—$1.95)

☐ **KINFLICKS by Lisa Alther.** (#E7390—$2.25)

☐ **RIVER RISING by Jessica North.** (#E7391—$1.75)

☐ **THE HIGH VALLEY by Jessica North.** (#W5929—$1.50)

☐ **LOVER: CONFESSIONS OF A ONE NIGHT STAND by Lawrence Edwards.**
(#J7392—$1.95)

☐ **THE KILLING GIFT by Bari Wood.** (#J7350—$1.95)

☐ **WHITE FIRES BURNING by Catherine Dillon.**
(#E7351—$1.75)

☐ **CONSTANTINE CAY by Catherine Dillon.**
(#W6892—$1.50)

THE NEW AMERICAN LIBRARY, INC.,
P.O. Box 999, Bergenfield, New Jersey 07621

Please send me the SIGNET BOOKS I have checked above. I am enclosing $_____(check or money order—no currency or C.O.D.'s). Please include the list price plus 35¢ a copy to cover handling and mailing costs. (Prices and numbers are subject to change without notice.)

Name_____

Address_____

City_____State_____Zip Code_____
Allow at least 4 weeks for delivery

Other SIGNET Bestsellers You'll Enjoy Reading

☐ **THE SECRET LIST OF HEINRICH ROEHM by Michael Barak.** (#E7352—$1.75)

☐ **FOREVER AMBER by Kathleen Winsor.**
(#J7360—$1.95)

☐ **SMOULDERING FIRES by Anya Seton.**
(#J7276—$1.95)

☐ **HARVEST OF DESIRE by Rochelle Larkin.**
(#J7277—$1.95)

☐ **THE HOUSE ON THE LEFT BANK by Velda Johnston.**
(#W7279—$1.50)

☐ **A ROOM WITH DARK MIRRORS by Velda Johnston.**
(#W7143—$1.50)

☐ **THE PERSIAN PRICE by Evelyn Anthony.**
(#J7254—$1.95)

☐ **EARTHSOUND by Arthur Herzog.** (#E7255—$1.75)

☐ **THE DEVIL'S OWN by Christopher Nicole.**
(#J7256—$1.95)

☐ **THE GREEK TREASURE by Irving Stone.**
(#E7211—$2.25)

☐ **THE GATES OF HELL by Harrison Salisbury.**
(#E7213—$2.25)

☐ **TERMS OF ENDEARMENT by Larry McMurtry.**
(#J7173—$1.95)

☐ **THE KITCHEN SINK PAPERS by Mike McGrady.**
(#J7212—$1.95)

☐ **ROSE: MY LIFE IN SERVICE by Rosina Harrison.**
(#J7174—$1.95)

☐ **THE FINAL FIRE by Dennis Smith.** (#J7141—$1.95)

THE NEW AMERICAN LIBRARY, INC.,
P.O. Box 999, Bergenfield, New Jersey 07621

Please send me the SIGNET BOOKS I have checked above. I am enclosing $_____(check or money order—no currency or C.O.D.'s). Please include the list price plus 35¢ a copy to cover handling and mailing costs. (Prices and numbers are subject to change without notice.)

Name_____

Address_____

City_____State_____Zip Code_____
Allow at least 4 weeks for delivery